I0600066

Angel's Fall

The Phantom Saga

Jessica Mason

Published by Murmuration Books, 2024.

This is a work of fiction. Similarities to real people, places, or events are entirely coincidental.

ANGEL'S FALL

Second edition. May, 2025.

ISBN: 979-8-9986338-2-9

Written by Jessica Mason.

Table of Contents

For every phantom phan who wanted a different end to the story. This one is for all of us.

Author's Note

Angel's Fall is a dark, historical romance with adult themes and explicit content. This includes light bondage and domination, semi-public sex, explicit language, violence, off-page sexual assault of a secondary character, and discussion of suicide. For more detailed triggers and other information, please consult my website: www.jessicamasonauthor.com[1].

Thank you for reading.

1. http://www.jessicamasonauthor.com

Foreword

So, do we now come to the end of the Opera Ghost's love story? We have followed this specter through shadows and trials to what surely must be the conclusion of the tale. We know how it ends, this story we have learned so well. Grand opera must conclude in tragedy, with lovers torn asunder as they sing their arias of love and death. That is the way of things.

But what if it isn't? What if the story we know is just a shadow on the wall? What if the real ending is one yet to be unmasked? Not all operas end in tragedy – just ask Figaro. What is more, this is not a fable of ghosts and restless spirits. This is a love story.

A love story about angels.

So, once more, let us begin.

Prelude

M eg tried to be quiet entering the flat, but the floor had decided it was the perfect morning to try out-singing the entire Opera chorus. Maybe it was the first hint of spring; the warming air making the boards groan under every careful step Meg took. All her training in the *corps de ballet* couldn't keep the noise from echoing in the stillness and alerting the woman waiting for her by the fire. Maybe her mother was scowling at being awoken so early. Or was it still late?

"Where in the name of God have you been, Margaret Giry?"

Meg hunched her shoulders meekly. She was doomed. "I told you: the masquerade. I lost track of time."

"Did you now?" Madame Giry, as she was known among the other box keepers, demanded as she stood. "And with whom did you do that losing?"

"I was with Blanche and Marie!" Meg gulped as her mother continued to glare. "For the most part."

"Who else?"

"Cécile Jammes?"

Her mother didn't like Jammes much. To be fair, neither did Meg. When they had first met, she had been impressed by the older dancer's confidence and the way she held herself above all the squabbling and rivalries among the petits rats. Jammes had always seemed to be playing a game no one else knew and Meg had been fascinated by it. The elder Giry had always been suspicious of

1

Jammes, however. Jammes had been in such sour moods lately that Meg had begun avoiding her.

"And what did you get up to with her?"

"Nothing! I more... interrupted her. I tried to apologize. Then I got lost." Meg wasn't lying. She *had* found herself lost at the masquerade and she *had* stumbled backstage to find Jammes in the arms of a paramour. It had not been the embrace that had shocked Meg – she was used to such things in the Opera. She had gasped only when she realized that Jammes' lover was not a man. It was one of the dressers: Julianne Bonet, clothed in a soldier's uniform.

The women had not seen Meg, only heard her, but her interruption had been enough to send Jammes running and leave Meg in a fog for an hour. She had drifted, thinking of how different it had been to see the two kissing in that little corner. It was so different from the patrons who would yank girls (some younger than Meg's fourteen years) to sit on their knees as they watched rehearsal. Or haul them off to some hidden corner of the Opera to do things that Meg wished she didn't know about.

"How long were you lost? Who found you?" her mother demanded, reading Meg's thoughts. "Was it one of the patrons?"

"No!" Meg cried, aghast.

"I've told you, you don't need them. *He* takes care of us so you don't have to do those things!"

"I know! I didn't do anything with anyone!" Meg *was* lying this time. She had wanted to feel what those women had. The idea had stuck in her head rather persistently after what she had seen. She'd wanted to have her own secret, seductive encounter even before she had seen the other couple that had taken her breath away even more. "I saw him."

"The Ghost?" Her mother straightened as she smiled dimly, pride radiating off her as it always did when she discussed the very particular owner of Box Five on the grand tier. "How do you know? Wasn't everyone in their masks?"

"I knew it was him. I could feel it." Meg shivered to recall the incredible aura that had radiated from Red Death as he had stalked the party. "He was dressed all in red with the most fantastic mask, like a death's head. It was truly awful, that head, just like I've heard the Ghost described, but then..." Meg sighed and her mother raised an eyebrow.

"Then what?"

"Do you remember how you told me you thought the Ghost might have a lady?" Meg was breathless as she said it. "After he asked you to bring him flowers a lady might like?"

"That was months ago, before Christine Daaé bewitched him."

"Maybe it was her. A woman all in black danced with Red Death, with the Ghost. The way she looked at him, Mama. I don't even know the words." Meg knew how it had made her feel though – a hundred times curiouser and lonelier. There had been such love and promise and defiance and sin in that woman's eyes as she had looked at Red Death. Everyone had just assumed that they were a normal couple, not a ghost and a siren. Meg might have been the only one to have still believed, and that made it all the more enchanting. Death and his maiden, celebrating into the night.

"You don't need those words," her mother admonished.

"I'm not a child anymore, you know," Meg pouted. "I can take care of myself. I made it home in one piece, didn't I?"

"After how many hours lost in dreams?" her mother snapped, and Meg looked away. She didn't want any more questions because her mother didn't need to know how Meg had searched for a good hour through the raucous, masked crowd for a familiar set of eyes. She'd found them at last, and the flutist to whom they belonged. Meg and Pierre had kissed in a stairwell until the chiming of a clock had drawn Meg away.

"Mother, please."

"Get to bed. We have church in a few hours."

Meg nodded and obeyed, skittering off to her room to remove her butterfly costume. She could still feel that thrill, like a healing burn on her skin, even as she slunk between cold sheets. The thrill of lips upon her, hands upon her waist... And no more. Those stolen kisses had been all she needed to warm her. She knew it wasn't the same as whatever it was Jammes had, or Red Death's lady; but it was something. A little spark. The morning star before dawn.

Meg closed her eyes, her mother's voice loud in her mind to remind her who ruled the morning star. The devil had many temptations, and a ghost, of all things, kept Meg safe from many of them. Meg didn't have to supplement their rent by selling herself to a patron as so many other dancers did, because the Ghost added to her mother's pay. Meg didn't have to worry her mother that she wouldn't come home after being carried off in some patron's carriage. She was glad of that and grateful to the Ghost because she didn't want that.

Meg wanted something different. She wanted starlight and fire and hidden embraces. She wanted whatever it was that made those lovers burn.

1. Ashes

"**A**re you sure that's all?" Antoine de Martiniac's voice was raw from a night of revelations and carousing, and Raoul de Chagny was sick of hearing it.

"Yes. That's everything." Raoul rubbed his hand over his face. He needed sleep and a shave, and probably looked as awful as he felt. The alcohol from the masquerade had worn off hours ago, and he had not been in the mood for more. Planning how to avenge one's father's death had a way of dampening the mood. Even Philippe had switched to coffee while he listened to Raoul's fragmented story.

"Then start again from the beginning," Antoine barked. His icy blue eyes were as wild as they had been hours ago, when he had revealed that the villain who had sent so many – including Antoine's own father – to a fiery death was the same Erik who had enchanted the woman Raoul loved, Christine Daaé.

"Must I?" Raoul groaned.

"Yes. Even the parts that make you look like a lovesick fool." It was Philippe who replied. Raoul's older brother was usually so jovial; the warm, laughing center of every crowd, who never took anything too seriously except money. It was sobering and unsettling for Raoul to see his brother with a grim expression as they sat in the parlor next to a dying fire. Even his thin mustache looked solemn. "Start with when you first heard him. When you were listening at Christine's door."

"I thought it was just a man in her dressing room," Raoul told the two older men for the third (or was it fourth?) time. The sky outside was brightening now. How long had they been at this? "After I saw Christine sing at the New Year's gala."

"When she laughed at you after you accosted her at the reception," Antoine scoffed. "You always forget to mention that part."

"She only laughed at me because *he* was watching her and influencing her!" Raoul wished with all his heart he had stayed home that fateful night. Maybe then he wouldn't have seen the girl he loved as a young man thrust onto the stage of the Palais Garnier when La Carlotta had become indisposed. Raoul blinked as a new thought occurred to him. "He did it."

"What?" Philippe asked.

"Erik," Raoul spat the name. "The villain must have arranged for Christine to sing. He made Carlotta sick."

"Adèle did say something about the bitch claiming to have been poisoned," Antoine mused. "I never took it seriously."

"He wanted his student on the stage!" Raoul exclaimed. "Erik put Christine there and in return, she gave him—"

"Her soul," Philippe finished with utter derision in his voice. "You listened at the door like a common thief and heard her say she gave him her soul."

Raoul shuddered at the memory of the pure devotion in Christine's voice that night. "She did."

"But then, when you snuck in after she left to confront the man, the dressing room was empty," Antoine finished.

"He was using the mirror. Somehow, he hides behind it." Raoul wondered if the fiend had been there, laughing at the fool on the other side of the mirror.

"And after that, you wrote to her. She didn't reply, yet you still thought it was a good idea to carry her to her room after she fainted on the stage after *Faust*," Philippe recited. "After she once again took Carlotta's place, when the Signora was tricked out of performing."

"Our Phantom's work again," Antoine remarked, twining his long fingers together. Philippe raised an eyebrow. "It had to have been."

"Sorelli said the whole company blamed the ghost for driving the old managers away too," Philippe added. "Maybe he cleared them out to help Christine. Carlotta had her claws deep in Debienne and Poligny."

"She has her claws deep in Firmin Richard now," Antoine said. "But back to our dear Raoul. You saw her that night. Then she disappeared from her room. Now we know how she was taken."

"You didn't believe me at the time." Raoul scowled.

"Because you have the tendency to be an idiot when it comes to that girl," Philippe drawled. "Then you saw her the next day. She was upset."

"Very." Raoul remembered the pale, stricken face of his old friend that cold morning after *Faust*. When she had been accosted by a man whose part in this mystery Raoul still did not understand. "I thought she was upset because of that Persian fellow harassing her, but then she started talking about—"

"What have you neglected to mention now?" Antoine's thin lips curling into a sneer.

"That she was talking about angels," Philippe finished for his brother and Raoul balked at him. "I remember things too, you know."

"She said she had thought her teacher was an angel. I thought she was being metaphorical or superstitious! She was always a fanciful girl. Now I think she might have really meant it. This *Erik* convinced her he was her angel of music. That's not so far from an opera ghost."

"You should have hauled her off to a madhouse right then," Antoine scoffed.

"She wasn't mad, that's the whole point!" Raoul snarled back. "She is a victim here." He bit his tongue and did not say how he had encouraged Christine to give her 'angel' a chance because signs from heaven did not need to be literal angels. Fate had presented this teacher to Christine, Raoul had told her. Only now did Raoul know it was the work of the devil.

"The next time you saw her was after Carlotta had her fired. She was trying to talk to the woman," Philippe pushed on. Raoul blushed at that memory too. He had held Christine and taken her to supper. Everything had been so normal. "I surmise the discussion with her rival didn't go well."

"Sorelli was gabbing on about some stagehands who broke their faces in a fight around the same time. They blamed the Ghost for it," Philippe mused. "If they went with Carlotta to accost Christine, maybe they ran into her protector. So he may leave the Opera?"

"Then he made our favorite diva croak like a toad at *Faust*," Antoine continued. "I must say, I can't fault him for that. It was her best performance."

"I saw Christine that night too," Raoul muttered.

"With the degenerate," Philippe added.

"I'd rather have Christine pretending an affair with a sodomite than actually—" Raoul stopped himself, unwilling to imagine what Erik had forced Christine to actually do. "Rameau is harmless."

"The next time I saw her was outside the Opera again," Raoul pushed on.

"With my help, and Adèle's. Which we both regret providing," said Antoine as Raoul rolled his eyes.

"I was foolish. I knew that she was being manipulated and controlled," Raoul recounted. "I told her so and kissed her as if I could break the spell."

"As we have established, you are a romantic fool." Philippe had pity in his voice that Raoul hated.

"And you were a fool again when you accosted her after the premiere of *Rigoletto*," Antoine went on. "Her beneficent *angel* probably heard you professing your great love for her and went into a fit of jealous rage."

"Are you implying *I* am the reason he killed that stagehand?" Raoul sprang up, ready to fall upon his brother's friend.

"Raoul, calm down!" Philippe barked, holding Raoul back. "We don't know why he killed Joseph Buquet. Or if he did."

"He did. I'm sure of it." Raoul fell back into his chair. Now came the most humiliating part of the tale. "I just don't know how Christine could have gone back to him once again knowing that, or how she could have refused me."

"You mean when you proposed the next morning?" Philippe raised his hands when Raoul sent him a dire glare. "You're right though. We should have known something was amiss when she rejected you so cruelly. No sane woman would do that."

"I didn't want to think about it." Raoul blushed to recall the days after he had been left alone in the Madeleine waiting for Christine. He had wanted to marry her since he was fifteen. His foolish heart still wanted nothing more than to lock her away from all this horror. In the days after her rejection he had indulged every vice he had. It had only been a dire warning that had brought him back to reality.

"You believe it was that Persian who tipped you off about the two of them going to the Bois after that?" Philippe went on.

"I don't know, but that's the only time I've seen the villain, before tonight," Raoul replied.

"I think the masquerade was technically last night," Philippe groaned.

"Did he look different? Erik, I mean," Antoine asked, his eyes fixed on Raoul and filling with fervor once again. "When you saw him and Christine in the Bois that night, did his face look like a skull?"

"He had a black cape and a wide-brimmed hat, felt maybe. His face looked like death. I thought it was another mask," Raoul answered softly. "It made more sense than a living corpse trying to kiss Christine."

"He must have her under quite the spell," Philippe grumbled and Antoine gave a scoff.

"He does!" Raoul sat upright again, anger surging. "It's his voice! It acts on her like magic. He's using his voice and his control of her career to manipulate her!"

"Does believing that make it easier on you?" Antoine's lip curled. "I've never seen anything uglier than the face of Red Death. I remember thinking that six years ago before he killed our fathers. That even the devil couldn't concoct something more hideous. Yet your Christine returns to him! Defends him! Probably even spreads—"

Antoine crumpled to the floor with the force of Raoul's blow. Philippe, surprisingly, had not moved to stop his brother from striking. "She is *not* acting of her own accord. He has bewitched her," Raoul gritted out as Antoine massaged his jaw and struggled back into his chair. "I saw it last night when I watched her go through the mirror."

Raoul held back the final bit of the confession, as he had all night. That he had heard her speak the name before her strange angel had come to abduct her again. 'Poor Erik,' she had sighed. Not poor Raoul. Poor *Erik*. The memory sparked a rage in him that made his smarting fist tighten again.

"Should we start in her dressing room? See if we can find Erik behind that mirror?" Philippe offered, but the other men shook their heads.

"That's just the door. The whole Opera is his labyrinth," Antoine said. "In or out of the Opera, we're facing a monster who will not hesitate to kill. He nearly strangled Raoul in the Bois. Only Christine saved him."

"Christine is the key." Raoul saw her face in his memory, turned to her mirror in absolute ecstasy, and a fresh burst of rage filled his heart. "We have to save Christine from him first."

"And how do you propose we *find* her to do the saving, if she's with him?" Philippe scoffed.

"Adèle might know something she hasn't mentioned," Antoine offered. "I could ask her."

"She's furious with you after the scene you made last night." Philippe turned to Raoul. "But she's always liked you, little brother. Perhaps after church, you can go."

"Church?" Raoul furrowed his brow.

"It's Lent," Philippe replied with a put-upon scowl.

"Since when have you cared about Shrovetide?" Antoine asked.

"Since the two of you started talking so cavalierly about killing a man. I think it might do you some good to remember what today is about." Philippe looked grimly at his younger brother and Raoul shivered. "Remember: thou art dust, and to dust you shall return."

There was no dawn in the underground. Erik had come to accept that years ago. More than accept it, he enjoyed making his life in a place divorced from arbitrary ideas like hours and dates on a calendar. When you lived outside of time and the world, nothing could hurt you. It was safe in the quiet dark next to the lake, tucked into the foundations of the grandest opera house in

Europe. Yes, he was a ghost, trapped in the shadows, but phantoms were not subject to the rules and vicissitudes of mortal men.

The ivory keys beneath his hands, only slightly paler than his skin, sang softly of loneliness and protection, of being untouched by the living world. Down here in the dark, he could sing forever, and no one could stop him or harm him, not even time. He liked losing himself in a book or a new invention or composition, only to find he had been transported through days. It was so easy to disappear.

Or it had been, before Christine Daaé walked into his life.

Erik stopped playing as he listened for movement from the adjacent room. Silence answered. He took up his quill to scratch a few more notes onto the parchment in front of him and considered the changes his Christine had wrought in his lonely existence.

His angel had come to him in the rain, fate placing her in the orbit of the famous Opera Ghost at just the right moment. Fate had taken pains in those early days to let him see her kindness and how lost she was. It had been a simple thing to reward a gentle soul by restoring her faith. Erik had shown her that ghosts were real, but Christine had not come to the Opera looking for ghosts.

It had been easy to become her Angel of Music, no different than pretending to be a ghost. But ghosts did not lust as he had for her, and angels did not sing their willing students to ecstasy as she had begged him to do. By the time Erik had realized he loved her, he had been lost entirely. So was she.

Erik smiled, the action still alien without the pressure of his mask against his face. Christine didn't let him wear it when they were alone anymore, especially when they made love. Such a contrast to the first time he had bound her and blindfolded her just to caress her, doing all he could to hide. He had thought nothing would match the thrill of her skin beneath his fingers. How wrong he had been.

With each encounter, she amazed him. Last night more than ever, when she had trapped him beneath her and let him spill inside her, speaking an impossible confession.

He had woken next to her hours ago, and for a while, he had stayed, drinking in her beauty in the dim candlelight. Just as she had transformed his world all those months ago, now she had put an entire symphony into his brain with the miracle of her kindness. Her kiss.

Her love.

Erik knew of no other way to celebrate this miracle than through his music. So he had slunk from their bed to play and transcribe a fraction of the awe and disbelief and fear and love in his soul.

Erik didn't look at the clock on the mantle to see the hour. He didn't want to know how close he might be to reality's return and the end of these dreams. Even after so many nights as Christine's lover, he still feared the dawn beside her. Or maybe it was the simple fact that, in his heart, he knew that he was a monster undeserving of her light. He would keep that light, even so. He'd do anything to keep it.

"I knew I'd find you here." Christine's voice came from behind him in answer to a silent prayer.

It was like the sun breaking over a mountain at dawn, turning to see her. The sky brightened as she smiled, gentle and indulgent, and the warmth of day returned as she drew near.

"I am sorry if I woke you. I was inspired," Erik murmured, taking in the beauty of the woman draped in dark sheets.

Perhaps there were those in the world above who would not find her perfect. They might deride the roundness of her hips and belly, the asymmetry of her eyes, the mess of her dark hair from a night of exertion, or the weakness of her chin. To Erik, she was nothing short of a goddess.

"I don't fully believe that," Christine admonished as she took her place next to him on the piano bench. "I think you ran off because you were afraid that I'd wake up and take it back. As if that were possible."

"Anything is possible." It was strange – after so many years of hiding his ruined face, with its corpse's sunken nose and hideous scars – how odd it felt for his bare cheeks to heat with embarrassment.

"I meant it." Christine caught Erik's chin with her finger to make him look at her. She looked back at his face with all its horrors... and smiled. She kissed him softly and held his gaze as she drew away. A miracle once again. "I love you. You can't run from it."

Words failed him, even as unheard music surged through his soul. He twined his fingers with hers as he kissed her, for it was all he could do to express his awe and need. He wanted to hold her forever; freeze this instant and those words for all time. Could he ever ask for such a gift? Even as the kiss deepened, the answer flared in his mind. Erik sprang up.

"I said not to run!"

"Stay there! I – I have to find something." Erik fled to his room. The ebony casket on his dresser was dusty. He hadn't touched the little box in years, but its contents were still there. The cool, solid feel of metal in his hand soothed his rising nerves as he returned to find Christine standing in wait.

"Erik, what is that?"

"I told you about the party at my father's house and being captured. The fire. I never told you why they thought I was a thief." Even as he spoke, the memory of that awful night made the scars across his shoulder and chest prickle. His father's pained voice calling out for his son at last echoed in his mind. Erik tightened his grip as Christine gave his hand a dubious look.

"Was it because you actually stole something?"

Erik gave a shrug that Christine answered with an indulgent scowl. "I felt entitled to this, but technically, I was not within any conventional legal rights in taking it."

"I'll ask again: what is it?"

Erik's fist clasped harder around the hard-won prize. "I didn't see my grandmother, the Baroness, very often as a child, but I knew her. For the longest time, I thought she was just a kind aristocrat that cared for us. When I learned who my real father was, it all made sense. The next time I saw her after that, I confronted her and asked her if I was so ugly because of what father had done to my mother."

"What did she say to that?" Christine asked as she caressed Erik's arm, offering comfort in the face of darkness.

"She said with personal certainty that children born of crimes and violence were not doomed by that, because the opposite wasn't true. My father was born of love and look how he turned out. Maybe there was hope for me." Erik gave a laugh.

"She was right, but why did she think so?" Christine asked sternly.

"Because she loved my grandfather, the old Baron. He had fought his parents for the right to marry her since she was below his station. His wedding ring bore his family motto. *Sic itur ad astra.* It means 'so goes one to the star and immortality'." Erik opened his hand and showed Christine the plain gold band, the engraving barely visible within.

"You stole your grandfather's ring?"

"I meant to, but when I finally had a chance to look at my prize, I found I had taken the wrong one. Maybe my grandmother took it off when he died." Erik toyed with the ring. It would fit one of his thin fingers if he tried.

"How do you know it's hers?"

"She showed me the engraving, that day. The promise that at least one man in my family knew how to love. *Amor ultra astra.*"

"Love past the stars," Christine whispered. She had grown still beside Erik, her eyes on the ring. "Why were you thinking of that today?"

"I'm not asking you to marry, don't worry," Erik said too quickly, and Christine raised an eyebrow. "I only ask for you to wear this as a symbol of the promises already given."

"That I am yours." Christine touched the gold band in Erik's palm.

"That you will always come back to me after you go up to the world above. That you will call this your home and stay here with me." Erik's heart seized as he asked it. He had never been so bold. "I love you and—"

"Yes," Christine said before he could make more of a fool of himself. "I will wear your ring, Erik."

Christine swallowed and presented her hand. Her right hand. Because this was not a wedding band and never could be for them. It was something less and more.

Trembling, Erik placed the ring on Christine's finger, surprised once again at how this woman could render him utterly helpless. He stared at the ring, shining in the candlelight and caught his breath in awe before he kissed Christine, sealing the vow.

What a picture they had to make, Erik thought distantly, as Christine's lips opened against his. A man with the face of death embracing an angel, two bodies in the shadows below Paris, tangled together, at the cusp of becoming one.

"You are everything to me, Christine Daaé."

"Would you believe me if I said the same was true of you?" Christine was breathless, her face full of something warm and kind. Was this what love looked like? Erik was not sure. He had never seen love in this light.

"No, but I hope you will try to convince me." Erik relinquished his last drop of composure as Christine smirked, and the sheet that had been concealing her nakedness fell away. Erik drew back to drink in her beauty, her utter perfection. "That's a good start."

"You're awful." Christine shook her head. Erik's hands swept over her and she sighed in delight, eyes falling shut so she didn't see his mask of arrogance fall away.

"I know," he whispered. "Will you tell Adèle that you won't need your room at her flat anymore? Tell her you've found a new home. Today," Erik begged but tried to make it sound like a command.

"As soon as I can. Then I'll come home and—" She held a finger to Erik's lips before he could speak. "When she asks, I'll confirm what she's known for a while. That I've made the awful mistake of falling in love and there is no cure for it."

The February sky was dark gray, barely penetrated by the dim morning sun. Shaya scowled at it as he rose from his prayers. If he didn't have to face Mecca to prostrate himself before Allah, he wouldn't even know which direction the sun was coming from. He had made a study of Paris's avenues and boulevards in his first months here, so he knew where East was, even on mornings like this when he was forced to do his duty to God in a hidden alley a few streets away from the Opera.

Shaya could have said his prayers at home, with Darius beside him, if he were a different man. That man could have been enjoying a strong cup of hot chocolate (one of the few inventions of this land that he enjoyed unabashedly) next to a warm fire right now. Instead, the inferno in his brain had driven him from home in the dark of the morning, leaving their fire to gutter to ashes for Darius to rekindle alone. Shaya had left a note, assuring his longtime companion (it was a fiction to call him a manservant anymore) that he was alive and Erik had not killed him at last. He had failed to mention what he meant to do.

He had sought Erik's ruin for years, and now that the monster admitted his great love for Christine Daaé, it was within reach. Shaya would need agents to help. Ideally, it would be the young Vicomte de Chagny, who foolishly loved Daaé, but Shaya could bring others to his cause. Recruiting spies was easy, if one had the right leverage. After a night of sin for Mardi Gras, the denizens of the Opera would all be on their way to beg absolution as Lent began, and leverage would abound.

Paris was full of churches, chapels, basilicas, and grand cathedrals, but the Opera folk tended to flock to one in particular. The Madeleine was a short walk from the Palais Garnier, and the building modeled on a Greek temple was a fitting place of worship for artists who were no better than pagans most days.

Shaya pulled his coat tighter as he watched hungover scene painters and choristers file up the stairs into the grand façade for services. They passed by those exiting, who had come earlier to have their foreheads marked with an ashen cross they would bear like the mark of Cain all day. Shaya had never really understood the ritual, but none of these people would understand why he had made the Hajj in his youth, so he didn't begrudge them.

He recognized many faces as he drew closer. There was Gerard Gabriel, the chorus director, looking bleary and yawning as he entered the church, with Carlos Fontana, the lead tenor, limping behind him. Did Gabriel look guilty? Was he too high of a mark for Shaya? He had clearly been influenced by "the Ghost" when it came to Christine, but he also thought Shaya *was* the Phantom, or some agent for him. Would it be worth his time to try and convince him they had a common enemy?

Shaya shook his head and fished in his pocket for his bag of tobacco and papers, only to discover those were in another coat. Or that Darius had removed them *again* because he hated the habit. He sighed in annoyance as he looked up, just in time to catch swift movement across the square.

A woman rushed towards a gaggle of ballet dancers (Shaya could tell their vocation from their identical chignons and the way they moved like reeds in the winter wind). He recognized her. There were only so many young ladies with dark brown skin and sparkling eyes who frequented the areas around the Opera, and Christine Daaé's dresser and friend Julianne Bonet was one of them.

Shaya watched as Bonet accosted one of the dancers, an older girl with dark blonde hair. Cécile Jammes. The dancer had been involved in the discovery of Joseph Buquet's body, and Shaya knew her. Bonet grabbed the dancer by the elbow with a sort of desperate possessiveness that interested Shaya greatly.

He skirted the square, keeping his eyes on his prey while Bonet tugged Jammes away from her friends and towards the row of shops near the grand church, closer to Shaya. Perhaps fate was smiling on him today.

"Are you really serious about this?" Bonet was asking heatedly as Shaya came within earshot, secreted in front of a shuttered mustard shop.

"Just because you don't care about our souls doesn't mean I feel the same way," Jammes snapped back.

"So give up meat for Lent like everyone else and confess your sins! You don't have to give up *us*." That certainly was interesting.

"Be quiet! There are normal people about!" Jammes hissed, confirming Shaya's suspicions. "Anyway, you should be happy. It frees you up to dote over your precious Christine."

"Christine is my friend and she's—" Shaya peered around the corner in time to see Bonet bite her lip, holding back a secret she couldn't reveal. "I don't care for her the way I care for you." Shaya couldn't see Jammes' expression, only Bonet's, and she looked hurt by whatever she saw in her paramour's face. "I love—"

"Don't say it!" Jammes admonished. "It's a sin!"

"Love is never a sin," Bonet replied quietly.

Shaya's heart seized. They were simple words, but somehow, they had made it to Julianne from the man who had spoken them to Shaya and Erik, so long ago.

"Go home, Julianne. Or better yet, go to church."

"I don't need to anoint myself with ashes to pretend to be holy," Bonet spat and turned away. "Neither do you, Cécile."

Jammes remained still as stone while Bonet stalked away, her back turned to the grand façade of the Madeleine. When Shaya moved so that he could see her face, he saw a tear on her cheek.

"An interesting choice in lovers, but not the strangest I have heard of in the Opera," Shaya said lightly as he stepped towards the dancer. Jammes went pale. He wondered if it was just his words or if she, like so many of the petits rats, feared the infamous 'Persian' as much as the Opera Ghost.

"What did you hear?" Jammes asked.

"Enough that if I were to share it, it would cause quite a scandal for you." Shaya smirked. "I don't think the chaperones would want such a dangerous influence around young girls."

Jammes sneered. "No one would believe you. Why would you tell anyway?"

"Because secrets are my business. I'll keep yours if you trade me something better."

"What?" Jammes blinked. She looked overwhelmed and Shaya was sympathetic. This was a lot for one morning, but she had to be prepared for a bit of intrigue at the Opera.

"You know things, Mademoiselle. About ghosts and stagehands hung above the stage. Things that are far more valuable than the sins of a ballet rat."

"Don't you work for him? Doesn't he know everything?" Jammes asked with narrowed eyes.

Shaya shook his head slowly. "I am his greatest enemy, Mademoiselle. I assure you any secrets you share with me will help to destroy him." There was nothing more to say, for now. "Good day, Mademoiselle Jammes. May God be with you."

Shaya knew Jammes glared at him as he walked away. It truly was a blessed day. He could hear the sound of the great organ inside the Madeleine as he walked beside the church in its cold shadow. Shrovetide had begun; the last gasp of winter when things were leanest and darkest. But that meant that spring would come soon. So too would the triumph he had awaited and sought for years. He could feel it in his soul.

The world was always a bit too bright when Christine stepped out of the cellars of the Opera and into the world of the living. Today she felt especially out of place with Erik's ring glittering upon her hand. A promise to the man she loved.

The thought echoed in her mind as she strode down the *Rue des Petits Champs* towards the flat of Adèle Valerius. Months ago, she had been content to love an angel. Now, she was certain in her love for a man. Love damned them both, but knowing that was better than lying to herself or hurting him by not telling him the truth. Erik was brave enough to love her despite the pain, so she had decided to be brave as well.

Christine cast her eyes away from the crowd around the Basilica of *Notre Dame des Victoires*, the faithful lining up to be marked for the season of Lent. She had gone last year, when she was failing and faithless at the conservatoire. She had not been able to see how a few ashes on her forehead would make her life any better. This year, she had spent the morning in delicious sin and intended to bide all of Shrovetide indulging her lusts and vices.

The door to Adèle's flat swung open and Christine took in the sight of the parlor. It had appeared so grand to Christine months ago, when the mezzo soprano she had been assigned to understudy had taken her under her wing and offered her a place to call home. Now, Christine saw the dust and the frayed edges. The walls were lined with posters and pictures of Adèle's past glories and a single portrait of the great love whose loss had hardened her friend's heart.

Even back then, Christine had not felt at home here. In those days, she had made her real home in a hidden corner of the cellars with a set piece as her bed and a bower of silken flowers above her. Now, her home lay deeper in the dark, and her bower was a canopy carved to look like a forest at night. She had thought of Erik's secret house on the lake below the Opera as home for weeks now. That was the place she was safe, where she didn't have to hide herself in any way. Erik saw all of her and thought she was beautiful. He knew all her crimes and still forgave her.

Christine's mind filled with the image of Joseph Buquet's body falling into the emptiness of the flies, his neck snapping before her eyes. The moment the life left his body repeated often in the theater of her mind, and what frightened her most was not the awful memory, but how each time she recalled it, it shocked her less. She had pushed that man to his end to save Erik. She would do it again.

A woman like her – prepared to do such things for a man who had taken lives and committed crimes far worse – didn't deserve the light of the living world. She deserved his ring on her finger, marking her. She deserved to go back to the dark to her terrible love.

Christine shook herself from her reverie and moved through the parlor.

"Adèle? Are you home?" Christine called. A tired groan came from the bedroom, followed by shuffling and swearing.

"What are you doing here this early?" Adèle demanded as she stumbled from her boudoir, tightening her robe over her ample curves. "In fact, what are you doing here at all?"

"That's what I need to talk about. I came to get the last of my things. I won't be needing the room anymore."

A wry smile warmed Adèle's face. "Well, it's about time your mysterious teacher found a place to house you. Do you need a suitcase?"

"I would appreciate that." Christine smiled as they entered the simple bedroom where she had never slept well. The maid must have tidied. The last Christine remembered seeing this room, the bed had been in shambles after she had made love to her angel there for the first time.

"I hope wherever your protector is putting you up, it has thicker walls," Adèle commented, following Christine's gaze. The Christine of even a week ago would have blushed at the comment, but today's Christine only smirked.

"It does. And very few neighbors."

"Lucky girl." Adèle retreated as Christine gathered her meager possessions from the drawers and returned with a worn bag made of an old carpet. "Don't worry about returning that. I won't need it. You might."

"What do you mean?"

"I'm happy for you moving up in the world, but you must be careful. Letting a man keep you can be dangerous. Gilded or not it's still a cage," Adèle said. "I have my own flat for a reason."

"It's not like that. He and I..." Christine touched the ring on her finger to steady herself. "It's different."

"So it's love?" It was a resigned statement rife with disappointment. Christine shrugged in reply and returned to packing her things. "Are you still taking precautions? Nothing is going to ruin your career or your sweet dreams of romance faster than a welp in your belly."

Christine blanched. "Yes. Mostly."

There had been a moment in his arms after the masquerade when everything had felt *possible*. When she hadn't just accepted that she loved a man with the face of death who hid from the world in the dark – she had dreamed for a second of *more*. Something more that could grow from them, from their love.

"I'm going to make you some special tea, just in case. In fact, you can have my supply of 'just in case' when you go." Adèle wafted from the room before Christine could protest and she followed with her full bag, pausing briefly to look back at the room she was leaving behind. The absence of any sort of regret comforted her.

In the parlor, Adèle fussed with a teacup and a tin of herbs that Christine knew were meant to keep a woman free of the burden of a child. She handed Christine the cup with a stern expression as Christine hesitated. She should drink it, she knew; to stem the risk brought on by her stupidity and passions, even if the danger was meager.

Until last night, they – or more accurately *Erik* – had been careful. He had never spilled inside her, saving her from the doom of continuing his bloodline. She hadn't told him the real reason he need not fear, but that was one secret she wanted to keep, for a little while more at least. She took the tea without protest. It tasted of bitter earth and summer sky. How strange.

"Good girl, nothing can drive a man away from his kept woman faster."

"For the last time, Adèle, I'm not being kept," Christine huffed.

"You know, I wouldn't have to be so worried if I knew more about your mysterious lover." Adèle took a seat near the enameled fireplace and gave Christine an accusing look.

"He's extremely private," Christine muttered.

"There's private and then there's a bloody ghost." Christine's choked on her tea, but Adèle didn't see as she heaved a dramatic sigh and let her head fall back. "The way that man makes you sing *and* hit your high notes, shall we say. I'm jealous."

"Are you finally going to look for someone better than Antoine?" Christine chuckled.

"Why do you think I'm giving you my supplies?" Adèle replied with a fresh scowl. "To think I wasted so much time at the masquerade with him, and he had the audacity to lose his mind before I had a proper final ride on that pretty cock of his."

"I'm going to ignore that second part. And ask what you mean by 'lose his mind'?"

"He went mad after Red Death put a curse on him at the masquerade, the fool."

"What?" Christine asked, unable to keep the dread from her voice. She had stopped Erik – clad in macabre crimson splendor – from exacting his wrath upon some fool at the masquerade. Had that been Antoine?

"I forgot, you weren't there. You missed quite the spectacle. For a while, we all thought it was the Phantom himself who'd stepped out of hell, or wherever it is he keeps his residence below. Red Death, he named himself, this man in a mask like nothing anyone had ever seen. I've never seen anything uglier." Adèle shuddered and it stabbed Christine to the heart. "Antoine, the idiot, tried to touch him. The thing caught him, nearly broke his wrist, and Antoine lost his mind. He was raving when Sorelli and I took him home."

"Raving about Red Death?"

"Said he was a ghost. Not the Opera Ghost, mind you, a different sort of ghost. I think." Adèle threw up her hands and shook her head. "An idiot, like I said."

"You don't think it was the Opera Ghost?" Christine asked carefully.

"Well, we all did until some little trollop decided to *dance* with the man. The girl looked entirely enamored of him, and I can't imagine any ghost inspiring such *admiration*."

"Maybe you need a more vivid imagination." Adèle looked at her curiously and Christine gave a falsely innocent shrug.

"And what were you doing last night, by the way?" Adèle asked with a sly smile. "It had to have been enjoyable if you're leaving my nest for good this morning—"

A knock at the door cut off the older woman. "Odd time for visitors." Adèle went to the door, uncaring for any modesty regarding her lack of dress. Christine admired that. "May I—Monsieur de Chagny?"

Christine spun at the name, hoping against hope that she wouldn't see the younger of the Chagny brothers at Adèle's door, but she had no such luck.

"I'm glad you're home," Raoul said. "I was hoping you could – *Christine?*"

Christine's heart was a stone in her chest as Raoul stared at her over Adèle's shoulder.

Last night, she had broken his heart on purpose. It had been as awful as pushing Joseph Buquet to his doom, but just as inevitable. Raoul had seen her and Erik together, caught in an embrace in the *Bois de Boulogne*. Only her promise that she would drive the boy she had once loved away had kept Erik from madness and desolation. At the masquerade, Raoul had called her a whore incapable of love and more. So why was he *there*?

"What are you doing here?" Christine demanded, forcing herself to stand and face the man who was looking at her with an undisguised mix of wonder and horror. "If you came looking for me, I think I made it very clear—"

"You had chosen *him*. I remember. I came here to ask Madame Valerius if she would be of help with Antoine. He's doing poorly and—" Raoul swallowed and shook his head. "I doubt you care."

"Neither of us do," Adèle grumbled. "So you can be on your way."

Adèle began to close the door, but Raoul stopped her, pushing into the flat with eyes fixed on Christine. "I will confess to being surprised to find you here, of all places. Though I am relieved. Have you come to your senses when it comes to your illustrious angel?"

"That does not concern you." Christine had to remain calm...

"Does it concern your friend here then? Or anyone who cares for you? Don't you think she should know the danger you've put yourself in?" Raoul's eyes were wide and bright. Christine began to tremble.

"Danger?" Adèle scoffed.

"Yes, danger!" Raoul cried. "Christine will lie and say she is safe, but she knows. She must know that the man who has ensnared her is the worst sort of villain."

"What on earth are you on about, boy? You sound as mad as Antoine!" Adèle laid a hand on Raoul's heaving chest, but he shook her away.

"Please, Christine, reassure your friend that you are safe!" Raoul pushed. "Tell her you won't be descending into the netherworld any time soon. Or that you've come to your senses!"

"Raoul, stop! Please!" Christine cried, raising her hands as Raoul pressed towards her, senseless of Adèle trying to hold him back. Raoul's fury froze and he stared at Christine's hands. "You have no right to speak to me like this."

"No one has the right to speak to her like that," Adèle hissed in agreement. "You're not her husband or her fiancé, dear God."

"Then who is?" Raoul asked flatly. Christine retracted her hand, but it was too late. Raoul had seen the ring. "Who gave you that? Is it a wedding ring?"

"Wedding rings go on the left hand," Christine protested, holding her hand to her chest to calm her pounding heart. "And as I have tried again and again to make clear: I owe you no explanations for my life, nor who I spend it with!"

"So it is from him. Your angel." Something grim settled on Raoul's face. "Your Erik."

Christine felt as if the room turned upside down. As if the world had started spinning like a whirlpool and she was about to drown. Blood pounded in her ears and her guts scurried in terror around her insides as her panic rose.

"*Where did you hear that name?*"

Raoul's face hardened further. "From your own lips. Last night in your dressing room."

"You were spying on me?" Christine fumbled for the arm of her chair, her legs failing her as she stumbled back and sat.

"A voice from the walls inspires you to slavish ecstasy and you fault *me* for trying to get to the truth of whoever it is who had ensnared you?"

Christine was going to be sick. Adèle ran to her, kneeling to embrace her. "Raoul, you don't know what—"

"I know what I saw. I know who it is that has trapped you in these lies and plots." Raoul looked mad and triumphant. Did he still think he would save her? It would be the death of him. Or Erik. Or both

"You must forget that name," Christine declared, grabbing Adèle's arm. "If you want both of us – *all* of us – to be safe, please, forget that name!"

"So you admit he is dangerous!" Raoul crowed, undeterred.

"No!" Christine heaved a sob, quaking in panic.

"Get out of my home, young man," Adèle intervened, pulling Christine close. The firm warmth of her body against Christine was like a port in a storm and Christine clung to it. "You've done quite enough. Go tell Antoine he can go fuck himself while you're at it."

"I won't go until I know Christine is safe!" Raoul shouted, and Christine covered her ears. Everything she had done had been for nothing! Raoul was still as foolish and focused as ever.

"Raoul, I can explain everything, I promise you!" Christine heard herself say from a hundred miles away as she turned her face from Adèle's shoulder. "But please, don't speak of this to anyone! Give me time and I swear I will explain. I can't right now. I—"

"Will you promise to meet me tomorrow? At that café where we had supper? At six o'clock?"

Christine couldn't even remember the name of the place but she nodded. "Yes. I promise."

"Now get the hell out," Adèle snarled. Raoul gave a final scowl before turning and storming out the door. "Christine, what was he on about? Are you really in danger?"

"No, I..." Christine swallowed, trying to calm her pounding heart. She focused on the details of the physical world around her. The feel of Adèle's linen shift against her hands. The smell of soap. The heat of the fire. "I'm not in danger."

"But Raoul is? Your Erik would hurt him?" Christine blinked up at Adèle, shocked again to hear that name in a mortal mouth. "Christine, I knew. I heard you that night, remember? You called that name. Several times."

"Goddamnit," Christine groaned.

"You need to stop being a fool about this affair, right now." Adèle held her firmly and breathed slowly, forcing Christine to match her. "This is what you do: You take your things and go to Erik. I will tell people you still live here. No one will know you aren't with Robert. And yes, I know Robert is sleeping with Moncharmin. I'm not a fool."

"Why are you—"

"Because I see it in your face when you talk about this man. You truly love him. You're practically marked with it, like one of those dusty crosses on your head."

"What else do I do?" Each word hurt. All of it hurt so much now that she admitted what Erik was to her.

"Do what we do best. Act." Christine looked up at her friend. "We play our parts. We make the fools in the audience think we are fragile damsels in need of rescue. It's easier for them that way, rather than meeting us as people. Make Raoul think he's saving you and then send him away with that."

"Erik won't..." Christine bit her tongue. It felt like a sin to speak his name, even now.

"If you love him, you'll make him understand what you have to do."

2. Leading Roles

Erik felt light as he walked the empty halls of his Opera. Lighter than he had felt in ages. Finally, the things he loved were safe. His angel and his home. Their home? Erik paused in the silent hall and smiled. As mad as it sounded, it was true. He would enjoy it more once he dealt with his administrative duties.

"Sweet Christ, my back," a low voice groaned further down the hall behind the very door to which Erik was headed. "I told you we should have just gone to your flat."

The only response was a rather piteous moan. The first speaker answered with a sonorous laugh that Erik recognized. It was Robert Rameau, the lead bass. Which meant that the other man inside the office where Erik had been heading was Rameau's lover, Armand Moncharmin, the artistic manager of the Paris Opera.

"How are you not hungover?" Moncharmin asked, voice thick with suffering, as Erik approached. "You had more last night than me."

"I told you: champagne is poison. Stick to sherry and you won't regret a thing in the morning."

Moncharmin made another pained sound. Erik glanced into the office. It was less opulent than the rest of the Opera, but the two men sprawled on the floor among discarded clothes, half under the desk, did increase the air of decadence.

"You are the devil," Moncharmin muttered, rubbing his eyes as Rameau leaned in to kiss him with a tender smile.

Erik watched the intimate moment with a twinge in his gut. He glimpsed encounters like these all the time as a ghost, though he tried to avoid it. His discretion was not out of any respect for the privacy; more so because catching an assignation had always reminded him of his own isolation. Now, it reminded him of what he loved, and how dangerous it remained. The lightness that had buoyed Erik all morning faded, and he saw a similar darkness in Moncharmin's face as his lover pulled away.

"You should go," Moncharmin said softly.

"Why? It's not like I have rehearsal," Rameau replied. Erik could hear something hesitant in the deep voice; something longing for more. Moncharmin stood by way of answering. "Armand."

"I have to work," Moncharmin sighed. "I'm assembling a full proposal for Richard on why we should mount our first production of Wagner."

"Of course you are." Rameau's exhale was wistful and resigned.

Erik retreated to an alcove in the hall as Rameau made himself decent and took his time exiting the office. Erik wondered if there was a final kiss, something to remind the two of whatever passion had led them to that office together the night before. Something to get them through the day alone. He hoped so, but the melancholy on Rameau's face indicated there had not been.

Erik waited from the shadows as Rameau's footsteps retreated. That was his life so often: waiting. Hiding. Watching the dramas of other people who had no idea how lucky they were to walk in the sun. Christine had changed that, given him someone to go home to. Yet Erik still knew that loneliness. Just like he was sure Armand Moncharmin did.

Perhaps that was why the Opera Ghost found himself standing at the manager's office door, clearly visible when Moncharmin looked up. There was no fear in his face, just quiet resignation.

"You didn't need to send him away. This place is a tomb on days like this."

To Erik's surprise, Moncharmin gave a tired smile. "I know. But it makes things difficult, having him here." The manager stepped behind his desk – which was just as mussed and disheveled as he was – and began sorting through the chaos. "Not in the way you're thinking though."

"Bold of you to assume how I think."

"He's not distracting," Moncharmin went on, straightening a pile of papers. "It's just that a domestic morning with him reminds me too much of—"

"All the things you cannot have." Erik gave a rueful smile at the edge of his mask. "You think having those things more will make it even harder to give them up?"

"Yes," Moncharmin chuckled and adjusted his spectacles.

"But they're already too hard to give up. Why not savor as much as you can?" Erik thought back to the morning and wanting to hold Christine until the world turned to dust around them. And the wrenching pain of watching her leave.

"You have a surprising depth of opinions on love for a phantom," Moncharmin remarked. "I thought your expertise only extended to music."

"It is music I am here to serve, but it is not all I am." Erik gave a shrug that made him appear, he hoped, less nervous than he felt.

"No, it would seem not. You, my friend, are something more." Erik began to feel a tightness in his chest as Moncharmin's sharp eyes remained on him, peering curiously through his spectacles. "Did you always attend the masquerades? I enjoy them. Having a night to be anything I want is liberating."

"As I said: I find it better to enjoy what I can, when I can," Erik answered. Moncharmin gave a nod and Erik flexed his fists. How did people do this? Just talk? Moncharmin righted a crooked stack of scores, with the largest on top. "So you are taking my advice? *Lohengrin?*"

"Richard and the patrons will have a fit about putting on our first Wagner, but the public has an appetite for it. I think we can find the right cast." Moncharmin held the ghost's gaze. "We may have to find someone to help Fontana, or another Swan Knight altogether. Valerius does deserve a role like Ortrud though, and Robert would enjoy being a king rather than a villain for once."

"And Elsa?" It was a role with greater vocal demands than Christine had ever undertaken.

"Mademoiselle Daaé will still be our poor martyr," Moncharmin nodded. "Another woman deceived and used who will die for love. As if there were any other kind in grand opera."

"There used to be," Erik replied wistfully. He turned away, glancing over his shoulder one last time. "I will leave you to your work."

"Do send my regards and compliments to your Queen of the Night. She was quite the sight, dancing with Red Death."

Erik wondered if he had made another impulsive mistake by speaking to Moncharmin like a fellow man. He knew what Erik was and could ruin everything. But Erik knew what he was, and there was a sort of equality there. Moncharmin was not the sort to tear away the mask of another.

"I shall. Until we meet again, *Monsieur le Directeur*" Erik threw his voice so it echoed through the office before disappearing down the hall. He did need to maintain some level of mystery.

Erik mused on the conversation as he made his rounds of the Palais Garnier, wafting like a shadow through the Grand Foyer and salons, each room covered in so much golden ornamentation and extravagant murals that the effect was like being encased in a great jewel box. Today the hall was still littered with the detritus of the masquerade the night before. A mask here, a shattered glass there, a feather and a crown cast into a corner.

The *grand escalier* was Erik's favorite, even after years. The marble of cream and peach and mauve and teal, the sweeping curves of the banisters, the nymphs raising their unlit torches to the sky. A dim beam of sunlight shone down into the empty, echoing space, reminding Erik of the one above his lake that let in just enough light to his underworld that he could see across the water in the day. All of it – the stone in the same color of flushed skin, the curves and frolicking nymphs, even the light shining into the darkness – made him think of Christine and long for her return. Perhaps she was on her way home even now.

How strange, that he could miss her so much after such a short time.

The thought of her moved him like the wind, and he found himself slipping through the door to the darkened auditorium and passing beneath the unlit chandelier. The massive ornament of crystal and brass hung like a dull bauble, an extinguished sun amidst the painted clouds. Erik wasn't concerned with that. His road took him through the orchestra and under the stage, then directly down. Through the ropes and cellars and scenery, right down to the darkest reaches of the Opera, to where he would find her. Or wait for her forever.

"Where have you been?"

Raoul had barely shut the door before his sister's cry echoed through the front hall of the manor. He was reminded of being caught stealing sweets from the kitchen as a child and was glad of the ashen cross on his forehead as an excuse. "Church."

"Why didn't you wait for us?" Sabine was marked too. She must have gone with Philippe while Raoul was off getting his head spun about again. "My maid told me you got in late and were up until dawn carousing with those idiots."

"One of those idiots is our brother and the head of this family."

"Says who? I didn't elect him." Sabine grabbed Raoul by the shoulder, forcing him to stand for an examination. Raoul knew he must look ghastly, and indeed, he wanted nothing more than to fall into bed and pretend the last days had been nothing but a dream.

"Luckily we're monarchists." Philippe's voice came from the parlor door and Sabine released the youngest Chagny. "Raoul was running an errand for me and went on his own to church, little sister. It's fine."

"It's not fine. Every time he leaves the house, he comes back injured or heartbroken!" Sabine looked truly concerned and it made Raoul feel small again, but not unpleasantly so. He was lucky to have a family that cared so much.

"He was checking in on a friend. He wasn't with the little strumpet, I assure you," Philippe sighed, and Raoul's warm feelings evaporated. He tried to hide the guilt in his face, but that had never worked with his siblings. "For God's sake, Raoul, you didn't! Did you?"

"I knew it!" Sabine crowed. "Has she not hurt you enough?"

"Is Antoine still here?" Raoul avoided Sabine's eyes as he rushed to the parlor where he had last seen his new ally in the war against this phantom.

"We're not done!" Sabine cried.

"Don't worry, I'll throttle him for both of us." Philippe followed Raoul into the parlor. Antoine was still there, sprawled asleep on the couch, his long legs hanging over the edge. The slam of the door behind Philippe startled him awake.

"What in the devil?" Antoine groaned.

"Raoul met with the whore," Philippe answered.

Raoul bristled. "She's not! There is no way under heaven she has allowed herself to be touched by that *thing*! And I didn't mean to. She was with Adèle."

Antoine stood (remarkably composed for a man who had just been unconscious) and glared at Raoul. "And what exactly did you discuss with your sweet Christine?"

Raoul gulped. It had seemed so righteous and correct to confront her. She had been wearing a ring from another man! A man who had murdered and destroyed so many lives! "I—"

"What did you do?" Philippe demanded.

"I told her I knew who her angel was. That I knew his name was Erik and that I'd been listening when he took her," Raoul sputtered, hoping the words would sound less foolish if they got out faster.

"You absolute fucking moron," Antoine growled, advancing on Raoul like a hungry wolf. "You idiot child!"

Antoine's hand flew back, and Raoul shut his eyes, bracing for the blow. Instead, he heard a muffled struggle. When he looked, Philippe was holding back his best friend from striking his brother.

"Control yourself!" Philippe bellowed, pushing Antoine back.

"We had one advantage against the monster!" Antoine cried, though he didn't struggle. "He didn't know that he'd revealed himself! Now he will!"

"She might not tell him!" Raoul protested. "Christine says knowing his name puts me in danger! She won't tell him if it means I'll be hurt."

"How do you know that?" Antoine sneered.

"He does have a point," Philippe said. "There's nothing in how your little bohemian has behaved to indicate she won't run right to her master and confess all."

"She promised she'd meet me tomorrow and explain!" Raoul whined.

Philippe looked ill. "And you believed her?"

"You've doomed this enterprise before it's even begun, you ass." Antoine began to move towards the door. "I see I'll have to take this into my own hands."

"If you go near Christine, it will be the last thing you do," Raoul snarled.

Antoine scoffed. "Rest assured, my besotted little friend, I have no intention of harming her."

"What are you going to do? Nothing rash, I hope," Philippe asked. "Unless it's going to the police like I've been saying all along we should do."

"The police are more useless than this idiot," Antoine replied. "I have other ideas." Without another word, Antoine threw open the parlor door to reveal Sabine waiting outside. The blond man's whole aura changed when he saw her, going from cold fury to oily obeisance as he bowed low. He took Sabine's hand and kissed it. "My dear lady, I will see you soon." Then was gone, leaving the whole family gaping after him.

"What on earth is going on? What are you all up to?" Sabine asked. Raoul glanced to Philippe for guidance.

"You needn't concern yourself," Philippe reassured her.

"I hope they were berating you about your ridiculous plan to go to the North Pole," Sabine asked.

Raoul had to think for a few beats as to what she meant. He'd almost forgotten that he had committed himself to the dangerous arctic voyage that left in two weeks, all because Christine had spurned him.

"I'm reconsidering, yes," Raoul replied, and the way Sabine smiled at the reassurance made his heart ache. "I'll know more tomorrow. Right now, I just need to rest."

"That does sound nice," Philippe agreed. "We will see you at dinner, dear sister."

Raoul's head was swimming by the time he was in his room, barely aware how he'd made it there. It was all too much. Too overwhelming. His world kept turning itself upside down and inside out.

Yet he was so sure of what needed to be done. Erik had stolen his father from him. That was a fact. Erik thought he could take Christine from Raoul. That was a fact too. The monster thought he could trap her with the promise of glory and golden rings, once again snatching from Raoul what he cared for most in the world.

Raoul would not let him. He would die before he let that creature have her. That was the thought he kept returning to as he slipped into the oblivion of sleep.

C hristine was still unaccustomed to finding her way to the house on the lake alone. That was the reason, she told herself, that she took so long to get home. Not a sick terror in her gut of what she had to confess to Erik. Of what she knew she had to do.

The dark fled only slightly from the lantern in her hand. She was not a part of it, as Erik was, at least not yet. She tried, sometimes, to imagine him in the light. What would he look like with the sun on his face? Every time she tried to picture Erik walking in a daytime garden or a green field, the image changed to a procession through a street full of jeering people as Erik was led to his execution.

Christine would not let that happen. She couldn't. She'd die if she lost him.

Her feet were like lead by the time she reached the hidden dock and triggered Erik's lock with a rhythm by Mozart. She found her lover exactly where she expected him to be, at the piano, engrossed in the same composition she had found him with earlier this morning. His attention was so focused he didn't even stop writing when she closed the door behind her.

She loved this place, this sanctuary below the stage. It was a lovely flat if you ignored the lack of windows. The ceiling painted with stars made up for it. The main parlor was full of candles, books, and musical instruments, dominated by the huge pipe organ opposite the door out to the lake. Erik's room was to the right and Christine's was to the left, both bedrooms filled with pictures and elegant hangings. The plush carpets and rich textures of the place made it feel so warm, even underground.

To the rear of the parlor, a door on the right went to Erik's workshop, where he built and explored and used his wondrous mind. It made Christine smile to think about it and then blush at her gratitude for all the other things Erik's clever hands could do. There was no room on the left to mirror the workshop, which was curious. Christine wasn't sure what filled that empty space and she always forgot to ask. The incredible man who built this all had a way of distracting her.

She surveyed her dark Angel of Music. His shirt was nearly the same color as his pale skin, half unbuttoned as if he had been so consumed with music, he had forgotten. He was so happy and unguarded like this – when the fire of eternal art was blazing inside him. She hated that she had to tear it away.

"Have you decided what it is yet?" Christine asked, and Erik looked up from his work. He had discarded his mask, and his long black hair was unkempt, framing his poor face as it lit with an expression of adoration.

"I think it might be an opera if I'm not careful. It's just an overture for now." Before Christine could speak again, he took her in his arms, kissing her like he hadn't seen her in years. She surrendered to it without a thought. "I'm glad you're home," Erik whispered, pulling back, and Christine was sure her heart would shatter.

"What did you do while I was gone?" she heard herself ask. "Did you go above?"

"I did. I had a pleasant conversation with Armand Moncharmin." Erik's scarred face was smug in a way that told Christine she had not misheard him.

"A *conversation*?"

"Face to face," Erik confirmed. "Well, face to mask. Same idea."

"What? Why?" Christine was not at all prepared for this sort of answer. Or for Erik to act so cavalier with their secrets. "You've gone to incredible lengths to make yourself a ghost and you just *talked* to one of the managers?"

"He looked lonely." Erik gave an infuriating shrug. "I do take pity on lost souls in my Opera once in a while. He'd just sent your dear Robert away. He won't reveal anything, just like we won't."

"And what, pray tell, did you discuss?"

"The next great triumph of the Paris Opera that will have all of Europe talking," Erik answered proudly, and the glimmer in his eye was as alarming as him conversing with another person. "Moncharmin has been swayed to finally attempt Wagner here."

"*Wagner*?" Christine squawked. "There will be a riot!"

"It will be quite an event," Erik grinned. "It won't be *The Ring*, of course. *Lohengrin* should be accessible enough for Paris."

"*Lohengrin*?" Christine echoed. Erik had played her a great deal of Wagner, and she'd heard bits of Wagner's epic opera about the doomed Swan Knight over the years, especially the wedding march, but performing it was as distant and intimidating as a mountain range and made her just as cold. Erik strode towards his shelf of scores. "I have it here somewhere..."

"I would have thought you would lobby for *Romeo and Juliette* to be mounted here at last. Or Mozart like we've talked about!"

Christine lamented, stomach twisting. "But you must have your modernism."

"It's not for me, it's for the Opera. And *you*."

"How is this for me?" Christine nearly shrieked.

Erik cocked his head, a few strands of dark hair falling in his face. "You'll be incredible as Elsa."

Christine blinked. "Erik, I'm years from even touching a role like that! You know that."

"You underestimate yourself," Erik countered, turning away again. Christine grabbed for the nearest wall, new horror and panic joining the throng in her mind that had been growing all day. She was going to faint...

"How could you demand this of me and not ask?" Christine couldn't breathe. This was too much. He was asking *too much*.

"You can do this. I promise." Erik said it kindly, but it made Christine want to crumble to the floor. And she began to.

"I can't do any of it! I can't—"

Erik had her in his grasp before she could fall, pulling her to his chest and touching her face with tender care that made the burden in her heart all the heavier. "Christine, what's wrong? What happened at Adèle's? You're more upset than any opera is worth."

Christine screwed her eyes shut and buried her face against the exposed skin of his chest, listening to the steady beat of his heart. "He was there. Raoul."

It was like Erik turned to stone at the sound of his rival's name, his arms tightening around Christine as his body went terrifyingly still.

"*Why?*" His tone made Christine shudder. She tried to stem her fear with the feel of Erik safe in her arms, but there was nothing safe about him in that moment.

"He was hiding in the dressing room last night when you came for me. He heard you. Erik, he heard me say your name! He knows who you are."

"What?" Erik pulled back, holding Christine by the shoulders, and once again like there was no solid ground beneath her. "That coward was hiding? I will have his hide!"

"No!" Christine cried, grabbing Erik as if she could keep him in check with pure will. "I told him not to speak of it to anyone! I told him if he wanted to be safe, he'd keep it to himself and I'd explain!" Fresh tears burned at the corners of Christine's eyes.

"How do you intend to *explain* this? He won't rest now!" Erik countered. "He won't give up until he's saved the damsel from the hideous monster. From the man *he knows I am*."

Christine braced herself. She knew what had to be done if she wanted to keep her angel safe in the dark. Even if it was terrible. She would do it.

"So I'll make him think he can save me." Christine waited, watching Erik as her words settled in his mind. She waited for his fury or panic, but there was only devastation. "I'm going to meet him tomorrow. Outside the Opera. I'm going to lie to him as much as I have to. I'll convince him of whatever he needs to believe and keep him in check *until he leaves*."

"What?" Erik asked. She could see moisture at the edges of his deep amber eyes now too.

"He's going to the North Pole! He'll be gone in a fortnight. Forever."

"That's a fortnight too long," Erik protested, violently wringing his hands through his hair. "Anything could happen in that time. You could—"

Christine grabbed Erik's wrists, forcing him to look at her, forcing him to remember that she was there and close. She placed her hand against his palm so he could see the ring. His ring.

"I swear I won't do anything you're dreading. I won't take this off. I'll still be *yours*." The way Erik changed as he looked at the ring was like a curtain rising.

Christine seized on the vulnerability and kissed him. She didn't know how to speak to this man, not really. Theirs had always been a connection beyond words, of flesh and music and tethered souls. There were no words that could calm him or keep him or convince him, only the truth that had been there since her first fumbling quests for ecstasy at the behest of a fallen angel.

"I'll always be yours," she murmured against his unmasked cheek.

"Show me." The command in Erik's voice was like nothing she had heard since he had been an unseen angel. There was power in it, unquestionable and undeniable, and it made Christine tremble. He knew she would give him anything. She would let him take it now.

She kissed him again and pressed herself against the growing hardness at his groin, stoking the fire. Erik's hands swept up her body, possessive and powerful, caressing her breasts and then finding the neckline of her dress, undoing her buttons with a thief's skill as Christine tried her best to aid him. They fumbled until just her chemise hid her breasts and Christine gasped as Erik tore the fabric apart, exposing her to the cold air and the starving attentions of his mouth.

He lifted her by the hips as he took one of her tight nipples into his mouth, sending Christine's mind into a fog of lust. Soon she was on his bed and he was tearing at her skirts and underthings, exposing the body that was his to claim. He drew back when she was bare, looming above her on his knees with the dark branches of his bed's canopy spreading like wings behind him. Christine was breathless below him, thighs clasped loosely and her chest heaving.

"I said: show me," Erik ordered and pushed her legs apart.

Christine groaned as he *observed* her, and of their own accord, her hands moved to her slickened sex. "This is what you do to me. This is you."

Erik pushed her hands away as he fell between her thighs and began to devour. He knew every way to touch her, which flick of his tongue or graze of a finger would send cascades of pleasure through her. Her hips rose and fell, chasing his mouth and begging for more.

She felt the climax rising inside her as he slid two fingers into her in perfect rhythm. The peak of pleasure began to tighten in her gut... Then Erik's fingers and mouth were gone, and Christine cried out in shock at the denial.

Erik's eyes were dark and deadly as she looked to him. He wiped her glistening wetness from his mouth with the back of his hand and grinned. "Not yet."

Christine bit her lip. The feeling of being at his mercy, under his control like never before since unmasking him, made her dizzy. She nodded. "I won't come until you allow it, I promise."

"I think I'll test that." Erik's voice resonated straight to her core. Suddenly, not coming at that very instant was a daunting task. Even more so when his mouth returned to her cunt, lapping languidly at the most sensitive parts of her. His fingers joined, gradually slipping inside her, making Christine feel every second of pleasure.

"Fuck," Christine heard herself gasp, no other more civilized word coming to mind as he continued. The vibrations of his smug laughter against her sex sent another delicious wave of sensation through her. She reeled, clasping at the sheets and trying to control her ragged breath, anything to hold back and obey even as he hooked his finger inside of her and made her scream. Her hips rose off the bed, but she held back. For him, she held back. At last, he gave her mercy and drew away.

"Impressive," Erik purred. Suddenly his mouth was on hers again, and she tasted herself on his lips, pungent and sweet. The kiss was dizzying, almost enough to make her forget that his body was between her splayed legs now. The feel of his cock at her entrance brought her back.

"Please," she begged.

Her angel obliged, but not as she hoped. Erik entered with slow, agonizing precision, not faltering until he filled her completely, stretching her wide. Then, with the same steady, unbearably careful pace, he drew out as Christine choked on groans of agony and delight. Again, he slid into her, letting her feel every centimeter of him until she was sure she would burst, before retreating again. Again and again, meticulous and perfect and wonderful, but not enough to finish her. Not enough at all.

"Good. So good." Christine opened her eyes at the words, looking up at the lover above her, spurred on by his praise. His gold eyes were dark with lust, his hair a mess, and his pale, scarred skin shining with sweat. She wrapped her legs around his narrow hips and swallowed.

"More. Give me more," she begged. "Let me show you how good I can be."

"As you wish," Erik replied, voice ragged. Finally, blessedly, he began to fuck into her with fierce power that made her keen anew.

"Yes, oh God! Give me everything," Christine cried, holding on for dear life with each brutal thrust, her whole body shaking with the effort of caging her pleasure.

Erik twined his fingers in her hair and pulled, sending new shocks to her core. Christine reached up to the headboard, frantically bracing herself as her ruthless lover continued to pound into her, unrelenting and unquestionable. She felt that telltale tightening again and bit down on the only thing close, the shoulder of the man driving her mad with need. The man who she needed to trust her.

"Almost. Almost, my love, just a few moments longer," Erik rasped in her ear.

Christine whimpered, because the love and trust in his voice was perfect. She needed to give him this, but she was so *close*. She was going to die if she didn't find release soon.

"Please, please," she babbled, her body as tight as a violin string ready to snap. "*Please*. Erik... God... Please. I need to come."

"Who do you belong to?" His rhythm grew erratic, his muscles tight. He was close too.

"You. I belong to you," Christine nearly wept. "I love *you*."

"Now," Erik cried, convulsing as he came, and Christine followed with a ragged gasp. The climax tossed her like a bird in a storm, cascading through her with bolts of lightning that blinded her as Erik poured out his seed, groaning with the same pleasure.

He panted as he collapsed on the bed beside her, spent. Christine was entirely unable to move, the pinnacle still close and comforting, like the warmth of a fire.

"I love you," Erik said softly.

Christine turned to see him staring at her through the shadows. She pulled him close, resting her head against his heart. The beat of it was always a comfort, and she would not lose it.

"You can't hide in here forever."

Shaya rose from the prayer mat to see Darius at his door. Only a year younger than Shaya, he had always had a softer face and manner. His jaw was rounded while Shaya's was sharp, and his eyes were always soft and kind, despite the darkness he'd seen. Which was what made it all the more concerning to see him looking angry.

"I'm not hiding," Shaya lied.

"What happened last night? Did you see Daaé? Is she safe?" Darius asked, proving his kindness once again with his concern for Erik's whore.

"She's more than safe. She's *his*. Body and soul," Shaya replied darkly. "He loves her."

"I don't like how pleased you seem about a revelation you should have already guessed." Darius stood aside as Shaya strode from his room back into the humble parlor of their flat.

"Don't you see? That's what's going to kill him. This love will destroy him."

"Like Ramin?" Shaya's heart collapsed at the sound of his brother's name. The brother who had died because Erik had corrupted him, like everything else he touched. "And then you'll have your justice?"

"Yes, exactly. That's always been the goal. Why are you acting so concerned now?"

"Because for a few hours last night, I was worried you were dead, and I didn't like it."

"We've always known the risks of this endeavor, but we do it because it's righteous," Shaya protested, suddenly uncomfortable under Darius's implacable gaze.

"*You* do it, and I support you because it is the only thing keeping you alive and sane," Darius replied. "If Erik loves her, he will kill to keep her – you know that."

"I won't be the one who takes her," Shaya protested. "I'll only guide the one who will."

"The Vicomte who's done with her? What if she's loyal to Erik? What if she loves him in return like—"

"No one could ever love that monster, not if they've seen what he is!" Shaya roared. He pushed the memory of Daaé dancing with

Red Death from his mind, as well as her words of pity and dewy eyes. "She's a fool who's been ensnared and blinded by ambition."

"I think you're the one who's being blind." Darius looked so forlorn. Shaya could not understand it. "But say you're right, and this is how he's destroyed. What then?"

"What do you mean?" Shaya stared at the man who had followed an exile from Persia across the world, the most loyal and true person he'd ever known.

"I thought I made it clear: I don't want to lose you." Darius sighed. "Or for you to lose your soul."

"You don't think it's already lost? After all the monsters I've served and the people I've failed?" Shaya found himself laughing, hollow and cold. "I was lost and fallen when Ramin died. All I've ever been meant to do since then is bring that monster down with me."

"It doesn't have to be that way. By Allah, we can just... leave it. We can just move on from all this hate," Darius entreated, his eyes watery and soft. Again, Shaya heard himself laugh.

"And what would I do then?" He had never considered it, the question of who he might be free of Erik's shadow, however that came to be.

"We would live," Darius said, like the optimist he had been decades ago when he had first come into Shaya's employ. That was what Shaya cared for the most in him, but today, that hope was misplaced.

"I will live when Erik is dead or in a cage, not before." Shaya grabbed his coat and yanked open the door.

He had never been good with fights. He was a spy, not a soldier. He preferred to hide away and avoid confrontation. When that didn't work, he ran like he was doing now. It was a bad habit for Shaya to go to the Opera whenever his thoughts were unsettled. It wasn't a long walk from his flat on the *Rue de Rivoli*, and as the sun set it wasn't terribly cold.

He found himself in his preferred alcove, searching his pockets for tobacco as he watched the *Rue Scribe* side of the Opera, where there were entrances for everyone from performers to horses.

Shaya didn't know what he was looking for. Just watching, as always. Waiting as he had for years. It was so close now: Erik's demise. Maybe tonight he'd find something new to spur it on. Perhaps he'd see the little Vicomte sulking, or Christine sneaking back to her lover's lair...

Or the fiend himself.

Shaya stood straighter, mesmerized by the sight of a tall figure in a black cape and felt hat slinking along the side of the Opera. Was he wearing a black mask for a change? The shadow made its way along the side of the Opera, as if inspecting it, until it came to the gate of the stables.

Shaya held his breath. Was this one of Erik's secret ways into his domain? That would explain his tendency to steal the horses and disappear. Had the Phantom now made an error out of some misplaced sense of security? The figure in the felt hat and mask stepped into the stables and disappeared from view. Shaya sprang into action, jogging across the empty street and to the stable gate. The head groom was snoring loudly, reminding Shaya that anyone could come and go without notice.

Including the shadow, who had left the door into the Opera proper ajar.

Shaya should have felt triumphant, but it was another mistake, and Erik did not make mistakes that often. He considered following, but the Opera was a dark maze this time of night, and he had already pushed Erik's hospitality too far in recent weeks. And if he died tonight, Darius would never let him hear the end of it.

Still, the image of the Phantom walking along the *Rue Scribe* unsettled Shaya. Why would Erik be so bold or foolish? Why would he go in through a door when Shaya knew the villain had secret ways in and out of the Opera?

A horse whinnied, startling Shaya from his thoughts. He turned to see the white stallion Erik was fond of glaring at him from its stable. Shaya gave the beast a nod and stole back out through the gate into the darkening night.

He should go back home, he knew that. The best course was to apologize to Darius, tell him he was grateful for years of loyalty, and promise he would be careful. There was something anxious in his gut now though, a shadow of fear that he could not place. Was Darius right to fear that not everyone entangled in Erik's web would escape with their lives?

For once, there was no music in Erik's head to push him from the warmth of his bed with Christine beside him. Even if there was, he wouldn't follow it. Not tonight. Tonight he just wanted to hold her, watch her as she rested peacefully and breathed. She was here for now, no matter what she had to undertake tomorrow to placate that awful boy.

Erik sighed. He didn't want to keep thinking about it, but all the parts of his mind that were usually humming with song were focused on every way this could go wrong. How he might lose her. Even thinking back to the way she gave herself to him, to her dozens of promises that she was his, wouldn't make the noise stop. It had been going for an hour.

He ran his hands through his hair and stifled a groan as he looked to the ceiling, crisscrossed by the branches of the bower that he had carved so carefully. He wanted to sleep. He had just started getting used to how safe and good it felt to rest next to someone he loved...

"You're thinking very loudly, you know," Christine's soft voice cut through his turmoil, and he turned to her in surprise.

"I'm sorry. I didn't mean to wake you."

She gave a tired smile. "How many times must I tell you? Everything will be fine."

"What if he doesn't believe you? He knows so much already."

"You've told me many times how people believe what they want, despite all the evidence to the contrary. There is nothing I can say that would make him believe I have chosen you of my own free will."

"I still don't believe that half the time."

Christine sent him a scowl. "So we will use that. We will tell him the lie he's told himself this whole time, the one he wants to hear."

"And that will make him want to stay, not encourage him to leave on that foolish expedition," Erik lamented, lungs and heart seizing up. "He won't abandon you to a monster."

"I can convince him that my teacher wishes me to only love music, and no mortal man," she countered. "His imagination will do the rest. He'll forget what he suspects. I'll tell him half the truth – that your voice speaks to my soul – and he'll follow the path. It will work. I swear it will."

"I believe you, in here." Erik pressed his hand against his heart. "I trust you."

Christine pressed into him, twining her fingers into his hair and stroking his brow. How incredible it still was that she could look at his face and touch it with such compassion and care. "And what about in here?" she asked with a kiss upon his forehead.

"In there... It's always a bit of a mess in there," Erik confessed. More words bubbled in his throat then stuck there, fear holding them back.

"What is it?" Christine asked, and something about the softness of her voice and the warmth of their bed made him brave.

"Sometimes, it's like my mind is full of ghosts. Always whispering. Always cruel. They remind me of what I am, what I've done, what I deserve, and all the disasters in store."

"Would it matter if I told you not to listen to them?" Christine asked, kindness in her eyes that Erik could hardly believe.

"I'm not sure – they're very persistent."

"I'll drown them out then." Erik did not resist as Christine pulled him towards her, wrapping him in her arms and pressing his head against the perfect, warm skin of her chest. And then she began to sing.

He had sung her to sleep so many times, but never had their roles been reversed. Never had she been the one to offer perfect music as comfort. It was a wordless song that sounded like moonlight and ancient pines, and it acted like magic, as music so often did. It drove away the fear and the dreams. For now, at least, he was safe.

3. The Garden Path

Raoul had arrived far too early at the café to meet Christine. It wouldn't do to drink several bottles of red wine like he wanted to, no matter how tempting. He had opted instead for a café au lait at half past four o'clock. And then another half an hour later. Now, it was well past five, he was sipping on the dregs of his fourth, and the omnibuses rolling by were making his skeleton vibrate.

"You're being very stupid, you know. More so than usual." Raoul nearly jumped out of his skin at the sound of Antoine's voice from behind. Before the younger man could protest, Antoine took the seat across from him that Raoul had been saving for Christine.

"I thought you were done with me?" Raoul snapped.

"I said I was taking things into my own hands." Antoine picked up Raoul's empty cup and looked into it scornfully. He hailed a waiter without hesitation, signaling for more. "I came to remind you that whatever your little songbird says, it's going to be a lie."

"You don't know her."

"She's a woman," Antoine sneered. "A woman of the theater, no less. Lying is all whores like her know how to do."

"I'm sure *you* know a lot about whores. They're the only women who will have you." Raoul did include that debauched creature Valerius in that number.

"Well we all can't be sweet virgins, hanging on nanny's apron strings still, can we?" Antoine gave a self-satisfied smirk.

"I'm not a—"

"Of course not, dear boy. You've seen so much of the world in your vast travels on the sea."

Raoul clenched his fist but held back his ire. Everything about Antoine was designed for provocation, down to the entitled way he took the cup of coffee the waiter brought and sipped slowly, peering at Raoul over the edge. "Did you have a purpose here other than to insult me and the woman I still intend to marry?"

"Speaking of marriage, I wanted to give you fair warning. I'm going to ask Philippe for Sabine's hand tomorrow." Antoine smiled but it did not reach his icy eyes.

"What if I object?"

Of course, Antoine chuckled. "I came to give you notice, not ask for permission. As my future brother-in-law, I wanted to keep an eye on you and remind you of the real objective."

"To save Christine?"

"To *end Erik*, you imbecile. If you can use her for that, then have at it, but don't trust her. I want to save you from that heartache."

"I don't believe that for a second," Raoul spat, and Antoine flashed a knowing grin.

"No, I supposed you wouldn't. But your heart *is* soft, Raoul." Something about the way Antoine looked at him made Raoul's skin squirm. "It makes me doubt your resolve."

"What?"

"If you can so easily be swayed to give Daaé another chance to deceive you, then I wonder how quickly you'll lose your spine when the time comes to destroy this fiend." There was no jest or humor remaining to mask the darkness in Antoine's words or eyes.

"*I* was the one who proposed—" Raoul looked around the half-empty café, wondering if any of these Parisians going about their day would care about their plot. "*Eliminating* him."

"Could you do it though?" Antoine asked, eyes drilling into Raoul. "Could you look a man in his face, however horrid it might be, and kill him? Could you point a gun at that monster and pull the trigger knowing what it might mean for your precious soul?"

Raoul swallowed. He didn't know. He hadn't thought of it that way. "I—"

"It's one thing to dream about it, but it's another thing to do it."

Raoul suddenly had the wild impression that this was not the first time Antoine had considered such questions. And this was a man he was supposed to let near his sister? "Have you—"

"She's here." Antoine rose as he looked toward the window of the café where Christine had appeared.

Raoul's relief and awe were instant. He had been prepared to return home tonight, once again betrayed and abandoned by Christine, yet here she was, stepping in from the chill of the evening with reddened cheeks and a tired smile when she caught Raoul's eyes. There was such sadness in her face. Surely, she was suffering as he was. She had to be.

Raoul smiled back in spite of himself before turning to dismiss Antoine, but the cad was already gone. It was no matter. Christine was here, and he would finally have his answers.

"You came." Raoul took Christine's hands. She was wearing demure white gloves, which stood in stark contrast to the heavy black traveling cloak she wore with the hood down. Raoul had seen her in it many times before and honestly disliked the garment.

"I promised I would." Christine sounded utterly exhausted. What had the poor thing been through? "I hope I didn't make you wait too long."

"I passed the time. Please! Sit."

Christine took the seat across from Raoul, and her beauty and warmth were a welcome change from Antoine's coldness. "I know you have questions. About..."

"About Erik," Raoul finished, and Christine flinched. "Yes, indeed I do have questions about the man whose name you won't speak and makes you tremble." Raoul remembered why he had spent the last few days so upset with Christine. "Yet fills you with such musical ecstasy."

"You make it sound very untoward," Christine muttered, blush now coloring her cheeks. Raoul bit back a scoff at her sudden modesty.

"You mean to assure me that your connection with this—" Christine looked up, breath shuddering again. "This *man*, if he can be called that, is purely artistic? I saw you with him in the Bois, Christine. He tried to kiss you."

"That wasn't what it looked like. We were moved by the music. It was no more than what would happen on stage with Carlos Fontana," Christine offered carefully. Raoul's mind went back to that night. *Was* he sure of what he'd seen in the dark? "It was a performance."

"It wasn't a performance when he attacked me," Raoul countered, his throat smarting at the memory.

"He was defending himself."

"I guess it makes sense that the monster didn't wish to be discovered. And after the masquerade?"

"When you decided to spy on me?" Christine's eyes flashed with indignation, but Raoul pushed away his shame.

"I'm glad I did. I saw your face when he called to you through the walls," Raoul pushed on. He remembered that voice, the incomparable beauty in it, the one blessing God had given this hideous creature. "I saw your joy! The way that music *enflamed* you."

"Raoul, his voice..." Christine's defiance faded and she avoided Raoul's eyes in what had to be shame for her wanton display. "It has power over me. I am not myself when he sings, nor when I sing for him. I cannot explain it."

"Has he—" Raoul swallowed. There was so much he was afraid to learn, but he had to know. "Has it been, as you said, untoward? Has he used this *power* to compromise you?"

"Do you mean to ask if I am still good? Still pure? You have been so quick to question my virtue lately," Christine asked back, righteous sparks in her eyes. "He has never compelled me to any sin against my will if that's what you wish to know. He would never."

Raoul stared into Christine's hazel eyes and tried to find deceit there. She'd never been a good liar, even as a child, at least not with him. He saw no sign of falseness now.

"If he has not ruined you, then you can still be free!"

Christine looked even more crestfallen, shaking her head. "That is my tragedy, Raoul," she sighed. "There's no escaping. I cannot leave him. I cannot refuse him. I have not been able to since the first time I heard his voice."

"And how did that happen?" Raoul pushed. "I'm curious how a man becomes an angel."

"He took pity on me and offered to teach me, when I first came to the Opera," she answered, voice unsteady. "And I told you, I thought it was a miracle, that he was an angel from heaven. He accepted the mask I gave him. I learned only later that I was wrong." A sob caught in Christine's throat, and more of the coldness and resentment that had frozen Raoul's heart melted away.

"But you went back? Why!"

"For pity, Raoul!" Christine groaned. "You have seen him. You know what he is and when I saw that face after I tore off his mask in fury, I was terrified, but then he *wept*. He sang. I could not abandon such a tragic creature."

"He is a villain!" Raoul cried, and another customer at the café shot them a look. Raoul cleared his throat. "The monster lied to you, then made you pity him so you would go back!"

"I went back because I had to! For that pity and that voice and that music, I went back. I swore anew to be his. I have to be if I am to continue in my career!" Christine's eyes were so bright now. "To live and breathe for music is all I have ever wanted. Don't you remember? It's what I promised Papa I would do. My teacher has made my dreams come true. Music is all I have ever lived for and it is all he has ever lived for. Neither of us can give it up."

"So you still belong to your angel?" Raoul asked softly, mind turning. Of course a monster that ugly, that murderous, could never dream of touching her. It all finally came into place. "But only for music?"

"He insists on it." Christine glanced around, as if she was used to being watched. "He's terribly jealous, you see. Not just of you – of any man that might distract me from my music. From *his music*. Raoul, this is why I cannot marry and I never will."

"Which is why you have continued to refuse me at every turn, even though it is against the will of your heart," Raoul surmised slowly. It all – finally – made sense!

"I had no choice," Christine lamented.

"And Rameau?" Raoul asked, and Christine looked down. "That's why he's made you take on that charade. So no man would pursue you and you can remain dedicated to music and to him."

"I have made a vow to him, Raoul, to serve music alone. As long as I do that, I am safe." Christine looked into his eyes at last with terrifying intensity. "*You* remain safe."

Raoul's blood froze as another puzzle piece fell into place. "You have been protecting me all along, haven't you?"

"He is more dangerous than you can understand."

"Oh, I understand how dangerous he is. Better than you ever will," Raoul snarled, and Christine looked taken aback. He wanted to tell her, wanted her to *know* that her angel and jailer had the blood of Raoul's family on his hands.

"But now there is at least a chance I can save you for good," Christine said, pulling Raoul back.

"How?" Raoul balked. It was absurd, for he was the one who was meant to save her, now more than ever.

"You are leaving in two weeks, are you not?" Christine asked carefully. All hope fell out of Raoul's chest like a mishandled plate clattering to the floor and smashing.

"I can't leave now! Not knowing you are in such danger and that this fiend walks free!" Raoul cried so loudly that several other patrons turned to look at them.

"You must!" Christine hissed, grabbing Raoul's hands and holding him tight. Her eyes were wild with fear. "Raoul, you *have to go*. For my sake! I can live knowing you are out there in the world, free on your adventures, holding your love for me in your heart. It's the only way I can go on."

Raoul imagined himself in the frozen wastes, a portrait of his beloved clasped near his heart. So romantic. So operatic. The notion was tempting. Yet, how could he let his family go unavenged? He had to find this monster and Christine remained the key. He had to save her and convince her to reveal her teacher's secrets. And maybe this was his chance.

"I can't leave without knowing you are safe, in every way," Raoul said slowly as his mind worked. "I would need assurances."

"Assurances?"

"I want to see you as much as I can, in the Opera," Raoul began. "I want to know your world as he does. For these few weeks, share with me all your secrets and joys, as when we were children. I want to be your suitor and fiancé for a fortnight, and then, when those days are over, I will go. Can you grant me that?"

Christine looked down, twisting her fingers nervously. "Yes, I can. I cannot say if it will make it harder, to send you off after such a time."

"Let it be my gift to you: a few scraps of joy before you give up the dream of love," Raoul offered, the lie coming easily, and Christine smiled.

"A moment in the sun before Persephone returns to the underworld," she whispered. Raoul knew his Greek stories well enough, and he didn't like that implication.

"Shall we begin now?" he offered. "We can share a meal like civilized folk, and then I can walk you home." It was a challenge for her: to prove she was not returning to the Opera to be shut away by her dark teacher again.

"That would be lovely," Christine replied, warmth returning to her face. "Tell me more about your time on the sea."

Raoul smiled and signaled a waiter, a bubble of triumph growing in his chest. This would work. He would have the pleasure of two weeks with the woman he loved and hopefully it would be enough to convince her to let these dreams go. She would have to once he found her teacher. Now, he had an excuse to be in the Opera, to explore, and a way to learn Erik's secrets. Then Raoul would destroy him. He would lie to Christine, tell her he was bound north. And when it was time for him to leave, he would not go. He would save her and she would thank him.

This was how he would find the minotaur at the center of the labyrinth.

Christine leaned on the door of the flat she no longer thought of as home once it clicked shut and let out a long sigh.

"You look exhausted." Adèle's voice came from by the fire. "Which of your paramours has you looking so put upon?"

"The one who is determined to save the sweet maiden from the clutches of the monster, of course."

"So you've taken my advice?"

Christine pushed off the door and ambled to the chair across from Adèle, who was settled in her shawl with a glass of wine and the evening edition of *Le Gaulois*. "It's worked, I think. I've convinced him that, to save me, he has to leave Paris, and I'll remain here mourning him and devoted only to art." The words tasted like offal in Christine's mouth. "He believed every lie."

"Then why are you back here?"

"Because he wanted to have dinner with me and walk me home, like a proper gentleman." She chafed at the memory of how Raoul had bowed to her at the door before pressing a demure kiss to her hand.

Adèle smirked. "At least you had a pretty face to look at."

"No pretty face could make up for the boredom of a man talking about boats *for an hour*," Christine groaned. "All without asking me a single question."

"Ah, poor girl," Adèle chuckled. "I've been to those dinners. Antoine liked to talk about hunting. He fancies himself such a tracker. As if he didn't have a game warden sneaking foxes into his path all his life."

Christine rubbed her brow, somehow sitting there doing nothing had tired her just as much as playing her role. She wanted to go home. "Erik's different. When he talks, I know he wants me to understand and ask questions."

"Are you going back to him tonight?"

"Raoul walked me home to make sure I didn't. He wants to trust me, but he's not entirely sure of my fidelity. Not that I can blame him." The leaden weight of dinner in her stomach became uneasy with the thought. She was a liar and a harlot. Every suspicion Raoul had of her was true.

"Don't look at yourself the way they do, my dear girl," Adèle admonished. "That is the way towards madness."

"What do you mean?"

"Men like Raoul – most men, if I'm being honest," Adèle began thoughtfully, eyes drifting to the fire. "They see us as things. We're no more than a prize mare or a beautiful painting, a treasure to adorn their halls in their pursuit of glory. They treat us with the same judgment they'd apply to those things. Are our hips wide enough for breeding? Are our tits high enough and our skin clear? Are we willing to bend over for a fucking and pray for our souls the next day? When we fail at one thing, just one, we are cast off and forgotten."

"Raoul thinks more highly of me than that," Christine argued despite herself. "At least I would hope so."

"He's always been quick to call you a whore when you strayed off the path," Adèle countered. Christine opened her mouth to remind Adèle that he wasn't wrong, but the older woman cut her off. "You're not, my sweet girl. You are no whore."

"You don't think so?" Christine asked, shocked that Adèle would contradict her and shocked that at some point she had accepted that title as true.

"That word..." Adèle mused. "Men love to use it when women don't behave the way they want. Especially women like us who make our own money or take our own pleasure. If you don't need them and enjoy yourself, you're a strumpet, a scarlet woman, a hussy. But you are not their insults and names for you. You are yourself, nothing more or less."

Christine was surprised this time by the warmth in her chest and the tears stinging at her eyes. "You're very smart, you know that? You don't show it off enough."

"Men don't like that either. My husband did though – when I'd challenge him on some idea of history or philosophy. He was a professor." Adèle looked towards the old photograph above the fireplace and smiled sadly. "He had all sorts of wild ideas."

"Is that why you married him?"

Adèle chuckled deep in her throat. "That. And the fact he could fuck like a steam locomotive and knew music better than me."

Christine burst out laughing, and Adèle grinned for a moment until sadness fell over her face. "How long ago did he die?"

"It will be ten years in May," Adèle replied. "I loved him for his ideals until he was stupid enough to die for them. He fought with the national guard on the side of the Paris Commune. Didn't even have the decency to let me say goodbye. My dear professor."

"I'm sorry." It was automatic to say it, and perhaps it was empty, but Adèle reached across the space between them and squeezed Christine's hand even so. "It will be three years since I lost my father soon. It never gets easier."

They sat in silence, their ghosts lingering in the deepening shadows until Adèle shook herself from the reverie. "I think you've waited long enough for your dashing hero to be gone. You should be safe to go home."

Christine nodded, noticing that she hadn't even taken off Erik's cloak. It was just as much a consolation to wear it as his hidden ring was. A piece of her angel wrapping her in his wings.

"I'll see you tomorrow. I imagine the managers may have some interesting announcements." Christine rose.

Adèle gifted her with a knowingly raised eyebrow. "What kind of announcements?"

"You may want to study your Wagner. I know you have some lying around." Christine winked. "Good luck."

"You as well. I think you'll need it more," Adèle smiled.

Christine found her way back onto the quiet *Rue Notre Dame des Victoires* and let the cool air of the night clear her mind as she breathed in the scent of the city. It wasn't unpleasant at all. Or perhaps she was used to the smell of soot and horses and cooking and a million people now. She still preferred the smell of Erik's home; of candles and musk and paper and something exotic she could never name.

She would have to tell Erik the awful news that Raoul would be coming to see her regularly at the Opera. Erik was going to hate that as much as she did, but they both had to remember it was temporary. And that she would always return to the dark. Another thing fate had left her no choice in.

Shaya was good at following people. It wasn't ego to think so – merely a fact. One that he had proven again tonight to be true. Christine Daaé had not noticed him trailing her and the dashing Vicomte back to her flat. When the young man had left the way he came, minutes later, Shaya had considered following and telling him the truth at last. It was high time Chagny knew what he was facing, but some instinct had stopped Shaya's feet.

He was glad of the impulse now, as he followed Christine through the gaslit streets of Paris. He stayed a good distance back, quietly blending in with the other meager foot traffic, careful and calm. He knew where she was going and didn't have to follow close.

Erik, it seemed, did not trust his soubrette either.

Shaya caught sight of the cloaked shadow near where the *Rue des Petits Champs* met the *Rue Sainte-Anne*. Interesting that once again Erik should be so cavalier about being seen, but perhaps his suspicion of Christine had made him foolish. That suspicion was warranted, given that she was consorting with his rival in secret after rejecting him at the masquerade. It made Shaya smile to think that that shadow had been watching to see her betrayal. Now, Erik wanted to assure that she went back to her prison.

Shaya followed the shadow that followed Christine all the way back to the perimeter of the Opera and watched in fascination as first Christine, then the shade, entered the stables on the *Rue Scribe*. That was where he had gone before and disappeared into the Opera. Tonight Shaya would find where they went.

He risked more speed as he rushed to the stables, listening to the horses' agitated whinnies, and beyond their noise, the sound of footsteps on stone. Shaya turned into the stable just in time to see the shadow disappearing through a wall that was not a wall at all. It was one of Erik's hidden doors into his domain, and Shaya was finally going to enter it.

He had to be careful, Shaya told himself, as he stepped into the cold, moist air of the tunnel, so different from the earthy scent of the stable. What if Erik had seen the girl consorting with his rival? How would he punish her? Shaya did not admire Christine Daaé, but he did not want her to die.

Somewhere ahead of him, a match flared and the Ghost hissed a profanity. Strange, Erik had never needed a light before. Shaya followed the glint of flame – a candle perhaps – further down the corridor, taking a right where the path forked. The sound of footsteps was closer now, as was the frustrated huffing. It made Shaya laugh to himself, how this woman and her betrayal had stripped the supposed phantom of all his magic and mystique.

"Damnit," the ghost hissed from ahead, and Shaya knew why. They were no longer in the cellars proper but among the sets and scenery stored below the stage. Christine had gone the wrong way – away from the lake. But why? No matter. It was Shaya's opportunity to distract Erik and perhaps save her if she was trying to elude him.

"Did you lose something?" Shaya asked coolly, stepping from the shadows.

The familiar silhouette, with its felt hat and dark cape, turned to Shaya, who waited to see the blaze of fury in the unearthly eyes behind the mask. But there was none.

This was not Erik.

"I don't need you interfering right now," the shade growled and pounced on Shaya before he could run. The hands on Shaya's throat were strong and ferocious, and for a delirious moment, Shaya wondered if this imposter was about to kill him exactly as Erik would have. That was his last thought before his head hit the wall behind him and everything went black.

Erik's whole body ached from playing so long, but he refused to stand from the organ. Instead he kept his bleary eyes on the notes he scrawled on the parchment in front of him. As long as he didn't look away from his music and into his empty house, everything was fine. Christine was going to come back and everything would be handled, just like she promised.

Or she's run off with him already, a ghost whispered in his ear, and Erik batted it away.

"She'll be back soon," Erik said aloud, repeating the mantra that had kept him (relatively) sane for the last few hours. Soon she would be in his arms again, and this gnawing, sickening fear in his gut would abate with the warmth of her touch.

Think of her return, he told himself as a new chord echoed from the pipes with the ecstasy of a first kiss. Music was no different than making love when you came down to it. The way the chords and melodies moved from dissonance and tension to resolution, then pushed towards the next cadence, the next climax; it was all like the ebb and flow of passion.

This melody here, it was a kiss at his lover's pulse point, teasing and light. It repeated itself and expanded, growing more intricate just as his lips might trail down a long, delicate neck. In a deeper range, it became his hands on hot skin, modulating into an aching parallel minor as need and desire grew. His feet worked the pedals of the mighty instrument before him, the bass notes rumbling like thunder.

How he wanted her. In every way. In every moment. He needed her like air. The music rose to a pounding climax, as inevitable and explosive as spilling into her had felt when she had said she loved him. The final cadence echoed through the shadows and Erik found himself panting, the sound echoing in the room as if there was another breathing just as hard behind him.

Erik turned to see his angel, standing in their home once again.

"I missed you too," Christine murmured as she charged toward him and took him in her arms. She kissed him hard, hungry and sweet, and smiled when she drew away.

"You're back," Erik gasped, hating the pale cast to her skin in contrast to her dark brown dress with its high, conservative collar. "Is it done?"

Christine's face fell immediately, along with Erik's heart. "He's placated again, but what he wants... You won't like it."

"Did he propose again?" Erik could not keep the contempt from his voice, even though it made Christine scowl.

"He wants to see me daily at the Opera. Have me spend my spare time showing him around or just listening to him prattle on," Christine replied and Erik let out a squawk of indignation. "Until he leaves!"

"In *my* opera? He'll have you playing guide and..."

"What is it?" Christine grasped his arm as Erik winced at the thought. "You know I won't enjoy it."

"But he'll be up there, with you, seeing all the things that I haven't even had the chance to show you yet," Erik confessed, his voice small. Christine laid her palm against his bare cheek, forcing him to look at her.

"Then show me now," Christine grinned. Erik froze, not understanding - even less so when Christine began to unbutton her dress. "I'm not wearing this any longer than I have to. I can be casual at home, can't I? Here. You can have this one for now."

"What?" Erik asked as Christine took the cloak she had borrowed from him and wrapped it around his shoulders.

"Just for tonight, so it will smell like you again. I like that about it," Christine explained. "Come along, *Monsieur le Fantôme*."

That was how Erik found himself cloaked in black, guiding a young lady in nothing but her corset and petticoats through the empty salons of the Opera Garnier in the quiet of the evening. He haunted Christine's steps, as he had for so long, filled with wonder and love.

Erik loved her defiance; he loved to see her traipsing about the ornate halls in her underthings because she could, especially with the shadow of a ghost following her. It was dark without most of the gaslights and candelabras lit, but he only saw light when Christine looked over her shoulder to smile at him.

They explored the rotunda meant only for the subscribers and richest patrons and he showed her where Charles Garnier had hidden his name and the dedication year of the opera in the filigreed ceiling around a chandelier's chain. They took in the fountain below the stairs as Christine trailed her hands over the intricate mosaics and carvings that festooned every surface, and Erik explained how they had taken almost the entire fourteen years of the Opera's construction to complete.

They walked the shadowed stairs (Erik noting how the scandalously bare skin of his companion matched the color of some of the marbles) and into the *grand salon* built to emulate the hall of mirrors in Versailles. It was a place for the patrons to pretend they were kings, even though the emperor who had commissioned their Palais was long-deposed.

Further into the gr*and salon*, he showed her another spot where Garnier had hidden his face upon a statue of Hermes, with his wife's countenance there as well, and Erik wondered if this building or any of its inhabitants would remember him when he was gone, decades or centuries on.

They went backstage through the unassuming door that divided the gilded lobbies from the plain world of the artists and found their way to the great stage. The fire curtain was raised, and Christine commented on the irony of a curtain painted to look like a different curtain and Erik laughed, noting that it was all illusion in the end.

The stage was set for the opening scene of *Faust* – the damned doctor's laboratory. Painted flats stood in for walls, but the table littered with books and scientific equipment was real enough. Erik watched as Christine approached, tripping slightly on the raked angle of the stage and giggling.

"It's a miracle I've never fallen on my ass with this slope," Christine commented, and Erik laughed. "The price we artists must pay so the half of the audience that bothers to pay attention sees everything."

"I've seen enough dancers fall." Erik stepped onto the stage. He could feel the ghost of the audience's gaze on him as he took in the great auditorium, lit only by the meager glow of the ghost light at center stage. He was wearing his mask, despite Christine's objections, but he was glad of the protection in such an exposed place.

"I'm sure ghostly laughter didn't make them feel any better."

Erik shrugged and floated towards Christine, noting how her pale skin glowed in the shadows, beckoning him like a beacon.

"Have you ever seen Charles Garnier?" she asked. "I hear he visits."

"Once, from afar." Erik recalled how tired the architect of the Opera had looked as he lingered at the foot of the *grand escalier* to observe the crowds filling his creation. "Part of me wanted to thank him for building my home."

"And part of you wanted to share your many suggestions on ways he could have improved the design."

"You know me too well."

"What would you change?" Christine asked, looking out towards the auditorium as she leaned on Faust's worktable.

Erik had an answer ready. "The chandelier is a bit much, honestly, especially when it's always on during performances. All it does is make it easier for the rich to look at each other and gossip. Another thing the patrons have ruined."

He watched as Christine's expression darkened to match the bitterness in his voice. "Don't think about him right now."

"I can't help it," Erik sighed as he took in her beauty. "It's worse than sharing you with an audience."

"Yet you manage that. Because you know I sing for you. Every note. It will be the same with him." Erik took a step towards her and Christine gave a wicked smile as she sat herself on the table and toyed with the lacy border of her chemise and corset. "When I sing, your music is inside me. Do you know I can feel it as surely as if you're making love to me?"

"Can you?" Erik purred as Christine stretched languidly on the table. "How scandalous."

"I can feel it right now," she went on, tugging her petticoat up and exposing her thigh. "Nearly."

"Well, you're not singing." Erik's mouth went dry as she smiled, pulling the petticoat higher.

"Love is a rebellious bird who none can tame and will not come when called." The seductive notes of Carmen's "Habanera" echoed through the empty theater with pure sensuality. It drew Erik like a moth to a flame, driving away any thoughts but the woman performing for him alone, as she continued to run her hands over her body.

Erik knew what she was doing, the seduction and distraction she offered as her defiant songs seeped into his blood. He was grateful for it, as much as he was enthralled. He approached beside the table, drawn to her light, and caressed her as she stretched and preened before him, casually knocking the props aside.

"Nothing helps, neither threats nor prayers. One man speaks well, another is silent. It's the other I prefer, he is quiet, but I like his looks." Christine's eyes were dark as she sang to him, and Erik's hands moved over her breasts and hips and thighs of their own power, insistent and seeking.

Her song became a sigh as he touched her, pressing right above her cunt. There was so little fabric between them that Erik could feel her rising heat. His cock answered it, beginning to stiffen beneath his cloak. Christine gasped when Erik withdrew his hand but sang on.

"Oh love, oh love," Christine called, her melody husky as Erik pulled her by the arms through the books and bric-a-brac, dragging her gently to the edge of the table so he could reach all of her, his hands sweeping over her stomach to her eagerly parted thighs once again. *"Oh love, oh love..."*

Erik kissed her at the end of the phrase and they became the music in turn, her mouth opening to his as she twisted to embrace him. He pulled her close, groaning as she wrapped her legs around him. More blood raced to his cock as Christine's body met his, and he ached for her. He wanted her. He *always* wanted her and somehow, she wanted him in return. When his hands slipped up her thighs, delving into her wet sex, she answered by groping at his tightening trousers.

"Right here?" Erik asked as Christine freed his cock and let him pull her to the edge of the table while he remained standing.

"I want to feel this, the next time I sing here," Christine purred back. "I want you to remember how every time I'm on this stage, you're inside me."

Erik entered her in one swift, inevitable motion, sheathing himself in her body as she cried out. He fumbled at her corset fastening as he thrust into her, frenzied and feral, as desperate for her skin beneath his hands as he was for the tight welcome of her cunt.

In a few breaths, her breasts were free, and she leaned back on the table to display herself as Erik fucked into her. He watched the perfect globes bounce with each movement, her nipples dark and tight. He listened to her moans and the slick sound of their bodies meeting. It was obscene – to have her here, to claim her like this, in the place where all of Paris would watch her sing a few nights hence. Erik loved it.

"Harder," Christine gasped, and Erik obliged, the table rattling beneath her as their bodies joined.

"He'll have you during the day," Erik panted, drawing forth a perfect symphony of ecstasy from his diva's throat. "But I have this. Only I know you like this."

"Yes!" Christine cried as he drove into her, his pleasure racing towards its peak, heat and passion consuming them as one.

The sound she made as she came, back arching off the table, was music, a secret song bursting forth just for him as she clamped around him and sent him over the edge with her. Erik moaned in harmony with her body as he spilled, pleasure transporting him to a realm where their souls were nothing but song, mixed together as one. Entwined and tangled forever.

"I'm going to take you home now," Erik purred, as he laid his masked cheek against his lover's flushed chest and licked at her nipple. He would take her back to his hidden abode, far from all prying eyes and cruel judgments. "I'm going to take you home and have you again and again. I'm going to fuck you with my tongue and my hands and my cock. I'm going to make you come so hard so many times, you won't be able to walk tomorrow without thinking of me."

"Please," Christine whimpered in reply. "Make me remember."

Erik smiled and yanked her into his arms. He would remind them both tonight of what they were. Of how desire and love would forever bind them. He would make sure Christine knew that no foolish boy who thought he was a hero could ever take her away.

The *Place de L'Opéra,* Raoul had found, was never truly quiet. It was chaos before a performance, of course, but there were people at the great crossroads at all times of the day, coming and going. He was glad of it. He'd had the carriage drop him off in front of the Madeleine, ostensibly to pray at the huge church before embarking on a day of errands and preparation for his voyage. Or so he had told his family.

In all truth, Raoul hated the Madeleine more than ever now. He had detested its pagan design and gaudy celebration of a whore *before* Christine had jilted him there (on Erik's orders). Now, even looking at it made his blood boil. Raoul shook the memory from his head as he entered the Opera through the rear entrance on the *Boulevard Haussmann.* It was still early and only a few artists and musicians had arrived so far. His appointment with Christine was not until later in the morning, and he was glad of it. He had other business.

Raoul recognized the bespectacled secretary standing watch at the door of Messieurs Richard and Moncharmin. The little man looked rather green this morning as he stared at the doors, unaware there was a patron waiting to be served beside him. Raoul coughed loudly and the man jumped.

"Oh, Monsieur de Chagny!"

"Are they available?" Raoul asked, already impatient.

"No, Monsieur, they are in a meeting regarding a new production and—"

"You have no vision," a voice cried from behind the door and the secretary gulped. "It will be a sensation!"

"It will cause a riot! The patrons' patience is already wearing thin. This will ruin it." Raoul recognized Richard's more measured (and perpetually annoyed) tones.

"Damn the patrons, we won't need them with the sales this will win us!" The other voice (Moncharmin, obviously) replied. Raoul raised an eyebrow and the secretary beside him looked absolutely beside himself.

"So you're doubly a fool," Richard said, voice closer now. Before Raoul could think, the door swung open. "Oh, perfect."

"Good day, Monsieur Richard." Raoul looked over the older, bald man's shoulder towards his colleague. "Monsieur Moncharmin," Raoul added coolly.

"What do you want, Monsieur?" Richard asked, impatient as ever.

"To discuss an important matter with one or both of you," Raoul said proudly. "The influence of the so-called Opera Ghost on this institution."

It was Moncharmin who laughed first, drawing a glare from Raoul and a dubious look from Richard. "I think you have been spending too much time with the petits rats. That's just a legend."

"What happened to La Carlotta right on your stage wasn't a legend," Raoul countered. "Nor was the thing stalking about the masquerade as Red Death."

"Yes, indeed, that was an ingenious costume," Moncharmin scoffed. Raoul elected to continue ignoring him in favor of watching Richard.

"What is your point, young man?" the balding manager asked with a sigh.

"That someone is abusing you and the people in your employ!"

"They – just like us – are in the employ of the National Academy of Music, Monsieur," Richard answered, and Raoul opened his mouth to protest. "I do see your point when it comes to these ridiculous stories and the undue influence they have," he went on in a growl directed at Moncharmin. The other manager rolled his eyes.

"What are you going to do about it?" Raoul asked.

"Why, nothing, Monsieur." Richard began to push Raoul bodily from the office.

"You can't mean that!" Raoul protested as he found himself guided into the hall and away from the gaping eyes of the secretary.

"I don't," Richard hissed. Raoul blinked at the older man, expecting some joke, but Richard's face was deadly serious. "But must say so while in the hearing of the so-called artistic manager of this cursed place."

"What are you implying?"

"I'm not implying anything. I am telling you that I know the ghost has insinuated himself into every damn aspect of this place, including the mind of Monsieur Moncharmin. I am done with it,"

Richard whispered, as if afraid the walls had ears. He might be right.

"I assure you, Monsieur: I am your ally in this pursuit. I am trying to find a way to destroy him," Raoul said as quietly as he could, trying to sense if there were unearthly eyes watching. "I am trying to find a way down to him."

"Down?"

"He lives far below, and I mean to find him," Raoul answered. "As soon as I can."

"You'll need keys then. Rémy! Bring me your keys!" Richard yelled back over his shoulder, and the secretary came running. He handed over the ring of keys with a quizzical look before Richard batted him away. "I don't have mine at the moment, but these will do for you. Good luck. I hope you don't end up like Buquet. The police inquiry would be interminable."

"Thank you, Monsieur." The keys dangled heavy in Raoul's hand as the manager left. Raoul grinned as he rushed away, imagining the cowed look on Antoine's face when he returned home with the news! Yes, it would be the foolish sailor who found the lair of their fathers' killer, not the pompous baronet trying to worm his way into their family.

Every door Raoul encountered opened for him (with some trial and error) and soon he was descending deeper into the theater's depths than he ever had before.

The cellars were dark, with very few gaslights illuminated at this hour. Raoul had to stop and take a lantern from a storeroom before going further. The place where he had found himself was eerie and strange. First, he saw woods, then a desert, then walls. It took him several turns to understand he had found himself among the sets and scenery from dormant productions.

He really should have consulted a plan of some sort before throwing himself down here, he thought, just as a bone-chilling moan sounded from behind a flat.

"Who's there?" Raoul asked aloud before he could stop himself. If Erik had come to torment him, he was ready... Except he was unarmed and didn't know his way out and perhaps, maybe, this had been a bad idea.

"Here," the voice groaned, obviously in pain. And also obviously not the voice of an angel. Raoul rushed around the *trompe-l'œil* sunset separating him from the man in distress and stopped dead in his tracks. The man's customary Astrakhan hat was on the floor beside him and he looked extremely worse for wear.

"You," Raoul exclaimed as the fellow he'd only ever heard called "the Persian" met his eyes. "Did *he* do this to you?"

The Persian rubbed his head and stood. "To whom do you refer, Monsieur de Chagny? I will need a name."

"To Erik!" Raoul cried. The Persian's eyes brightened before darting around them to the shadows.

"It's not wise to speak the devil on the borders of hell, Monsieur, lest we call him down upon us."

"So it was him who left you like this?" Raoul pushed. On impulse, he fetched the man's hat and handed it back to him. "I can't imagine you're shocked after *you* sent me to the Bois to be assaulted by him as well!"

"I am sorry for the danger I placed you in that night." The Persian dusted off the dark fur of his cap. "I was also the one who delivered you home. But to answer your first question, no. It was not our mutual friend who did this to me. At least I don't think it was."

"What do you mean?" Raoul asked as the Persian looked about to the shadows once again.

"We shouldn't talk here. He might spy us."

"Where can we talk then?" Raoul demanded. "Because you are going to tell me everything you know about this man in a ghost's mask right now."

"There's a café across the *Rue Auber*. We can talk there," the Persian replied.

The man knew his way about the Opera far better than Raoul did. In minutes, they were leaving the great building back into the damp February chill and crossing to the café. They found themselves seats, and a waiter provided them with a pot of coffee and two cups without prompting.

"Ah, perfect. You Frenchmen do know how to brew a decent coffee, I will give you that," the Persian mused as Raoul stared at him. "Would you like some? I certainly need it." He rubbed his throat and shuddered.

"Do you have a name?" Raoul demanded. "I can't just call you 'Persian' if we are to be allies."

"I have not yet decided to commit myself as your ally, but I am called Shaya Motlagh. Thank you for finally asking."

"Not yet committed—" Raoul blustered. Motlagh, unperturbed, began pouring.

"You see, Monsieur le Vicomte, you are unpredictable. You rush into dangerous situations without any regard for your safety – like the Bois or that cellar where you found me. And one minute, you are ready to die for Christine Daaé; the next, to cast her aside. I am forced to doubt your conviction."

"You do not need to doubt it anymore," Raoul growled.

"Has Daaé once again assured you of her virtue and devotion?"

"This isn't just about her anymore."

"Are you so concerned with the safety of the Opera?" He took a slow sip of coffee and looked over the cup at Raoul. "I wouldn't have guessed such selflessness in a young noble like you."

"The monster killed my father," Raoul spat, the words bitter and cold in his mouth. He didn't like thinking of it – the truth of what Erik had destroyed.

Across the table, Motlagh carefully set down his cup and nodded. "He killed my brother. I guess I was wrong."

"About what?"

"We are already allies, Monsieur. Let us begin our work this instant."

4. Shades

The room that had been hers in her first weeks in the house on the lake still felt so comfortable to Christine as she lingered there to dress. Erik had taken such care to fill it with her things, making the chamber full of stolen paintings and out-of-date furniture truly hers.

Yet, it was lonely there without him, the pit in her stomach growing deeper as rehearsal drew near. She stared at the blank space above her vanity where a mirror would be in a normal room as she yawned. She wished she could crawl into the warm bed and sleep the day away.

It was so much easier to pretend there was no world up there that wanted to chase Christine's lover down and pillory her for protecting him. Just like it was easier to do what she had done last night and let his music and her desire overcome her entirely. Erik had kept his promise: she could still feel the ache of their lovemaking between her thighs, and it was delicious. Her skin prickled with gooseflesh as the same eyes that continuously enthralled her settled upon her.

"You look nervous," Erik murmured as Christine looked up at him. Christine could see similar apprehension in the scarred landscape of his face.

"Help me with this first." Christine indicated the half-buttoned back of her dark green dress. Erik obeyed, and she took a deep breath as he set to work behind her with deft fingers.

"I'm not used to attending to your buttons to get your clothes *on*. This is a new experience."

"At least you know the geography." She swallowed, looking down as the dress tightened around her bust as Erik finished, yards of moss-colored taffeta swathing her body like a secret only he knew. "He's going to be there. Today."

Erik froze behind her. "So soon?" When Christine turned to him, Erik's eyes were hard and his jaw tense. "You really think he'll believe this charade for a fortnight?"

"I told you: he'll believe because I will make him," Christine countered. "So I can protect you."

Erik's anxiety melted away the instant her palm came to rest against his cheek. He covered her hand with his, caressing the gold ring that signified her promise. "You shouldn't have to..."

"It's too late. But I swear to you, it won't be real. It's just another scene. I won't take this off and you'll know the truth."

"And while you play this role, what will I do?" Erik demanded, pressing his forehead to her and rending her heart with the pain in his voice and eyes. "Do you expect me to watch while that boy follows you about my opera?"

"You can watch and see it when I don't offer him anything a good virginal girl wouldn't. I'll blush when he tries to take my hand. I'll protest if he tries to kiss me." Erik closed his eyes, then opened them as Christine wove her fingers lovingly through his hair. "Or, you can have mercy on yourself, which I would prefer."

"You think I'll be able to stay away?" Erik asked with a bitter laugh.

"If I beg it of you, maybe." Christine pressed a kiss to his desiccated cheek. "I don't want you in any more pain. Turn to music. Let it distract you and save you like always."

Erik gripped her tightly, as if he was holding onto solid ground in hopes that his fears would not wash him away. "What kind of music would you have me use to fill the day?"

"An opera," Christine whispered back, tears threatening as she considered the beauty and absurdity of it. "Your opera, the one you've started already."

"An opera," Erik echoed, inspiration sparking in his eyes and giving Christine the barest glimmer of hope. "In two weeks?"

"Stranger things have happened." She tried to smile. "And this opera, it won't be a tragedy like all the others. The lovers will end up together, happy and alive?"

"I will try," Erik replied before Christine kissed him with every ounce of love and tenderness she could muster.

"You will," she breathed as their lips parted. "You will write me music like nothing before, and you'll be safe here. And then tonight, I'll come back to you. Take me up now, so I can come back home soon."

"Not soon enough," Erik sighed, but let her go.

"It won't be long, I swear."

Christine thought on that promise as they ascended from the cellars, her hand in Erik's as always as he led them through the labyrinth of corridors, sets, and stairs that protected his home. All too soon they were in the passage behind the mirror of her dressing room, reality waiting for her on the other side of the glass.

"I always hate this part," Erik vocalized for them both as he hung the lantern. "I hate it more now."

"I won't be far," Christine tried to reassure him, heart smarting at the sight of his furrowed brow and desolate expression. She'd never seen him look so vulnerable up here. Because he had never come up with her unmasked. That was how much he trusted her. "I'll be with you like you're with me," she tried again, taking his hand. "I love you."

Such simple words, but they meant everything. It was just as simple to surrender to the embrace when he kissed her, fiercely asserting his claim on her mouth along with her body and soul. "I wish I could show, right now, how I love you in return," Erik purred against her cheek.

"I'd be late—" Christine protested, catching her breath and fighting to keep her own need in check. Erik groaned in frustration. "You can have me tonight. Before or after our lesson. I want to give you my voice too. I haven't sung with you for days."

"I will leave that up to you, my mistress, my ruler," Erik sighed, hands sweeping over her. "Whatever you want is yours."

"I will be at the door from the stable at seven sharp and you can have all of this off me by a quarter past."

Erik triggered the mirror as he let her slip from his arms and into her darkened dressing room. In a blink, the glass slid back into place, but the light from the lantern meant she could still see him there, unmasked and yet perfect. Christine placed her palm against the cold, cruel barrier between them and Erik did the same.

"I love you, my angel," Erik spoke, those words in his unearthly voice sending new tremors through Christine's soul. There was nothing she could do but nod before rushing from the room, lust aching between her thighs.

Christine wondered how flushed she looked as she arrived on the stage, one of the first principals to do so, and tried to straighten her hair and dress as best she could. Today would be a simple, un-costumed run of *Faust* to refamiliarize the company with the production before they returned to it in a few days.

A few members of the chorus were already on the stage, and some of the musicians were tuning in the pit. Christine's chest tightened anytime one of them looked up at her. She didn't even want to look to the audience to see if Raoul had arrived. She settled for smiling to herself as she surveyed the table at center stage where she'd given herself last night.

"Ah, I see you've recovered from Mardi Gras as well." Christine turned to see Robert Rameau smiling at her. The caddish bass who pretended to be her lover (or one of them) was always a comforting presence.

"I don't know if I'd go that far," Christine sighed. Robert chuckled as he looked her over and his eyes fell on the ring on her finger.

"Did I give you that?" the basso asked without a speck of judgment or suspicion. "Just so I know if we're engaged."

"That's the other hand," Christine muttered. "But yes, it's from my not-so-secret lover. The speech along with it was very romantic."

"Well, good job to me then." Robert looked out into the audience, and Christine's gaze followed his. To her shock, there was absolutely no one in the seats. "Were you expecting someone to be here?"

"Raoul de Chagny will be here periodically to see me in the next few weeks," Christine explained. "As a dear friend who wishes to spend time with me before he embarks on a long sea voyage, of course."

"No threat to the man who gave you that ring," Robert followed. "Or I hope not, for my own sake. Yours too."

"None at all." Christine squinted at the sea of red velvet – the bathtub, as it was called – and wondering if she was missing something with her nearsightedness. "I thought he'd be here today."

"Maybe he's busy doing something noble or naval, or whatever a young man like him does." Robert shrugged and Christine gave a distracted nod in return.

"Maybe."

Where on earth could he be, and why did it make the pit in her stomach grow to consider it?

S haya was not sure what to think of the young Vicomte de Chagny, even after hearing the young man's narrative of what he knew (or thought he knew) of Erik. The boy was brave, certainly, but the stupid kind of brave that only a young person could fully embody.

"So your plan was to just... wander into the cellars and find the way into Erik's house?" Shaya said. "When you know better than most that he's a killer?"

"You make it sound stupid when you put it that way," Raoul grumbled.

"That's because it was."

"Having the keys gave me confidence," the young man huffed, reminding Shaya all too much of Ramin as a schoolboy when Shaya had been the one to catch him trying to sneak out of lessons to attend a fair.

"You're lucky you only found me," Shaya reprimanded.

"He wouldn't kill me. Christine would not allow it."

"And you truly believe this woman has the capacity to control him or keep him at bay while you two – what? Play with your hearts the way children play with balls? While you also try to uncover his secret?"

"Christine is an innocent victim here," Raoul repeated for what had to be the third time that morning. Shaya wanted very much to protest, but it would do no good right now to tell the boy how wrong he was.

"Of course," Shaya settled on saying.

"Now that you are willing to help, we can find the fiend!" Raoul went on, fire in his face.

"When will you hear me, Monsieur? It's not that easy," Shaya sighed. "I've been watching Erik for years, trying to find a way to draw him out in the open someplace he's vulnerable."

"You said you have some hope now of a way in" Raoul pushed back, still caught on the confession Shaya had made of the hidden door he'd seen Erik enter in the third cellar, part of a set for *Le Roi de Lahore.* "We have to go there!"

"And fall right into one of his traps?" Shaya laughed back. "No, it's too dangerous."

"So you're a coward then?" the Vicomte scoffed, lightly pounding on the table between them so that the empty coffee cups clattered.

"Do not mistake me, boy. I have seen horrors that you could not dream, all created by Erik's hands. I have seen men driven out of their minds by his inventions. I've seen him kill in the blink of an eye." He watched as the Vicomte's ruddy complexion became ashen. "I watched that monster corrupt and destroy my own brother. I waited years for justice, because I knew if he killed me, there would be no one left to hold him in check. Do not presume to lecture *me* on cowardice."

"I'm sorry," Raoul muttered, avoiding Shaya's eyes. "That must mean you understand how much I need to save Christine and destroy him. I just want to do something!"

"We need to find a time when we know he's distracted by your little songbird," Shaya countered. "Do you think she would tell you when they have these lessons of theirs?"

"I believe so. Then you'll show me what you can, down there?"

"I'll try, but you must listen to my every instruction. You're a naval man, aren't you? I will be your captain and I will expect complete obedience, for the sake of your very life." Shaya watched as a muscle twitched in the boy's jaw.

"Yes, Monsieur."

"One thing I will tell you now, if you are stupid enough to go back down into his domain alone again: keep your hand at the level of your eye."

"Is this some Eastern superstition?" the boy scoffed, and Shaya fought the urge to box his ears.

"Did you hear nothing I told you of his executions in Persia?" Shaya snapped. "The Punjab Lasso can kill you before you even know it's coming. It's a whip, it goes around your neck and garrotes you *unless you stop it with your hand.*"

"Oh," Raoul said. Shaya wondered how Erik hadn't killed this fool already. "I'll remember."

"Do try. Now, I think you're late for an appointment." The boy jumped and pulled out his (impressively golden) pocket watch and swore softly. "Will you be escorting Daaé home?"

"If she lets me, but I guess if she goes off to him..." The boy looked so young and unsure all of a sudden. Shaya very much didn't want to tell the poor, besotted fool that Daaé had snuck from her flat the night before after Raoul had left her there.

"Let her. It's best. Then find me and we'll begin." Raoul nodded and turned to the exit before looking back at Shaya.

"You think she's safe? That he won't hurt her?" Raoul asked with genuine fear in his voice. "Everything you've told me... I fear for her even more now."

"He won't hurt the thing he wants to keep and control. You and I are in far more danger if that makes you feel better."

"It doesn't. Goodbye."

Shaya watched the handsome young noble leave the café. Once again, the memory of Ramin surged into his mind. Shaya's brother had been older than this green boy when Erik's evil cut his life off, but he'd had the same headstrong determination. Ramin had also thought the one he was so infatuated with had a chance of being saved, like Raoul did with Daaé. Ramin had been wrong, but Shaya found himself hoping that Raoul was not. If there was hope for Daaé to be torn from Erik's clutches, there was hope that he could make Erik suffer all the more.

E rik was not sure what to do. The half-written composition he had been commanded to create sat on the music stand above his piano keys, mocking him. He had doffed his jacket and vest and sat in shirt sleeves with his unruly black hair falling in his eyes, probably looking the very picture of a tortured artist (if said artist had been decaying in a crypt for a few years, granted). At the time he most needed to escape his troubles into the calming waters of sound, he found the spring dry.

"Fuck it." Erik rose, finally daring to look at the clock. It was a little past five, blessedly closer to his appointment with Christine than it had been the last time he looked. It was late enough to give up.

It's not that he hadn't tried. The melodies that had consumed him yesterday were still there, resonant and ringing in his mind, but the idea of Christine walking his opera with *that boy* had installed a nest of wasps in his brain that would not stop buzzing. Every time he tried to add a line of notes or, gods forbid, consider what sort of story this opera could tell, his thoughts returned to them.

Erik grabbed his cloak and mask and stalked from his home. There was safety in covering himself and letting the darkness surround him. Several openings above the lake to the world above assured that it was always a sort of eerie twilight when he polled the boat across the crystalline waters, but it was far darker than in his home and it gave him some ease to become a shadow again.

What would the boy say about him? What lies might he tell – or worse – what truths? What if he whispered into Christine's ear that she was ensnared to the devil, that she had sold her soul for music and fame and sins of the flesh? What if he convinced her that she was better off in the world above? The little fool could tell her that Erik was a killer, a monster, a thief, and a deceiver – and it would all be right!

She promised, a ghost in his mind responded, barely audible over the noise. *She knows you are more.*

"What if that's not enough," Erik found himself whispering aloud as he came to the shore. He moored the boat, trying to let the physical toil ground him, but the relief was only temporary. That horrible 'what if' was still ringing in his head.

Erik knew he shouldn't go up. Christine had told him not to torture himself, but he just wanted to look. He wanted to see her and know she was *pretending* to be something else, to belong to someone else to save him. Because she said she loved him and she had to mean it.

Erik quickly found his way to the third cellar, past the furnaces and in among the maze of machinery, sets, and close, dark corridors. This was the place for ghosts, everyone in the Opera knew it. Erik, being one such ghost, rarely stopped to take in the unsettling feel of the place, but today it struck him like a cold blast. Something felt *wrong*.

Erik paused, listening to the shadows around him as his senses prickled. He had spent his whole life afraid of people and being forced on display for them, and he was hyperaware of what it felt like to be watched or even be near another person. He felt that now. Was it Shaya? Or the boy? Were they snooping where they shouldn't be, or was it something else?

Erik moved slowly, hiding behind sets and backdrops, moving them when he could. If someone had come into his labyrinth, he would not make it easy for them to depart. It was slow work, but the feeling of someone intruding didn't dissipate until he was closer to the stage. A stage which was empty, Erik saw to his dismay when he emerged into box five.

His anxiety surged, like a predator seizing on his guts and twisting them around its claws. What if she was gone? What if it had all been a distraction? What if someone else had interfered? Erik scaled the edge of the box and column, jumping effortlessly to the stage with no care at all of being seen. Let someone earn themselves a new legend of the Phantom to tell if he was caught.

The wings were empty and the halls towards the dressing rooms were deserted too. The singers and musicians were gone, and only a few workers remained. Soon they would retreat too, but maybe one of them was there. Maybe one who knew Christine...

Erik followed the familiar path towards the costumers that he had taken so many times when Christine had been employed there. Sure enough, Julianne Bonet was one of the final women to emerge from the workshop as Erik watched. Should he talk to her? She might not even know where Christine was. Perhaps it was better to follow? Erik blinked back to reality from the fog of indecision and realized he had already lost track of his mark.

"Damnit," he whispered, turning the corner of the hall to come face to face with the woman he had misplaced.

"She's off with him up in the west rotunda, I think." Bonet said without flinching when Erik met her eyes. "I saw them go off together after the run-through. I wanted to say something, but she was too fast. I don't think she wants to talk to me."

"You're her closest friend," Erik replied without thinking (unsurprising, as he'd been doing very little of that today).

"I was, until lately and all of this." Bonet did not have to explain what she meant or gesture at Erik for him to comprehend. "I don't think she wants to hear me tell her to stop lying to people she cares for."

"Sometimes lies are necessary," Erik shot back even as his skin began to crawl under Julianne's discerning gaze.

"Did you know? About her and the Vicomte?" she demanded, and Erik nodded. "Good. I think. Or not. Actually, I don't care. Just tell her to talk to me tomorrow, alright? I need her."

"I shall." Before Erik could disappear, Bonet turned away and vanished herself.

Erik raced away towards the dancer's rotunda, located beneath one of the two smaller domes that flanked the Opera. It was a lovely spot, and he was filled with new envy that the boy was the one who would share it with Christine, even for an hour.

Erik soon found himself at the door to the rotunda, his heart pounding as he listened.

"I don't think I can come." The sound of Christine's voice, firm and cool, was a balm on Erik's soul. "But if they're not actually engaged yet, I don't see why we need to worry about a party that I wouldn't be wanted at anyway."

"I want you there." Erik cringed. As much as he loved hearing Christine, he hated the little noble's whining. "I'll need you to keep me from making a scene and telling Sabine what a fool she'd be to marry that man."

"You could talk to her, you know, before he proposes. She deserves to know about him and Adèle." There was kindness in Christine's words because she was always kind, even to little shits who didn't deserve it.

"She knows." The boy paused. Erik could imagine the vacant look on his face. "Or I think she does. It doesn't matter. To Philippe, Antoine is family, so Sabine marrying him won't be too much of a change."

"One day, I'm sure you'll tell me why Philippe feels that way," Christine replied and there was uncharacteristic silence. It worried

Erik enough that he chanced glancing through the door to see a horribly serious expression on the young man's face.

"I don't think you'll like the story." The young man looked so sad for an instant, Erik almost forgot to hate him. Almost. "I miss my father. He'd know what to say to her. And me."

"He'd never let you see me," Christine countered. If that was the case, Erik regretted that the old Comte was dead.

"Your father would do the same," the boy chuckled. "He was always against romance of any kind. Any story he told with love in it ended badly. Maybe he knew something we don't."

"He did," Christine said softly. "He knew what it was like to lose someone you love. Maybe Sabine is better off marrying a man she only cares for just enough to tolerate for security."

"No matter how we're connected, I still don't want a man I can't trust as a husband for my sister," the boy went on with a sigh, moving to the round window that looked out on the street below. That left Christine to look over her shoulder towards the door where Erik hid. And give a quiet smile.

"Trust is a hard thing. It's precious and rare," Christine said, and Erik was suddenly awash in guilt. "Even when someone is true, doubt can creep in. Both sides need to be patient as much as they're trusting." Christine's eyes were not on the boy, but on the shadows. She sensed Erik there and somehow, she forgave him.

"I don't see how that's relevant to Sabine's situation," the boy huffed, turning to look at Christine just as she returned her attentions to him.

"I was just thinking aloud. I'm quite tired though. Would you mind taking me to the front?" Erik's heart ached again. He didn't deserve her. Neither of them did.

"Can I not escort you home myself again?" the interloper asked. Christine shook her head and the boy's face fell. "Oh. You have... another engagement?"

"I have a promise to keep that I've explained many times."

"Is it just a lesson?" Once again, Christine nodded, and Erik smiled to himself. They were due for a lesson, but that would have to wait for other promises Christine had made to be fulfilled. "Very well then."

Erik raced from the hall the moment the pair moved, clinging to the surge of hope and peace that just seeing her had brought, not his guilt at having been caught spying. Christine had not forbidden Erik from watching her, just encouraged him to spare himself. He hoped she was not too angry.

Not soon enough, he found himself by his door from the stables, catching the scent of hay and horses through the opening. The passage felt different. The way that it had been different in the third cellar earlier. Had he left the door ajar? That was unlike him, even though he had been distracted of late.

He examined the entrance to his secret world and indeed, it was open. He pressed through and the horses whinnied in interest as he made the door secure before examining around it. Had Shaya been snooping in here again?

"It wasn't I!" Erik spun to see Jean-Paul Lachenal, the chief groom of the stables whom he often delighted in tormenting. His usually red cheeks had faded to chalk white behind his gray mustache at the sight of the Phantom. "I swear it, Monsieur! Someone was here and opened that door, but not me! I would never interfere with your affairs!"

"I believe you," Erik intoned, and even the reassurance made the man tremble. "You won't let anyone else in the stables but Opera employees anymore, will you?"

"I haven't!" Jean-Paul stammered. "I mean – I won't! Ever again!"

"Good. Now go find your wine and throw it out. It's not too late for you to be sober for Lent," Erik ordered. The man looked like he'd been asked to cut off his leg, but he nodded and rushed away. Erik was only slightly reassured, the feeling of unease that had been bubbling in him all day once again reaching a boil.

"What did you say to that poor man?"

Erik blinked at the sight of Christine silhouetted in the gaslight from the street. Once again, his salvation had appeared at the gate from the *Rue Scribe*, her beautiful face flushed and a tender smile upon her lips.

"Nothing that matters."

Christine ran to him through the shadows, letting him pull her into his secret passage and kiss her. She kissed him back, gentle and warm, her lips driving out the demons that had taken up residence in his brain all day. He didn't want to let her go and he told her so with each knead of his lips against hers.

"Were you that worried?" she asked softly as she pulled away after an interminable kiss, her hazel eyes meeting Erik's.

"I couldn't help it." It felt so good, just holding her close, and he never wanted to let her go again. "May I take you home?"

"Please." Christine's voice was husky as she placed her palm against his pounding heart. "We have promises to keep."

Raoul had circled the entire Opera twice looking for The Persian and he was beginning to think this was all some sort of joke in poor taste by the strange man. The details of what Shaya Motlagh had told him of Erik's time as an architect and executioner in the court of the Shah made Raoul shiver more than the late winter chill as he rushed along the *Rue Auber* beneath the gaslights.

It was all so much worse than he had imagined. Raoul had known the Opera Ghost was capable of murder since he had found the body of Joseph Buquet above the stage, then he had learned of Erik's role in the fire that had claimed his father's life. All those killings could be explained, perhaps, as acts of a man under the delusion he was defending himself. But that could not be said of this monster's crimes in the East. He had killed with finesse and glee, ruthless with his victims. He had *tortured* them.

Raoul stopped in his tracks, looking up at the lofty walls of the Palais Garnier. Somewhere beneath that great edifice, Christine was with the angel who was really a devil. Was she in ecstasy as she sang with him? Was she moved by the pity she claimed for this deformed genius? Was she scared? Was she safe?

"I'll find you, Erik," Raoul seethed at the silent walls of stone, fists contracting.

"You won't find him out here."

Raoul turned to the man in the fur cap, whose face was just as wry as his voice. "Where have you been? I've been looking for you for an age."

"My apologies. I had to return home and assure my servant that I was still alive. He gets very worried."

Raoul rolled his eyes. "You shouldn't let a valet get so familiar. How can you afford a servant anyway? Does the stalking of ghosts pay a salary?"

"I have a pension from the Persian court and Darius is more—"

"Are we going back in? Christine is with him right now, distracting him with a lesson," Raoul cut him off. He had no time for pleasantries. "And are you ever going to tell me how you ended up in such a state this morning that you had to assure anyone of your survival?"

"Eventually." The Persian nodded for Raoul to follow. They were headed, he deduced, to the entrance used by the artists, which Motlagh patiently waited for Raoul to unlock it with his borrowed keys. "This way. We're going down."

Raoul followed Motlagh down a narrow stair to an alcove where he found a small dim lantern. It was cold, and the air made

Raoul think of the times he'd visited inside his family crypt. "This place is so grim. It fits *him*."

"Hand at the level of your eye, Monsieur," Motlagh chided, making the gesture himself. Raoul complied grudgingly. "And I wouldn't tempt fate by insulting him aloud, even with such a precaution."

"I told you, Christine said they had an appointment." Raoul shuddered. He did not like the smug look he caught on the Persian's face at that.

"I'm glad you trust her," Motlagh muttered as they descended a set of stairs and found themselves in another dark corridor with gray concrete walls, but now there was a strange light from far off. "The furnaces," Motlagh explained before Raoul could ask. "They're always going this time of year. You know you're getting closer to the lake when you see them."

"If he lives near the lake, why don't we just go there and go across?"

"Because he has traps set in it too, fool," the Persian hissed. "I was lucky to get out of one such snare alive."

"But you did get out," Raoul pushed, suspicious. "Did he—"

"He saved my life out of a sense of obligation," the Persian went on, and Raoul's trust diminished again. Clearly this man had conflicted loyalties if he'd hunted Erik for so long and let him live.

"Why the hell is there a lake under an opera anyway?" Raoul wondered what the thing looked like. In his imagination, it was an entire lagoon, cattails and frogs and all – but that was probably inaccurate.

"When they were building, I believe they found a stream—"

"What was that?" Raoul hissed, grabbing the Persian's arm and stopping him. They listened in frozen silence for several heartbeats before the sound came again: footsteps.

"Someone is coming. Get back," Motlagh ordered. Raoul did as he was told, ducking away and then down into a corner, pressing himself against a wall as the Persian hid their lamp. "Is it he?" Raoul whispered, suddenly reassured by the feeling of his hand right by his brow.

"Erik doesn't make a sound when he walks," the Persian hissed back. "Now be quiet."

Raoul held his breath, sure Motlagh was doing the same beside him. The steps approached, and Raoul wondered if it was just some fireman. They patrolled the Opera all the time, didn't they? Making sure this new monument didn't suffer the same fiery fate as the old theater of the *Rue Le Peletier*. But there was no clink of keys and no light coming towards them as the steps continued.

Then Raoul saw it: a tall shadow in a wide felt hat, its face obscured. The shade was the same height as Erik, but his eyes... There was no fire in them. Raoul could not make out any eyes at all as the figure passed by where they had hidden themselves.

Only when the shade was long gone and the sound of footsteps had faded did they rise. Raoul turned to see that his guide looked rather ashen.

"If that was not him—"

"That was the one who caught me and left me for dead last night," the Persian replied. "I guess now is the time to tell you: I met that same shadow last night, and he assaulted me. He said he didn't want me interfering. I have as much of a clue who it is as you. Which is to say none at all."

"Someone *else* is down here, sneaking about that's not him?" Raoul pressed as they continued their journey. "Who could it be?"

"The police, perhaps? Some liaison for the managers?" The Persian shrugged. "I would have heard if they were making a move."

"If he – the shade – if he injured you, perhaps he's on Erik's side!" Raoul cried before remembering that Erik himself could still be close if they were unlucky.

"No one is on Erik's side," the Persian countered.

Raoul scowled into the deepening shadows. Where in God's name were they now? It was dank and stony, and it made his skin crawl to imagine Christine trapped in such a funereal place.

"Don't be so sure." Raoul had his suspicions of many people, especially the other men who were too supportive of Christine, like Moncharmin or... "What if it was Rameau?"

"The bass?" The Persian sounded unconvinced. "What reason would he have to help Erik?"

"He's entwined in this too!" Raoul went on, focusing on his theory and his apprehension rising at the first sound of running water in the distant dark. "He's been pretending to be Christine's lover to cover up her connections to Erik and his own degeneracy. Maybe—"

"Stop," Motlagh commanded suddenly, and Raoul nearly tripped over where the other man had frozen in front of him. "Shit."

"What? Is it him? Is he coming back?" Raoul could not hear any footsteps, only the soft rush of a stream somewhere. It was like no stream he'd ever heard above ground, he considered, especially as the noise grew *louder* while the two men remained stock still. "What on earth is that noise?"

Raoul looked towards where the sound was coming from and yelped. A head with no body, glowing like it was on fire, was approaching! And the sound – not like water anymore, but a terrible hissing, scratching noise – was moving with it!

"Get against the wall! Don't move! It can make them angry!" Motlagh warned and Raoul obeyed, afraid to ask what 'they' were. He knew he was about to find out. "Allah protect us."

"Make way!" the glowing head called and Raoul's heart leapt as something skittered over his foot, then something else against his leg. "Make way for the ratcatcher!"

"Jesus Christ in heaven," Raoul groaned as the horrible realization of what the sound was hit him.

It was *rats*. Hundreds of rats scurrying over their feet and legs as the ratcatcher drew near. It was just a man with a bright lantern on his face, drawing the vermin to him, Raoul saw now, but, oh God, there were so many! Thousands of tiny claws skittered over his legs, greasy fur and a hundred sinewy tails following.

"Make way for me and my rats!" the man whooped, and surely any man that undertook such an occupation had to be completely mad. He clearly saw Shaya and Raoul cowering as he drove his horde of rodents through the cellars, and he laughed as the torrent of squirming vermin engulfed them like a wave all the way up to their thighs and hips. The vermin scrambled across his groin and Raoul was glad the wall was there to keep him from expiring in pure disgust.

It went on forever, an endless parade of rats as their master's light faded down into the hall, until finally the last little creature scurried past. Raoul nearly collapsed, fighting the urge to vomit.

"You knew *that* was down here too?!" he managed to cry. He didn't care that the Persian looked ashen too.

"I never know when he's going to be making his rounds, I assure you that—"

"You can assure me of nothing!" Raoul yelled, and he didn't care that his voice was ringing through the dark. "You are useless! You don't know who this shade is! You won't take me to the lake! You send me into *that*, and for what? Why are we here?"

"If you mean to hunt him, you must know the territory."

"So that I can be just as much of a coward as you? No! There has to be a better way! This is madness!"

"Monsieur!" Shaya called as Raoul rushed away. He had no idea where he was going, but finding his way out couldn't be so hard. He'd been a fool all day and he was done with it. It would be better, he was sure of it, to spend his time trying to win Christine's confidence so she would betray her teacher.

His poor Christine, wherever she was now, Raoul prayed she was safe from all this horror and darkness so far below.

Christine nestled closer to the warmth of the lover sleeping beside her and mused on all the ways he had made her ache today, for better or worse. All day her heart had stung with guilt, not just for the fear Erik felt each time she left, but also for Raoul, who did not deserve such lies. At least she could tell herself there was a good reason for it all. With Erik, at least she knew how to console him. She smiled against the pillow, happy for the way her thighs and ass still twinged with the echo of their coupling.

It had been fast and slow all at the same time when they arrived home. In seconds, just as promised, Erik had rendered her bare and begging in his bed. He'd taken her on her knees, fucking her so thoroughly she saw stars.

Christine had surrendered to being possessed. She loved the way Erik's cock filled her as he fucked her in that position. She loved the way he made her grip the bed for support, even as she hated how he was hidden from her eyes. He was hers: the hands on her hips as she sped to climax, the frantic rhythm as he claimed her. Her terrible angel had made her scream so loud she was sure the Opera above might hear.

Christine found herself blushing at the memory and coughed softly into the pillow, reminding herself of the other pleasures they'd taken after. Well, it *should* have been a pleasure to sing for him, but tonight they had begun on *Lohengrin*, just one scene, and it had left her voice tired and irritated.

She closed her eyes and tried to think about the beauty of the music instead. Her teacher had played for her afterwards when he saw that she was tired. The violin had filled her mind with melody until her eyes had drooped and he'd ushered them to bed. She could still hear it if she listened.

Even with her eyes open now, the notes were there, familiar and comforting. Maybe tea would ease her throat and help her sleep, she thought as she rose, wrapping herself in her red robe.

The music went on, louder now, and Christine stopped at the door. She recognized *The Resurrection of Lazarus*, but this wasn't how Erik played it. It was familiar in a way that made her heart ache anew. She stepped into the parlor and stared at the player standing by the crackling fire.

He'd always loved that spot, either to play or tell stories, especially at the end. He finished a phrase and turned to her, not annoyed at all by her interruption. The violinist's smile was a little sad, even when she was a child, and it was the same now.

"There you are. I thought you'd be out sooner," he said, setting down his instrument and beckoning her closer.

"I'm sorry, Papa. I must have lost track of time," Christine answered, voice shaking.

She wanted to embrace him. It had been so long since he'd been able to hug her. He'd been so weak before. Now, he looked healthier than she had seen him in years, and it made her so happy. Even so, Christine stayed a foot away. Was he mad at her for being late? He looked glad to see her, but also disappointed.

"Sit. Have some tea, you need it," her father ordered. Christine poured for him first and then herself, taking a place in the chair next to him. Should she have sat at his feet, like in the old days? She wanted so much to look into his dark eyes and count the wrinkles around them again.

"Are you—"

"Drink." Her father nodded to the cup in Christine's hand and she did as she was told. "I don't like this Wagner nonsense. Your teacher certainly shouldn't have you singing it after so many exertions today." He made a tsking sound over his tea and Christine looked down in shame.

"Erik thinks I can do it."

"The role doesn't suit you. He's asking too much." Her father sighed and shook his head. "Your angel is meant to protect you. Not ruin you."

"He's not—"

"That's not even to mention these silly romantic notions he's inspired." His tone was familiar. Christine had endured this conversation many times before, when her father had warned her to stay away from Raoul because he would break her heart. "He'll break your heart too, when you lose him."

"He won't – I won't lose him," Christine stammered, staring at her father's worn shoes. They'd walked so many long miles, those shoes. He'd always hated replacing them and said it was about finding the right pair and not that they could never afford it.

"As long as you keep him *here*, keep him a dream, you won't," her father answered, certain and calm. "He's not real now and that's good. Keep him an angel, like he was meant to be. Not a man. Never a husband."

Christine looked down at her hands. Where was her ring? Where had it gone? She had promised to keep it safe...

"Does he know – why you can't be a real wife? You should tell him. It might make him feel better," her father went on, and Christine felt a fresh stab of shame. "It's better for your career. For the music."

"My career isn't—"

"Look at me, my child." Christine's eyes shot up. Her father's face was no longer warm and vital. He was growing pale and thin, wasting away before her eyes all over again. "The music is what is real, Christine, and it's all that matters. That's what will be there when he's gone."

"Not again, please," Christine begged, reaching for her father's hand as it turned to dust and his face became a corpse's above her with wide, worried eyes. Golden eyes. "No!"

"Christine!"

She gasped awake to the reality of Erik's hands on her arms, shaking her. She threw herself against his chest, a sob tearing from her throat. "Oh God."

"It was a nightmare," Erik cooed in her ear, stroking her hair as she wept. He was so solid and warm as he held her, the living thrum of his heart against her ear the most important sound in the world.

"Erik." His name was all she could manage as she pulled him to her tighter. If she held on hard enough, he'd stay. She could feel his ring on her finger again, solid and heavy as a chain keeping her in the here and now.

"I'm here," replied her angel. "Whatever you saw, it wasn't real."

She couldn't tell him why those words drew more tears from her eyes.

5. Family

Raoul missed rising early. He had formed the habit from months at sea when he had slept rocked by the waves and sailors were expected to be up and working before the morning bell even rang, if they knew what was good for them. Now, he slept in a soft feather bed alone, rather than bunked amongst half a dozen snoring men, and he tossed and turned with worry after late nights of misadventures. He rued how soft he had become as he rose and rang for his valet to dress him.

"Is Mademoiselle Sabine still in?" he asked the valet as he brushed the shoulders of Raoul's jacket.

"Yes, she's at breakfast with Comte Philippe. The Baron de Martiniac has joined them," the valet stammered. Raoul huffed and bolted from his bedroom down to the small dining room where breakfast was being served.

"Ah, there he is!" Antoine piped up first. "I was hoping you would be here for the official event."

"What event?" Raoul asked, not hiding his scowl.

"We don't need it to be anything more than it is," Sabine muttered, a slight blush on her cheek. Raoul blanched. He was too late.

"Still, I should like to formally ask to join the family with the whole family here." Antoine grinned like a wolf. "What do you say, my lovely Sabine, will you have me as a husband?"

"I guess so," Sabine smirked.

"Now, when will we have the party? Before our dear Raoul takes to the sea again, I hope," Philippe said. Raoul hated the way that made Sabine's face fall.

"You're not still intending to go to the North Pole, are you little brother?" Sabine asked. "Please make this the true happiest day of – well, at least my week – and tell me you are staying."

"I'm staying," Raoul heard himself say. In truth, he had decided it days ago, when he had resolved to kill the man that had taken his father and threatened to take Christine.

"Oh, Raoul, thank you! You don't know what it means that you will be there for the wedding," Sabine beamed.

"Congratulations to you both."

"Thank you, dear brother," Antoine said, ending the reverie. "Speaking of romance, how is Mademoiselle Daaé? Yes, we all know you were seeing her yesterday. Philippe was just telling us that you can't be dissuaded from her."

"Could she be invited to the engagement party?" Raoul blurted out.

"I will invite her myself if we see her at the Opera tonight," Sabine smiled, and Philippe looked at her in shock. "What? I'm feeling celebratory. Indulge me."

"We should go consult with Madame Cayette about the scheduling and arrangements." Philippe looked positively joyful. He rose and offered a hand to his sister. "I will be giving you away at your wedding, won't I?"

Sabine grinned as she took her brother's hand and followed him from the room, sending Antoine another cool smile as they left. Raoul marked how when Sabine was gone Antoine's mask of warmth and chivalry fell away.

"So, what did you learn yesterday skulking around the Opera?" Antoine asked. "I hope humiliating yourself with that little minx had some benefit."

"For your information, I did learn quite a bit. I met—" Raoul stopped himself. He didn't want Antoine to know he'd enlisted help, as useless as the Persian had proved. "I met with some obstacles. It's hard to get down to the lake – where he is. There are more hazards than just him down there."

"Hazards?" Antoine scoffed. "It's just a cellar, Raoul. Albeit one with an impressive little pond."

"A pond full of booby traps apparently. And you can tell me it's just a cellar again when you meet the rat catcher." Raoul shivered as he recalled a thousand little claws over his lower half.

"Sounds dark and dangerous. Did you faint?" Antoine sneered, and Raoul had endured quite enough.

He stomped from the salon and back to his room. The display he had created the week before of all the evidence and clues about Erik was still there on his desk. There was more to be added now, and at least putting it there would give him some piece of mind until he saw Christine again tonight. Until he could start anew trying to win her over to his side and learn what he could from her. He needed to record the entire narrative in the meantime, and so he began to write.

Erik adjusted the white tie at his throat, noting how the fabric felt more restrictive than usual today. It always happened when his mind or spirit was not at ease that even the texture of cloth on his skin became irritating, and every buckle and button was too tight. The mask was the worst: hot and hard against his face, the hooks that kept it in place heavy behind his ears.

There were times when his formal clothes, cape, hat, and mask were the armor between him and the cruel world. Right now they were just another uncomfortable wall separating him from humanity.

Maybe Christine will understand, he thought as he crossed the parlor to her room to see if she was ready to be escorted up. She wanted to be there early before the performance to see Julianne, since Erik had delivered her friend's message. Which was why he was surprised to see her still in just her underthings. She was sitting on the bed with her back to him, her shoulders slumped.

"Are you alright?" he asked, and Christine jumped. She had to have been in deep thought not to have sensed him. "What's wrong?"

"It's nothing, I—" She was holding something in her hand, and Erik saw a red stain on the white fabric.

"Are you hurt?"

Christine's face softened with amusement. "I'm fine. It's just the monthly curse. It snuck up on me."

It took Erik several seconds before he comprehended. "Oh."

"You need not trouble yourself," Christine said, but there was still something sad in her eyes that left Erik perplexed.

"Aren't you relieved to be...safe?" He couldn't think of a better word for her being free of an unwanted child for another month. He'd been careful until recently, to protect them both. That had changed the night she told him she loved him.

"I am, of course." Christine looked down and Erik was not sure she meant it. "It's just an inconvenient time, as always, with a performance tonight and everything else. And I don't want to disappoint you."

"Why would you disappoint me?" Erik sat beside her and lifted her chin so she'd look at him. Her eyes warmed as she smiled. "Do you think I care if I can only hold you?"

"You might."

"I have told you before that I'd give anything just to spend a few moments more each day in your light. I don't care about anything else." Erik was surprised when she embraced him, but glad that wrapping her in his thin arms could perhaps bring some comfort.

"Help me into my dress then." Christine gave an elegant little sniffle when she drew back. Erik obeyed, assisting with the skirt first then the separate piece for the top.

"It's curious to me, you know, how dresses like these are lies," Erik commented and received a perplexed look. "Two pieces made to look like it's one dress. It's a deception."

"All fashion is deception; you should know that," Christine chuckled, turning to look at him as she straightened her bodice before touching his mask. "Do you ever think of changing it? Your mask, I mean."

"Changing it how?"

"I don't know. Maybe add a beard or something?" Erik laughed and was glad of her smile.

"Perhaps glasses too? I do worry I'll start to need them as much as you soon." That suggestion received a light glare even as the idea planted itself in Erik's mind. "I did think about it, years ago: making a mask that would let me move about more easily, like a normal man. It just always felt like a bit too much of a lie."

"As we've discussed, it's all lies and artifice, the face put out to the world," Christine countered. "Would it really be so bad to have the option?"

"Would you want that? For me to..." Erik shook his head. The thought of going *up there* anymore even with a mask that made him look something like a normal man was still so strange and frightening.

"Maybe. One day." Another shadow of melancholy passed over Christine's eyes.

"It wouldn't hurt for me to have another project to distract me."

"Not at all, *Monsieur le Fantôme*," Christine smiled at the title. "I don't think that name would work at all if you were to walk among the living. What is your surname, anyway? I've never asked."

"I've never used one," Erik replied with a shrug. "I certainly don't want my father's name."

"What about your mother? What was her last name?"

"Gilbride," Erik answered quietly. "It means a servant of Brigid. She's a goddess or a Saint in Ireland, depending on who you ask. She watches over smiths and bards and sacred fires."

"Erik Gilbride. I like that." It sounded so wonderful on her tongue. "I think he would look dashing with a beard."

Erik thought about it as they ascended to the Opera above, arm in arm, discussing the merits of Gounod over Meyerbeer and Halévy. They had walked like this in the catacombs and the Bois at night, but what would it be like to stroll with her above with no one looking at him like a freak or a monster? Would Erik feel brave with such a wondrous creature on his arm, or would all that old fear still rule him?

Too soon, they were at the stables again. They had decided together it was best for Christine to be seen more often than not going into the Opera rather than appearing at random from her room.

"Will you be watching from your box?" Christine asked at the threshold. Pale daylight stained the stones when the passage opened and the horses whinnied.

"It wouldn't do for the ghost to miss a performance. Madame Giry would worry. Will you be going to see the patrons after?" There were few things he hated more than how artists like Christine had to bow and scrape before the patrons after a performance. He hated it all the more knowing the boy would be there.

"I have to." The depth of regret in Christine's voice stemmed some of Erik's jealousy. "I'm going to sing for you tonight. Think about that. Only you."

"I will treasure every note," Erik whispered.

"Let it inspire you. I'm still expecting my opera on time." Erik was sure she meant it as a jest, something to distract him and lift his spirits, so he did not say or do anything to betray the way it made him squirm to think of composing a full opera. The first one was unfinished, and she never needed to know about that bloody business, did she? His *Don Juan Triumphant*...

"I will try." Erik was glad it made her smile.

"I'll be here. I promise." Christine pulled him into a kiss. It was such a miracle, every time her soft, living lips met his dead ones; such a reminder of the undeserved grace she gave him every moment she allowed him at her side and in her bed.

Erik held on for as long as he could before letting her go, the feel of her fingertips lingering in his hand for a few seconds more driving away the dread in his heart. Then he watched her go back out into the world through the deserted stable. Once again retreating to a world where he could not follow.

He lingered, unsure of what to do with himself now that he was alone once again. It was such a strange thing, to be made conscious of his solitude after so many years. He had grown so used to being alone; so unknown and unseen that he forgot his own humanity and need for the world. But ever since Christine, he had been so aware of it again, and so tired of the days in the dark with nothing but his thoughts.

Erik stepped out of the passage into the stable and walked to César's stall. The white stallion snorted in recognition before letting Erik pet his nose and scratch his flank. He'd always loved animals. Animals didn't care about the differences in human faces and yet it was always such a precious thing when one trusted you.

César huffed and nudged Erik's hand with his snout, soft nostrils flaring as he nipped at him.

"Are you hungry? Hasn't Jean-Paul provided your oats for the day?" To Erik's surprise when he looked, César's feed bag was indeed empty. "I'll take your complaints to the management."

Erik took the empty bag towards the storeroom where Jean-Paul liked to pass out, disappointed in the man for so quickly defying Erik's orders to sober up. But the storeroom was empty. Erik took on the work and filled the bag. He did the same for the rest of the horses, though he stopped short of doing any dirtier work. Where could the man be? Why did it make his anxieties flare again to worry about it?

U nlike her first days in the Opera chorus, when Christine had spent many a rehearsal wondering if the people whispering backstage were talking about her, now she knew that the murmurs and sidelong glances of the petits rats, chorus, and stagehands were indeed aimed at the woman who had somehow become a diva in such a short time. She tried to ignore it most days, but it was hard. Today she had meant to look for Julianne, but instead found herself behind a flat listening to a discussion where she was the topic.

"She's not even that good," one woman was saying, in a tone of pure disgust. "She thinks she can just waltz in off the street, fuck a bass or a vicomte, and then be the toast of the town!"

"Never paid her dues, the little bitch," another voice agreed. Christine's eyes stung. She knew that voice – it belonged to an alto who had always been kind to her face. "Not that I mind her ruining La Carlotta, but at least that bitch knew how to play the game. Daaé just comes in here and thinks she's better than everyone because of some witchcraft she's managed on the ghost or the managers or whoever."

"I want to claw my ears out when she sings the Jewel Song – too much vibrato! *And* she sings it like Marguerite has already been corrupted. It's wanton."

"She wouldn't be anything without—"

"Don't listen to them." Christine turned at the sound of Julianne's voice as she placed a hand on Christine's shoulder.

"I've been looking for you," Christine exclaimed, throwing her arms around her friend. "I'm so sorry I've been gone so much."

"You should be," Julianne replied with no venom. "Come on. We have to get you dressed and solve all my problems." She pulled Christine towards the dressing rooms, leaving the gossipers behind.

"Only yours?" Christine laughed.

"Oh yes. Your problems are far too complicated for a mere mortal. And it's my turn to be in crisis."

"What's going on?" Christine swallowed down the guilt of always being the one at the center of every drama. "Is it Jammes?" she asked once they were safely behind the door of dressing room thirteen.

"Of course it's Cécile. She's given me up for Lent, and it's my fault." Julianne slumped onto the chaise.

"How could her fear be your fault?" Christine countered, taking a place beside her friend. "I didn't think she was that concerned about the rules or sin or whatever."

"I told her I loved her," Julianne sighed. "It was at the masquerade. I wore a suit so we could dance together, and we did! I said it when we were kissing backstage, and someone saw us and she ran away! The next day she's claiming we're a sin. How do I prove to her we're not?"

"I'm so sorry." Christine took Julianne's hand. "I don't know if that's something that can be proven. If someone saw you, she might be worried. Or she could be fearful for another reason."

"I know we can't be together like normal, but—" Julianne lamented.

"No, I just meant love. It's terrifying. I didn't want to admit I was in love until I thought about how awful it would feel to lose...him. So I told him I loved him and I've agreed to live with him. Officially. Because I realized how much it would hurt for him to go on thinking I didn't and how I want all the time with him I can have."

"I think she knows – how much it hurts for me. Should I tell her more?"

"I don't think you can force it, if she's afraid, and certainly not if she doesn't feel the same way. Maybe tell her you'll wait? Or that this is enough the way it is?"

"Is it though?" Julianne asked back. "Can half a life be enough?"

Christine swallowed. "I think so, if there's enough love."

"Are you sure?"

Christine closed her eyes. She wasn't sure, but this was what she had: Erik and the Opera and the music. It had to be enough. She shivered to recall the dream of her father telling her as much.

"I should start getting dressed and warmed up." Christine ignored Julianne's concerned look. "I can talk to Jammes, if that would help?"

Julianne winced. "She doesn't like you much."

"Because I'm a backstabbing whore who doesn't deserve this role or any?" Christine tried to laugh.

"Because she was convinced for a while that we were having an affair, remember?" Julianne chided, shaking her head. "I told her you were very much taken."

"I'm sure she was relieved." Christine drifted to where her costume for *Faust* hung ready to be laced on.

"You shouldn't listen to those bitter shrews. They only gossip and ignore your talent because they're jealous. They couldn't even dream of being half as good as you."

"But they're right," Christine argued reflexively. "I was *given* all of this."

"By someone who recognizes that you're extraordinary." Christine smiled at that. "Don't tell me you don't trust your illustrious teacher."

"I trust him more than anything." Christine thought of seeing her blood-stained chemise this morning and the few secrets he didn't know. Her gut ached for a new reason.

All too soon, she was dressed and running through scales, then behind a scrim as the illusion of Marguerite, there only to tempt Faust. She felt that way on stage sometimes, she mused, as if when she stepped under the gaze of a thousand members of the audience, she ceased to be a person or even a character. Marguerite was an idea, a symbol, and she, Christine, disappeared and didn't matter. At least not to them. She mattered to the man who had filled her and claimed her on this very stage, and they would never know.

Christine sensed Erik watching. When her time to sing came, she felt his love through the limelights and the smoke and the sound. When she sang of jewels and angels and love, she sang to him. Carlos Fontana was there, holding her in his arms, but he was just an illusion too, as empty as the applause. Erik was there, watching in the dark, and his ears and admiration were all that mattered. When the crowd rose to their feet in ovations, she looked up to box five and smiled at the shadow there.

She was exhausted when it came time to put on a new costume, this time her favored gown of crocus-purple silk. She wondered if Erik would be watching from somewhere, hidden in the walls of the mirrored Salon du Danse. She hoped not, knowing it would only make him suffer more. At least this was the only time she'd see

Raoul today. Soon he would be gone, but what then? Just more of this? More empty performances just to survive?

Christine winced as Julianne tightened the bodice of her dress and aggravated her cramped womb, then pushed down another insane wave of disappointment. She should be glad her blood had come. She should be relieved to be free, just like Erik said.

"Are you alright?"

Christine turned to her, plastering on a smile. "I will be when it's over and I'm home."

"I didn't think you even remembered Adèle's address."

Christine found herself giving a genuine, secret grin. "I didn't say I was going to Adèle's. I said I was going home."

"Well then, get going so you can do that," Julianne chuckled.

It was more performing when she met Robert Rameau in the hall for him to escort her, more false smiles and straight spines for everyone to see. She swept past the women of the chorus who sneered at her, and into the Salon du Danse to more worthless applause. The managers were there already and Moncharmin tapped his glass as soon as he saw Christine to gather the attention of the masses.

"*Mesdames et Messieurs!*" Moncharmin crowed. For a moment, Christine thought he was looking to her for reassurance before Robert gave him a smile. "We are happy for you to be the first to hear an exciting announcement. Before the end of the year, we will be bringing to the Paris Opera a work unlike any we have staged in this theater's brief history. Our first work by the great Richard Wagner—"

The room exploded in chatter before he could finish.

"Well, there we are," Robert murmured at Christine's side.

"And it shall be *Lohengrin*!" Moncharmin cried over the din before Richard pulled him into a corner.

"German opera? *Here?*"

Christine turned at the familiar sound of Philippe de Chagny's voice to see that he was flanked by Raoul and, unfortunately, Antoine de Martiniac. Between Antoine and Raoul was a handsome woman who Christine had not spoken to since she was seventeen and being told Raoul could no longer see her. Sabine de Chagny was radiant, her brown hair perfectly coiffed, her modest pink dress as perfectly executed as her polite smile. She was in sharp contrast to Raoul, who looked rather green and grumpy.

"It's high time we do something more modern," Robert said. "Don't you agree, my dear?" It took Christine a beat to realize he was speaking to her.

"Oh. Yes, it will be different, but that's not always bad," Christine muttered.

"You are the expert, Mademoiselle Daaé." Sabine made it sound like an insult. "I must say, it is so amazing to hear the little girl who used to sing for the gardener at the house in Perros on the stage of the National Academy of Music."

"Amazing, yes, but not surprising," Raoul piped in.

Christine smiled politely. She had no idea how to speak with him while there were so many others looking on, all of whom had completely different ideas about who she was and what she and Raoul were. And none of them were right. At least she didn't feel the telltale shivers that told her Erik was close.

"Indeed, my brother is your greatest admirer. Musically." Sabine grinned as she took Antoine's arm. "And my future husband and I have been discussing the celebration of our engagement—"

"Oh, congratulations." Christine tried not to be obvious in looking around the room for Adèle. Hearing her old lover was to be married might ruin her night. Christine hoped she had escaped early.

"*And*," Sabine went on, the coldness in her smile so clear Christine saw Raoul's eyes widen in worry. "My dear brother has suggested you entertain at the party."

"Entertain?" Christine noted the way the color drained from Raoul's face. She met her old love's eyes with a challenge even so. "You wish to invite me to your house... as entertainment?"

"We do understand if you cannot make it on short notice. Artists like you are in such demand," Antoine added. Christine wanted to slap him.

"I will consider it." She turned to her escort. "Robert, we should congratulate our managers on their announcement."

"Indeed we should, my dear." The bass swept her around and Christine was quite satisfied to turn her back on Raoul for once. She knew in a day or two he would come groveling. It only reminded her that there was no future there. Either he would go away or maybe perhaps his family would save her from him. Either way, soon there would only be Erik and wouldn't that be enough?

They found themselves in the circle of artists and patrons waiting to speak to Richard and Moncharmin. Christine's mind drifted back to the house on the lake, where it was all quiet and there were no cruel insults or callous lies. Maybe, she thought, and not for the first time, she could go down and never come back up, just like Erik had done.

"I'm sure he'll be fine. We have Monsieur Fauré as well as Inspector Mifroid looking into the whole thing now," Richard was huffing. Christine cocked her head.

"Was someone hurt?" she asked no one in particular. It was Carlos Fontana who turned to her to give her a look like she was a child late to school. "Did you not hear? They found a man beaten to a pulp near the stables. He claims it was the ghost."

Shaya was glad he hadn't bothered attending another performance of *Faust* that night. The commotion around the Opera was much more interesting. So far, he had seen three gendarmes come and go, near to the stables, and one man with bruises and wounds being questioned.

Shaya recognized the man too: the head groom of the stables. When had he been assaulted? As far as Shaya could remember, he had been in one piece yesterday. What could he possibly have done to displease Erik in that time? That was the question that drove him back into the stables once again, skirting the police on the street.

"Amateurs," Shaya grumbled under his breath as he examined the ill-lit space and found his clues immediately. Shovels and bags were on the ground by one bay's stall, as if there had been a struggle. The horse snorted at him as he drew closer, examining the paddock. "Too bad you can't speak," he said softly to the animal.

"She'd tell you this wasn't me, Daroga."

Shaya was proud of himself for not jumping when Erik's voice cut through the gloom. He turned to his nemesis and looked him over. Did he look... tired?

"I already knew that," Shaya replied coolly. Erik stepped further into the light, looking at the mess on the floor. "You have a fox in your hen house, I think the saying goes."

"So it would seem." Erik kneeled to touch where the dust on the floor had been disturbed. "And here I was thinking you had a fellow spy on your side."

Shaya swallowed as Erik rose again, reminding Shaya of his considerable height. "I don't need spies, Erik, just patience. I'm sure you know your sweet student is spending her days with the Vicomte before he departs for the north."

"I'm aware," Erik growled in return.

"Soon enough she'll turn on you and tell the boy everything." Shaya didn't care if Erik knew he was helping Raoul. In fact, it delighted him to think how the suspicion would worm its way into Erik's brain. "Or tell him more."

Shaya braced himself as he watched Erik's hand twitch into a fist. The only thing that was keeping him from being throttled right now was probably their relatively public location and some lingering compunctions from Erik.

"You could just leave us alone, you know," Erik muttered as his hand relaxed. "Let Ramin's memory rest. Live your own goddamn life instead of spending every day trying to destroy mine as if it will bring him back."

Now it was Shaya's turn to fight the urge to strike the man in front of him. "You'll suffer just like I have. I promise."

"Get out of here before I run out of patience, Daroga." Shaya was more than happy to comply, turning his back on the monster in the shadows with no fear. He knew he'd struck a blow, knew that Erik was obsessive and paranoid (with good reason), and that the insult to him and Christine would work into his soul like poison. Hopefully, Raoul de Chagny, fool that he was, would prove Shaya right.

E rik was not sure how long he had been sitting on the ground with his back against the wall, head in his hands. It had been long enough for the cold to seep into bones. It was comforting, in a way. The chill didn't feel good, but it felt real. It was solid and quiet while everything in his head kept getting louder. Why was it so loud? He should be happy – or something like happy. Christine had sung like her soul was on fire tonight, awing all of Paris, but where was she now?

He'd come right to the stables when he heard someone had been hurt, berating himself for not investigating further earlier in the day. Now, Jean-Paul was beaten and bruised, and everyone thought it was the ghost. But it hadn't been him! Or had it? Erik could not help but wonder. What if he was so broken that he had done something awful and forgotten it?

No, Shaya had said there was someone else in the Opera. Why did that even matter with Christine off at the party laughing with that boy?

"Erik? What are you doing here?"

He looked up, certain she was a dream. Christine knelt and pulled him out of the darkness. "I'm sorry, I—" She embraced him before he could finish, so tight it pushed the air from his lungs.

"I heard about Jean-Paul. I thought something had happened to you and I was so scared," Christine whimpered into his shoulder.

"I'm fine. It wasn't me. I didn't—"

"I know," Christine cut him off, pulling back to look at him carefully, hand against his masked cheek. "I know you wouldn't hurt him."

Erik wanted to say she was wrong. He'd hurt so many people, but he was speechless, overcome by the trust and love in her eyes. "We need to go. I'll explain at home."

"Alright."

Erik held Christine's hand tighter than usual as he led her down to the lake, listening at every juncture for some noise, waiting to feel something wrong. Luckily, there was nothing, barely even the sound of rats or dripping water. Soon enough, they were safe between the double casing in the candle-lit parlor he had built.

"Someone has been trespassing; someone who wants people to believe they are me," Erik answered before Christine could even voice the question. She grimaced in confusion as she came close to him, touching him gently as if to soothe him.

"Who? Why?"

"I don't know." Erik huffed in surprise when Christine threw her arms around him again. "What's wrong?"

"I told you, I was scared," she whispered before she kissed him. Why did kissing her make it all go away? All the fear, all the shame and doubt. When her lips were on him, there was nothing but good in his world, and he was safe again. How did she accomplish such magic?

"I'm fine," he sighed against her cheek. "Though I think I was more worried than you."

"About what?" Christine asked, pulling away to reveal debauched lips and heavy eyes. "Are you still convinced I won't return?"

"Every time," Erik confessed, looking down in guilt.

Christine answered his doubt by pulling off his mask. It was another kind of witchcraft, the way she looked at him with such tenderness every time his awful face was revealed. "One day I hope I will be able to convince you that I'll always return."

"I hope so too."

Christine pulled him towards his room, and he followed with no resistance. It was strangely relaxed, the way she began to undress him once they were behind his door and surrounded by the dark hangings of his bedchamber. Domestic, even. He helped her in turn, undoing the laces and buttons on her violet gown, and soon, they were free of everything but her chemise and his trousers.

"Come here," Christine commanded, guiding him to the bed until he was sitting on the edge. When she knelt before him, he suppressed a gasp.

"You don't need to," he gulped, even as her hands pushed his knees apart and she nuzzled his thigh. "I don't expect—"

"Let me." It was such a simple request, but the way she spoke it – husky and soft, looking up at him from beneath her dark lashes – left Erik breathless. "Please."

He nodded, words failing him as Christine undid the fastenings of his trousers and took his stiffening member in hand, stroking him to full hardness before licking at the tip. He groaned as her lips encircled him, soft and careful. His eyes fell closed in pleasure, his head falling back as her mouth welcomed him slowly, teasing him with her tongue and sucking in turn. When she hummed, it sent lightning through him, and he gasped when she added her hands at the base.

"Christine..." he exhaled her name, hands knitting into the sheets as his body grew tense and bliss zinged in his veins.

She sped up her attentions and he forced himself to open his eyes. The sight was perfect and obscene when he looked down, his cock disappearing into the throat that so recently had let forth music that had thrilled him and the audience alike. But this was his alone.

Christine squeezed his thighs as she met his eyes, bobbing her head and taking him deeper. Was she encouraging him? His body responded before his mind, his hips fucking upward as his climax built at the base of his spine. He didn't want to hurt her. He didn't want to lose control, but her mouth was tight and warm and she was all his, on her knees before him, and it felt so good to be *seen* and trusted.

Erik cried out, grabbing Christine's hair as she worked her throat in some incredible way, and he came. She held him in place as he did, swallowing down his spend in another act that left him awestruck.

"More often than not, I think you must be a dream." Erik fell back onto the bed. He loved the way she laughed at that, how warm and kind it was. "How else could someone like me deserve you?"

"Let's not wake then, either of us," Christine murmured back. He followed her bonelessly as she guided him up towards the pillows and settled her head on his chest. "Just hold me forever."

"As you wish." Erik was so tired, all the things he had been afraid of were far away, and the woman he loved was right here, kissing a scar on his chest. He pulled her to him and kissed her mouth, amazed again at the bitter aftertaste still on her tongue. "Forever and a day."

The brothel where Philippe had brought them was surprisingly elegant, Raoul noted. The walls were papered in gilded patterns, the paintings of succulent nudes were competent, and the whole place was draped in red velvet. On further thought, it wasn't so different from the Opera – the goods on display just had fewer clothes on. Raoul was watching as his brother examined a girl on a little pedestal, draped in black silk, with a connoisseur's eye.

Philippe shook his head and said something to the madame, who gave a polite smile before escorting the whore away.

"That's the third one you've sent back," Antoine sighed from his place on a divan with two well-paid but bored-looking women draped over him, already at work.

"Some of us have standards," Philippe grumbled in reply.

"That's why I'm marrying your sister," Antoine sneered, and Raoul shot up from his seat. "Oh for God's sake, calm down. How did your brother end up the only one in the family with a sense of fun?"

"You're right. I don't even want to be here," Raoul snapped back.

"Well, I'm sure you won't be long when it's time," Antoine said with utter smugness over the head of the whore licking at his chest. "Philippe, you have instructed him on how it's done, haven't you?"

"Honestly, Antoine. You think I didn't see to my little brother's education long before this?" Philippe called back.

Raoul sat down, trying not to blush. Now that he looked more carefully, he was sure he had indeed been to this house of ill repute before, when he was halfway through his seventeenth year and still heartsick over Christine. It *had* been fast, but he had certainly improved in the years since.

"Ah, yes, that's what I was looking for," Philippe crowed as the madame escorted a new girl into the room. A girl with dark hair, hazel eyes, tanned skin, and soft curves. In the low light, if Raoul squinted, she could be Christine. That was what Philippe had been looking for. "This is my brother, young lady. Please fuck what little brains he has right out of his head."

The whore smiled like a cat spying a mouse and approached Raoul with an extended hand.

"Unless you'd like us to get you a boy so you can pretend you're at sea," Antoine called just as Philippe took one of the girls from his lap and attacked her with kisses while she squealed.

"Fuck off," Raoul shot back as he let himself be dragged away to a side room with Antoine's laughter ringing in his ear. There was a large inviting couch full of pillows in the center of the room, and the whore guide Raoul there. She didn't move like Christine, but from the back, she was close enough. She let her silk robe fall to the floor with a giggle and Raoul surveyed her exposed body.

"How do you like it, Monsieur?" the girl asked with a smirk. Christine would never look so eager or proud. She would never reach for him like this wanton thing and massage him through his pants. Raoul batted her hand away even as he stiffened.

"I want you to pretend like you're a lady. A good, pure one," Raoul ordered.

"You want me to act like yours is the first cock I've ever had? No one else has ever fucked me so good?" The whore smirked again as Raoul's throat bobbed. He gave a quick nod in confirmation. "I'm sure that won't be too hard for me. Now, are you? Hard for me, that is?"

"Stop talking. A lady would never say anything so obscene," Raoul growled as he grabbed the whore and spun her. He didn't want to see that feline smile any longer. "Get on you fucking knees and do your job."

H er place next to Erik in his bed was still warm when Christine returned to it from the washroom. The clock in the corner said it was close to four in the morning and she very much wanted to sleep again. Even if more dreams came. There was part of her that wanted nothing more than to see her father's face again, even in sleep, but there was the other part that was so afraid of seeing him or the dozen other horrors of late that haunted her dreams. Buquet's body falling into the void on its rope and becoming Raoul's or Erik's.

"So I'm not the only one who can think too loudly."

Christine turned from the edge of the bed to see Erik looking at her with a soft expression, his hair a messy halo. "I'm sorry, I didn't mean to wake you," she whispered as he pulled her into his arms.

"Don't ever be sorry for that," Erik murmured back, nuzzling into her hair. "Will you tell me what's wrong, or must I guess?"

"I lied to you, earlier today – yesterday – whenever it was." Erik's whole body went tense in panic, and Christine shifted to meet his eyes. "About not being disappointed that I wasn't—" She swallowed. It was foolish to not even say the word, but even that felt like bad luck.

"You want a child?" Erik asked with a new sort of terror in his voice that Christine could not help but laugh at.

"No. I mean, I don't know." She squeezed his shoulder to comfort him. "It's just that... I have to confess something."

"I don't understand." Erik looked so strangely innocent and confused, ruined face and all, there in the shelter of her arms.

"When I was eighteen and Papa was getting very sick, I got sick too," Christine began, thinking back to the fear in those months. "For a few days, I was afraid I'd never sing again, but I pulled through. Mostly."

"Mostly?"

"I told you about the doctor we worked for and lived with, Doctor Mainville," Christine went on. "He told me after I got better that the disease meant I might not be able to have children. I thought it was so odd to say that, but now, maybe, I think he was right, and—"

Erik pulled her to him before the tears could come. "I'm sorry. I don't know if that's even the right thing to say, but I am."

"I don't even know what I feel or why." Somehow, it was safer to whisper it into her lover's shoulder in the dark. "I know it would ruin everything and I wouldn't be ready and all of that, but I think I was hoping for some sign I wasn't broken or—"

"You're *not* broken." Erik hooked a finger under her chin to make her look into his eyes. Christine opened her mouth to protest. "And I don't say that because I don't want you having a child. That's not for me to decide for you, I know. I mean to say that either way, whatever happens; to me, you will never be broken. You're perfect."

"You know I'm not," Christine breathed back. "More than anyone, you know what I've done."

"And more than anyone, I know that you are good," Erik protested, twining his fingers into her hair, a familiar gesture for them now. "Your soul isn't tainted. Not like mine."

It was her turn now to argue. "You know I don't think that."

Erik shook his head ruefully. "You are too kind, as always. I lied to you too, you know. Or omitted." Christine blinked in concern. "You told me to write an opera, and I didn't tell you that I've already written one. Or started to."

"That's not really the same—"

Erik's frown stopped her. There was something deadly in his eyes. "I had the idea decades ago, to rewrite a story of damnation into triumph. That's why I called it *Don Juan Triumphant*. It was an idea that kept coming back to me in my darkest moments. When I was hurt in the fire – when I left my father to die – I ran here, to the Opera, and began to compose. And more than that."

Christine tightened her grip, holding on to the warmth of Erik's body against hers as cold and darkness seeped into his voice. "More?"

"I was delirious with fever from old wounds and new. I didn't just write an opera, I devised a plan. It was more than music – it was the design for the end of the Opera above me and everyone in it."

"Erik..."

"I have conceived of evil beyond your dreams," he pushed on. "You say you love me, for all the terrible things that means and that you are willing to do. But what I was willing to do for hate..."

"Imagining is not doing." Christine stared into his golden eyes, hearing her own words of consolation to the killer who shared her bed. "And you didn't do it. You said you started your *Don Juan*, but you never finished it."

"I thought I would though; that I'd take the score to my tomb with me and—" Erik shook his head. "My better angels stopped me. Still, what I want to say is that I know what darkness is – what broken is. And that is not you."

"It's not you either. I won't allow it to be. Do you hear me? That's all done. It's in the ashes with your lasso." Erik opened his mouth, perhaps to protest or confess more, but Christine stopped him with a kiss, deep and tender. "Do you hear me?"

"Yes," Erik replied, utter devotion in his eyes now, and it terrified Christine to think of the power she had over a man who confessed to such crimes. Or maybe that power was as much of an illusion as anything else.

"Hold me, please," Christine ordered, and again, Erik complied, pulling her against his scarred skin. "Tell me that it's better this way, if I can't bear a child."

"It's better for my bloodline not to carry on, but I think you'd be a good mother, if you wanted to be," Erik said, and it stung Christine's heart in a new way. "What we have now, it's good enough. Remember that we have this. Close your eyes and forget everything else but this."

Christine tried. It was easier when he began to sing; easier to forget all the pain and death and loss and useless dreams. Her hopes of a normal life that would never be real were as futile as Erik's plans to destroy everything above. It was all dreams. All illusion and nothing more.

6. Seen

Friday, the day of prayer, was when Shaya felt the most alien in Paris. Usually, he and Darius made do with their prayers at home, but sometimes, he needed the consolation of knowing he was not the only follower of the Prophet in the city filled with churches and idols. So once in a while, they would go to the *Père Lachaise* cemetery, where the Ottoman consulate had built a small mosque so that fellow Muslims could pray for their dead. The building was crumbling, but Shaya was just a bit closer to Allah within its walls, listening to the chants and prayers.

He bent his head to the prayer mat, the woven texture so familiar, just like the prayers. *Allah give me strength to bring justice. Allah let my brother be avenged. I am so close.* "Please," Shaya said aloud and saw Darius glance at him from the corner of his eye.

"So, no luck yet?" Darius asked when they were out, looking for a cab home from the eleventh *arrondissement*. "I assume you would tell me if you had made any progress, even though you know I'll reprimand you."

"I thought I had some hope in working with the Vicomte, but it's been a series of dead ends," Shaya sighed. "He's been hounding Christine Daaé for over a week. He thinks he can get her to turn on Erik, but he won't take any advice on how to do that." Shaya thought back to his few brief conversations with Raoul over the past week. He had sought the boy out carefully, slipping him a note through Jammes the ballerina and meeting him in the café across the *Rue Auber*.

"I admire your persistence in trying to reason with a young man who is certain of what he believes and knows," Darius laughed. "Do you remember how stubborn you were at twenty-three?"

"I wish I could forget."

"Don't worry. I'll never let you," Darius replied. "Your father warned me how hard it would be to keep you in check. Sounds like now you have to deal with yet another young man with no interest in logic or truth or, heaven forbid, the knowledge and expertise of another."

"I wasn't that bad."

"Oh, you were, but you had redeeming qualities. You had a sense of justice. You loved your country and your family."

"And they're all gone," Shaya whispered. "All but the justice."

"Not all of them," Darius said softly as they both shivered when the wind rose.

E rik had gone from not caring at all what day it was to counting them fastidiously, or at least counting down the days until the boy left for the north. From his place in the walls, he watched Christine in the Opera's halls and told himself that there would only be a few more days before the little inconvenience was gone. Indeed, it was the very topic of the conversation Erik was currently observing.

"Do you know how long the voyage will be?" Christine asked as she and the boy passed where Erik was hidden.

"I'm not sure, it will depend on the weather. Signs point to a mild spring, so we're hopeful." The boy sounded bored.

"I'm looking forward to spring. I've had enough of the clouds and gray," Christine replied, and it made Erik wince. He wouldn't know what the weather was, would he? It had been so long since he'd been outside in the day.

"Sabine wants a May wedding," the boy went on. "I've told her that's far too soon, but she's insistent. I guess she's waited long enough."

"I'm sure," Christine's voice grew distant as she and the boy continued on their way. "Have she and—"

Erik turned away in his secret passage before he had to hear more about the little vicomtesse's marriage. Christine was a master at small talk, Erik had discovered in the long days of checking in on her (just checking, not watching... constantly) and that boy. He slipped back through the shadows, considering what to do with the long empty hours that lay before him without her.

It never used to be this way. He had always been able to distract himself with some new contraption or composition. But he was unable to regain his mind now that there was love in his life. She had changed everything, and now all the pursuits he had once turned to in order to fill his lonely days were empty, even haunting the halls.

He drifted towards the manager's office, curious as to if he'd catch another fight about the upcoming productions, or even about himself. It was time for his salary to be paid again, and Richard had been adamant that no more thousand-franc notes were to go missing under his watch. Thwarting the ass could be a bit of fun.

Erik smiled to himself, feeling the movement of his cheek against his mask. He noticed it more often nowadays, when he took it off at home with Christine. He had done as she asked, in one of his many attempts at distraction, and begun to make a new one that looked like a normal, bearded face. It was an interesting endeavor, to be sure, made easier by the copious amounts of supplies available to him in the Opera. He had something quite passable as a face now, with the suggested beard and glasses. It might make him appear like a regular man if he paired it with a hat and no one looked at him too closely.

It was a strange thing to consider – going out and about in the living world – as he slunk under the boards of the manager's office to haunt them.

"You can't be serious," Moncharmin was lamenting as Erik arrived. "She'll never do it."

"She will if I pay her enough. And luckily, you already provided the cash," Richard snapped. "You'd be amazed to learn what people will look past when money is involved, Armand."

"That money is to placate him, not to provoke him!" Moncharmin screeched. Erik wondered who Richard could possibly mean to pay off with the Opera Ghost's salary.

"It only makes him bolder!"

"And walking about with it pinned into your pocket only makes you look like a fool!" Moncharmin barked back and Erik wondered if that was intentional on his part. Moncharmin did know that the walls had ears, and while Christine was the only one in the Opera who could sense Erik without fail, many felt the change in the air when the ghost was listening.

"So I'm the fool? For refusing to kiss the ring of a charlatan?"

Well, Erik certainly didn't like *that* sort of disrespect. He heard the creak of the chair above him as Richard sat for emphasis. He was right above the Ghost's trap door, just in reach.

"How many times must I warn you, Firmin, this is no joke or trick." Moncharmin's voice was much louder when Erik softly opened the trap door. Erik took one brief second to savor the slightly less stale air in the office compared to the space beneath its floor.

His skills as a pickpocket remained unmatched, Erik thought to himself as he easily dipped his hand into Richard's pocket and undid the safety pin the manager had used to secure the wad of money. As if a little piece of metal could stop a phantom.

In a heartbeat, Erik was back in the passage, a small fortune secure in his hands. It was best not to linger, as much as he wanted to hear Richard's reaction, and it might not be the wisest thing to wander around the Opera with so much money.

He walked cautiously to the cellars, on guard as he had been since Jean-Paul's attack and Shaya's confession. He still felt it, just as Moncharmin must have in that office – the instinct he was not alone in his kingdom. But who would come down and interlope? It wasn't the boy, that was for sure.

Just as the thought occurred to him, Erik stopped on a stair into the third cellar, a shadow of movement catching his eyes. Yes, there it was again: someone moving between the set pieces that concealed the entrance into the torture chamber. At least that door was shut, sparing Erik the mess of confession and body disposal.

Erik followed soundlessly after the shadow in the unlit maze of backdrops, scrims, and machinery. The interloper was dressed in black, just like Erik, with a felt hat and a long cape. Whoever it was had the specific intent of looking like the ghost. They (Erik did not want to assume it was a man) were methodically looking for something, that much was clear, and Erik wondered if Shaya had told someone about the secret entrance behind the backdrop from *Le Roi de Lahore.*

The shade stopped, looking over their shoulder. Erik saw for the first time that his doppelgänger had gone so far as to wear a mask. It was a black domino, not a white mask covering the entire face like Erik's, leaving only his lips visible. Erik remained hidden in shadow, but the shade continued to scan the dark. Again, a remarkable example of how humans know when a predator is close.

Erik held his breath and reached for his Punjab Lasso on instinct, only to remember when he found just money in his hidden pocket that Christine had burned it weeks ago. She wanted Erik to be done with his horrors – with tortures and plans to burn down the world. It was truly only her grace and mercy that was keeping this shadow alive right now.

Erik retreated, dark thoughts following him as he took a different path down to the lake. Who had that been? Why did the shade feel familiar but also so dangerous? Had he been a fool not to seize the intruder and unmask them? What would he have done with them after? He had no idea what to do with himself most days – how would he deal with a prisoner?

Erik entered his home and lit more candles, their light illuminating the brass pipes of his great organ. Cecilia loomed there, calling him to her comfort. It was not her that drew his attention, but the great, red-bound score on the shelf beside her. Then of course there were the two little caskets on the mantle above the fire. Christine had never noticed them.

He opened the casket on the left, the memory of Christine bright in his mind, thinking how she had held him through the nights as they had muddled through these weeks of deceptions. The bronze scorpion waited there, ready to strike, and Erik stood ready to turn it. One turn of that little trigger, and it would all be over. Lake water would drown the cache that could end them all. He would truly kill the monster he had been before her.

But what if he still needed it? What if one day she didn't come back? Erik closed the casket and turned away from its twin as well, where the grasshopper waited with its deadly trigger. He didn't need it today, but with that boy above, so close to her, he could not yet let it go.

Raoul was tired of seeing the same story over and over, he thought to himself as he squirmed in his box while Carlos

Fontana sang of seduction on the stage. More than that, he was more uncomfortable each time he heard Christine sing, knowing who she sang for. She had sworn up and down that her teacher had not corrupted her body, but it was clear in how she sang that he had done *something* to her soul. It was obscene, the passion she brought to each note as virginal Gilda was deflowered by the Count...

Raoul rose from his seat and strode from the family box they had leased for years. He didn't want to see any more displays. He didn't want to hear Christine sing for the thing that lived in the shadows. The creature Raoul was no closer to destroying after so many days of trying. Time was running out.

Each day, they grew closer to when Christine believed he was leaving. Each day, he saw her and tried to make her speak of Erik and his secrets, but she refused. He followed her through the Opera and like he had when, as a child, he had tried to catch cats in the stables. Christine was always running a few feet ahead of him, impossible to capture and pin down.

Raoul's feet took him automatically to the door from the lobby to backstage. It was quite hard to find if one didn't know where to look, but thanks to his adventures with Christine and continued explorations of the Opera, he knew it well now. Not as well as *Erik*, of course, but well enough.

"Monsieur, you can't go in there!" a voice called as Raoul grasped the door handle. He turned to see a concierge rushing towards him, panting and moist with sweat.

"I am a friend of Mademoiselle Daaé," Raoul protested and opened the door. To his horror, the concierge threw himself in front of Raoul and closed the door again.

"That is all well and good, Monsieur, but *no one* is allowed backstage that is not part of the company."

Raoul huffed in annoyance and strode to the nearby coat room. The attendant sputtered when Raoul grabbed a paper and quill from the counter and scrawled a note.

My darling,

I miss you and wish I could be with you behind the curtain. Please order this imbecile to let me in.

He pressed the note into the hands of the concierge and glared. "If you won't admit me, take this to Mademoiselle Daaé and let her tell you to let me back there. I want to see her."

The concierge scowled before disappearing through the door and loudly locking it behind him. Raoul was left alone in the lobby by the entrance to the boxes, save for the various other box attendants who were staring at him darkly. Especially one older woman with wild eyes by the final box before the premiere seats.

"Tired of artifice and pretense?"

Raoul turned on his heel to see Shaya Motlagh, his Astrakhan hat neatly in place, eyes as sharp and knowing as ever. Raoul gave a sidelong glance to the listening box keepers and strode towards the *grand escalier*, knowing the Persian would follow. Once they were away from prying eyes and ears, he turned on the man.

"I am tired of the theater, yes. Are you tired of sulking around cellars doing nothing?" Raoul snapped.

"I assume you remain unable to turn Daaé to your cause and she has not betrayed him yet." Raoul's jaw fell slack as the man laughed again. "She remains under Erik's thrall, trapped in this place like his pet."

"I don't like your implications," Raoul replied. "And Christine leaves the Opera all the time, even if she won't see me outside these walls thanks to some command from him. It's not like she lives here."

The Persian looked carefully at Raoul. "You must know she visits him below. And stays there to do who knows what."

"*Music*. She goes for music and, yes, I believe in the past she spent the—" he swallowed, hating the idea of his almost-fiancé sleeping in the underground home of that phantom. "But that has been rare. He treats her as a student and she goes home to Valerius. Adèle has assured me of that many times! So has Christine!"

"Of course. Your Christine remains a paragon of virtue."

"She does," Raoul sneered. It was as if Shaya had dropped a burr in his brain, the idea of what Christine did with her teacher poking and piercing his thoughts. "Do not try to find me again unless you have useful information."

Raoul turned and headed back to the door that separated him from Christine's world. He was just in time to see the concierge exit with a note in his hand. Was it from Christine? Raoul rushed to the man as he walked resolutely to...the wild-eyed box keeper at the end of the row of doors?

"Did you speak to her?" Raoul demanded as the man handed his note to the woman. "Who is that from?"

"I couldn't find her, Monsieur. Another performer had a message," the man said as the old woman smirked and pocketed the missive. Raoul had half a mind to throttle her, her coworker, *and* whoever it was receiving correspondence in box five.

"I suggest you return to your seat, Monsieur," the woman stated with more smugness than necessary for the occasion. "You may see Mademoiselle Daaé on stage and she will be as captivating as always."

Raoul scowled and stalked away towards where he hoped there was still alcohol being served.

God, he hated this. He hated not knowing what the next day would bring, he hated knowing that Christine was under the influence of a monster and a murderer. Most of all, he hated that he had no choice but to just let it continue.

Christine stormed off the stage as the final curtain fell after bows, the applause still echoing behind her. Julianne was at her elbow immediately, eyebrows high.

"Get me out of this." Christine tugged at the itchy collar of her doublet. She liked the pants she wore for Gilda's masculine disguise at the end of *Rigoletto*, but not the high, tight collar with excessive ruffles.

"Still angry at your vicomte for trying to get back here?" Julianne asked.

"Of course I am," Christine grumbled as they made their way towards the dressing room, no care for propriety as Christine fully removed the doublet and handed it to Julianne. "The nerve of that man to think he can just demand to be seen while I'm working."

"A man like Raoul doesn't think what you do is work," Julianne laughed in reply. "Performing on stage is a folly while you wait to find a husband."

"I hate that you're right," Christine sighed as they reached her dressing room door.

"Will you tell him off at the reception?"

"Even if I did, he wouldn't hear." Christine pushed away a fresh wave of exhaustion and frustration, the kind that had been hammering the shoreline of her mind for weeks. It was better than the rage she had experienced upon seeing Raoul's note – his *demand* that she play another part for him in the midst of doing the same thing on stage. After unsubtly pestering her every day for information about Erik or a sign she'd betray her teacher.

"It will be done soon," Julianne consoled as she opened Christine's dressing room door.

The air was electric when Christine stepped inside, and she could not help but smile. Her missive to Erik had been delivered in her small rebellion against Raoul. She stripped off her trousers quickly and handed them off. "I can finish on my own," she told

Julianne, feeling her angel watching from the other side of the great mirror.

"What about getting you dressed for the reception?" There was a knowing tone in Julianne's voice that made Christine smirk.

"I'm very tired, if you would not mind giving my regrets to Robert and the managers," Christine said, and Julianne nodded with a dark chuckle.

As soon as she was alone, Christine locked the door and turned to the mirror. She caught her reflection and saw the wanton way her breasts were pushing against her corset, her skin flushed under her chemise.

"Beautiful," Erik's voice whispered before the glass slid aside and he pulled her to him. The mirror closed behind Christine as she surrendered to his kiss, melting at the way his long hands swept over her body.

"You got my message," Christine cooed as her masked lover kissed down her throat and worked to undo her corset.

"I've never received a more welcome note," Erik replied, halfway done with his work. "Then again I don't get much mail."

"I meant it," Christine hummed as her corset fell to the ground in the close confines of the passage behind the mirror. "I want you in me. I've needed it since Act Two."

Erik seized her, enveloping her in his dark embrace. She was breathless with that need as she kissed him and pulled off his mask so she could feel his cheeks. He spun her, so her ass was against his thighs and she could feel his hardening desire. He kissed ravenously along her neck and shoulders, pawing at her hips and belly through her chemise.

"Christine?" Raoul's voice came accompanied by an insistent knock, and Erik paused with his hand on her breasts. "Are you in there?"

"For God's sake," Christine groaned softly. She had never been happier to have locked her dressing room door.

"Come back another night, Monsieur, Mademoiselle Daaé is busy," Erik purred into her ear. Christine found herself grinning as he moved again, pulling down her chemise so that her tight nipples were exposed to the cool air before he took them between his fingers, twisting them gently so that Christine gasped.

"Not busy enough," Christine exhaled, her head falling back against Erik's chest.

"So impatient," Erik responded, licking her ear and making her legs go wobbly. He knew exactly what he was doing and what it did to her, judging by how he snaked an arm around her waist to hold her up from collapsing. "Shall I—"

A horribly distinct sound came from the other side of the mirror: the lock rattling as a key was inserted. Erik froze, gripping Christine tight, and her eyes flew open in horror. They held their breaths as the door opened and Raoul stepped into the room. His curious face was illuminated by the gaslight as he tucked a large ring of keys into his waistcoat.

"Impertinent little swine," Erik breathed against Christine's ear. She shared the sentiment. How dare Raoul invade her room again. Had she not given him enough?

A distant voice chided Christine that Raoul was right not to trust her, but she wanted that persistent voice to leave her alone too. She didn't want the reminder of her deceit and descent into the gutter. She wanted her rage and the heat still pulsing between her legs. She wanted defiance and freedom the only way she could find it.

Slowly, her eyes on Raoul on the other side of the mirror, she grasped Erik's hand where he held it tight against her ribs and guided it downward. She felt him tense as his finger raked through her ruff, but he did not resist.

"Don't stop," Christine ordered in the softest whisper before biting back a gasp as Erik's perfect fingers slipped inside her.

"Don't close your eyes," he commanded in turn, and Christine understood why. He wanted her to see – to look at the man on the other side of the glass who could not comprehend giving her pleasure and sin like this. Raoul turned towards the mirror, and Christine shuddered at the sight of his unfocused gaze while Erik's fingers worked in and out of her, paying special attention to the sensitive nub that made her spasm and brace herself against the glass.

It was torture to stay silent as Erik touched her in every way he knew to drive her mad. She bit her lips hard as her body sang and hummed with pleasure while Raoul paced an arm's length away, only separated from her by glass. She was so close, the wrongness of it all making each rub of her angel's hand all the more delightful.

Then Erik's hand was gone, and Christine nearly collapsed, stuttering forward silently as Erik took her by the hips and pushed her pantalettes down and off. She stifled an ecstatic sound and flattened her palms on the mirror to support herself as the lover behind her filled her with his cock.

"Where are you?" Raoul demanded as he stared into the mirror, and Christine could feel Erik looking right into his rival's eyes in pure triumph.

I'm right here, he seemed to say, and who could tell if they were real words whispered in Christine's ears or magic in her mind. She was too far gone to care, riding waves of pleasure as her angel fucked her fast and silent, her nipples grazing the cold glass as she arched to meet him. *I'm here, Monsieur, her lover and her hope and her doom, and you will never know. I am hers as she is mine.*

Christine looked up to see Erik's hand entwine with hers and the ring she had been forced to remove for the performance slip into place. She wanted to scream her climax, but held it in, throwing back her head and closing her eyes at last so that finally, there was nothing but them. Nothing but this. Nothing but the feel of Erik coming with her, filling her with his warm seed as his hand dug into her hip hard enough to leave a mark.

She fell back against him, gasping for breath as he stroked her face. She wanted to keep her eyes closed forever. Only Erik's embrace prevented her from falling. In fact, she was flying. Erik lifted her up with such ease, carrying her through the dark like a bride over the threshold.

"You don't need to carry me," Christine murmured against his shoulder.

"Nonsense." The journey down always went so quickly when he was the guide, even with no light. Soon enough, they were at the lake, and she was wrapped in his cape as he poled the boat over the still waters. Was he Chiron or Hades? She wasn't sure. She was his in the underworld either way.

Shaya knew it was a risk going backstage, but he wanted not only to see what Daaé and Erik were up to, but the de Chagny boy as well. It was easy to slip in, not through the door de Chagny had been harassing, but around through the back. He kept out of the way as dancers and musicians prepared to go home after the performance – or parade themselves for the patrons in the Salon du Danse. Shaya placed himself in a secluded corner near Daaé's dressing room and simply waited, and it did not take long for him to hear the distinctly disgruntled voice of Raoul.

"What do you mean she's gone home?" the young man was fuming in the face of Daaé's dresser.

"It was a very trying performance, Monsieur," Bonet replied, tired and annoyed. "She left as soon as the curtain was down."

"With no message for me?" Raoul asked back as Shaya peered around the corner. Bonet shrugged and shook her head. "For God's sake, were you not watching her?"

"Watching her?" Bonet echoed. "I watched her leave and go home. I dressed her myself."

Raoul did not look like he believed the woman, and Shaya was dubious as well. It was all too convenient for Christine to disappear again when Raoul was so eager to see her. "Are you—" Raoul began.

"Good night, Monsieur," Bonet cut in and swept past him towards Shaya. He assumed she was on her way to harass the poor dancer she continued to corrupt. Raoul sighed powerfully just as Shaya stepped out to reveal himself.

"She's with him. You know it. I know it. She'll be there with him in the morning too." Shaya took some pleasure in how the words cut the young noble.

"Because of me – because I attempted to see her when it was *his* time. Do you think she is safe?"

"No one is safe from Erik. He destroys and corrupts anything he touches. It is only a matter of time before he does one of those to her, no matter how he claims to love her."

"Christine would never submit," Raoul muttered, the unspoken words lingering in the air – that she might not have a choice. "Good night, Monsieur. As I said, come to me when you have something useful to share."

Shaya nodded and turned away, following where Bonet had gone. The halls were quieter now, enough that he could hear voices in one of the dressing rooms, though he could not make them out well. They sounded more sad than angry, and so it did not surprise him to see Jammes emerge, wiping her eyes.

Shaya followed, not concerned at all with whatever sins they were bickering over, only that it made his agent more likely to confide something. Once the dancer was further removed from Bonet and the dressing rooms, Shaya cleared his throat. Jammes jumped and turned to him with a glare that was far crueler than Raoul's.

"I'm not carrying more messages," Jammes declared.

"I'm not interested in messages. I'm interested in if you've learned anything interesting. About Christine Daaé specifically."

"Why do you care about that slut?"

"You seem quite certain she's a woman of loose morals," Shaya said carefully. "Why so?"

Jammes peered at him suspiciously, her hands knitting nervously into the fabric of her dress. Shaya inclined his head with a look that held all the threat needed to untangle her tongue. "Julianne was trying to make the case to me that we could – never mind. She told me Christine was brave enough to live with her lover! Not just be kept by him but to live in sin with him! The harlot."

"Do you know who that lover is?" Shaya asked – she could mean Rameau or it could be a rumor about de Chagny.

"None of the men she goes about with, that's for sure," Jammes scoffed, and Shaya felt a surge of triumph. "Why do you care?"

"Thank you, Mademoiselle, you've been of great service."

Shaya turned without another word and strode towards the exit. He had no more need of the Opera tonight. He needed to bide his time, make sure he revealed the depth of Christine Daaé's duplicity at the right moment. Raoul de Chagny would soon know where his beloved spent her nights, and then, he would be ready to do what needed to be done.

E rik smiled from the door as he watched his lover stir. Christine was never more beautiful than in the soft quiet of the morning, when she lay rumpled and relaxed in his bed, the sheets pooled around her as one nude leg escaped into the open air. He watched as she stretched, arms extending above her head, a bare breast escaping the cover. Had they not already thoroughly enjoyed themselves before he went to fetch her morning refreshments, his cock would have stirred at the sight.

"You're lurking," Christine yawned.

"You can't blame me for staring." Erik savored Christine's warm expression as she turned towards him. "When the most beautiful creature I've ever seen is just laying there, I have no choice but to appreciate."

"You're not just stuck in ghostly habits?"

"Or it could be that."

Christine smiled, eyes falling on the cups he carried. "Is that coffee or tea? Please say coffee."

Erik handed her the café au lait she so adored. She moaned obscenely at the first sip as he sat on the edge of the bed beside her. "This means we'll need to wait until at least afternoon for a lesson."

"Oh no, what shall we do to pass the time?" Christine smirked back.

Erik shook his head in awe as he took his own sip of coffee. "I'm sure we'll think of something productive. We certainly can't spend the whole day here."

"Why can't we?" Christine smiled back. "This is the first day in a week no one expects me anywhere. Well, I guess Raoul expects me to be at church, but at least I—" Erik flinched at the name and Christine stopped cold. "I'm sorry."

"Don't apologize. You can talk about him. Just..." Erik swallowed. "Not too nicely, if you don't mind."

"Shall I tell you that he invited me to join his family at their church? Not to sit beside them of course, but he offered for me to be in the back row so he could wave," Christine said with delicious venom in her voice.

"What an absolute ass," Erik chuckled as they both sipped.

"He also was groveling for me to come to that damn engagement party tonight," Christine went on. "Remember? The one his sister invited me to as *entertainment*?"

"So they inherited idiocy with their false titles, how lovely." Erik knew Christine didn't really think that of her handsome knight, but it made him happy that she was willing to pretend.

"I almost feel sorry for her to be marrying an ass like Antoine de Martiniac."

Christine jumped as Erik's cup clattered to the floor. He stared at her, an electric shock echoing down to his bones. "*Who?*"

Christine rushed to put down her cup so she could take Erik's now-empty hand. "Antoine de Martiniac. You know him. Don't you? He was Adèle's patron until she came to her senses. He's a cad. Even Raoul dislikes him."

Not even the sound of the boy's name spoken with such familiarity could startle Erik from the shock of hearing the other name. "I never pay attention to those pigs, you know that."

"You've met him. He was the one who tried to grab you at the masquerade who you frightened out of his wits."

Erik remembered the fool who had sought to touch Red Death and looking into icy eyes behind a black domino. Eyes that had been so familiar. He had forgotten them in the chaos of that evening, but now they burned in Erik's memory. "I thought I was dreaming. Is he a Baron?"

"I think so. Erik, what is wrong?" Christine asked, her hands on his wrists the only anchor as his mind spun with fresh horror.

"De Martiniac...was my father's name. Baron Alfred de Martiniac." He hadn't spoken that title in decades, perhaps ever. It tasted like bile on his tongue to name the creature who had raped and destroyed his mother; the noble scion who Erik had left to die burning in his own manor.

"Oh my God. Does that mean Antoine is—"

"I never considered it," Erik cut her off, not ready to hear the word yet. "And that makes me a fool. I knew my father married. Some poor woman was bought off to be his wife. I never thought he'd breed another monster."

"Erik, you are not—" Christine stopped when he looked at her, face stricken.

"Is he? This Antoine, is he a monster?" Erik asked, trying to think if he had ever seen the man's face. Every pompous, leering patron looked like his father when he bothered to glance at them, maybe that's how he had missed it.

"He's an odious scoundrel, but not a monster." The feel of Christine's hand on his face brought Erik back from his thoughts. "And neither are you."

"I've always known I had family, out there in the world, but never thought about a brother," Erik whispered. "I don't know what to think."

"The only family that should matter to you is right here, in this room," Christine broke in, once more steering his thoughts away from the abyss. "Stay with me, right now. Just breathe."

Erik didn't resist as she pulled him into her arms, wrapping him in tenderness that was safe and solid and real, her bare skin against his as warm as the life in her steady breath. He tried to match her inhales and exhales to stop the shadows and ghosts in his head from rioting. He concentrated on the texture of her hair, the smell of their sheets. He held onto her as the world he knew melted and reformed around him.

He had a brother. The monstrous father had an heir who meant to marry into the very family that wanted to steal Christine away.

He had a brother who had no idea that his bastard sibling had ended their father's life in merciless flames.

7. Cloak and Dagger

Raoul's gut was unsettled, and not just because the wine Vincenzo kept in his little garret tasted closer to vinegar than fruit. He kept drinking it, even though it was barely past noon on a Sunday. As Vincenzo had declared before pushing the bottle into Raoul's hands and pulling off his suspenders, it could count as communion. For a few minutes, as he'd taken his pleasure with his shipmate, Raoul had felt just a bit more human. Now the fucking was done, and his brain was afire once more.

"You know, I could get offended that you look so far off after all that," Vincenzo said from where he was sprawled on his bed, staring at Raoul as he dressed. "And that you're getting on your way so quickly."

"Lucky for us, you're not sentimental."

"I'm just patient." Raoul turned to Vincenzo in confusion, and the other man cocked his head, smiling playfully as his dark curls danced about his face. "I'll have you mostly to myself again in a few days. When we set sail."

"Oh. That." Raoul's stomach fell. "I'm... not sure if I'm going north."

"Not sure? Raoul, the expedition needs you," Vincenzo replied with uncharacteristic seriousness. "You're a trusted officer. Men signed onto this adventure because they knew you were brave enough to do it too. And now you're thinking about abandoning it?"

"It's complicated. My family needs me here," Raoul muttered. It was half true.

"You're the second son. No one needs you as much as the men on that ship," Vincenzo countered. "Be honest: you're still pining after your soprano, thinking you can marry her. As if she'd take you."

"She would! But there's more than that—" Suddenly, the weight of all of it – of Christine and his father and all the intrigues and lies and revenge – was suffocating. Raoul collapsed on the end of the bed, his head in his hands. "I have to stay to make things right."

"What the hell does that mean?"

Raoul took a deep breath, remembering the face of Red Death and the skulls and angels on his father's ornate tomb. They'd given him nightmares for weeks, so had the knowledge of how Georges de Chagny had burned to death. "I'm planning on killing a man. The man who killed my father."

"What in the sweet name of fuck are you talking about?" Vincenzo forced Raoul to look at him. "I can't possibly have heard you say you want to kill someone."

"I don't *want* to. But I have to. To save Christine and avenge my father, I have to kill this man. I have no choice."

"Bullshit! You could keep your promises to the expedition and just leave. You could walk away from whatever operatic entanglement you've found yourself in and live your life!"

"Can I?" Raoul asked back, again feeling like the weight of the world was on him. "It doesn't feel that way."

"You can. Dear God, Raoul, I know you," Vincenzo said with more sincerity than Raoul had ever seen from him. "You're a romantic and an idealist and a brave, good man. You're not a killer."

Raoul recalled Antoine saying as much. No one thought he could do what needed to be done. They thought he was soft and foolish and easily led astray, like a child fighting shadows. "I need to be, to avenge—"

"Killing someone won't bring your father back, but it will damn your soul."

Raoul scoffed and looked down at the other man's still naked body. "You're concerned with salvation after what you just did?"

"What *we* just did," Vincenzo corrected, and Raoul shook his head.

"I'm not like you," Raoul declared, rising and grabbing his jacket. "And I'm not as weak and foolish as everyone thinks."

"I didn't say that! I'm trying to help!"

Raoul pushed Vincenzo away when he tried to come near. "I'm going to be late for the party. Good day."

Raoul did not look back as he stormed out of the building and into the bracing cold. Winter was hanging on fiercely, even though spring was only weeks away now. That was the reason for the expedition's timing. They were to sail north from Le Havre before stopping to resupply in Bergen before the long voyage north. Their mission wasn't even to reach the pole, but to find the wreckage of another ship that had disappeared three years before on the ice.

Raoul shivered as he put on his jacket. He wondered how cold it would be in those still waters, where ice floes and bergs made passage almost impossible. He'd spoken to a whaler once, who had spent three years along the cold coast of Greenland hunting the great beasts for their oil. He'd said it was so quiet out there you could hear the snow landing on the sea.

Raoul wished he was there, away from his family and his past and his useless love. He could disappear into the north and never return. He could be happy. If only he could let go.

He was surprised when he found himself at his own doorstep, his feet sore from the long walk full of dark thoughts. Servants were already hard at work filling the Chagny manor with flowers and food, and no one even spoke to Raoul as he went to his room to change. His valet ignored the stench of liquor and cigarettes on his clothes as he helped Raoul into his evening attire for the party. Soon enough he was gone, leaving Raoul to stare at his useless mural of evidence about Erik and his handwritten accounts.

Vincenzo was right – killing Erik would not bring back Raoul's father. It could save Christine, but was she worth that? Would it damn his soul to take a life? Surely, it would be like killing in war. It would be righteous. And Erik wasn't a person, he was a monster.

Still, Raoul thought back to when he was twelve, and his father and Philippe had taken him hunting for the first time. They'd spied a handsome stag, and their valet had readied the gun before placing it in Raoul's hands. It had been so heavy. He had felt his father watching him, and all he could think with his childish heart was how beautiful the creature was and how little he wanted to end its life. What gave him the right? He'd aimed for the tree beside it and scared the poor thing off. His father had found it again later and shot the beast with no hesitation.

Raoul shuddered in shame for the coward he had been and the killer he might become. The fire was low in the grate, and the chill of evening had crept into the corners. It reminded him of the Opera; the way the light never fully pierced the dark shadows that hung like cobwebs. It was eerie, how the dark made him feel like he was being watched. Perhaps because he was.

Why did he feel that way now? Raoul wondered as another shiver rippled down his spine. Why could he suddenly not shake the sense that if he turned quickly enough, he would see shining eyes watching him from the dark outside his window?

Raoul was perfectly still, closing his eyes and letting himself feel the weight of a gaze upon him. What would he do if he turned to see Erik right there? Where was his pistol? He opened his eyes and spun.

There they were! Gold eyes in the dark! He rushed to his bedside where his revolver was hidden. By the time it was in his hand, the lights – those two stars watching him – were gone. He was about to run out onto the balcony, screaming into the night when his door burst open.

"What on earth are you doing with that?" Antoine demanded when he saw the gun in Raoul's hand.

"I thought I saw—" Raoul realized how insane it sounded. "I saw something outside. Maybe. There were glowing eyes!"

"Did you nearly just shoot a cat thinking it was a ghost?" Antoine snatched the revolver from Raoul's hands. "Put that down, you idiot, and come downstairs. Your whore is here."

"What?"

Antoine rolled his eyes. "Do you have to think *which one*? Daaé, you fool. She's claiming you invited her as a guest, and Sabine is worried she'll be offended by the entertainment we did manage to snag. Come and sort it out."

"Christine is here?" Raoul's heart leapt and he raced from the room, leaving the darkness outside his window and whatever creature was hiding there far behind.

C hristine had never been to the de Chagny manor in the *Faubourg Saint Germain*. She had expected it to be grand and ostentatious like the foyers and salons of the Opera, but it was surprisingly old-fashioned and conservative. This was the home of old money, everything about the place declared, from the dour portraits of dead counts and countesses on the walls by the main stair to the dark wood and heavy stone the place was built from.

Christine felt like there was no fresh air in the place, perhaps due to the nervousness eating up her insides.

"You're really here!" Raoul's voice cut through Christine's thoughts. She forced herself to smile as he bounded down the stairs to her and grasped her hands. She was glad of her long gloves. "I'm so glad! Don't tell me – you knew how much I was worried after last night."

"What?" Christine asked before she could stop herself.

"You disappeared again," Raoul whined.

"I just went home. I was so tired. I've been in bed most of the day." Like so many things she told Raoul, it wasn't entirely a lie. She had been home and spent most of the day in bed – albeit not alone.

"You poor thing. No matter. I can't tell you how happy it makes me to see you in the real world." Raoul grinned, boyish and bright.

"I hope you don't mind that I changed my mind at the last minute. I am still invited, aren't I?" It was Raoul's turn to look rather sick, and Christine sighed. "There was no amended invitation, was there? You told me to come knowing I wouldn't."

"I didn't think *he* would allow it!" Raoul protested.

Christine could hardly tell Raoul that *he* and his ridiculous need to see the brother he had not known existed was the reason she was there.

I just need to see him, Erik had begged. Christine would be the distraction, the spy, sent to learn anything she could, while Erik confirmed his worst fears from the shadows. What was the point, she had demanded, and there had been no answer. *Please*, he had said, so small and soft, and she had crumbled.

"He commanded it," Christine repeated the lie she had rehearsed in their carriage ride across the Seine. "He said that I had brought him so much joy, it was only fair that I could do the same for you before you left."

"How compassionate." Raoul made it sound like an insult.

"I did want to try again with your family, even if it's in vain," Christine added. "May I enter?" She glanced through the double doors towards the grand dining room and parlor to where dozens of people with more money than she could ever conceive of were chatting demurely.

"Yes, of course." Raoul looked terribly apprehensive, and Christine noted that he didn't offer his arm as he showed her to the party. She felt more exposed than she ever had on stage as the guests turned to look at her and whisper behind their fans. What was this bagatelle from the Opera doing here?

Raoul led her to a discrete spot by a gilded fireplace. Christine glanced to the windows out into the garden and was happy to not see any shadows watching.

"I'll go find Sabine," Raoul offered, and before Christine could protest or grab his arm to keep him close, he was gone.

Christine surveyed the room. She had glimpsed Antoine de Martiniac when she had been shown in, conversing with the butler who had admitted her, but she couldn't see him anywhere now. Nor could she spot Philippe. Some of the faces were familiar, perhaps from the Opera, but no one spoke to her or held eye contact with her for more than a heartbeat.

"This is quite a surprise." Of all the people Christine had expected to turn and see in the Chagny home, Firmin Richard was not one of them. "Did they change their mind about Madame Cruvelli?"

"Excuse me?" Christine asked, stomach twisting. She had never liked Firmin Richard, not since he had unceremoniously fired her at Carlotta's behest. Now, every time she saw him, the shame and fear of that awful day echoed through her so powerfully that her whole body shook.

"Oh, you haven't heard?" Richard asked with a cruel smirk. "We've made an offer to Sophie Cruvelli to sing Elsa if we end up going through with this *Lohengrin* nonsense. She's sung the role elsewhere and has the maturity for it. I hope you didn't think *you* would be cast – you're still so young and we wouldn't want to destroy such an instrument before it's flowered."

Christine dug her nails into her palms to steady herself. She didn't know what to feel when something had been taken from her that she was not even sure she had wanted. "I – I had not heard."

"Well, she's around here somewhere. I suggested her to the Vicomtesse when you begged off performing for whatever reason it was. Best to let the patrons and the audiences in the Faubourg get to know her."

Christine glanced around the room, as if she would recognize her new rival – was that who this was? She didn't even know. She needed to sit down. "I should be happy to greet her."

"Do be kind. She has sung Marguerite, but she's too old now, and won't step on your toes, I promise. We don't need another great artist to suffer poor Carlotta's fate."

Christine made her face stony. "What happened to Carlotta was—"

"Have you heard the latest? On her condition?" Richard went on. "Her family from America wants her sent to an asylum or private hospital. For her health, they say."

"What?" Christine recalled hearing one such rumor, but she had dismissed it. The thought of that woman – terrible as she had been – locked away made Christine feel even sicker.

"I just thought you should know." Richard gave Christine one final cold look before crossing the room to go into the main parlor with the other invited guests. Christine simultaneously wanted to throttle Erik for making her come here and fall into his arms for comfort. Was he out there in the night somewhere trying to spy Antoine and confirm their connection? Would she be able to feel him if he wasn't looking at her?

Christine leaned against the fireplace, trying to settle her wrecked nerves. God, where was a servant with a tray of alcohol when it was needed? Not that drinking would make this go away. She was so tired.

She was tired of playing her part, tired of the empty applause that did nothing to lift her soul. She was tired of how, after every triumph, she had to start all over again from nothing. Tired of knowing that without constant vigilance and backstabbing, her career would be gone.

There were so many people who wanted her to just disappear. People she didn't even know hated her for daring to step on stage and sing well. Had Madame Cruvelli already been warned to stay away from that Daaé bitch for her own good? Christine had half a mind to tell the woman she was welcome to Elsa and any other role she wanted. Christine was ready to be done with it all.

But then what? Could she run away from music? From *Erik*? Could she take Raoul's offered hand and marry into this world? Christine took in the faces of the women at the party. She watched as their smiling masks fell away when their husbands yawned. One downed too much champagne, another stared longingly out the window. Then there were the dowagers – wrapped in lace and mourning black, hidden away in the corners like old furniture to watch the world that had forgotten them go by. Christine didn't want that either.

"Oh no, I've offended you!" Christine jumped as Sabine de Chagny appeared with Raoul at her side. Of course the one man she wanted to see wasn't there. It gave her another reason to resent Antoine.

"What?" Christine asked automatically.

"By engaging Madame Cruvelli. I didn't think you wanted to perform! Maybe we can—"

Raoul grabbed his sister's arm and shook his head. "Sabine, I told you, I invited Christine as a guest so she could wish you well."

"You didn't need to do that. We have already received her congratulations." Sabine gave one of those perfectly cold aristocratic smiles that did not reach her eyes. "I guess now that Mademoiselle Daaé is here, she is welcome to stay for a while. Unfortunately, we do not have room at the table for supper, but her carriage can take her home."

"I came in a cab," Christine countered flatly, unable to count the various subtle ways she had just been insulted.

"My goodness, how quaint. I've never done that. It just frightens me too much, the idea of some stranger driving me around and what they might do to a lone woman," Sabine cooed.

"We'll send her home in ours," Raoul offered, and Christine wanted to scream. That meant leaving Erik behind. "Until then perhaps – ah, there they are."

Christine turned to see who Raoul was looking at over her shoulder and was confronted with the very face she had been waiting to see: Antoine de Martiniac, standing next to Philippe de Chagny.

"Good evening, Mademoiselle," Antoine said with a smile just as false as Sabine's. Christine watched him as he joined his fiancé, linking his arm with hers.

"Yes, hello. We didn't know to expect you," Philippe added, far warmer.

"So I've been told. Many times." Christine sent a quick glare towards Raoul, and he blanched. "I won't impose too long."

"You don't have to—" Raoul began, but Sabine cut him off with a sour look.

"We are always happy to welcome artists when we can as patrons," Philippe said.

"I must confess I did not even know you were courting Mademoiselle de Chagny," Christine tried, looking closely at Antoine for what might be the first time. He was tall and angular, like Erik in his way, with a strong jaw and sharp cheekbones. Maybe there was a resemblance, but it stopped at his eyes. Their icy blue was a complete contrast to Erik's warm gold.

"One might say he has been courting her for years," Philippe answered with a genuine smile.

"You two are close friends, of course. Raoul has mentioned it." Christine had no idea what she was meant to ask or investigate, just that she had agreed to.

"Really? Was he complimentary?" Antoine asked back. Christine noted the pointedly disapproving look Raoul gave.

"Lamenting would be a good word for it. You're a bad influence," Raoul countered. "I hope my sister will reform you."

"I don't want such talk at my party," Sabine said firmly. "I think it's time for supper. Good night, Mademoiselle. I'm sorry you won't be able to hear Madame Cruvelli. She'll be singing after dinner. You may go meet her, if you like, she's somewhere about... Maybe in the kitchens with the other hired help."

On cue, a bell rang, and all the well-dressed guests began moving, circulating around Christine like a river around a stone. She was too insulted, confused, and exhausted to move.

"I'll see you soon," Raoul stammered, bringing Christine back as his family pulled away. "I'll send my man with the carriage!"

Christine only nodded in reply and walked out alone into the cold night as servants and guests stared. She wanted to crawl back into the warm bed she had shared this morning before she had spoken and ruined everything. She wanted to burrow away from the sins of the past and the damnation of the future and forget. That was impossible now.

The rumble of the fine de Chagny carriage coming to a halt in front of her shocked her from her thoughts. The footman who had followed her outside rushed to open the door and help her in, and Christine had no choice but to go. Now she was leaving Erik alone to spy on these vipers and make who knows what kind of idiotic decisions on impulse.

"Please come back to me," she found herself whispering as she rolled away from the grand old manor and into the night, towards the flat that was no longer home. "Please be safe."

Erik was accustomed to spying on people from hidden passages and behind the curtains of his theater, not through windows while he perched on ledges and narrow gutters in the cold night. This was much more difficult, especially considering that he had nearly been discovered already when he had made the mistake of looking in the wrong room to see the boy.

The boy... who had an impressive collection of evidence regarding the Phantom *and* had caught Erik snooping. Erik had ducked away and into the garden (glad the fool had been slow with his trigger finger) and tried in vain to find someplace unexposed to look in on the party.

It was harder than he had anticipated, with a few people taking the night air and more lingering close to the windows. That hadn't mattered when Erik's quarry had joined them on the terrace overlooking the garden. From the bushes, Erik had glimpsed him, peering out into the night.

It had been (ironically) like seeing a ghost, Erik thought as he carefully made his way along the edge of the roof in the dark, trying to embody the cat he had been named for. It was hard when the sight of the new Baron de Martiniac had left him so shaken. To see a younger, slightly changed version of his father's face... Erik had needed to compose himself, and in that time, everyone had gone in. So now he was doing his best to peer into the dining room to catch a glimpse of his brother, or Christine.

There was no sign of her, which was troubling. Had she been turned away at the door? Was she on the way back to the Opera without him? This had all been a terrible idea.

His thoughts froze as his eyes settled upon the face of Antoine de Martiniac once again. He was seated next to the woman Erik recognized as Sabine de Chagny. He had no interest in her, just in her fiancé. The man was charming. He laughed and smiled at the guests, but it was all so clearly a façade. He had the same ruthlessness in his eyes that Erik remembered from his father, and none of the joviality. It was as if any soft edge the man had ever possessed had been honed to razor sharpness.

There was no reason to keep watching other than to torture himself, and yet, Erik could not look away. What did it mean that this man existed? What did it change? Was it some joke of fate that this man was entangled with Erik's greatest enemy?

There was, apparently, a pause between courses, and the well-heeled guests rose from the table. De Martiniac wafted towards the door to the terrace, and Erik leapt silently from his perch and into the garden once again, this time close enough to hear his brother speak.

"Where is that useless man with the cigars, Philippe?" Erik knew it was Antoine's voice without looking. He had their father's tone.

"He's probably the one Raoul sent off with Daaé to whatever hovel she calls home." That was Philippe. Erik was immensely thankful for the information.

"I still can't believe that woman dared to show her face here," a third male voice chimed in, one Erik did not know.

"Oh, Louis, haven't you heard? My idiot brother still thinks he's going to marry the baggage, as if that's what opera wenches are for," Philippe laughed. Erik clenched his fists.

"My goodness, that would be a scandal. But I thought Raoul was going back abroad?" the other man asked. A pause.

"He's reconsidering," de Martiniac answered, and Erik's heart seized again. "Sabine made him promise to stay for the wedding."

Philippe sighed. "That boy will be the death of me."

"You used to say that about me," Antoine laughed back. There were clicks, and in seconds, the air was full of cigar smoke, heavy and sweet.

"How did you convince an angel like Sabine to marry you, you rogue?" the stranger asked, coughing.

"Antoine's been family for years. We're just formalizing it," Philippe replied. "When men have a bond like ours, it's important to build on it."

"What are you talking about, old man?" the stranger asked.

"Philippe is being poetic. He means to say he adopted me after our fathers died together."

"And after you frittered away your inheritance, don't forget that..." Erik did not hear the rest, the blood rushing to his head was too loud.

Died *together*? That couldn't be. Could it? There had been other men at that party, other guests who had perished in the fire when Erik left Alfred de Martiniac to burn... Had Raoul and Philippe de Chagny's father been one of them?

Shit.

The bushes rustled as Erik fell to his knees, and the men above went silent.

Shit.

"You should talk to your groundskeeper about whatever vermin has been sneaking into the garden in the off season," de Martiniac said, pointed and threatening.

Erik's instinct to live was the only thing that kept him from bolting right there and running into the street to get home as soon as possible. He stayed frozen as the small talk resumed – politics and hate for the Germans and something about a dowry. He didn't care. Finally, the men went in, and Erik ran.

It was a far different thing to get back to his part of the city from the refined *Faubourg Saint Germain* than it had been to get there. It was colder on foot, and Christine's gentle worry had been replaced by a whole host of voices in his mind screaming that he was a monstrous fool in every sense. His lungs were burning from the pace he kept, but soon enough, he was near the *Rue Notre Dame des Victoires* and Adèle Valerius's flat.

Erik didn't wait to scale the side of the building, dashing up a gutter pipe and to the window that had been Christine's. It was more important to find her right now than to be subtle. Christine's old room was dark and cold when he entered through the window. The bed where he and Christine had first made love was neatly made, not a wrinkle in sight. There was light from under the door and hushed voices. Once again, Erik found himself an eavesdropper.

"You can't let them get into your head – the managers or those bitches in the chorus or whoever this new singer is. You sing because you love it, right? Not to be the star." Adèle's voice was warm and comforting, and yet the words were nearly as alarming to Erik as what he'd heard in that garden.

"Then why does being on stage even matter?" Christine replied. "I'd be just as happy singing with him alone forever." That was a consolation, but still concerning. And likely something Erik was not meant to hear.

What the hell was he supposed to do now? Open the door and give Valerius the fright of her life? He settled for making himself known by knocking a chair over so it clattered loudly.

"What was that?" Adèle asked as Christine sighed in annoyance. It was only slightly embarrassing.

"I'll check," Christine said, and Erik stood back from the door as she opened it. "For God's sake, how did you get in?" she demanded tiredly as she met Erik's eyes.

"What on – Jesus fuck!" Adèle exclaimed as she saw the legendary Phantom of the Opera standing in her spare room.

"Adèle, I don't believe you've been formally introduced to Erik," Christine's voice was annoyed, not angry, but Adèle's shocked look didn't necessarily calm Erik's frayed nerves. At least he had his mask.

"Good evening, Madame. I hope you will forgive me for dropping in," Erik intoned, inclining his head politely. He did still have manners. "I was anxious to find Christine. We were... separated unexpectedly."

"Was it that unexpected?" Christine grumbled.

"You're welcome any time," Adèle replied, clearly trying to keep her calm. "But I do have a door."

"My apologies again," Erik muttered.

"I had no idea Christine's paramour was so... famous." Adèle looked Erik up and down, and he fought the urge to squirm. "Wonders never cease, I guess."

"I think it's best if we go," Christine cut in, taking Erik's hand. "Through the front door if you don't mind? Goodbye, Adèle. I'll see you tomorrow."

"Good night, Madame." Erik followed without protest as Christine pulled him down the stairs. They were half out the door, into the open street, when she pulled him to her and, to his utter shock, kissed him.

He had never kissed her in the open like this. The closest they had come was the Bois, before their disastrous discovery by the boy, but this was different. This was like coming home. It was comfort and need, on both their parts. It was a deep kiss, soft and longing, and Erik wished dearly that he could remove his mask and fully enjoy it.

Christine's eyes were an ocean when she drew away, full of feeling and unshed tears glittering in the gaslight.

"Did you find him?" she asked. "Did you see?"

"I saw enough," Erik answered, chest tightening once more. "It is – *he* is..." He shook his head.

"He's not your father. He's awful, but he's not evil."

Erik wanted to say so much. He wanted to confess that his evil was even greater than Christine knew, and that he recognized the monstrousness in Antoine de Martiniac like looking in a mirror. Christine would only say that was his paranoia and pain speaking. He couldn't tell her the rest. Not yet.

"Let's go home. You can tell me what you and Adèle were gossiping about," Erik offered weakly.

"I'd rather not. It's foolish anyway." Christine looked away, and Erik saw in her the same hesitance he felt. If he was going to hide tonight, he'd let her do the same.

"Come." He took her arm and bent his head so that the brim of his hat shadowed his mask. It terrified him to walk about in the world he had forsaken. But the woman he loved was walking with him. Through their gloves, he could feel the ring she wore.

The last time they had walked this street had been in the other direction, the night they had sent Joseph Buquet to his doom. Erik had already absolved her of that, taking the sin for her and adding it to the catalogue of his own. He would do anything for her, to keep her safe, even walk with her in the terrible mortal world until he could bear it no more.

Shaya clenched his fists in triumph from his place in the alleyway across from Adèle Valerius's flat. He had them. He had them both – Erik and his whore. He had waited in the cold for hours, hoping to confirm that Daaé was absent from the flat before she had arrived in a fine carriage and his confidence had faltered. Maybe, he had thought, just maybe, she would leave, and he could spring his snare.

Then lo and behold, a miracle. Erik himself had descended on the flat to accost her and force her back. He had watched in horror as the fiend had broken in, and then disgust as he hauled the girl out and claimed her mouth. He shuddered to think how Erik had warped the poor thing's mind and corrupted her soul. It would be up to de Chagny to save her if he still wanted to. But now, finally, he would know what she was.

Shaya headed in the opposite direction from the lovers and managed to hail a cab at the *Place Des Victoires*. The driver made no comment when Shaya told him to head to the *Faubourg Saint Germain*. The entire ride, Shaya felt more excitement than he had in years, his mind buzzing. Now, Raoul would act. Whatever he did, it would shatter all the illusions.

It appeared some sort of party just ending as Shaya's cab deposited him in front of the Chagny manor, with well-dressed ladies and gentlemen awaiting their carriages near the gate. Shaya pushed through the crowd, ignoring the scandalized huffs of the departing guests, and found a footman.

"Where is Monsieur le Vicomte? I need to speak with him urgently." The man rolled his eyes, but went inside, and no one chided Shaya for following. He waited, nearly bouncing until the young Vicomte emerged from a side room in a cloud of cigar smoke with a tall, blond man beside him.

"What is the meaning of this, Motlagh? You didn't even give the man your card!" Raoul demanded. Shaya did not like the way the other man looked him up and down.

"I have what you demanded." Shaya watched Raoul's face harden in interest.

"This way," Raoul hissed, nodding towards a much smaller drawing room, opposite where he'd emerged from. To Shaya's shock, the other man followed.

"Monsieur, I must insist this discussion be in private," Shaya said as Raoul closed them all in.

"Anything you have to say about Erik, Monsieur de Martiniac can hear. He is just as invested in bringing the creature to justice as I am. Antoine can be trusted."

"Come now, *Monsieur le Perse*. Tell us what your spying has revealed," the other man – Antoine – said with a cool sneer, and Shaya bristled. Raoul nodded for Shaya to speak.

"You've claimed over and over that your Mademoiselle Daaé is good and pure. Even that she spends her nights at home when she is not in his grasp." Shaya savored the way Raoul's noble jawline began to twitch. "What if I were to tell you she no longer lives with Madame Valerius and has not slept under that roof for at least two weeks?"

"I have seen her home personally," Raoul snarled. "I sent her in my carriage tonight!"

"And she enjoyed her friend's company briefly before her teacher came to escort her back to his kingdom," Shaya declared. "I saw it myself."

"You saw him take her? How?" Raoul sputtered, wringing his hands through his hair.

"I told you she was a lying little minx." Raoul and Shaya turned to see Antoine smiling dangerously. "She's been playing you for a fool, just like he has."

"Shut up, you don't know that. Neither of you know! Who told you this?" Raoul demanded, rounding on Shaya.

"I have my sources. You can go look right now and find her bed at that house empty."

"What a wonderful idea," Antoine purred and that made Shaya cold. "Raoul, it's time to finally act."

"What?" Raoul asked, but Antoine was already hauling him away.

"You'll need me if you're going after him," Shaya protested as he followed the men out the door.

"We'll come find you if that's the case," Antoine called over his shoulder. Shaya watched the men rush away, his excitement now replaced by dread. It was not de Chagny's rage at fully discovering Christine's betrayal that he feared, but the unknown factor of the man he had just met. He was so cold, and yet, so familiar in a way Shaya could not place, and it filled him with fear.

The dream, as so many dreams were, was the same and different every time. Christine knew it wasn't real. She knew her father lay dead and buried, but Christine still worried that he would be mad at her for not practicing. She hadn't played violin in years. Now he was demanding she perform for everyone.

The theater was crowded and cavernous at the same time, and the instrument was huge in her small hands.

"I don't want to anymore. I'm scared."

"Again, from the beginning. Don't disappoint me again," her father ordered from the conductor's podium. She began to play, the notes of *The Resurrection of Lazarus* as familiar as breathing.

"Stop!" Raoul cried as he struck the instrument from her hands, and her father jumped onto the stage in rage.

"Get out of here, boy. I told you before, you don't deserve her," her father growled in the voice that made her so afraid. Would he yell at her next, then go off to mourn in his room before begging her forgiveness? She hated when he did that, but it hadn't happened for so long...

"She doesn't deserve me, but I will take her anyway," Raoul declared, grabbing her and ripping at her dress. Christine screamed. Where was her angel? Why had he sent her out on stage alone again?

She didn't want this. She had to wake up.

She sat up in bed with a gasp and Erik stirred beside her. "Christine, what's wrong?"

"I—" she panted, the dream still lingering around her like fog.

"Another nightmare?" he asked as he took her in his arms. "You've had them every night."

"I'm sorry. I don't know what's wrong with me." She threw her head against his chest as she stifled a sob, her night dress twisting around her.

"You don't need to be sorry," Erik whispered. "I just wish you would tell me what's been tormenting you."

"I see my father," she breathed. "And he's so angry and he wants so much from me that I can't do, and then..." She shook her head, tears staining Erik's bare shoulder.

"Shhh, it's just dreams," her lover cooed, and Christine surged up to kiss him. Erik's response was hesitant, scared even, like when she had first given him her lips. Why was he afraid of her now? Why hadn't he made love to her tonight and sung her to sleep instead? Why wouldn't he free her from fear with lust when she needed it?

"I need you," she sighed against his mouth, sweeping her hands over his rough skin.

"Christine…" The way he said her name was still a drug, even if it sounded like he wanted to argue that she couldn't fuck her way out of her problems. That didn't mean she couldn't escape for a little while with him.

She pushed Erik back on the bed, straddling him as she yanked off her gown. She ground herself against his manhood, feeling it respond as she watched his head fall back. "Please," she entreated before kissing again, her hand dipping between them to free the hard organ of his lust.

"Yes," Erik exhaled, gripping her hips. She guided him into her slickness, groaning at the familiar feeling of being stretched and filled. How was it so good when everything around them was darkness? Why did she feel like she was the light reflected in his eyes as she began to move with him inside her? Did any answer matter but this?

"I love you," she moaned as she rode him, her hips meeting his rhythm as his thumb pressed on that magic place above her entrance. Each touch was electric and wiped away all her nightmares and fear. "Don't let go of me. Please don't let go."

"Never," Erik swore.

Christine threw her head back, her breasts rising and falling in a frantic tempo as she chased her little death in the darkness.

"Why are we waiting, for fuck's sake?" Antoine demanded as he threw the nub of another cigarette onto the ground.

"Maybe she'll come home, or we'll see a light," Raoul argued, shivering. He couldn't tell Antoine the real reason – that he was terrified of what sort of truth they might uncover if they confronted Valerius or Christine.

"Come on, you pansy, no more dallying." Antoine strode across the street to the building's blue door. Raoul rushed over, impressed to see Antoine using a key. "Adèle forgot to ask for it back."

Antoine gave Raoul a chilling wink and rushed through the door, practically bounding up the steps. He knocked loudly before he began to fumble with the key, and Raoul began to wonder how much Antoine had drunk at the party.

"Adèle! Darling!" Antoine called as he pushed his way into the flat. The woman in question was entering the parlor, obviously having just been woken up. She looked indecent in her nightdress and robe, and Raoul tried not to blush.

"Antoine? What the hell are you doing here? What's going on!" Adèle demanded as Antoine advanced on her. "Why is this boy with you?"

"Where is Christine? I need to see her immediately," Raoul asked back. The panic in Adèle's face made him sick. "Where is she?"

"She's—" Adèle began, but Raoul could not wait. He ran to Christine's door and opened it, only to see an empty room and a neatly made bed. "She didn't come home tonight. She must be staying at the Opera. She does that often."

"At the Opera?" Antoine scoffed. "How clever of you to not lie completely."

"I'm not—" Antoine's slap cut off Adèle's words, and the woman crumpled to the floor, holding her cheek. Raoul sprang forward, but Antoine caught him by the throat, holding him back in an iron grip.

"My future brother-in-law asked you a question," Antoine said calmly. "Please answer. We know Christine came here tonight and left. Where did she go?"

"She didn't say." Adèle stared up at Antoine with pure hate in her eyes. Antoine laughed as he let go of Raoul and advanced on the prone woman. He grabbed her by the hair and hauled her up as she whimpered.

"And when was the last time she spent the night here?" Antoine asked, and Adèle looked frantically between the two men.

"Last night! She lives here!" Adèle answered, voice high and panicked.

"You're lying," Raoul stated, suddenly numb. "You've been lying for her for who knows how long."

"What Christine does with herself is no concern of yours!" Adèle snarled. Antoine struck her roughly again, in the stomach this time. Raoul winced but did not move.

"Tell us more, my darling," Antoine ordered, sweeter than Raoul had ever heard him speak. "Did you teach her how to moan and beg like a whore too?"

Adèle glared at Antoine with a fury Raoul had never seen before spitting in his face. Raoul turned away when the blow fell this time, bracing himself against the sound of Antoine's fists doing their work until the sound of sobs broke through.

When Raoul dared to look, the sight turned his stomach. Antoine was still holding Adèle by the hair, and her eyes were burning with fury as red marks bloomed on her face to match her bleeding lip. "Go ahead. Tell us the truth, you wretched slut."

"At least her lover actually made her come," Adèle hissed. "She didn't have to fake it like I did with you, you useless bastard."

Raoul was not prepared for how his vision went red at the words. "No! You're lying!"

"Why would I lie now?" Adèle sneered as the blood dripped down her chin, defiance in her eyes. "I heard them. I heard her calling his name as he fucked her so hard the wall was shaking! You should hear the way she talked about him, little boy."

"Stop," Raoul nearly wept, but Adèle went on with a laugh.

"You'll never measure up – you know that? Even if you steal her away, you'll never give it to her as good as he did, you—" Another slap cut off Adèle's words. Raoul was shocked to see his own hand hanging in the air, palm smarting.

Antoine chuckled and began to pull Adèle away. "Raoul, this next part may be too much for an innocent soul like yours to see, but if you like, you can have a go when I'm done." It was like he was discussing dinner plans.

Adèle was struggling furiously, but she was no match for the brute dragging her through the door. Throwing her onto her bed.

"Antoine, no! Wait!" Raoul bellowed even as Adèle screamed. It was too late. The door slammed in Raoul's face and the lock clicked shut.

8. Liars

E rik was rather familiar with what most people called a sense of dread. A connoisseur, one might even say. The one that had haunted him since waking this morning was of an interesting variety – it was the sort that made the world seem just slightly off its normal angle, about to tip. He told himself, as he went about the morning, that it was all in his head. This, despite knowing from years of experience that his gut was usually right. He didn't want it to be. He wanted things as they were and for nothing to change.

He didn't want to tell Christine he was the reason her sweet young hero was fatherless now. He didn't want to be the one to shatter her again, so he was silent and ignored the fear gnawing inside him. A lesson with his angel would be an antidote, or so he had thought. They had sung together, losing themselves in Mozart and Rossini. It all changed again when they had turned to *Faust*, and discussed what Christine might improve for the next performance. A shadow had fallen over her, and her voice had lost its brilliance like tarnished silver.

Now it was time for her to return above, and the dread was even stronger than before. Did Christine feel it too? She looked as if she was going off to do chores, not to the career she had dreamed of her whole life – the one Erik had moved heaven and earth to give her. Even the colors of the shadows in the cellars and passages were ever so slightly changed, which he could attribute to the imminent return of spring, but something told him this was different.

"They may discuss *Lohengrin* today, after the musical run-through," Erik said by way of small talk as they came to the stable exit. They were being careful today, in light of everything.

"Oh. That. I hope not," Christine muttered. "I don't think they will. Don't they wait until March for new casting and such?"

"It's been March for several days. I think," Erik replied, concerned first by her hesitancy and then more so by the crestfallen look on her face.

"It has?"

"Are you still unsure about the role?" Erik pushed back.

"Yes, but I don't think it will matter. Couldn't you convince them to do *Roméo et Juliette*? I could die again in a part that suits me better." Christine sighed as Erik stared. "I'm sorry. I don't mean to be ungrateful, but... Never mind."

"What's wrong? Do you not want it?" He wasn't even sure what he was talking about – the role or everything they had built.

"I don't know what I want," Christine whispered. "I just want to rest."

"It will be better when he's gone. Only a few more days."

"What if it's not? What happens when there's some other patron or rival or..." She bit her lips and shook her head.

"We'll face it," Erik offered, even as his panic was rising.

"Together?" Christine added. "Were you going to say that? Or will I just be your mask or your soldier again while you wait in the shadows?"

"Where else would I go?" Erik heard himself snap back in horror. "*They* won't have me in the sun."

"*They* aren't the ones who decided that," Christine snapped, and Erik wondered when this had become a quarrel.

"It will be better when he is gone," Erik repeated like a spell. Christine frowned but nodded. "We can talk more later."

Christine said no more as she turned and stepped into the milky light of afternoon where Erik could not – or would not – follow. Did her eyes sting when she stepped out into the cloudy day?

Erik took his customary path back down through the dark. The feeling of someone intruding into his realm was absent today. No one had disturbed any of the traps or triggers near the lake, but how did it fare above? He had no idea how Richard had reacted to the loss of the money from his pocket. That was worth investigating.

The passages and halls were more claustrophobic than ever today. The journey to the managers' office was so long, even for a shadow and a ghost. Once there, Erik crouched under his trap door and waited for someone to speak, muscles cramping and lungs full of dust as a rat scurried by.

He hated this.

Erik hated being locked below the feet of the living like a corpse in a grave. A worm in the dirt. He hated listening and haunting and watching when it was so easy for everyone to just *do* things. He was trapped and, damn it, it was *their* fault, not his. He had not chosen his face, nor the evils mankind had inflicted on him. He was not to be blamed for wanting some goddamn peace. He had spent six years chasing it, alone in the dark! Now he had her, and here he was, hiding in the grimy blackness still.

"I can't believe you did it!" Erik jumped, nearly cracking his skull as the door above burst open and Armand Moncharmin began yelling. "You went behind my back and contacted that woman, and now everyone is talking about it!"

"Sophie Cruvelli is one of the foremost sopranos on the continent, and her agreement to sing some of *Lohengrin* in concert is just a trial," Richard replied without missing a beat, his voice measured and calm, filling Erik with fury.

"We agreed Daaé would sing it!" Moncharmin bellowed on Erik's behalf.

"There are other singers in the world, including ones who are mature enough to handle such a part," Richard drawled. "Daaé will get there eventually, but I thought you and your ghost wouldn't mind me saving her voice and her reputation."

"So now you believe?" Moncharmin said.

"I have always known that there was someone in this Opera making trouble," Richard answered, and Erik's anger grew. "Some charlatan who hides away and steals from honest men. Who kills and threatens to keep his favorite on the stage, as if an opera someone will forget the next morning is worth murder and extortion."

"And you wish to provoke such a person?" Moncharmin scoffed. "Are you mad?"

"I simply do not care anymore and have decided to make this creature's life – or afterlife – as miserable as I can. I'm returning the favor he has done for me and so many others." Richard sounded positively gleeful. *How dare he...*

"There will be consequences for this," Moncharmin warned, speaking for Erik once again.

"What can he do? Kill *me*?" Richard laughed again. "I'm not some stagehand. I *matter*. He won't touch me or any of my allies unless he wants all the commissaries in Paris swarming this place. If he's found, he'll be lucky if the chorus kills him before he's thrown in prison. Now, he just gets to suffer until he makes a mistake. Or another mistake. There have been so many—"

"Messieurs?" Rémy interrupted. "I've just been handed a note I think you should know about."

"From the ghost?" Richard asked, still sounding amused.

"I'm not sure," Rémy replied. Erik didn't recall sending any missives recently.

"What is this?" Moncharmin huffed. "It says Adèle Valerius is indisposed. It is unknown when or if she will be able to return to the stage... Dear God, where did you get this?"

"A boy brought it just now. It's not signed. No return address," Rémy stammered.

"For God's sake, prepare her understudy – she does have one still, doesn't she?" There was a flurry of steps above as Erik himself rushed from his hiding spot.

What on earth had happened to Adèle, and how was it already being pinned on him? She had been fine last night. Was this the disaster his intuition had warned him of?

He needed to make sure that the woman was alright. He needed to talk to Christine about this nonsense regarding the casting and Richard's vow of defiance – which was meant to hurt them both.

Erik followed the road to the costumers automatically, his mind returning to the simpler days when Christine was just a seamstress who believed in an angel. Who smiled so brightly at the sound of his voice and sang with nothing but joy. Now, she sang with fire and sadness that Erik had given her to replace that joy and he wondered if he would ever see her smile like that again.

He had to wait forever for his quarry to leave the costume workshop to walk alone. Julianne was at least polite enough to only gasp and swear when Erik appeared before her in the hall, rather than scream. Small miracles.

"What the hell are you doing—"

"You need to go see what has happened to Adèle Valerius," Erik cut her off. "Something is wrong. The managers have been told she's ill, but not by her."

"What have you done now?" Julianne demanded, and Erik glared back.

"I have done nothing, that's why I am concerned. Now go," he hissed. Julianne only stared stonily back at him, unmoving. "Please?"

"Fine." Julianne turned down the hall. Erik watched as she went, once again feeling helpless, useless, and full of dread. What good was a ghost, anyway? Fear only went so far, and it always turned around to hurt him more. The same was true of loyalty.

One person in the world saw him as a man, not a monster or a thing. And even she saw how incomplete he was and berated him for sending her out to fight the battles and face the world while he hid. What was he to do otherwise? He was a creature of shadow, a corpse and phantom. He did not belong out there in the living world when even the memory of the sun hurt his haunted eyes.

C hristine's mind drifted from boredom to annoyance as Robert Rameau and Carlos Fontana plotted her downfall. Or Marguerite's. The more she thought about her poor character in *Faust*, the angrier she became.

Faust fell in love with the image of Marguerite when Satan showed it to him, not with *her*. The brilliant doctor did not sell his soul for youth or riches, but on the promise of a virgin he could seduce. Poor Marguerite was bought with jewels, tricked away from her sweet suitor Siebel. Then Faust bedded her and left her with a child in her belly that she killed. Her only redemption came from turning to God when Faust and the devil sought her soul. Was Marguerite a fool too? The woman should just have stayed with Siebel and his flowers.

"Let us rest for a while," Claude Bosarge declared, bringing Christine back to reality. It was interesting to see how the orchestra conductor ran the rehearsal in contrast to Gerard Gabriel, who had left halfway through when word came that Adèle was ill. Christine had wanted to go with him. "Ten minutes, then we'll return to the trio, and after that, if we have time, Mademoiselle Caron again."

Christine glanced at said mademoiselle, a woman she had barely met before today when she had stepped in for Adèle as an understudy. Christine had resented the interloper for taking Adèle's indisposition as an opportunity to show off before she realized those bitter words sounded like Carlotta. Christine didn't want to be that woman. Not anymore.

Rehearsal felt wrong without Adèle there. She was never late, let alone absent, and she had been fine last night. Christine was truly worried for her friend. At least they had been spared the indignity of discussing new productions.

Worrying about a friend and fuming about the helpless fools she had to play was better than thinking about how she had entirely forgotten what day tomorrow was. She felt like even more of a failure as a daughter. How could she have just *forgotten*? How had she been so deep in Erik's underworld that she had missed the days passing above?

Christine drifted towards the walls, trying to sense if there was an angel lurking there. She didn't know if she even wanted him to be close today. The escape he offered was just another dead end in the maze. When he found her again, she'd have to tell him about the role she didn't have and the career she didn't want and her father and why she wanted to start running towards the sea and not come back.

She turned her attention to the door that had just opened and was surprised to see it was Gabriel who came in, looking more serious than usual as he strode to Bosarge and spoke quietly to the conductor. Christine did not like the way he frowned.

"Mesdames and Messieurs, we have a change to rehearsal," Bosarge called to the crowd. "Monsieur Gabriel and I will be working with Mademoiselle Caron, as we have been notified that Madame Valerius will not be able to perform on Thursday."

"What's happened to Adèle?" Robert asked before Christine could.

"Yes, is she alright?" Christine still demanded, coming to stand by the bass.

The look on Gabriel's face was answer enough as he glanced between Robert and Christine. "No. She is not. Your dresser is there with her attending to her—" Gabriel looked overcome as he shook his head, reminding Christine that he was one of Adèle's lovers. "She won't talk. But she's... hurt. Beaten."

"What?" Christine gasped, her stomach plummeting. "Who hurt her?"

"That bastard de Martiniac, if I were to hazard a guess," Robert muttered, and Gabriel looked away.

"I think he did more than beat her," Gabriel said, sad and low. "I should have been there."

"I'll kill him," Christine breathed. "I need to see her."

She rushed from the rehearsal room toward the stage door, heart pounding with the fear that, somehow, this was her fault. The sound of yelling stopped her in her tracks before she came to the exit, for one voice was familiar.

"For God's sake, let me in! You know me!" Raoul's voice boomed from the door, and Christine's panic grew.

"He's my guest, let him in," Christine heard herself say, rushing to the door then nearly tripping at the absolute devastation in Raoul's face when he looked at her. She had never seen the man look so dire. "Raoul, what's—"

"Let me by, you oaf!" Raoul shoved past the doorman only to grab Christine by the arm and pull her towards the hall she had just come from.

"Raoul, what's going on? I need to get to Adèle!"

"That whore can wait. I want you to tell me the truth," Raoul entreated as they came to a standstill, holding Christine so she was forced to look into his red-rimmed eyes. He was unshaven and disheveled, and he looked as if he had not changed since Christine had left him last night. "I need to know where you spend your nights."

Christine's heart was going to shatter her chest, fear and shame and panic all surging through her at once. She saw the doorman watching out of the corner of her eye and looked frantically towards the shadows she knew had ears.

"Not here, please. My dressing room—"

Raoul shook his head, gripping her tighter, eyes wild. "No. Somewhere he cannot follow or hear. I don't trust anything you say if he's listening."

Christine swallowed, glancing towards the street through a dingy window, where faint daylight still remained. She couldn't go out there, but she could go up. "Follow me," she ordered and set off on a path she'd only taken once before.

Up to the flies where she had watched Buquet die and up higher still she rushed, confident Raoul was behind her, but never looking back. Her mind was not on her feet as they carried her skyward on narrow metal steps in close spirals, trying to guess what Raoul knew and plan what she might say. The daylight was the one place Erik would not go, or so she hoped Raoul believed. She didn't know if she was afraid to face Raoul's condemnations alone or if she needed the shelter of her angel's wings.

The air was warmer than she had expected when they stepped onto the roof, the copper dome above the auditorium warmed by the glancing rays of the late afternoon sun. She didn't stray near the edge, but rather towards the place behind the dome, to the very feet of Apollo thrusting his golden lyre to the sky.

Christine looked up to the cold, handsome face of the god of musicians. He who had raped and chased in the name of love, who had cursed and destroyed artists and oracles, and who now looked over Paris with placid calm.

"No further," Raoul commanded, and Christine dared to turn to him again. "Confess your lies. Tell me that you've been spending the nights with him. I know you haven't been at home."

"How—"

"Your friend told Antoine. She told him everything," Raoul confessed as if it caused him terrible pain to say it. It hurt Christine too, as the pieces came together at last.

"Adèle," she whispered in horror. "Did Antoine—"

"He got answers," Raoul spat, looking sickened before shaking his head. "It doesn't matter how. I know you've lied! I want to know why! I want to know what else *he* has done to you and made you hide! That woman said such awful things! That she saw you and your lover! That you told her how he..." Raoul looked like he was about to wretch. "She deserved what he did to her."

Christine braced herself against the cold stone of the Opera, staring in horror at the man before her. Gone was the sweet, bumbling boy she had loved years ago. Gone too was the bashful sailor that had pined for her hand. In his place was a thing made of rage and judgment animated by pitiful despair. A man who had allowed her friend to be beaten and worse, just so he could call Christine to account.

"Were you there?" Christine asked softly. "When that bastard beat this all out of her? *Were you there?*"

"I am not the one answering questions right now!" Raoul spat, grabbing Christine and shaking her with force that only strengthened her resolve. "I want you to tell me that trollop lied! I refuse to believe that you have shared the bed of that monster – that corpse!"

"I thought you wanted the truth," Christine hissed back and watched Raoul's face darken further. "Adèle didn't lie – how could she? I'm the one who has lied, just like you said, and I am exhausted by it. Don't you want to hear how every horrible thing you've ever suspected of me is true?"

"Tell me he forced you," Raoul gritted out. Christine shook her head, defiant. "No. I won't believe that. You're lying for him again!"

"Is it so hard to comprehend?" she nearly laughed. "You said it yourself! He inspired ecstasy in me with merely his voice. He always has. I have always *wanted* him. Why are you arguing now? That's what you and your friend beat Adèle to learn, and it's all true!"

"No!" Raoul cried and pushed her away.

"Do you want to know all the details?" Christine went on, rage rising. "Shall I tell you all the ways he fucks me? All the places he's had me? How hard he makes me come?"

Raoul spun to look at her, utter disgust on his handsome face. "Stop!"

"Shall I tell you how I gave myself to him before you ever returned to my life?" she pushed on, lifted by the freedom of speaking the truth at last and the power of finally hurting the man who shamed her for it. "How I wanted him when he was nothing more than a shadow?"

Raoul stared at her as the wind picked up around them and seemed to carry the sound of triumphant laughter.

"Why would you lie to me then, if you are so happy as his whore?" Raoul seethed in return. "Why string me along?"

"I tried to tell you!" Christine yelled back. "I tried again and again to *tell you* I was not free! And you would not leave me alone! You hunted him and pursued me no matter what I told you!"

"I want to save you from a monster!" Raoul wailed in return.

"I am not his prisoner!" The words rang out through the fading day beneath Apollo's golden lyre, and Raoul looked at her like she was a madwoman. Maybe she was. Maybe she was Marguerite, reduced to the worst now her innocence was lost. "If you want to save me, you will have to do it by force, because I have chosen him even if it damns me!"

"You don't know what you're saying."

"Don't you see? You were right," Christine went on as the weight of her terrible love pressed on her heart. "Everything you've said has been *right*! You were the one who knew before I could even admit it to myself what I felt for him. I return to him because, despite myself, despite everything, I—"

"Don't say it!" Christine flinched as Raoul seized her once more. "I will not hear it. I will not believe it! He's controlling you! You're still lying for him because you're ashamed of what he's done and the whore he's made you!"

"*Stop calling me a whore*," Christine growled, as she looked to the ring on her finger, glistening in the setting sun. "I'm his, Raoul, but I have not been taken or bought."

"I will not allow it. Whether he has stolen you or tricked you into giving your soul, you belong to *a murderer*!" Raoul railed, his hands a vice on her arms. "He killed Buquet and so many more! The Persian – has he told you what that monster did in his country?"

"Erik told me," Christine whispered in reply, tears falling freely, finally unable to confess more. She couldn't tell Raoul she was bound to Erik because her love had made her a killer too. That Buquet's blood was on her hands. "I know everything."

"Do you? Did he tell you how he tortured people? How he took delight in driving them mad in his chambers of horrors and strangling them to death?" Raoul pushed back, and it was Christine's turn to look away. "I'm sure he's made it sound so tragic!

A poor freak driven to kill, but he didn't just kill Persian – he killed men who mattered too. Good men!"

Christine's insides froze. "What are you—"

"Men like my father," Raoul said, incomprehensible words falling like stones and snuffing Christine's rage. *No*, the night itself seemed to sigh.

"No..." Christine breathed as well.

"He was hired to entertain at a hunting party for Antoine's father and caught stealing. They locked him and the gypsy mongrels he was with up in the cellar, but he broke out and set the place on fire. My father was there for the party." Raoul's eyes were moist now too. "Your Angel of Music destroyed my family. He left my father to die *in agony*."

"He didn't know—" Christine stammered, the foundation of lies and violence she had built upon for months finally crumbling under her.

"If it wasn't for that monster, we could have been together when we were young! I could have convinced Father to let me marry you if he had been alive!" Raoul went on. "Your Erik kept me from you then, and he keeps me from you now!"

"Raoul, he didn't intend—"

"I don't care, Christine! He is a killer, and I am going to bring him to justice!" Raoul screamed, the words ricocheting off the dome and into the night. *Justice*, the wind echoed. Gooseflesh rose on Christine's skin.

"No," she exhaled as Raoul shook her, forcing her to look into his enraged face.

"Your Erik is a monster, no matter how he's warped your mind. He kills and destroys everything he touches. He killed my father and he's destroyed you. You know it," Raoul entreated, his eyes wide and full of fury even as Christine crumbled. "Look at yourself, Christine, look what he's done to you. He makes you parade for the crowds, singing your pretty songs, and for what? His glory? Is *music* so precious you're willing to damn your soul for a hideous creature that's defiled you? I knew your father, Christine, and this is not the life he would want for you!"

"Raoul stop!" Christine sobbed. "Please stop. Please just go and leave this and—"

"I'm not going north. I never was. I am going to destroy him and save you. Then, *we will be together,*" he said, as if it wasn't utter madness. "When he's gone, you'll come to your senses. Once you're free."

"I am—" She couldn't say it – the word 'free.' She couldn't lie again.

Fresh tears sprang to Christine's eyes and she floundered for words. She couldn't say Raoul was wrong, because she had been broken and lost and Erik had given her all her dreams, and they had turned out to be hollow. Now, the one thing she had was cursed too. The man she loved, who she had given herself to, body and soul, had taken everything from the first boy that had held her heart. Who still somehow wanted her, despite her sins.

"I know what you are, Christine, and I'm still going to have you. I'm going to save you. He cannot stop us being together. When you're cured of this madness he's put into you, you'll be grateful." Raoul looked so convinced. For a heartbeat, Christine wanted to believe him. But the final rays of the sun faded from the sky and a telltale shiver ran down her spine.

"Raoul, leave now and never speak to me again. If you try to take me, he will kill you," Christine declared. "If you hurt me or come near me again, he will kill you."

"I will marry you before the week is out, I swear it," Raoul argued back, talking to the illusion of the girl he still wanted her to be. To seal the awful promise, he kissed her, hard and cold as Christine tried to writhe away. If the Punjab lasso had flown through the air to kill him that instant, Christine would not have been surprised, but no vengeance came.

"Goodbye, Raoul. Forever," Christine hissed as he finally let her squirm away. "Leave."

She did not look back as he stalked away. She could imagine the determination in his face that she knew would be her doom. She waited for the sound of the door crashing closed before she collapsed, weeping and shaking, to the cold roof. It was all done – her lies had found her and destroyed everything. One of the men who loved her would be dead by the spring, she knew it in her soul, and it would be her fault. She couldn't save them. She couldn't save herself.

Now she felt the ghost behind her. She had to turn and face the phantom who had stolen her soul and still possessed her heart. The man who had killed the father of the first boy she ever loved.

"Did you hear it all?" Christine asked Erik's shadow as it appeared beside hers.

"I heard enough." Even in the most terrible of moments, his voice sounded like an angel's. "Christine, I'm—"

"He wants revenge for his father and he won't stop." She turned to see her lover at last. Erik stood tall, mask shining in the twilight, his black cape fluttering like wings in the wind. Beneath the brim of his hat, his golden eyes glowed with pain, but not regret. "Did you know? About his father?"

"Yes. I—" Erik began, and Christine heaved another sobbing breath in shock. "Only since yesterday. At the—"

"You knew and didn't say anything?" she cried, jumping away as he reached for her.

"I didn't know how to tell you." That had been his excuse the first morning she had found herself in his bed. The first time he had destroyed her.

"You never do," Christine intoned numbly. "You hide, and you lurk, and you *wait*. I love a ghost who won't follow me into the world! Who leaves me alone to face every trial so *he* can be safe in the shadows. You can't even use a goddamn door to find me!"

"Christine, please, I can fix this," Erik protested, a storm in his eyes.

"Will you? Will you heal Adèle?" She spat and Erik winced. "You know what your brother did to her, don't you? Will you kill Antoine for that?"

"You'd ask that of me?" Erik replied in horror that made Christine want to laugh.

"Even if I did, you won't. It's too risky! You don't want to destroy everything you've built here. All your illusions and masks." Christine wondered if confessing to Raoul had burned away even the lies she told herself. "All you want is here, but you can't kill to keep it. Will you make it so that I don't hate it when I step out on the stage you put me on? Will you give me some goddamn hope that my life can be more than music and darkness? Because that's not enough."

"It's all I can give," Erik pled.

She wondered if there were tears under his mask. "It's *not enough*."

Christine ran past her angel, knowing he would not follow. She ran down the thousand steps through the flies where she had lost her soul, past the stage and corridors where she had lost her innocence, and finally out into the streets. She couldn't run home, because her home was gone, if it had ever existed. Still her feet carried her to the place where she would beg forgiveness. There was no place to go but to the first place she had lost her heart.

Shaya waited in the café and listened to the other people talk. There was a peculiar thing among these white Europeans: they would glance at him and decide based on his dress and skin that he was not one of them, and therefore, could not possibly understand them. They'd make no attempt to speak quietly or to even disguise their disgust that such *people* were all over the city now. As a spy, he didn't mind. Their prejudice allowed him to hear so much. But some days, it did weigh on him to be a pariah in a foreign city.

"Another understudy coming on? What's happening?" a man said over his coffee, and Shaya looked at the speaker in the reflection of the café window. He was not too well dressed; perhaps he was a musician or one of the secretaries? His companion was another man in a well-worn suit who looked tired.

"Do you think the ghost did her in? Valerius?" the second man asked. Shaya's ears perked. "Heard she'll be off the stage for a month."

"How'd you hear that?" the first man scoffed.

"From Hugh who heard it from Bosarge!"

"You're trusting a trumpet player? They're worse than tenors." So they were from the orchestra. "I heard from Giry in the ballet corps that she's just faking it for more money."

"Why the hell were you talking with the petits rats?"

"We weren't talking, I was just listening to them. That other dancer – the mean one, what's her name?"

"That's most of them."

"No, you know who I'm talking about; the head of the third row. Jammes!"

"What about her?" Shaya found himself holding his breath. "Well, she caused some sort of stir when she heard the news. Started ranting about the ghost and saying it was all him."

"See, like I told you!"

"And the reasonable ones told her she was being an idiot! They said the ghost has nothing against Valerius. She's friends with that witch Daaé."

"Well, as long as they keep the lights on, I honestly don't care who's singing up above. Though I don't know about this Wagner rumor..."

Shaya found himself walking to the door. He did not like what he had just heard. Had Raoul and his friend done something to Valerius? More likely, Erik had found out that Adèle had shared some secret with Raoul. The fiend had already broken into her home once, what was to stop him from doing it again?

That could mean de Chagny knew the truth, and perhaps, had confronted Christine. Shaya had to know. He had to be ready, he told himself as he rushed towards the Opera, only to see the subject of his musings speeding away from the building on foot. Christine Daaé looked devastated, running down the *Rue Auber* with no sense of propriety or discretion. That could only mean triumph for Shaya. He had no choice but to follow.

Raoul stormed into the house, his brain afire with rage with no place to direct it. He had never felt hate like this. Knowing the man who had ruined his life and Christine's was walking the world alive and free made his body tremble with helpless fury. Christine was fallen! And she refused to let him save her because that monster had corrupted her mind!

"Where have you been?" Philippe called, rushing down the stairs.

"Learning the truth," Raoul seethed back.

"Oh for God's sake, don't be dramatic now. One minute, we're enjoying cigars and brandy, the next, I hear you and Antoine have run off after that Persian fellow broke into the party!"

"That *Persian fellow* was doing us a great service. He told me the truth about Christine. Or tried to," Raoul spat, not resisting as Philippe pulled him into the drawing room. "And so Antoine and I..."

Raoul choked back a wave of sickness at the memory, not just of Adèle Valerius's cries for help, but his useless impotence on the wrong side of the door. He'd thought of running to the great church of *Notre Dame des Victoires* and confessing his sins, but he had been glued to the spot, listening to Antoine's brutality.

"Raoul!" The sound of his brother's voice shocked him from the memory. "What did you *do*?"

"What needed to be done," Raoul said. Philippe looked at him in bewildered horror. "I know the truth now."

"That Christine is a whore? I could have told you that! You didn't need to go off and do who knows what to—"

"She asked for it," Raoul snarled back, his blood boiling again at the memory of Adèle's insults. "Valerius has had half of Paris in her bed. It was just another night for her."

"Raoul, I say this as a brother who loves you: this has all gone too far." He sounded so sure and sincere, but Raoul shook his head. "Please, listen to me. You cannot fight an evil man by doing evil yourself! This has to stop. We are going to the police."

"What will the police do?" Raoul scoffed. "Erik lives across a lake of the dead, his house can't be found! We have to do it this way! Don't you want to avenge our father?" Raoul asked back, shaking his head.

"Vengeance won't resurrect him! It will only damn us and destroy the family we have left!" Philippe protested, grabbing Raoul and shaking him. "For God's sake, you've done enough! You can't think this is right!"

"Yesterday, I was unsure," Raoul replied, fire in his heart at the memory of his hesitation.

"I was afraid to do what was necessary. I was worried for my immortal soul, but no longer. Now I know the depths of Erik's evil. I know we are just. Killing him will be no worse than killing any loathsome animal."

"Glad to hear you've finally found your balls after Daaé stole them." Raoul looked up to see Antoine himself entering the parlor, looking as pristine as polished ivory. There was no mark on him of any sort of struggle or sleepless night, and his cool smile was so easy.

"No! You stop encouraging him! We need to be reasonable!" Philippe cried as Raoul's words dried up. "You two have gone mad."

"We're the only sane men in Paris," Antoine drawled. "Well, I am. Your little brother looks rather worse for wear. Where did you get off to?"

"I needed a drink," Raoul muttered. He'd actually needed several dozen, and then had spent hours praying and sobering up before his assault on the Opera. "I talked to Christine. She confirmed everything."

"You *what*?" Philippe gasped.

"She confessed it all: that he's defiled her for months. The monster has her head turned all around, but I'm going to—" Raoul choked on the words. "I'm going to save her."

"Raoul, she's already lost. Let her go and let this be over!" Philippe tried again.

"No! I will not let it go!" Raoul screamed so load the windows shook, and even Antoine looked shocked. "If I give up, he wins! I will not let him win! I will have her and I will destroy him! And I'm going to make it *hurt*."

"Exactly," Antoine said quietly, and the brothers turned to him. "That's how we destroy him. We take her and he'll come. It's simple."

Raoul looked out into the darkening night, where somewhere, Christine was still in danger, her soul falling deeper into sin with every passing hour that Erik lived. "We have to do it carefully. We'll need to draw her out of the Opera. Then there's the matter of what to do when we have him." Raoul smiled at the thought. He was not a torturer, not like the monster, but he still had imagination.

"You've lost your mind." Philippe threw up his hands and stalked from the drawing room. Raoul moved to follow, but Antoine held him back.

"Let him go," Antoine reprimanded. "We need to discuss our plan."

Raoul's face hardened as he looked at the man who smiled so easily after doing such terrible things. "*We* don't need to do anything. In fact, I think you should go. I need to think and I'm not sure I want you around Sabine after..." Raoul swallowed even as Antoine gave a wolfish grin.

"Oh come come, Sabine is a lady. She's not like Adèle," Antoine assured him. "And I will be marrying her, no matter what."

"Why does that sound like a threat?" Raoul asked, his stomach falling as he imagined his sister's wedding night with the beast before him.

"Because it is," Antoine replied easily. "I am marrying your sister and I swear I shall be as gentle as a lamb with her... Unless you try to get in my way. In that case, I may need to be more forceful as a husband. To remind both of you of your places."

"You wouldn't dare—" Raoul gasped as Antoine took his shoulder, holding him tight. He recalled the way Antoine had gripped his neck the night before and braced himself.

"I would. You know I would," Antoine said, eyes like ice before he smiled. "But you don't need to worry. Sabine is a good woman, the only good woman I know. There will be no need to be anything less than a gentleman. Now – to the plan. We do need to hurt him, you're right. I have some ideas."

The Opera had never felt so empty as Erik walked the dark halls and salons. There was no one in the galleries and rotundas, just the living shadow that stalked up the great staircase alone. It was cold and desolate, this palace to art and splendor. Erik hated it.

He hated the excess the upper classes had poured into this place to celebrate nothing but themselves and their power. He hated the cold marble and the shining crystal. And he hated the yawning depths beneath, where he had hidden for so long, a den for a wounded animal. Now, it was hollow – his nest of useless trinkets, filled with compositions no one would hear. Christine was gone, and he couldn't go home to their empty bed.

You did this. You drove her away with your monstrousness, the other ghosts whispered in his ears. *You're just as horrible as his other spawn, you coward. You fool.*

Erik turned, as if he could catch the memory that spoke, and gasped at the figure that met his eyes: a shade in a pale mask with glowing eyes. A phantom. Something so far from alive and human, it couldn't even step into the sun without fear.

"You fool," he said to his reflection, staring at himself for the first time in six years. "You coward."

His heart had pounded when he had followed them onto the roof. Even in the fading light he had shied away and kept to the shadows. The glancing sun that had caught in his eyes as it set and stung like acid in a wound. How could she ask him to be in that world when only a few moments of daylight were torture? And yet...

Christine had confessed to whom she belonged. She had been true until she had learned of another terrible lie. The boy was going to steal her away, and Erik was as trapped and helpless as if he were back in Klaus Steiner's mirrored torture chamber that he had built and rebuilt for himself throughout his cursed life. He was still a trapped child – still afraid to run to freedom even when the door was right there.

Even now, the door out to the balcony loomed behind him in his reflection and it might as well have been the false forest in the torture chamber below: an illusion meant to drive a man mad thinking he was free. What if the illusion wasn't the mirror?

If he was in a cage of his own making, then didn't he have the key?

Erik turned from his hated reflection, riding the impulse like a wave that pushed him to the door and out into the fresh air of the night. It was simple to climb and jump down from the balcony and onto the near-deserted *Avenue de L'Opéra*. He knew the way so well it was a trial not to run. His fear of humanity spurred him too. It terrified him to know people might see him and his mask, even with his hat low to shadow his face.

Not soon enough, he was on the *Rue Notre Dame des Victoires*, doing as Christine had asked and entering through the front of the building to climb the stairs to the Valerius flat.

He hesitated at the door, hand poised to knock. What on earth would he say, other than begging forgiveness? Was that worth anything? Especially when he didn't deserve an ounce of grace. Still, he had to try. He knocked. And waited.

After an agonizing span, the door of the flat swung open only to reveal the face of... Julianne Bonet. "Oh, it's you."

"Is she—"

"No. She's not here. Now fuck off." Erik blinked at the young woman whose dark eyes were full of defiance. "Or were you asking about Adèle? The woman who's actually been hurt. Or do you not care about that either?"

Erik's mouth hung open, a new shame creeping under his skin. He'd been enraged when he learned what Antoine had done, but it had been subsumed by so much else. "I do care. I... I'm sorry."

"Men are always sorry after the fact," a soft voice came from inside the flat, and Erik peeked around Julianne to see inside. Adèle was there, wrapped in blankets, the light from the fireplace illuminating her bruised face. "Doesn't ever change the past."

"I could kill him, if you'd like," Erik offered and ignored Julianne's look of horror in favor of meeting Adèle's tired eyes when she turned her head.

"Would you make it slow, if you do?" Adèle asked languidly.

"Very," Erik replied, and Adèle nodded.

"Good. Bring the whole damn Opera down too while you're at it." The bitter exhaustion in the woman's voice chilled Erik to the bone.

"I *am* sorry," he murmured. "Not that it matters. We had no idea that—"

"We?" Julianne scoffed. "You don't get to use that word. Not anymore."

"I know, I—" Erik protested as Julianne stepped so as to block Adèle from view.

"Like I told you, Christine is gone," Julianne went on.

"No, you said she wasn't here – have you seen her?" Erik asked, hope and fear surging at once.

"She came to apologize too," Adèle confessed while Julianne scowled. "She cried and begged forgiveness but didn't stay to take it."

"Where did she go?" Erik's pulse was racing.

"As if you could follow," Julianne snapped, and Erik cringed. "She's left the city."

"To go where?" Erik watched Julianne's eyes harden in deeper defiance. "Please. I just need to know."

"She didn't say exactly," Adèle answered. "Just that she was going home. I didn't think she had one."

"Thank you," Erik whispered, mind racing.

The door slammed in Erik's face before he could reply, and he was left in shock in the lonely hall, feeling like a fool again. A killer and a fool who no one believed was brave enough to follow his love. Were they right?

9. Lazarus

The Inn of the Setting Sun was as warm and welcoming as Christine had always dreamed. She'd been inside many times, of course, to the pub on the first floor where the people of Perros-Guirec gathered to drink and socialize with the scant travelers and merchants that came through the little town at the edge of the world. Until now, Christine had never been inside a room.

Under different circumstances, she would find the little chamber charming, with its cozy fireplace and bed covered in a warm quilt. Like most of the rooms, hers had windows looking west out to the sea at the sunset which gave the inn its name. She had spent most of the hours since she had awoken looking away from it, her eyes instead on the crackling fire.

Christine had traveled through the night on the last train from Paris, staring out the window while trying to sort out her thoughts and not weep when the memories came unbidden. She remembered the final summer in Perros with Raoul, when they had celebrated her seventeenth birthday together and sworn that by the next summer, they would be married and make their way in the world.

Then Raoul had left with no word. Only months later had Christine learned that the old Count had died and the Chagny chateau was to be sold. Would it have ended differently for them had Erik not set the fire that killed his own father and Raoul's?

Christine's father had been relieved, almost happy, that the boy who wanted to take his daughter from him was gone. They had traveled all over that fall, the last year they had done so, but it had been slow as it became clear that Papa was getting ill. In the spring, they had returned to Perros and then never left. Papa had continued her training and practice, letting Christine educate herself with books, but always kept her close.

It had not been until the fall of 1877, once Christine was twenty, that Papa had sent her off to audition for the Conservatoire in Rouen. Papa had called in a favor with an old acquaintance from his time in the opera orchestra in Nice. Christine had been so happy and hopeful when the audition had gone well, but then her chaperone, Doctor Mainville, had said it: that her father would rest easy knowing she had a future at the conservatoire. She had understood then that her father had finally let her audition because he was going to die soon.

It had been the longest train journey of her life. Even though she had nursed her father for two years, she had always thought he would get better, or at least *stay*. Papa couldn't die and leave her with so many dreams to fulfill without him.

"Do not worry, my Christine. I will send the angel of music to watch you and guide you. He will keep you safe and even keep up your lessons," her father had told her that night, the same old story from her childhood. She had believed it because the alternative was unthinkable. There was no world without Papa.

The toll of the bells in the church shook Christine from her thoughts and she forced herself to rise, despite her exhaustion. It was afternoon, and soon the sun would be gone again. She'd tried to sleep once she arrived, so late in the night it was morning, but the dreams had come again. Dreams mixed with memories of her father's cold hand in hers and his disappointed eyes watching from far across the sea. *I warned you, Christine. I tried to protect you, but you had to go looking for more.*

Christine had been out earlier, wrapped in Erik's dark cloak out of habit, his scent bringing her comfort even as it mixed with the wind off the sea. She had wandered Perros-Guirec for an hour before she had found the courage to knock on Doctor Mainville's door. He had looked so old compared to her memory, but he had smiled to see her and offered her tea. He too recalled the date and had been expecting her. It was the third year she had come back to Perros to honor her father's passing. She had nearly forgotten, and the shame burned in her like acid on her insides.

This year, at least, Christine had been brave enough to look at the precious relic the good doctor had sheltered. He had insisted Christine keep it. Now, it sat silent on her lap: the violin her father had lived by and played until the day he died. Would it still play, she wondered? She was afraid to try. Erik could tune it easily, of course. Her Angel of Music was a master of mending the broken and discarded so they could sound again, just as he had done with her.

The Angel of Music asks only for devotion and fidelity, and in turn, he will fill you with song. That's all you will need.

She understood now, why her father had wanted her to wait for an angel – because men were fickle and cruel and lied and died. Then what was left of you after?

Raoul's words had followed her too. *Look what he's done to you.* He was right. Christine didn't recognize herself anymore. Somewhere along the way, all the roles and costumes and music and dreams and lies had made her into a woman she didn't know. All she had known was that she was Erik's. That was all that made sense, because all she had been before him was Stellan Daaé's daughter. What was she without them?

I knew your father, Christine, and this is not the life he would want for you. But what had he wanted? Hadn't he wanted her safe from the world, safe from real love and loss, devoted only to music and the memory of him and nothing else? Her father wanted Christine to truly be that insipid girl who cared only for art – who she had convinced Raoul she was. Christine had hated that part.

It was anger that made Christine rise and cast the violin aside, anger that pushed her out of her room and down the cobblestone street to the church, through the drizzling rain. There were no people visible in the church in the middle of the afternoon on a cold, gray day, and fewer still in the cemetery to the side. Along the low stone walls, green shoots of crocuses had begun to pierce through the cold soil. Christine remembered how, three years ago to the day, she'd watched her father take his last breath and felt like spring would never come again.

The grave was humble, nothing but a headstone tucked towards the back of the churchyard, but still more dignified than the unfortunate souls relegated to rot in the charnel house, their bones piled neatly by the side of the church like so much gothic artwork, their names forgotten. Christine's father's name was carved in cold stone above where he rested in the ground, somewhere below her feet.

She stared at the simple inscription. *Stellan Daaé: beloved father and husband, now with the angels.*

Christine had fought with Doctor Mainville about the burial. Her father would want his final resting place to be in Sweden, his native soil, next to where his wife and son were buried in Upsala. But there had been no money for that – everything they had was to go to the conservatoire and Christine's survival. It was better this way, the doctor had rightly argued, to bury him near their new home in the land where he wanted Christine to thrive. At least here she could visit, stare at the place where his body lay, and wish he could hear her.

She wished so many things.

"Why did you send an angel that I couldn't keep?" Christine asked aloud, her voice so weak and thin no one would guess she could fill the glittering Paris Opera auditorium with sound. "Why did you fill my head with dreams and promises? You made me think that if I was good enough or achieved everything you wanted for me, that it would mean something. But I've done it all and more, and you're still gone. It still *hurts*."

That was the crux of it, wasn't it? Christine thought as a tear trickled down her cheek, mixing with the rain. She had spent so long dreaming and striving because she had been told she had no choice. Her grand career – the dream Erik had moved heaven and earth to make real for her – had been built on the lie that if she reached that pinnacle, there would be some reward or change.

"It was beautiful when I sang for him and you, like you both wanted me to. I was so happy and so proud. But none of the applause mattered, because the music was over and I had to go back to the world without you. Why didn't you tell me it was all so empty? Maybe you didn't know."

Christine laughed softly to herself, bitter and cold as the graves around her. "You never had a whole theater applauding you. The best you could hope for was a crowd at a country fair stopping for a few minutes to smile and throw us some coins. That was enough for you. You should have told me even that was just... temporary."

Christine held back a sob. It was all temporary. All fleeting and impermanent, and no one could change that. There was no immortality at the end of a performance, no life of love with no end after a lover's vow. Her father had made her believe that music was forever, unlike love that would leave her.

"You were wrong." It was a shock to say that aloud, speaking to the ghost that listened from her dreams as rain began to fall. "You taught me all my life that it was music and art that would endure, but they're just dreams too. You lost your love, so you never wanted me to feel that pain. Yet you didn't let me have a world beyond you, so when you left, I had nothing." Christine swallowed, a pit opening inside her. "*I* was nothing."

She recalled the shell she had been for so many years – faithless, hopeless. Nothing more than a trained bird singing the same songs in hopes an angel would finally hear.

"Then you sent me him."

It had been a miracle the night her Angel of Music had appeared. She knew – in her soul she *knew* – it was because of her father that Erik had found her. By some intervention of the divine or the world beyond, Erik had been there at the perfect moment and heard her prayers.

"And then I was his and I was happy – until I lost him. Until I learned he was just a man, not divine. Now, I love that man, and I fear losing him again, just like you. Why would you send me an angel that made it hurt so much more?" She balled her hands into fists.

"You broke me, Papa. You taught me to be afraid, then left me all alone with nothing but foolish dreams you knew would never replace you!" Her voice was rising even as the rain fell harder. "You were so hurt and so afraid. Why couldn't you have taught me to be brave so I didn't have to suffer like you?"

Christine fell to her knees before the gravestone. She wanted to shake it and smash it and scream until some sort of answer came. "You left me alone! And now he's going to do the same! He's going to die, just like you, and what do I do then?" she sobbed, pressing her palm against the unyielding stone. "What do I do now? When he's already just half there?"

No answer came from the marker, this inanimate thing standing in for a father long gone.

"He's just like you – I see it. He's so afraid to lose me that he won't live. And it's killing me. I don't know what's worse: knowing he's going to leave me just like you, or that he's never really even been there. But it hurts so much to love a ghost."

"Would you accept an idiot man instead?"

Christine stumbled as she stood, afraid to turn around. Surely it was some illusion, or she had finally succumbed to madness. It could not be Erik's voice she heard because that was impossible.

"Even if he was late in arriving."

Christine turned and gasped at the sight. Erik stood among the graves, a funeral figure in black with his deathly face covered in his white mask. Nonetheless, he was there, standing in the daylight. Months ago, a ghost had appeared to her out of the darkness, towering and terrible. Now, Erik stood before her in the rain, not in the sunlight, but in the day. Her ghost arising to breathe in this place of the dead. Another miracle.

Christine flew to him, and Erik caught her in his arms, tight and tender and real. "You found me," she whimpered into his sodden cloak as he cradled the back of her head.

"Always," he whispered in reply as she looked up into his eyes. They were a different color in the daylight, with no fires to reflect or shadows to defy. They were muted and so human. His mask was pale in the light too. There was rain dripping from his hat and in his hair, and it was all wondrous, because he had left the darkness for her, just for a moment.

Christine kissed him and held him close when he flinched in shock. It was wrong, perhaps, to kiss him here, on hallowed ground with the light of day upon them, but it was the only thing that felt right. His lips tasted of the rain, and he was warm and alive, right there. She pulled away and looked up at him in awe and love.

"I'm sorry," Erik said. "I'm sorry, for being mortal and a fool. I'm sorry I can't stop time and change the world. For all I didn't say, and—"

"It doesn't matter," Christine protested, even if it wasn't true. "You came. That's all I wanted." She kissed him again, still unsure if it was real.

"I wish I could give you more," Erik sighed in return, nothing but regret in his eyes.

"All I want is this. You here with me," Christine breathed. "All I want is to keep you, as long as I can."

"I will try to stay." Erik's fingers threaded with hers, where she still wore the ring. "I promise."

Shaya's footsteps were slow and defeated as he trekked through the Faubourg. He had been so certain a few days ago that by now Erik would be in chains, but now the key to his undoing had slipped through their fingers and they were all doomed. His only hope now rested with the young aristocrat from whom Erik had taken everything. He found the Chagny manor far less busy than before. The butler who answered the door looked harried and wan, but he escorted Shaya to the parlor, where he found Raoul de Chagny staring grimly at the fire.

"I've been waiting for you," Raoul said before Shaya could speak. "You were right. Adèle confirmed it all."

Shaya shook his head, thinking of the horrors Erik must have inflicted on the poor woman when he discovered she had shared his secrets. "You confronted Christine with this information?" Now it made sense why she had fled.

"Yes, and she..." Shaya watched as the young man waged a small battle with himself. "She made it clear that Erik has manipulated her into... giving her innocence."

"Is that what she told you?"

"She told me how he lied to her. How he abused her and seduced her," Raoul snapped. "He's used his music and all his masks to twist her mind. She doesn't even see reality anymore."

"So, she told you she cares for him," Shaya countered, and Raoul sent him a vicious frown.

"I trust what I see – what I know in my heart – not the lies *he* has made her tell. I see an innocent, naïve soul who was moved by pity and led into... corruption." Raoul looked sick. "Christine thinks there's no hope for herself. She thinks that now she's fallen no one will have her, but I will."

Shaya raised an eyebrow. He did admire the young man's optimism. "You want her? Knowing he's had her—"

"He *took* her," Raoul contradicted. "It's not the same."

Shaya nodded sullenly, remembering the last time he had seen his brother alive and all the lunacy Ramin had spoken then. "You're right. No one would willingly lie with that thing, even if they protest otherwise."

"Exactly. She's been driven to madness by him, but I'm going to save her – her life and her soul. When she is my wife, she will thank me."

"Wife?" Shaya tried not to sound too incredulous.

"I'm going to marry her, and when I do, she'll be pure again." Raoul seemed like he was repeating something he had told himself before. "She'll confess her sins and be absolved, with the right penance."

"Of course," Shaya muttered. "But to save her, you need to find her."

"That is the hard part," Raoul sighed. "It's impossible to get her out of that place with him watching. We've been wracking our brains and—"

"Monsieur, she's already fled," Shaya confessed at last.

Raoul turned to him. "What?"

"I saw her leave the Opera last night and I followed. First to her flat, then to the Saint-Lazare train station." The weight of failure settled on his shoulders again. "That is what I came to tell you. She's left the city and who knows if she will return."

"To where?" Raoul asked in horror. "Tell me you at least saw where she was headed."

"The train she boarded was bound for Brittany. That is all I know." Shaya was surprised to see Raoul's face brighten with hope. "I've tried to find some other clue, but—"

"I know where she's gone!" The pure glee in Raoul's face was concerning. "This is perfect. We can find her there! And bring her home!"

"What if she doesn't want to come?" Shaya asked, but Raoul waved him off as he rushed towards the door. "What if he's there too?"

Raoul spun back to Shaya with a new fire in his eyes that was nearly like delight. "All the better."

"You mean to confront him?" Shaya balked. "Alone?"

"No, we do this together – the three of us!" Raoul crowed, bounding from the parlor towards the stairs. "Antoine! Where the hell is he?"

"You want to involve *him*? He could be—" There was no more time to protest before the man himself emerged at the top of the stairs.

"What were you doing up there?" Raoul demanded. "Never mind. The time has come. We're going to retrieve Christine."

"Are we now? I'll need to stop at home for what we discussed," the taller man said with a smirk.

"What about your elder brother?" Shaya asked. "He'll want to know where you've gone. I know what it is to worry over a brother. You should inform him."

"He doesn't have the stomach for what will need to be done," Antoine replied, and Raoul's dark expression was in agreement. "Do you have the stomach, Persian?"

"What is it you intend to do?" Shaya asked. "I thought you meant to rescue her."

"Christine is not herself – she may resist or try to dissuade us from bringing Erik to justice." Raoul held Antoine's gaze as if repeating what he had been told. "We are simply prepared for that. If we need to hold him, we'll be ready for that too."

"Then we should be going, as soon as possible." Shaya was glad to finally be making a move against Erik, yet there was something off about this, something untoward. Were they walking into a trap? Or was he choosing the wrong allies?

The roiling sea looked as unsettled as Erik felt standing on the bluff overlooking it, even with Christine at his side, her hand in his. The wind and remnants of rain danced around them, wild and cold, and he could taste the salt of the surf on his lips.

"I almost forgot the smell," Erik murmured, amazed at all he had forgotten in his exile below Paris's streets.

Christine smiled, eyes on the horizon. "There are tide pools further down on the beach, the smell is strongest there. I'd beg to go and explore and come home smelling of brine. But this place, right here... this is where Papa liked to bring me. The wind is stronger here. He said it would carry the notes out farther when he played. So the mermaids could hear."

"How often did you come here?" Erik asked, and Christine smiled sadly.

It had been strange and terrible to stand with her next to the grave of the man who, in his strange way, had led Christine to him. Erik was familiar with the way graveyards felt empty and crowded all at the same time – of the strange feeling of exposure with the other ghosts watching one's private grief. So he had asked her, in a weak attempt to guide her toward hope and away from the pain of the past, to take him to some place where she remembered her father at his best. Or at his happiest.

"All the time," Christine answered softly, squeezing Erik's hand. "There's a little knoll down there, hidden from the wind. The first summer we came here, we camped there for a few nights, when it was mild and dry. You could see every star out here when it was night, and we'd have contests of who would see the most falling."

"I can imagine it."

"I came here after the funeral," Christine said. Erik turned to her, ready to argue that this excursion had been meant for better memories. "I stayed until dark, waiting."

"For an angel."

"I felt something though," she whispered. "I just didn't want it to be real because it...didn't match what I had hoped for."

She turned to Erik, meeting his eyes and letting him see the unshed tears in hers. "What was it?"

"I felt him, I think, but I felt him at peace, finally released and going home to Mama. And I didn't want it because it meant that he was truly gone. I wanted him to haunt me. And now..."

"Peace doesn't mean he's gone," Erik argued as a tear escaped down Christine's cheek. "Letting your pain and grief go doesn't mean he dies again. He's part of you. All the ones we love and lose are."

Erik thought back on all the love he had known before Christine – how every single person that had meant something to him was gone or dead, so many of them because of him. He thought of Ramin Motlagh smiling out onto the sea the day he was taken from this life.

"That's why we must hold on to the ones we have as tightly as we can, while they are here," Erik added, squeezing her hand and wishing he could indeed just keep her close forever.

"He spent his whole life after Mama died grieving her and refusing to let her go. I was supposed to do the same for him," Christine went on. "But I don't want that. I don't think he wants that for me anymore either. Or he shouldn't. I don't know."

"It's hard, letting go." Erik pushed the moisture from Christine's cheek with his thumb. "Even for ghosts."

"I think that's what love asks of us: to be brave." Christine echoed his gesture, her hand against the mask. "Are you still scared now?"

"Yes. I've been in terror since last night when I watched you leave," Erik confessed. "But it's been many different sorts since then. Getting on a goddamn train to get here was a unique kind of torture. I preferred the coach I had to take from Rennes."

It was a relief to see Christine smile, then laugh, even if it was at him. "I can't even imagine."

"At least I had this," Erik offered and fished his hand into his cape as Christine looked on in interest. She chuckled again when he produced his alternate mask – bearded and bespectacled, but passable as the face of a 'normal' person if one did not look for too long.

"You actually made it," Christine said. "Do you wear it over this one or on its own?"

"Two masks at once would be more discomfort than even I am prepared to endure for vanity." Erik was surprised to find himself smiling too. How was it so easy with her when they were so exposed and far from home?

"Would you like to put it on, for the walk back to town?" It was a kind question, but it assumed several things that Erik had not considered, and his bewilderment must have shown in his eyes.

"You're coming back to the inn with me. We'll walk in together and it will be fine. Where else would you go?"

"I came to take you home," Erik said. It was obviously the wrong answer. "Do you not want to go?"

"I don't know. Everything back at the Opera is such a mess," Christine sighed.

"Your career is there," Erik protested, and it only served to make her look sadder. "The career you... don't want anymore."

"I wanted it because he told me to." Christine glanced towards the cemetery and the grave Erik had found her berating. "I don't know if it's what I want. If I did, shouldn't it be a career that I earned on my own?"

"You did earn it."

"I know you think that *you* giving it all to me is the same and that I deserve it, but it feels wrong. Empty." She looked as if she were going to weep again. "Can't we just stay here? Forever?"

"You know I can't. We can't." Erik hated the truth of it.

"Then I just want to stay here and be free of it a little longer. Would you let me? Please?" She looked at him with pleading eyes.

"There will be so many people there. If I change masks, someone could see..." Erik stammered, noting that the tips of his fingers had started to go numb in panic.

"Are you scared right now, out here in the day with me? Even all alone?"

"Terrified," Erik nodded. "It hurts less than I thought it would at least. The sun. Thank God for the rain, I guess."

"It's not raining anymore."

Erik glanced to the horizon where a few shards of blue were visible. "Oh."

"Don't you want to feel it? The wind and the sun on your face?" Christine's fingers strayed to the edge of the mask and Erik caught them, his whole body tensing. "It's alright. I'm here."

"I know, but..." There it was: the fear. The fear that kept him a ghost, always halfway out of her grasp. Erik was so tired of it. "Alright."

He braced himself as Christine removed the mask and the fresh air finally touched his desiccated cheeks. He fully smelled the sea with the abbreviated gash he called a nose. His scars smarted as the sun found them, but he kept his focus on Christine's eyes and how bright green the daylight made them.

"There you are," Christine breathed and pressed a gentle kiss to his withered lips.

Maybe it was the retreat of her shadow. Maybe it was that moment that the sun chose to break through the clouds. Either way, when Christine pulled back, the full light of day hit Erik at last, searing his eyes with brightness as it warmed his skin. Erik fought to open his eyes, to experience the light of the sun for the first time in over six and half years and it hurt. But not when he looked at her instead; this angel who was brave enough to look at him in the light.

"You are the greatest of fools if you think you are nothing without me or your father, Christine Daaé. You are strong and brave and good and kind and so many wondrous things. You need to know that."

"Thank you," she said, eyes unreadable as the sun dipped once more behind a cloud. Even the brightest light didn't last.

With a nod, Erik replaced his old mask with the new one, grateful for Christine's smile as he did, and the reassurance of her hand in his as they turned away from the bluff and made their way back into the town. Christine spoke softly to him as they walked the old cobblestone streets, of her memories of the village and her happier days there. Erik kept his head low, inclined towards hers. For a few minutes, they were nothing more than a normal couple strolling the streets.

His anxiety flared again as they reached the inn. The woman at the front gave Christine a curious look, but Erik's beloved only smiled.

"I'm sorry if I failed to tell you my husband would be joining me. It must have slipped my mind after arriving so late. I hope you don't mind." Erik would be the worst of liars if he were to claim that hearing Christine call him 'husband' didn't make his heart burst with joy and pride. It was a dream of course, but a beautiful one, just like all of this. "Please send up supper in an hour or so."

Erik kept his head low as Christine guided him up the stairs and unlocked her humble room. It was so normal and welcoming. He drifted to the window as Christine stoked the fire, watching as the sun sank towards the sea, painting the sky purple and pink. When was the last time he had watched a sunset? He didn't even know.

"Beautiful," Erik mused as the sky entranced him.

"I still can't believe you're here." He turned to see Christine staring, as awestruck as she had been in the cemetery.

"I know it's rather out of character, but you know how I react when I'm told I can't or shouldn't do something," Erik replied with a shrug.

"Ever the rebel," she sighed, taking off the cloak he had given her. "You can take that off. It feels like talking to a stranger."

"That means it's working." Erik obeyed and unhooked the new mask from behind his ears. Christine helped him remove his hat and cloak.

It made his heart pound to be so exposed in an unfamiliar place, even with her hands reassuring against his chest. All of a sudden, the rashness of what he had done in coming here filled Erik's mind and it was hard to breathe.

"Are you cold? You're shaking," Christine asked softly, bestowing soothing strokes on his shoulders and face as he shook his head in the negative.

"I don't know what to do – up here in your world," Erik confessed, trying and failing to stem his rising panic. "I'm rather overwhelmed."

"Do what I do then: play the part."

"What part is that?" Erik grasped her hips, desperate for something solid and familiar amid so much newness and change. She continued to touch him, gentle and steady.

"Didn't you hear? You're my husband," she breathed, and Erik's heart leapt. "You've come to join me after a long journey. You've missed me."

"I have," he murmured as she pulled him down into a kiss. It was like falling into a dream, the feel of her soft lips on his once more mixed with the teasing flicks of her tongue. "I have missed you so much. My..." His voice caught on tears. "My wife."

"We're here now, together," Christine went on, her fingers straying to his collar, causing him to tense again, but she kept kissing him, her mouth chasing away all thoughts but her. She kissed down his neck, bold and sure. "And we'll wake together at dawn."

"We'll go home to our lovely flat above ground," Erik whispered back, drunk on the heat of her lips. "Where I keep you amused in the evenings. Shall I take you out on Sunday?"

"To see the first blooms at the Bois." He could hear the emotion in her voice too as they dreamed. "But first, let me see you, so you can make love to me."

He didn't fight as she undressed him, carefully removing the layers of clothes that served as his armor. He was too in awe, too in love. She kissed the scars on his bare chest and caressed the still-raw wound on his side from the knife he had taken for her. He'd take a thousand more stabbings and fires just to keep feeling the touch of her hand on his horrid skin. Or the pressure of her body against his rising desire.

"Now help me with this." She meant the fastenings of her simple blue dress, but even so, Erik's hands trembled as he undid the buttons and hooks. The sunset outside the window turned the whole room to gold as he exposed her skin, inch by inch. "You're so beautiful," he sighed aloud when the last undergarment joined the pile at her feet.

And she was. Christine's skin was like rose petals in the sunset light, all of it bare to Erik's starving eyes. Her round, perfect breasts and rigid nipples; the soft curves of her belly and hips and thighs. It all called to him, and he was being pulled by her tide when he embraced her. He needed to feel as well as see, taste the way the fading daylight made her warm. He lifted her to the bed, falling upon her with his hands and mouth once they were safe on the mattress. He took a nipple between his lips, suckling as she writhed in pleasure beneath him.

"Erik," she breathed. "My Erik."

It did something, to hear her call his name in this heady dream. Despite everything, this woman wanted him. Loved *him*. How it was possible, he still did not know, but he would rejoice in it.

He parted her thighs and took his honored place between them, kissing up her chest and claiming her mouth again as he did. She was so wet when his fingers found her, and her body arched to chase his touch as he stroked her open. She wanted and needed him, this wonder, this goddess. He could never be enough, but he would be damned if he didn't try to serve her even so.

"I love you," he gasped as he embraced her and filled her. She groaned her response, wrapping her legs and arms around him as he began to move inside her. She was hot and slick and close around him, her entire perfect body welcoming him and begging for more.

Still he began slow, drawing out the incandescent pleasure inch by inch, losing himself in the music of her sighs and the perfect heat at her core.

"Yes," Christine whimpered. "Erik. *Yes*. Just like that."

"Keep saying it," he begged in return, drunk on their ecstasy. "Keep saying my name."

"Erik." The name broke through her moans, and it spurred him on. He thrust harder and deeper, gaining speed as Christine hung onto him. "Erik, I—"

He caught her scream in a kiss as she came, her nails digging into his flesh as her body convulsed. He savored it for a fleeting second before he followed, his pleasure rising to a maddening peak as he lost himself in her. He was free and whole as he poured into her, and she sang out his name one more time. Perfect and sublime.

"*Erik.*"

Reality came back into focus slowly as he stared down at his lover's glorious face on the pillow beneath him. The last rays of the sunset were fading, and the shadows were returning to steal the vision of her away once again. For the first time in years, he hated the darkness.

"Will you do something for me, tonight?" Christine murmured, sweeping a hair from his face.

"Anything," Erik replied instantly, even if it wasn't true. "If it is within my power."

"I just want him to hear you play. I have his violin and I..." Erik kissed her forehead before more tears could come to her eyes.

"*The Resurrection of Lazarus*?" he asked by way of reply, and Christine nodded. "Of course."

Erik wished more than anything that he could do more than play for her departed father at his grave. He wished he was brave enough to walk with her in the daylight world. Would that he could play himself to a real resurrection, not this temporary reprieve. But he could still only summon ghosts.

R aoul had never liked train rides; they were loud and shaky. At least the first-class cabin was somewhat comfortable. He didn't want to think what the Persian was enduring in the inferior accommodations in the back. It hadn't just been appropriate for them to separate, it had given Raoul and Antoine ample time to discuss the different options for what they were about to do before the older man fell asleep.

Raoul didn't know how Antoine could sleep at a time like this, but finally, the train screeched to a halt at the Perros station. Raoul kicked his coconspirator in the ankles to wake him.

"We're here," Raoul said as Antoine yawned and stretched languidly.

"So I gathered. Did you sleep at all?" he asked, annoyingly relaxed.

"I had too much to think about," Raoul grumbled in reply. He wasn't sure if he'd ever sleep again after the last few days. He'd stolen a few hours, but every time dreams took him, he was tortured by visions of *them* – of Christine being ravaged and defiled by that monster. The only thing that kept him from going mad was the knowledge that soon he would be the one to hold Christine. Soon, she would be his, and it would be the monster who spent his remaining nights tortured by the idea of his beloved in another man's bed.

Antoine grunted as he took down his bag and handed another valise to Raoul. "God, these things are heavy."

"Stop whining and move," Raoul huffed. "I still want to know why you had all of this."

"No, you don't," Antoine replied with a sneer that made Raoul's skin crawl. They spotted Motlagh waiting on the platform, and Raoul did not break his pace to greet the man. They were so close he could feel it. Did soldiers feel like this going into battle? Tense and tight and strangely excited.

"Where are we going?" Motlagh asked as they left the station.

"There's only one inn. Unless she's taken a room with that doctor they used to live with, she'll be there," Raoul declared. "We'll start there. It's not far."

"You still haven't told me what you mean to do when you find her," the Persian demanded. Raoul quickened his pace and Antoine snickered. "Are you armed at least, in case he is here?"

"Very much so," Antoine answered. "Though of course we hope it will not come to pistols."

"Are you?" Raoul asked, and the Persian nodded. Raoul felt the weight of the gun in the inner pocket of his heavy coat and the bullets in the other. How his finger itched for the trigger.

"I still hope he's not beat us here, but if he has, we must be prepared," Motlagh said. "He is more dangerous, now that he knows what you know. After what he did to Valerius..."

Raoul's stride faltered, nearly tripping as he looked back at Antoine. "Valerius?"

"Did you not hear? She was beaten." The Persian looked sharply between the two. "I... assumed Erik found out that she revealed Christine's secrets. And took revenge."

"You – you think he would do that?" Raoul stammered and turned away. It would be much better if Motlagh thought it was Erik and not Antoine who had abused Valerius.

"Adèle didn't receive anything she hadn't begged for in the past," Antoine drawled, securing a look of horror from Shaya. "I'm sure."

"Erik is capable of anything," Raoul grunted as they turned onto the main street of Perros-Guirec. It had been over six years since he had set foot there. Six years since Erik had taken his father at the height of summer and Raoul had been summoned away, just days after Christine had been torn from him. He would not let it happen again.

"That is why I would like to know what you intend to do if we find him with her already," Motlagh demanded.

Antoine snickered. "You're not in charge here, Monsieur. You're just extra muscle."

"I had two men with me when I tried to take him before, and they were both dead within half a minute when we confronted him," the Persian said.

"We really don't care about your failures, old chap. Just do as you're told, and it will be easy," Antoine replied. Motlagh didn't seem to like that, but Raoul didn't care. They had reached the Inn of the Setting Sun.

"Stay here. I'll ask after her inside." Raoul did not wait for his companion's assent. The woman tending the table in the common room looked up in interest when Raoul entered and approached.

"I'm looking for a woman who may be staying here, a dear friend," Raoul began, fumbling for something that was not too far from the truth. "She's about this tall, with green eyes and dark hair. Pretty in a dark sort of way. Her name is Christine. Christine Daaé. She's travelling alone."

"There was a woman who came in late last night," the innkeeper answered slowly. "I don't recall her name. But she's not alone. Her husband joined her today."

Raoul's heart leapt to his throat. "Are they... Is she here now?"

If he caught the monster in the act of defiling her, Raoul would kill him. He would strangle the fiend with his bare hands, and no court on earth would convict him for the death. He blinked the vision away to see the innkeeper shaking her head.

"Where have they gone?" Raoul pressed. The woman looked hesitant, so Raoul seized her by the arms and shook her. "It is essential I find them! My friend – that's not her husband. She's in terrible danger!"

"They left just before you arrived! I think they went towards the church," the woman stammered. Raoul's excitement surged again as he rushed from the inn to find Antoine and the Persian staring icily at one another.

"We have to be quick! I know where they are!" Raoul cried as he ran, fumbling with the valise in his hand for the materials he was so worried he might need. "She's gone to the graveyard."

"You're not going to kill him in a house of God, are you?" Shaya asked. Raoul shook his head grimly, thinking back to his dreams and the constant vision of a corpse taking Christine's maidenhead against her will.

"I assure you, *Monsieur le Perse*, he will not die," Raoul muttered. "He deserves far more suffering."

It was different to be in the churchyard at night, Christine mused. Eerier and darker, of course, but beautiful in its own way. The light from the ever-burning candles in the church and the waxing moon above allowed them to see, and Erik held her hand as they made their way through the humble gravestones.

"Are you sure about this?" Erik asked.

"I need it," Christine whispered back. "I need him to hear you and know you. I need to feel him and say farewell."

Erik sighed beside her. It was a strange way to reconcile the lover she had killed for with the father whose death had destroyed her. They were not the same, her angel and the man who had promised him. But one could help her say goodbye to the other, and perhaps, let her soul be free. Free to do what, she did not know, but free, nonetheless.

"Thank you, if I didn't say it already," Christine added, lifting Erik's hand and kissing his knuckles. She met his shining, worried eyes as she did.

"I've never been so nervous before a performance," Erik murmured as they came to the grave where she had wept and protested that afternoon in the rain. Now, it was clear and silent and calm. "Are you sure no one will hear?"

"If they do, they will think it is a ghost."

Erik smiled weakly at the edge of his mask. "They won't be entirely wrong."

Christine could tell how tense he was to be out in the world again, even after all her reassurances. How could she convince him she would keep him safe? That was for another night perhaps.

She knelt before her father's grave, silently begging for forgiveness and a blessing. Erik stood behind the stone and lifted the violin to his chin below the mask and began to play, the lilting notes of the violin calling Lazarus up from his grave.

She had known the old Romani air since before she could speak. It had always been her father's favorite, this secret, magical song of The People. He had played it in his darkest moments, bringing his soul back from the brink of despair. Erik had played it for her when he was an angel hidden behind her mirror and made her feel that tenuous connection to the father she had lost. Now, he played above the place Stellan Daaé rested forever, and Christine could do nothing but weep.

It was pure beauty, this music. Pure love and hope ringing out through the cool March night under the moon. Christine felt the pull at her heart, the echo of an embrace, and the unmistakable swell of pride mixed with contrition. He had been wrong in so many ways, her father, to hold her too close and keep her wrapped in his despair and dreams. But he had loved her, and she sensed that love now as Erik played to the heavens.

Too soon it was over, and Christine was left looking up into Erik's masked face in the moonlight. She could see tears glistening in his golden eyes. She wished so dearly that he had not hidden his face for this, but there was only so much she could ask of him today. Even so, she wanted to ask more. She wanted to beg. He had told her there was nothing he would refuse her. If she asked him to stay here above, maybe he would...

"Erik, I—" she began as he reached out his hand to help her up.

"Get away from her!" A voice rang out through the dark. Christine turned in terror to see Raoul racing through the gravestones, face twisted with rage and a gun in his hand.

"No!" Christine screamed, rising on instinct to block Raoul's aim. "Please, no!"

"Out of the way!" Raoul cried as Christine threw herself at him, desperate to keep Erik safe. Raoul seized her and cast her to the ground. The sound of the gunshot hammered against her ears, rendering her deaf to her own screams as Erik dropped her father's violin and gripped his arm.

"Erik!" she cried as she struggled to stand, and Raoul grabbed her again with a grip like iron.

"Now!" Raoul cried in turn. Her relief at Raoul's failed shot evaporated as Christine saw Shaya Motlagh rushing towards Erik, gun aimed, and from the other side, Antoine de Martiniac. Erik moved to charge at Antoine, and the man aimed his own pistol. Not at Erik, but at her.

"Fight and she will suffer, monster!" Antoine yelled.

Erik froze. His petrified eyes locked with Christine's as pure terror filled every particle of her being. Raoul would not hurt her, but Antoine would, and Erik knew it.

"Christine..." Erik lamented, and the men seized him.

"Let him live and I will go with you!" Christine cried with all her strength and watched Erik crumble to his knees, eyes wild as he reached for her. "Please! Take me! Don't hurt him!" she screamed as she struggled to run. Raoul held her back.

"Christine, you need to calm down!" Raoul bellowed, but she saw that Antoine had something in his hand now that he was raising to use for a blow. Chains. Horrible, heavy *chains*.

Erik collapsed as Antoine brought the iron down on the back of his head, his mask falling to the ground beside the violin.

Christine screamed again, knowing what they meant to do; knowing that Erik would wake in a nightmare because of her. She screamed, piercing and raw, the sound echoing off the church walls and charnel house just as the notes of her father's violin had moments before. She screamed because it was her fault and now Erik would never trust the world above again. They were doomed entirely.

"Christine, stop!" she heard Raoul beg as he shook her. He placed his hand over her mouth to stifle her cries and her very breath. Suddenly, she was falling, collapsing into his grasp as the sweet smell of his hand filled her nose. Her strength was gone, and the world was fading to black.

Suddenly, there was nothing.

10. Shackles

Shaya could not help but smile at the sight of Erik, unconscious, in chains. The last time he had caught the creature in a seaside town with a stolen love, it had been Ramin's body that had ended up on the ground. Now, Erik was the one bleeding and defeated.

"I'll see you soon, old friend." Shaya ascended the steps of the crypt and into the church proper. The sight he found there was less alluring: Raoul de Chagny kneeling over Christine Daaé's unconscious form, caressing her face and straightening a few errant hairs.

"Antoine's getting the carriage. I'll need your help to move her," Raoul said as Shaya approached and grimaced. It had been one thing to help de Martiniac drag Erik's limp body from the graveyard into their makeshift dungeon, but it was quite another to transport an insensible woman.

"It was lucky for us that she fainted when she did," Shaya muttered.

"It was a blessing. Hopefully, she will sleep all the way home," Raoul replied, distracted. "She'll be relieved to wake up somewhere safe. Somewhere we can reason with her."

"Do you think you can?" Shaya asked darkly. "What I saw in the graveyard was a woman willing to do anything for a man she—"

"A man who has manipulated her, lied to her, and twisted her mind into thinking she—" Now Raoul looked ill. "She is simply a kind woman. She took pity on a deformed animal, and he used that to ruin her. Now she's safe."

"I hope you are right," Shaya said, eyes on the girl.

"Of course he's right. We have the fiend in chains – what could go wrong?" Antoine cut in, smirking as he sauntered down the aisle.

"Many things," Shaya warned with a sigh. "Don't invite a curse with overconfidence."

"Were you successful?" Raoul asked.

Antoine snickered. "You'll owe the carriage driver about a thousand francs when we get to the city, but we have our transport. Well, you two do. Or three, I guess."

"I thought I was to be the one to guard him?" Shaya demanded, suspicious.

"We thought it best that I be the one to stay behind as a guard," Antoine answered with a smirk. "All offense intended, I don't trust you with him."

"We'd like him alive, and you might not keep him that way," Raoul added.

"I've allowed him to live for three years," Shaya replied darkly.

"You've failed at apprehending him, you mean," Antoine drawled. "Now that we've captured him for you, who's to say you won't take your revenge before we can have ours?"

"He killed your *father*," Shaya snarled in reply. "You might feel the same."

"I never liked the man much." Antoine shrugged and Shaya turned to see if Raoul had any reaction. The young man was still intent on Christine's unconscious form.

"It's decided. Let's get her to the carriage," Raoul ordered, and Antoine moved to help. "No. I'll do it myself. You go tell the driver to have a smoke or a piss before we get going so he doesn't ask questions."

"Yes, *Monsieur le Vicomte*," Antoine sneered and strode from the deserted church.

"You trust him with Erik, but you don't want him touching her?" Shaya asked as he watched Raoul muddle through the unwieldy task of lifting a full-grown woman into his arms to spirit away.

"She's been defiled enough." Raoul touched Christine's pale face as they carried her. She made a soft sound as he did, brows furrowing, and Raoul caught his breath.

"Erik..." The name sighed from Christine's lips, and Raoul's face hardened.

"He haunts her even in her nightmares," Raoul declared.

Shaya's gut writhed. Christine had been ready to dive in front of a bullet for Erik, from what Shaya had seen. She had screamed for him, and it reminded Shaya so powerfully of the terrible moment years before. He remembered the bullet that had pierced Ramin's chest and the way he had fallen to the ground. Maybe Antoine was right, and he shouldn't be near Erik.

Raoul placed Christine with an exhausted huff. Shaya noted how the young man took care to make her comfortable even as she tried to stir, whimpering as she did. The young man took a handkerchief from his pocket to wipe her face, with curious care paid to her mouth and nose, and it seemed to calm her. It did the exact opposite to Shaya as he watched Raoul pocket the cloth.

"Wait here and watch her," Raoul ordered as he left the carriage. "I want to see him before we leave."

"Don't do anything rash," Shaya warned. "If he's awake, try not to let him rile you up or get into your head. His words are poison."

"Nothing he can say matters now that she's with us. Tell Antoine where to find me."

Shaya watched as the young man walked into the night. He comforted himself with the thought that, soon, they would be headed back to Paris to enlist the help of the managers and the police. Soon, it would all be over at last. Erik would never walk free again.

It was difficult for Erik to tell the difference between the pain throbbing at the back of his head, the searing pain on his right arm, and the general ache from his bruised ribs. It all hurt, but so did his position, with his arms pulled back and upwards. The pain that had awoken him, Erik realized, was that of his arms being hoisted up with cold shackles closed around his wrists. Because he had been taken. And Christine was theirs.

He forced his eyes open, his vision blurred at first as he took in his surroundings, watching two dim shadows move away from him. There were skulls in piles in one corner of the dark room, and a stack of what had to be coffins along the opposite wall. The damp, derelict smell was familiar, as was the uncomfortable sense of being where the living were not welcome. They were in a crypt, somewhere below the church in Perros.

Erik winced as he tried to move, the cruel angle of his arms aggravating where the bullet had grazed him. The wince in turn made the wound on his head smart. He could feel where it was tender and his hair was matted with blood. Perfect.

"It's even uglier when it moves," a voice Erik was beginning to know drawled. He forced himself to turn to his captors and open his bleary eyes. His erstwhile half-brother looked extremely smug, which was understandable, but the boy appeared utterly sickened to have Erik in his sights. Good.

"Where is Christine?" Erik asked as the two came closer to the pool of light cast by some candle or lantern above him that he couldn't see.

"She's safe. Recovering," the boy snapped, and Erik ground his teeth. Christine had offered herself in panic to save him, once again forced to be the sacrificial lamb. She had to hate all of them at this point. "Far away from you."

"Did you have to aim more guns at her?" Erik demanded, forcing himself to look directly at the boy. Let him take in the full horror of his face. Let him tremble at the fire in the Phantom's eyes. "Is she in chains too?"

"She's finally free," the boy countered. It occurred to Erik that, after months of mutual hatred, this was the first time he and the little welp had actually exchanged words.

"And very relieved to be so." It was de Martiniac who said it, provoking a sneer from Erik. He noted how only the boy cringed.

"I'm going to kill both of you. I think you are aware of that. But how it happens will be up to you. If you harm her in any way, I will make it slow and more painful than you can imagine."

"We are not the ones who hurt her," the boy seethed, baring his teeth as he advanced. "And I do not think you are in any position to be making threats, monster."

"These won't hold me forever," Erik smirked back, testing the strength of his chains. As he did, the boy, unfortunately, smiled.

"They don't have to. By this time tomorrow, you'll be in a real cell, in a jail, where you belong." The boy's smile broadened, and Erik fought a shiver. "Surrounded by guards, all of them looking at your hideous face. I gather you don't like cages."

"Then you'll be tried, convicted, and guillotined for your crimes," Antoine went on, cool and smug, but there was something more in his eyes. "Or perhaps, we'll be merciful – come visit you in your cell and help arrange your suicide. Either way, I'm sure there will be some doctors out there who'll want to study you. Preserve that awful visage in a jar for crowds to enjoy forever."

Erik missed his mask and how it would have made it easy to hide his emotions at that threat. As it was, he had to force his jaw not to clench, his eyes not to widen, his core not to shudder. His own brother was describing his worst nightmare, and he could not allow him to know how it terrified him. Defiance was all he had left.

"Christine will never allow that. She just saved me again. She won't let me die."

"She will be the first to testify against you, once her mind is clear," the boy said in triumph, and Erik made himself laugh. "And she will do it as my wife."

"You'll make your wife tell Paris all the things she and I did then?" Erik mocked. "Things I think *you* could not imagine, boy. Didn't you hear her say it? How she was mine in every way? Right under your nose—" Erik was able to brace himself for the kick the boy delivered to his ribs. The pain was worth it.

"Don't speak that way of her," the boy snarled, kneeling close and peering at his rival. "I know you forced her. Look at you. I've never seen anything more hideous and disgusting. The idea that any woman would touch you of her own free will is insane. She *thanked me* for saving her."

"It was touching to watch," Antoine added.

"Liar." Erik cast the man a glare. They were lying. Christine was somewhere above, worried sick and trusting that Erik would find a way out of this. He would find a way to take her home so they would never have to face this awful world again. After his revenge.

"She wept when we got her away, knowing she was free at last and that you were in chains," the boy mocked.

"I will never believe that," Erik hissed even as the image of it bored into his brain. "She loves me."

"No soul on earth could love you," the boy spat back, and Erik stiffened his spine. It was impossible to believe that he was loved, yes, but he would not let go of the miracle. He would trust her. He had to.

"Ask the Daroga if that's true. He'll have quite the tale to tell," Erik replied. "Is he watching her now, wherever you've hidden her away?"

"She's recovering, and happy to be rid of the vows you forced her to swear." With a gleeful flourish, the boy reached into his pocket and pulled out... Christine's ring. "She cast this thing off like a curse the first second she could."

"Liar," Erik repeated, even as the sight of the gold band glinting dimly in the light made his insides twist. The boy threw the treasure into the dusty shadows. "I'll give it back to her with your apologies when I see her again."

"I do admire his confidence," Antoine drawled.

The boy gave him his compatriot glare. "It's insanity. Delusion."

Erik's hate for the boy and the world and way of things he represented surged through him so powerfully that he nearly wretched. He had been so wrong to come above – such a fool. But they all would pay for reminding him that the living world was cursed.

"Perhaps," Antoine replied. "It is fascinating to consider how living with a face like that and living underground like some sort of mole or insect has twisted his mind."

"You know, Monsieur, we have not been formally introduced," Erik sneered, ignoring the furious boy in front of him in favor of speaking to his closest blood kin directly for the first time in his life. "Whom has this young idiot doomed along with himself?"

"Just another grieved son left fatherless because of you." Antoine gave an aloof shrug that Erik would have been proud of. They were related. "We'll be fast friends soon."

"If he tries to move or escape, break his hands," the boy ordered as he rose and met Antoine's eyes. "We'll return with every gendarme and commissary in Paris. The next time I see you, Erik, I'll be watching them put you in a cage where you belong."

"The next time we meet, my face will be the last thing you ever see, Monsieur de Chagny," Erik snarled. "I can't wait to have my hands around that pretty neck of yours. I'll watch the light fade from your eyes, and it will be beautiful when I send you to join your useless father."

The blow was more forceful than Erik had anticipated from such a soft, young thing, sending his head crashing back against whatever crypt he'd been chained to. It made him dizzy, along with the loss of blood. He couldn't focus on the sight of the boy walking away. He couldn't see anything, and maybe that was for the best. He would let the darkness swallow him now and find Christine in their dreams.

C hristine could not see because her eyes were too heavy to open. Why did she need to open them? She was warm and still so tired, and strong arms were holding her tight. All she could do was listen to the distant sounds of creaking and low rumbles, as if she were near a road. She could feel it too. She could feel the world moving, rocking her aching body. She could feel the angle of her neck. It hurt. Her corset was too tight with her body positioned this way. Why was she sleeping in it? When had she fallen asleep? Why had Erik left her dressed?

Erik.

Christine jumped, her eyes opening to searing light and her stomach lurching as she did. "Erik! Where is—" She gasped when the man beside her caught his in her arms. The man who was not Erik.

"He's gone!" Raoul smiled. Christine's heart shattered at the sight of him.

"What's going on?" she gritted out, trying to understand her surroundings. A carriage? With Shaya Motlagh across from them. "Where are we?"

"You're safe now. You've slept a good long while, poor thing," Raoul cooed.

Christine gripped her head, forcing herself to remember. The cemetery. *The Resurrection of Lazarus*. Raoul rushing in and firing at Erik as she screamed. Erik seized. All of it her fault.

"Where is he?" Christine demanded, looking frantically between Raoul and Shaya. "If he's hurt—"

"He's contained." It was Shaya who answered, soothing her like a wild creature. Christine recalled the sight of chains and heaved a sob. "He can't hurt anyone anymore. We're going to send the police, and then you can breathe easy."

"Let him go, please," Christine begged as tears welled in her eyes at the thought of Erik captive again. "You can't put him in jail. It will kill him!"

"We're going to bring him to justice, not kill him." Raoul tried once again to take Christine by the shoulders and she batted him away.

"What justice is that?" Christine spat. "For what?"

"Murder, Christine," Raoul said slowly, as if talking to a child. "The murder of my father, and Antoine's. And all the others he killed in that fire."

"No! He didn't mean to! He was trying to get away," Christine stammered.

"I know he's told you all sorts of lies and made his excuses." Raoul reached for her again. In the confines of the carriage there was nowhere she could retreat as he petted her hair and face. "There will be a trial. The truth will come out there."

Christine shook her head at the terrible thought of Erik in a public courtroom with onlookers jeering and gawking. "No. You *can't*."

"We have witnesses. Antoine was there! He saw him and knows everything that happened." How could he sound so optimistic and joyful about such a thing? "He'll testify."

"So Erik's life will rest on the word of a man who raped my friend? While you cowered in a corner!" Christine looked to Shaya, whose face had gone slack. "Did they neglect to mention that?"

"There was also Buquet," Shaya replied quietly.

"Erik did not kill Buquet!" Christine barked. The two men looked at her as if she had gone entirely mad. "I did."

The relief of saying it aloud at last was washed away by the pitying look Raoul gave her. "Did he make you think that? That his crime was your fault? Oh, my dear Christine..."

"Buquet came at Erik with a gun. I tried to stop him, just like last night," Christine went on, the visceral terror still resonating in her bones. "But we were on the catwalks, and he had a rope around his neck, and—"

"A rope Erik put there?" Shaya asked calmly.

"Erik is the one responsible for all of it," Raoul pushed on, as Christine shook her head. She was going to be sick, but she had to get out first.

"Let me out, wherever we are – let me out!" Christine yelled, throwing herself towards the door only to see the streets of Paris out the window. It was past dawn. "Dear God, how long was I—"

"You were exhausted, obviously," Raoul protested, taking her once again by the arms and holding her back, firm enough that she knew she would not be making a dramatic escape. "Don't be hysterical. I know it's hard to believe it's over, but it is!"

"I told you I would come with you if you let him go," Christine wept. "Just let him go."

"He will kill us all if we do that," Raoul argued as he again pulled her to his chest. "This is the only way for us to start our life."

"We have no life." Christine tried to push him away only to see her right hand was bare of the ring Erik had given her. Yesterday, she had held Erik in the sun and thought there was a chance for them. Now, it was all gone.

"You'll feel better when you've had more time to rest," Raoul admonished. "Here we are, finally home."

The carriage jolted to a stop. Christine fought the urge to be sick again as Raoul opened the door with a grin. She began to shiver, realizing they had taken Erik's cloak from her too. She had no scrap of him left. "You left my home in Perros, in chains," Christine murmured.

Raoul's sweet countenance finally darkened. "And if you wish him to remain in chains and not in the ground, you will come inside and try to be calm."

Christine did not resist as Raoul rushed her from the carriage and through a side door. Shaya followed as she was led up the stairs and into a finely appointed room that had to be Raoul's. Disconcertingly, there were bars across the windows outside.

"Those were installed yesterday. He's been here, spying on me. I had to be safe," Raoul explained. "Now you'll be safe too."

"I'm not staying here!" Christine balked. "Adèle needs me. Let me go home!"

"You're safer here for now, while your mind clears. I'll sleep elsewhere, I assure you. You can go home once the monster is fully in custody," Raoul declared as if she hadn't spoken, and Christine wanted to start screaming again. If she did, they'd just send for a doctor to drug her out of her hysteria, she was certain.

"How do you intend to explain my presence to your family?"

"They will understand, and so will you. You just need to rest and think," Raoul repeated. "I'll be back soon. I'll send up some food and have Sabine get you clean clothes. Just rest."

Before Christine could berate him again, Raoul swept out of the room, and she heard the lock click behind him. She was alone, helpless and defeated. She fell to the ground weeping again.

"Please," she whispered, clasping her hands to her chest and looking up through the impenetrable bars to the gray sky. There was no resort left now but prayer. "Please, God, Father, angels... Please help us. Please help him. Please."

No one would guess from the spring in Raoul's step the sort of adventures and trials he had endured in recent days. Perhaps it was due to the rest he had enjoyed on the carriage ride from Perros. Perhaps it was the morning air that carried a hint of spring's warmth. No matter the reason, Raoul was happier than he had been in weeks.

Yes, it was true that his poor Christine still needed time to unbind her soul from Erik's, but she was already seeing things clearer. In fact, he would go to the Madeleine next and find a priest familiar with the Opera denizens to see if he would take Christine's confession soon and offer her absolution. But first, he had a more important errand.

"Would you slow down," came the voice of the Persian from behind Raoul. He froze in his stride then turned.

"I'm sorry – I forgot you were there," Raoul confessed, half-honest (he had forgotten but he wasn't sorry). "I can manage talking to Richard on my own, thank you."

"I have questions for you." Motlagh looked dourer than the occasion demanded. "Such as: what did you use to make Christine so conveniently insensible for the journey and her rescue?"

Raoul frowned and avoided the eyes of the olive-skinned man, knowing they were full of judgment. "It was Antoine's idea."

"To drug her? Why on earth did he even have such chemicals?" the Persian hooted, and Raoul continued to look away.

"He said something about winning a bet with a surgeon. I didn't press the matter." Raoul was simply glad the plan had worked.

"Christine is right," Shaya sighed. "This is a dangerous man to trust with testifying or bringing Erik to justice."

"Antoine is nothing more than a means to an end," Raoul scoffed, waving Shaya off as he began to walk again.

"Like Adèle Valerius was?" Motlagh asked, not moving. Raoul paused, his back to the other man.

"Are you feeling some sort of guilt about how that lying slut was treated?" Raoul didn't recognize his own voice. "Were it not for the information *you* encouraged us to procure from her, I might be on the way to the North Pole right now. Imagine."

"And what does your brother think about such things?"

Raoul began moving again. "Philippe is weak, soft. He'll be grateful for the result when this is done."

"Is that why you're avoiding him?" There was mockery in the Persian's voice as it followed Raoul. "What about your sister?"

"Go home, Motlagh," Raoul spat over his shoulder. "To whatever empty hearth you warm yourself at. Prostrate yourself on your little rug, say your prayers, and prepare yourself. We'll need you well-rested when we bring the monster back."

There was silence behind Raoul, and he hoped that meant he was no longer being followed. He did not turn around to look for a while, not wanting to give the man any sort of satisfaction. Luckily when he did, the avenue was empty behind him. Raoul still quickened his pace, eager to move things along.

He had never visited Firmin Richard's home in the Faubourg, but he knew the address. It was humble, compared to the Chagny estate, but passable. The servant who answered the door when Raoul rang looked sleepy and annoyed at such an early caller.

"I must speak to Monsieur Richard immediately," Raoul said before the man could open his mouth. "Tell him it is the Vicomte de Chagny, here on a matter of life and death."

Raoul spent the tortuous minutes waiting in Richard's parlor rehearsing his words in his head. He needed Richard to go with him to the police – otherwise, no one would believe the fantastic story. Without someone to corroborate the tales of the Opera's 'hauntings' Raoul would sound like a madman, especially when he explained he had a man chained in a church crypt leagues away.

"Did you find our ghost?"

Raoul spun to face Richard, whose countenance was grim (even more so than usual). "Better. We caught him in the wild and we're holding him. We just need a force of some kind to bring him back to be jailed and stand trial."

"And you expect me to procure this force for you?" Richard asked back with a sigh.

"It's essential."

The man did not seem convinced. "What about my lead soprano? What have you done with her? She has a performance tomorrow, and I refuse to cancel it. No matter how much I'd like to fire the little baggage."

Raoul had not thought about that. "She's... recovering. It's been an ordeal."

"I'm sure," Richard sneered. "But unless you can assure me that she will sing *Faust* tomorrow, I don't know about helping you. Can't you just kill the thing and end all our miseries?"

"Death is too good for him," Raoul countered. "I assure you – she will sing. Will you come with me to the police?"

"When the hour is decent and I have seen Mademoiselle Daaé. To make my own assurances," Richard answered with a scowl as Raoul groaned. "Do not mistake me, Monsieur, I am glad to hear you have captured the creature, but I have important business to see to."

"What interests could possibly be more important than sending the criminal that has tormented your Opera for years to jail?" Raoul cried, and Richard rolled his eyes.

"You'll understand when you're older and you aren't living off a hoard of money that your ancestors stole for you."

Raoul opened his mouth to protest but Richard raised a hand. "I will see you and Mademoiselle Daaé in a few hours. I'm sure you can wait that long. It's not as if your prey is going anywhere, is he?"

At that Raoul smiled and let out a breath. "You're right. It won't hurt to let him linger in pain for a while. Waiting for the blow to fall, knowing that Christine is out of his reach. I'm sure it's torture. He deserves to enjoy it for a good stretch. I need to see a man at *L'Époque* before the evening paper is set as well."

"You're starting to see," Richard replied. Raoul's smile spread into a grin as he let himself imagine what Erik was thinking right now.

The light woke him, even though it was weak, along with the creak and slam of a door. Erik grunted as he forced his eyes open, resenting the stiffness in his bones and ache in his muscles that accompanied his more acute sources of pain. His temporary prison was slightly brighter now, pale shards of daylight sneaking in through hundred-year-old cracks in the stone foundation of the crypt. Along with the lantern that still burned, it gave Erik a decent view of Antoine de Martiniac as he walked towards him, a bundle in his hand.

"Ah, you're awake." The man's voice was conspicuously cheerful, as was his handsome face. "I hope you don't mind that I didn't bring any for you," Antoine went on, gesturing to the bread protruding from the bundle before setting it down. "The priest was happy to share. That, or he just threw it in for good measure along with what I paid for his silence."

"I was wondering how you'd deal with that," Erik muttered. "Plain bribery is so common though. I thought you at least would have more panache."

"You'd be amazed at what people will do for money." Antoine knelt so his face was at the same level as Erik's but remained safely out of reach. "Does that hurt?"

With difficulty, Erik followed Antoine's gaze to the bullet wound on his upper arm. It had scabbed but still looked angry. "I've had worse."

"I'm sure you have." To Erik's mild surprise, there was no snideness in the comment. "I'd offer to bandage it up if I thought I'd survive it."

"Why would you do that? It's not going to kill me if you're worried about me dying before all your glorious plans come crashing down around you."

Antoine chuckled and peered at Erik with a curious smile. "Perhaps I'm feeling brotherly."

Erik could not help but catch his breath at the words and the look of clear recognition in the eyes of his father's second son. "You know?"

"I wasn't sure – even with all the evidence – that you were the Erik our dear father called out for in his last moments. Until I saw this." Antoine picked the gold ring up off the ground where the boy had thrown it the night before and examined it thoughtfully.

"*Amor ultra astra*," Erik intoned as Antoine read the engraving.

"A match to Grandfather's." Surprising Erik once more, the other man reached into his jacket and pulled out a matching band. "*Sic itur ad astra*."

"I always wondered where that went."

"At least they're together now. Grandmama will be so happy to know." The venom returned to Antoine's face as he placed both rings in his pocket, causing Erik a fresh surge of rage at all this man and his kind had stolen from him. "Is this what you were stealing that night?"

"It was. You were there?"

"Yes. I was the one who encouraged Father to hire you for the party when we heard your name. I wanted to see the monstrous bastard I'd heard of for so much of my life."

"You knew about me?" Now this was one thing Erik had not expected. Antoine nodded. "Interesting. I had no idea you existed until three days ago. Maybe it's four. You must forgive me for losing track of time."

"You never wondered if he had an heir, or other bastards?" Antoine asked with something that passed for genuine curiosity.

"I tried to not think about what other ill-begotten offspring my father could have foisted on the world," Erik answered honestly.

"Well, he thought of you often. So did I." Antoine looked over Erik discerningly.

"I hope I don't fall short of your expectations," he intoned as his brother's eyes grew soft and thoughtful.

"Father loved to compare us when I disappointed him – which was often." Erik noted the way Antoine tensed, like he was bracing himself for a blow that would never come. "He'd be drunk or angry – or both – and say something about how his monstrous bastard was less of a useless failure than me. Between the lashes from his belt, of course."

"Am I supposed to pity you?" Erik sneered. "Because your father struck you before throwing you back into your gilded cage? You poor thing. It must have been wretched."

"Nothing compared to what you suffered, I'm sure," Antoine replied with a lack of malice that left Erik temporarily speechless. "Still. I had my trials. He drove my mother into an early grave too."

"Sounds like him," Erik intoned carefully.

"One night, I finally got him drunk enough to reveal what he did to your poor mother." Antoine shook his head with a sigh. "Grandmama told me more, years later. Oddly enough, it was after she had agreed with Father about cutting me off. From the money, that is. She said I was too much like my father and if I wasn't careful, I'd damn myself too. That's why you're in the goddamn will. Did you know that? The estate goes to the first born."

"As if that matters to anyone," Erik scoffed.

"It matters to her. Still does. She's still alive – Grandmama." Erik blinked in surprise. In his mind the one relation who had shown some hope for him had passed away years ago. "She thinks you'll come back someday. So she can apologize. Can you imagine? Meanwhile, my efforts to bankrupt my share of the estate are going swimmingly."

"Again, do you expect my pity?" Erik had to admit, despite his venom, that he was fascinated by the man in front of him, now that they were speaking. This new brother was a monster, just like their father, but so... familiar.

"Do you know what's worse than wanting a thing?" Antoine asked back wistfully. "When you want a thing, it's just this distant dream. But when you *have* the thing – like you having your way with that Daaé girl – and then lose it? That's worse."

"I will see Christine again," Erik seethed, hate surging again that this lout dared to compare the two of them.

"Only through prison bars or smiling up at you while you walk to the guillotine. Though now that I consider it, I don't know if I want such a fate for you."

Erik blinked, thrown back into reality. "What?"

"It's different now, after really seeing you. I feel this pull in my blood. Don't you feel it too?"

"I feel a lump on my head, a gash on my arm, and the serious need to piss, but no pull," Erik jeered back.

"What if I told you I was grateful to you – for ridding the world of our monstrous father?"

"Honestly? I wouldn't be surprised," Erik said, for the briefest moment seeing himself and not his father in the man across from him.

"You did the world a favor when you knocked that lamp into those rags and kindling." Antoine smiled, oblivious to how Erik froze at the words. How did he know... "I imagine it felt wonderful to leave him yelling your name."

"Not the word I would use."

"I'm going to bandage that now." Antoine nodded towards Erik's arm. "I'll need to undo one shackle. I trust you aren't interested in killing your own flesh and blood again. Or running off into broad daylight."

"You're placing a terrible amount of trust in me." Erik watched as Antoine took out the key to the chains and did what he promised. Erik's right arm fell from the chains and his brother did not take his eyes off of him.

"If you kill me, you prove you're a monster."

Erik smirked back. "No one needs proof of that." He whipped around the chain that held his other wrist as he kicked Antoine's legs out from under him. In a heartbeat, he had the cold links of iron around his brother's throat.

"Erik! Please!" the man sputtered as Erik cut off his airway.

"Monsters are not born, they are made, Christine told me that once," Erik purred into Antoine's ear as he struggled. "I am not a monster because of this face or because of the blood we share. I am a monster because of what has been done to me – what worthless pigs like you have done to me and so many others. And I intend to be every inch the monster when I take my revenge for these chains."

"*Please...*"

"But I am going to let you live, brother, don't fret. I want you to tell the Daroga and that miserable boy that I am coming to take what is mine." Antoine's hands ceased scrabbling at the chain and his body went limp. Erik released his grip and let him collapse onto the floor.

Despite the pain throughout his body, the thrill of violence gave Erik energy and speed. He freed his other wrist using his dear brother's discarded key and toyed with the idea of chaining him up, but that wouldn't do for his plans. He wanted the boy and the Daroga to wallow in their fear and to let Christine know he was on his way.

Erik faltered at the thought of Christine. The last thing he remembered from the cemetery was her offering herself to the boy so that Erik could live. He was alive – what sort of sacrifice had she been forced to make? No matter, he would make them pay. He had given the patrons and the aristocracy mercy for far too long, but now the boy and his brother had reminded Erik exactly who he was. Now, they all would know.

He grabbed the food and supplies Antoine had so helpfully provided and raced up the stairs from the crypt. The door opened, thankfully, back onto the cemetery, where his mask and the violin remained in the bright light of day. Near it he found the cloak he had given Christine, thrown on the ground. He wrapped himself in protection and steeled his heart.

The light hurt. Not because of the memory of his face exposed in the daylight six years before – the day he had been taken and abused and used by his own blood. When he had blamed himself for a crime that was not his for six years. No, the sun burned because he remembered Christine's lips against his in the sun and how he would never know such joy again. They were doomed to the darkness, the two of them, he knew that now. They would be safe while the world above burned.

S haya was not proud that he had done as the Vicomte had ordered and gone home. Even less so when Darius found him staring at the fire.

"Good, you're alive. I had my doubts when you didn't come home for the second night in a row." Darius handed Shaya a cup of strong tea. "I assume you didn't catch him, or you'd look happier."

"We did," Shaya murmured, and Darius's eyes widened.

"After all these years," his most loyal companion said, and Shaya's heart sank further. "And it feels empty?"

"It feels too easy. We caught him with her, out in the open like the fool in love that he is, and we took him. Put him in chains and threw him in a crypt."

"Where is he now?" Darius asked in horror.

"Still there. He's guarded by a truly odious friend of de Chagny," Shaya scoffed. "Antoine de Martiniac.

"Why does that name sound familiar?" Darius asked as he sat across from Shaya.

"He's a patron. A Baron of some kind. Or he was, before the revolution."

"Didn't Erik tell you and Ramin he was a baron's bastard? You had a list of names of families near Rouen when we first came to

France, when you were searching for him." Shaya gaped at Darius, a student at the feet of a master.

Shaya rushed to the shelf containing years' worth of supposition and clues regarding Erik and his past. He fumbled for the right volume until Darius calmly stepped beside him and pointed to it. "Thank you. I—"

"Would be lost and probably dead without me. I know," Darius sighed as Shaya flipped through the notebook. In the years pursuing Erik at the Opera, he had focused so much on his fear for the future that he had forgotten the dark secrets of Erik's past that had been shared with him and Ramin over long nights of conversation in Persia. There, finally, he found it: a list of barons in and around Rouen where Erik had been born.

Third on the list was Alfred de Martiniac.

"Antoine said he never liked his father. Erik was the one to kill him. What if it wasn't a coincidence that he was there that night?" Shaya thought aloud. "And what if they learn their connection?"

"You must tell de Chagny."

"I have a bad feeling about all of this," Shaya agreed, hurrying to the door. "I need to go with the police back to Perros if they've been summoned. Don't wait up for me."

"Don't die," Darius admonished as Shaya ran out of their flat and hailed a cab. His mind raced as the cab ambled towards the Faubourg. Somehow, it made sense. De Martiniac was so familiar – even the abhorrent things he had done proved he and Erik were fruits of the same poisoned tree. What if the two allied? What if Erik was able to use his silver tongue to set himself free?

The butler sighed when he saw Shaya at the door but did not protest when Shaya pushed past. He followed the sound of raised voices to the parlor.

"Raoul, this is absolute madness! You cannot keep that woman here like she's a prisoner!" It was Philippe who was speaking.

"I don't want her in our house either. I can't believe you expect me to let her take my clothes – as if they would even fit." Shaya assumed that was the voice of their sister.

"I am keeping her safe – from that monster and herself!" Raoul protested. "Please, Sabine. I need her decent when Richard arrives. I have to convince him she's ready to sing if he's to help us."

"Do you understand how absolutely insane you've gone?" Philippe thundered. "And that's to say nothing of this idea that she'll marry you! She has to be furious."

"Raoul wouldn't know, he's too afraid to speak with her," Sabine sniped. Shaya decided that he might like this woman. The bell rang at the door, and the butler cast Shaya one more tired look before going to answer.

"That could be Richard now," Raoul snapped.

The parlor door flew open to reveal the siblings, who all looked equally put out to see Shaya. "Good day," he grumbled.

"Please, Sabine, just do as you've been told," Raoul added towards his sister. The woman cast him a look that would have wilted flowers on the vine before storming up the stairs.

"What fresh madness have you brought to wave in front of my brother, Monsieur?" Philippe demanded of Shaya, who puffed his chest defiantly.

The butler returned with what looked like a telegram on a silver tray and whispered something into Raoul's ear. The younger man tore open the missive as he nodded at Shaya to speak.

"I'm here to warn you that I may have discovered something about your friend and Erik, a possible connection—" Shaya stopped, watching as the blood drained from Raoul's face. "What is it?" he asked grimly, though he already guessed the truth.

"Antoine he... he's been hurt," Raoul stammered.

Philippe grabbed the telegram in consternation. "Let me see that. 'Beast escaped. Too injured to pursue. He is coming.' Dear God in heaven."

Shaya sighed. "I—"

"Don't you dare say you warned me!" Raoul growled. "We need a plan. Everyone in this house is in danger!"

"And the Opera," Shaya added. To the shock of the men gathered in the foyer, the bell rang yet again.

"Now *that* will be Richard, and he'll certainly be happy to hear the madman who lives in his cellar is free again! And angry!" Philippe hissed. "Would you like to tell him, or shall I?"

Raoul swallowed, looking between Shaya and his brother desperately before his eyes cleared and his expression hardened. "This is better. No more charade of mercy or a trial for him. When he comes for her—"

"Are you suggesting another trap? At his opera?" Shaya balked.

"This time, we'll have more men, and—" Raoul looked towards Philippe, as if he would encourage him.

"You'll never convince Christine," Philippe admonished just as Firmin Richard entered the foyer and took in the men's grim faces.

"I see the news is not good," Richard drawled, giving Raoul the most withering of looks.

"Not right now, but it will be. I swear it will be," Raoul replied, and Shaya's gut filled once again with the sense of doom.

C hristine refused to rest in Raoul's bed, so she had taken up a spot in one of the chairs to stare at the opulent wallpaper for the last hour. She had already memorized the intricate pattern by the time her stomach truly started to growl for food. The last time she had eaten had been yesterday, wrapped in the sheets with Erik. It had been an unpretentious meal, bread and cheese and some stew, but it had been warm and the simple pleasure of eating in their warm, safe room at the Inn of the Setting Sun had made the food all the better. She had imagined with great hope what it would be like to see the dawn with him.

Now she wondered if she would ever see him again at all. At least alive.

Christine jumped from the chair, her head in her hands, pushing away the terrible thought. It had to join the other fears and imaginings of what Erik was doing right now. Was he in pain? How filled to bursting was he with hate and vindication? Because he had been right about the dangers of leaving his home. Such ideas were impossible to escape here, in a room that Raoul had filled with evidence and testimonials (intended for the police, she assumed) of all of Erik's crimes. All the reasons she could never escape.

The sound of the door opening was an unexpected shock, as was the fact that it was not Raoul who entered, but Sabine de Chagny with a maid in tow. She looked annoyed to even be looking at Christine.

"I'm sorry we've been so slow in attending to your needs, but I didn't want to," Sabine said.

"At least one member of this family is honest," Christine muttered.

"Yes, well, my brother cares about you to the point of madness, so I have to get you dressed. Yvette." Sabine sighed as the maid presented Christine with a plain, black dress as if it were a gift. "You're too tall and round to fit anything of mine, this was from a housekeeper who left. I think it will do."

"The clothes I have are fine. I'd like some food."

"Dinner is not until seven, and this is at least better than your traveling clothes or whatever it is you have on." Sabine looked Christine up and down.

"Am I to dine with the family or remain up here like a prisoner?"

"I can't imagine you'd be good company, but Raoul may demand it. I'd rather they send up a tray. I forgot to do it for lunch. Apologies."

"You make me not want to say what I must to you." Christine braced herself as the woman gave her another cold look.

"Do you have some fresh insult for my brother? The man who has – despite everything you've done to him – deigned to save you and redeem you with his name?"

"No, only for the man *you* intend to marry," Christine answered calmly. "Antoine is—"

"Yvette, leave us," Sabine snapped before Christine could finish. The maid gave them a nervous look and rushed from the room. "What do you have to say about my fiancé?"

"He raped and beat my friend. He's horrible." Christine didn't even try to keep the hate out of her voice. Sabine's face remained implacable.

"It's strange to hear such *critiques* from a woman who has been ruined. By a criminal and a killer, if I am not mistaken?" Sabine shrugged. "Is there anything else?"

"Don't you care?"

"Antoine has been stumbling into my room while Philippe passed out in a puddle of brandy for years. Nothing you could say of him would surprise me." Sabine's face was full of a brittle, hardened sort of fury as that not even her veneer of propriety could fully conceal. Christine was horrified.

"He's taken advantage—"

"I'm as ruined as you, but *I* understand that a man with a family name wanting me at my age and in my position is better than withering away to nothing. Or throwing my life away for some romantic dream," Sabine went on, as if she'd said it to herself a hundred times. "That's what you need to learn. Marry the man that will protect you from a world that would happily see women like us thrown to the wolves."

"I won't—" Christine began to protest, but Sabine raised her hand for silence.

"We can bear what happens in the dark –you know that as well as I. What we cannot do is survive alone. So be grateful, do your part, and marry the handsome rich man. At least the one who wants *you* actually loves you beyond all reason. Have his heirs and forget all the darkness. At least during the day. Pretend the rest is just bad dreams."

"I don't want to survive. I want to live," Christine whispered, and Sabine gave a scoff. Just in time, the door opened again. This time, it was Raoul. Christine's heart sank to see his ashen face.

"Thank you for helping her," Raoul told his sister. "Would you mind if Christine and I spoke alone?"

"I do mind, but no one cares, so go ahead." Sabine swept from the room. Raoul closed the door behind her.

"I want to go home," Christine said before Raoul could even begin, and he shook his head immediately.

"We will find you better accommodations soon, I promise," Raoul stammered, avoiding her eyes. At least he looked uncomfortable and guilty.

"What about Erik?" Christine demanded. "Where do you have him? Is he hurt? Do you truly intend to hand him over to the police, even if you know it will kill us both?"

Finally, Raoul looked at her, his eyes entreating and hopeful. "What if I were to let him go – on certain conditions? You told us, when we saved you, to take you and let him be. What if I did that?"

Christine stared at Raoul, horrified that once again she was being offered a devil's bargain to save one life at the price of her heart and soul, yet also filled with hope. "What do you mean?"

"Agree to marry me and start our life, and I will let him go free. He'll leave France and go to the Americas and never trouble us again. I'll even give him the money." Christine heard the words but they refused to make sense in her head.

"He'd never agree to that..."

"He would. He's already has."

"He's what?" The world was crumbling underneath Christine again.

"I had a telegram. From Antoine. A negotiation occurred. Erik will leave because he... He knows you would have a better life with me than he can offer. All he wants is to hear you sing one more time, tomorrow night, in *Faust*."

Christine sat on the bed, no longer able to support herself. "But the Opera is his home. He could never leave."

"Isn't it for the best?" Raoul entreated, kneeling before her and taking her limp hands in his. "We can be together, and he will live. We will all be free! Christine, isn't this what you meant when you said you'd go with me to save him?"

"And if I don't do this, you'll throw him in jail and parade him through the streets?" she asked back numbly.

"Christine, please. You can save us all – our souls and our lives." Raoul placed a tender hand on her cheek.

Christine did not bat it away. What was the point? "Will I be able to see him? To say goodbye?"

"After. If we can arrange for certain assurances to be made," Raoul replied, hesitant. Christine took a deep breath, choosing once again as Erik had taught her, to cling to the next moment and live and hope.

"Yes. I'll... Yes," she heard herself say and watched from miles away as Raoul embraced her. She was outside of her body when he kissed her, so distant that she did not even feel it. Her mind was with Erik, wherever he was. She would take this deal, this new prison of promises and hope that, somehow, her angel would be able to save her. If she could just save him first.

11. Gravity

Raoul had never been happier to see dawn break. He sank onto a chaise in relief, glancing to where Philippe had been asleep on a couch for hours. Raoul had kept watch all night, walking the halls, pistol at the ready. He had not slept, fueled by all the coffee the kitchen could brew him and elixirs from Antoine's valise of medicines. Those... and the fear that Erik could be around any corner.

Sometime near three o'clock, Raoul had seen eyes in the window and dashed out into the garden, only to catch an extremely angry cat before he returned to his patrol. It was at that point that Philippe had given up and decided to rest, claiming that Erik was too smart to try an assault on their home. Raoul hoped he was right, but he would not take any chances.

He couldn't let that thing near Christine again. That was why they had to keep her in his room with the windows barred and door locked. She had complained of the safety measures, protesting that if Erik was contained, there was no need for her to be shut away. Raoul had assured her it was just a precaution, surely, she knew better than anyone how dangerous and devious Erik could be. He couldn't tell her that the monster had already proven himself to be thus.

Raoul's patrol had taken him by his own door so many times he had lost count. He'd listened from the other side just as he had listened outside Christine's dressing room door months ago, and every time he had expected to hear that voice calling out to her, seeping in through the walls. He had only heard the sound of her breathing and weeping.

Raoul gazed out to the empty street, practically shaking with anticipation and readiness. (It could also be the substances he had used to stay awake.) They had made it through the night, and he had kept Christine safe. Soon, she would be done with her tears. Soon, Raoul would know her as his wife, and the memory of that thing would be erased from her mind and body...

"I need to call the priest," Raoul exclaimed.

Philippe startled awake from the couch. "You need to... What bloody time is it?"

"Seven o'clock in the morning. I need to get the priest and arrange for the marriage and our confessions." Raoul had no idea why Philippe was looking at him like he had gone mad. He was being perfectly reasonable.

"Not even God is awake this early," Philippe groaned. "It can wait."

"I'm tired of waiting." Raoul's leg bounced nervously as he tapped it.

"You always were impatient." Raoul turned to see his brother looking uncharacteristically affectionate. "You'd wake before dawn and run into my room when you were a wee thing and demand we play. Drove the nannies insane. Me too."

"But you always played with me, even when you were tired." Raoul smiled at the memory. "You were the best at all the games."

"To think that impatient little boy has grown into such a bold, impatient man," Philippe sighed. He stumbled from the couch and rang the bell to summon a servant. "Any word from... anyone?"

"Nothing. If Antoine is coming back, he hasn't decided to let us know."

"Maybe that's for the best. He's a bad influence on all of us."
Raoul gave his brother a surprised look. Philippe shrugged. "I'm
still hoping I can talk you out of all of this."

"The plan is sound."

"The plan is ridiculous," Philippe countered. "You're hoping to
lay a trap for a man who has already escaped you when you had him
in chains. A trap set in the opera house where he can walk through
the goddamn walls!"

"Our mistake last time was being merciful." Raoul clenched his
fists, imagining how much better things would be if he had not
aimed to hurt Erik in the cemetery and aimed instead to kill. As he
would tonight. "I will be ready for him when he shows himself."

"And if you succeed – somehow – what will you tell Christine?
After you've killed her lover and she finds out you lied?"

Raoul had already thought long and hard on that subject. "She
believes he is to be freed after hearing her sing, I will simply tell
her that he broke the deal with violence, and we had to defend
ourselves and her."

"What if that's what she wants though? For him to break free
and save her?" Philippe's expression was deathly serious. "She has
made it clear where her heart lies."

"She agreed to marry *me*," Raoul protested again, thinking back
to his elation at the sound of that simple word: yes. Christine had
kissed him, and all had been right in the world when he saw the
woman he loved begin to throw off the shackles Erik had placed on
her soul.

"What about Richard? I don't trust that man – he has some
other game here." Philippe approached his brother.

Raoul shook his head once again. "He's agreed to call up all the
firemen and have the police in the building. That's logical!"

"None of this is logical, Raoul," Philippe entreated. "When it goes wrong, who will have to save you? Me. Do you have any idea how unqualified I am for heroics?"

"Then don't come," Raoul snapped. "Have a brandy. Go find wherever Antoine is licking his wounds and leave this to the men of action. Now, I need to go."

Raoul bolted out of the parlor and into the coach house to rouse the groom who had audaciously fallen asleep as well. Soon enough, he was on his way across the Seine, to the church where he had always known Christine Daaé would say her vows. She needed to free her soul entirely first, and then she could be his.

Perhaps it could happen tonight. Perhaps once that thing was dead, Christine would rejoice and elope with him immediately without even waiting for Sunday. Then he could have her, at last. It made his cock twitch to think of it. He had seldom thought of Christine in such sinful terms, but to have their marriage so close meant he could not help it. He had dreamed of her since he was a boy, but as a distant, chaste ideal. Now, she would be his as a woman. He closed his eyes, imagined her voice...

Shall I tell you all the ways he fucks me? All the places he's had me? How hard he makes me come?

Raoul jumped in his seat as the carriage came to a stop, crying out in disgust. Christine hadn't meant that. She had said that just to placate Erik and drive Raoul away. She had lied.

Adèle's words haunted Raoul too. *No matter if you steal her away, you'll never give it to her as good as he did.* She was a liar too.

Raoul hid his face in shame, horrified to think on such things so close to a house of God. He looked up at the Madeleine in all her Romanesque glory. Christine was a free spirit, he'd always known she'd like this church dressed in a pagan costume. She was like Mary Magdalene now too: a fallen woman only God could redeem. She had to cleanse her soul and come to their marriage free and pure again. So did Raoul.

There was one young priest attending to the candles when Raoul entered, and he signaled to the man to meet him in the confessional. Raoul knelt in the close, dark space once the door closed behind him and crossed himself, exhaling and feeling his soul unburden as he did so.

"Good morning, my son. Do you wish to make a confession?" the voice came from the other side of the screen.

"Yes. Forgive me, Father, for I have sinned. It has been five days since my last confession," Raoul began.

E rik reached the one passage into the Opera from the catacombs, only to find it wide open, a sight which filled him with rage. It was a message from the other shade that haunted the underground, or the Daroga. It declared that Erik's way out had been found. It was open now to welcome him home, but Erik knew it would not be so later.

This was the final insult in a long journey of pain and humiliation, hiding from the searing light of day as best he could. Thoughts of revenge and hate had kept Erik moving, but more than anything memories of Christine had driven him, even as they were tainted with doubt. He remembered her cries and entreaties to the boy, that he could take her. She had done that to save her angel. What more had they made her do?

Christine didn't want their life in the dark and she was tired of the career Erik had forged for her. She wanted the daylight – the cursed sun that had tempted Erik, only to remind him why he was not welcome in its light. Did that mean she would see the world through the boy's eyes now? Would she want him? Erik had to take her back before she could be swayed, but what if it was too late? What if they were gone?

Erik found himself leaning against a cold stone wall, gasping for air, his mind spinning in terror building to rage. This was not the first time such an attack had taken him on the journey, but it was certainly the worst. His breathing was shallow, he shook from his legs to his fingertips, and his vision was tinged deadly red.

He hated them, all of them. His brother and the boy and all the rich and careless fools above. They had taken everything from him again and again, driven him to the dark for crimes that were not his. And now, after he had scraped together an existence in the shadows and dared to find love, they had stolen away everything *again*.

Erik hated them so much he could barely breathe. He had to force the air in and out of his throat, force himself to feel the concrete against his hands and the solid earth beneath his feet until the crimson fog of rage abated. He was not surprised to find that he was on his knees when he came back to himself, or that he had somehow come to the fourth cellar already. He stood and stalked towards the stairs that would take him into the Opera proper.

The Phantom was back in his safe haven, but he was not ready to return to his home. He didn't want to enter the house that he had shared with an angel for so brief a time without knowing how he could return her to his grasp. He sped up the stairs, eager instead to learn anything that had transpired in the Opera while they were gone.

As if on cue, a uniformed gendarme was the first thing he saw – in deep discussion with a fireman.

"What do you mean *lake*? Why is there a lake? Why does a bloody theater need five cellars anyway?"

"That lake is a reservoir, and it could save this bloody theater from turning to ashes like the old opera if needs be!" the fireman crowed.

"Well, my men aren't going down there. We'll stay up here and your lot can patrol the depths, if it's so important to the managers to have this place cleared."

Erik's rage rose again. Why were there police patrolling his opera? What was going on? He pressed himself against the wall and edged closer.

"What do they think they're doing, going after a damn ghost?" the fireman asked.

"It's not a ghost is what I hear. It's a madman who tried to kill the Vicomte de Chagny," the gendarme replied. Erik sneered. He wished more than anything that he *had* killed the boy months ago and spared everyone this trouble.

"It near killed two of my men last week, and many before that," the fireman said, and Erik's dreams of murder paused. When had he assaulted a fireman recently? It had to be the shade – the one who he had seen and who had gone after Jean-Paul. Another interloper whose death was now assured. "So my men won't go down there."

"Neither will mine," rumbled the gendarme (or perhaps he was a captain of some kind – Erik did not care, given all police were corrupt swine, and he made no distinctions between their ranks). "It doesn't matter. You're the one who has to explain this to your idiot managers."

"The hell I do..."

Erik didn't wait to hear more. He too had much to take up with the management.

The Ghost sped in the opposite direction from the men, then up and up, until he was in his hidden passages, his tension abating as he took his place in the tight space. Through the walls and hidden ways to his hiding place below the manager's office, his heartbeat in his ears drowning out the meaning of the voices above. He was sick with anticipation of what he would learn, but he had to if he was to make them all pay. He had to know their crimes to plan their punishment.

"I do not understand any of this," Moncharmin was saying as Erik finally forced himself to listen. "Why are the police here if—"

"As a precaution, to protect the girl and the Vicomte," Richard replied. Erik's heart leapt. "All you need to do is make sure your phantom knows that Mademoiselle Daaé will sing tonight."

"For her final performance?" Moncharmin finished, and Erik's miniscule hopes shattered. "You think I have some way to reach him? And you think I'll survive telling him this?"

"I frankly don't care," Richard said as Erik's blood began to rush. "Leave a note and the paper with that awful Giry woman at his box. She likes to carry his messages."

"I am not your errand boy!" Moncharmin crowed. "I am a manager of the Opera, and I demand to know what is going on!"

"You are a useless degenerate with divided loyalties who will do as he is told!" Richard thundered. "You will do it silently and without bothering me further, unless you would like me to enlighten the Minister of Fine Arts about the forty thousand francs you've stolen for a fucking ghost!"

Silence above. Erik imagined the look of shame and hurt on Moncharmin's face, something his spectacles and mustache could not hide. "You're a bastard. Whatever he does when he retaliates... you will deserve."

"Get out of my sight," Richard scoffed.

Erik followed Moncharmin's footsteps as they retreated. What did this all mean? A final performance? What sort of trap was being laid? Erik found himself free of the walls and following the younger manager like a shadow into a dark hall. The man paused mid-step and looked over his shoulder to meet Erik's eyes.

"Of course you're here now. Where have you been?" Moncharmin asked sadly as he turned. "Somewhere dirty and painful, by the looks of it."

Erik looked down at himself. He was a mess: clothes torn and covered in grime, to say nothing of his unmasked face. A face that did not seem to give Moncharmin too great of pause. "I was indisposed. Where is Christine?"

"At the home of her fiancé, under guard. I assume from you." Moncharmin held something out to Erik. It was a newspaper of all things, *L'Époque*, folded to the society section. "It's in there if you don't believe me. Christine Daaé is set to marry Raoul de Chagny. After her final performance tonight, she wishes to devote herself to her husband and family."

"No..." Erik whispered, fire in his throat and a strange melody in his mind. "It's a trick. It's a lie."

"It's a trap. They want you to see this, to know what their plans are. They want you to come for her," Moncharmin said, something like concern in his eyes.

"So he can kill me this time, and take her forever," Erik growled. "The little fool."

"I am telling you because I'm praying you will have mercy," Moncharmin sighed. "I can try to get her away – get her to you, so you can flee."

"There is nowhere to flee. They'll find me and take her again." Erik could see it now: a horde of police led by the Daroga and the boy descending towards his home. The music grew louder, screeching violins and thundering horns filling his mind. He knew the theme. "Unless they are too busy sorting through the rubble."

"Please, Monsieur." Moncharmin's face was so worried and sad, but Erik could hardly see it. "There are innocent people involved."

"Then it will be up to you to warn them, Armand," Erik replied softly. "You will know the signal. When the first beat sounds, warn them. They will have until the fifth to run."

"What does that mean?" The manager demanded even as Erik turned away, a cacophony in his head. "What does that mean!"

Erik descended to his realm, as swift as Hermes towards the river of the dead. He had no souls to guide to the Styx yet, but perhaps soon he would. The brutal chords of an opera never completed thundered in his mind as he rowed across dark waters and entered his home. He lit his candles and looked to the organ... and the shelf beside it. Erik followed the siren's song, the inevitable beat of the red leather score and all that lay within.

Don Juan Triumphant. His masterpiece of revenge. It was ready to be played at last. He seated himself at the organ and the first terrible chords sang from the pipes, the music of doom echoing in the dark.

Christine had slept – moving in between a chair, a chaise lounge, and even the floor in a quest for some sort of peace in this alien place – but she didn't feel like it. Her body ached, and her soul hurt more. It was a strange thing, to find a mirror in a bedroom, after so long without them in the house on the lake.

She stared for a while at her alien reflection: pale cheeks and red eyes and haunted expression. What had become of the version of herself she had seen in the dressing room mirror, when an angel had called to her from the glass and inspired her to divine ecstasy? Now she would only feel that in her dreams.

She looked at Raoul's chaotic desk and the letters she had penned there. So many goodbyes to so many people she was afraid she would never see after tonight and a few entreaties for forgiveness.

"Mademoiselle Daaé?" A voice she did not recognize came from outside the door, accompanied by a gentle knock. "Are you decent?"

"Depends on your definition," Christine grumbled back as she rose from her seat to greet the entering visitor. "I'm dressed at least."

"Oh, good." The door opened to reveal, of all people, a young priest. Of course she had made a joke about her fallen moral character to the clergy. "I am Father René." He held out a hand which Christine did not take.

"You're a bit early for last rites."

The young Father swallowed and withdrew his hand. "Your fiancé sent me to receive your confession."

"So my wanton soul will be cleansed before he lowers himself to take me in holy matrimony? Yes, I remember." Christine knew she should be playing along, but she was so tired and she did not think it would make too great a difference. "I haven't been to confession for... a very long time. Does Raoul know I was never even given a formal first communion or baptism? My father grew up among the Roma, and I grew up wild."

"I-I can't speak for the Vicomte," the priest stammered. "I can perform those rights as well, and your sins will be forgiven for you to begin a new life in Christ, embraced by God."

"It is not against God that I have sinned, I am sorry to say," Christine said, and Father René went as pale as his white collar. "I have failed the man I love over and over. That man is dangerous and I fear he has been lost to the darkness. But I love him, and for him, I have sworn to marry another. I will say marriage vows and not mean them, and it will be for love of a man who is not my husband. A man who taught me that love is never a sin."

"Oh," the priest muttered as he held Christine's gaze.

"Is that not what I am supposed to say?" she asked with a bitter laugh. "Because I don't need your forgiveness for my so-called sins of the flesh. They were wondrous and blessed in my mind. *You* cannot absolve me for all I have done to protect him, to save him. All the terrible lies I have told and lives I have torn apart. Because I do not deserve forgiveness."

"Everyone deserves forgiveness, Christine," Father René replied. Christine smiled because the man truly meant it.

"I am sorry to shock you, Father. I am not at my best today." Christine sat, finally, on Raoul's bed. Would that be their wedding bed? What would he expect of her – to just lie there and take him? She did not want to think of it beyond the hope that she could escape into her mind as easily when Raoul fucked her as when he kissed her.

"Mademoiselle, may I be forthright?" the priest asked, bringing Christine's attention back to him. To her surprise, there was nothing but kindness in his face. Christine nodded for him to go on. "I was told you were under some influence of evil, but I did not fully believe it."

"He is not evil, the man I love," Christine protested.

"I believe you." They were the simplest words, but it astonished Christine to hear them after so many men had told her that she could not trust herself. "I do not think a truly evil man could inspire such love. You are willing, if I understand right, to sacrifice your freedom to save this man's life?"

"I am, but I cannot believe, in my heart, that it is what he would want. I wish I could see him one more time before I do this." Tears pricked her eyes again. "I don't know what to do."

"I wish I could help," the priest confessed, and Christine gave a sad smile. "Is there nothing else I can offer you?"

"There is one person I have wronged to whom I should make amends." Christine crossed to the desk and selected one of the missives she had written. "Carlotta Zambelli. I took everything from her and I want to give it back. Will you take a letter to her for me?"

"The woman who sang like a toad? Who you replaced?" Christine raised an eyebrow. "My congregation is half of the Opera. I know things and I know who you are. The man you speak of, is he... the Phantom?"

"He is the Angel of Music," Christine countered sadly. "For me at least."

"Mademoiselle, are you—" The earnest question was interrupted by the opening of the door. Raoul stood in the entrance, perfectly dressed for the opera and smiling broadly.

"I hope you have had time to unburden yourself with the father," Christine's ostensible fiancé said. "It's time to go."

"Thank you, Father," Christine murmured and took Raoul's proffered arm.

It was strange to walk in the fresh air again, letting the rain kiss her cheeks. Christine breathed deeply, savoring the free air for what could be the last time.

"Soon it will be done." Raoul tried to sound reassuring. Christine only nodded.

It would all be over soon, but even now, Christine didn't know what that meant. She felt like a condemned woman on the road to execution, having given confession and now sent in the cart to the place of her final judgment. Could she sing for Erik one last time? Was he truly just going to let her go off to a life with his rival if she did? Or would he trick them? Would he take her one last time, even if it condemned them all?

The gendarmes assigned to the Opera refused to listen to Shaya. He was not surprised, but it was still infuriating. They were getting close to when Christine would arrive, and the trap would be ready to spring. But it would not matter if Erik was not actually trapped in the Opera. Shaya rushed through the halls, hoping to remedy that oversight.

Near a flight of stairs towards the furnaces, Shaya saw his chance in the personage of Firmin Richard. The manager looked just as he had the night before when Raoul had outlined his plan. Shaya had not advised against the scheme, for the idea that Erik would come for his love and expose himself while doing so was sound, but only if the correct precautions were taken.

"Once the audience is inside, make sure you are posted," Richard was telling a fireman.

"Monsieur Richard, a word!" Shaya called as he rushed to the man. "I once again entreat you to listen to me! Posting guards at doors is a waste!"

"And I once again entreat you to shut up and leave this business to those of us who know what we are doing," the manager snapped as the fireman retreated.

"I was—"

"A sheriff in some backwater sultanate. I know," Richard scoffed. "This is Paris and my opera."

"So you must know that he can get in and out of *his* opera without ever using a goddamn door?"

Richard sneered. "Indeed I do, good Monsieur. My agent made sure that entrance was wide open for him today. Then barred it after it was used."

"Your agent?" Shaya asked, mind racing.

"Did you think I was relying solely on the intelligence of the young Vicomte? I thought you were claiming to be wise in all things," Richard went on, pleased with himself.

"The shade. He's yours?"

Richard's smirk was all the confirmation Shaya needed. "What sort of game are you playing?"

"One you have no business interfering in. Don't you have to go lurk somewhere?"

"Something like that," Shaya said softly before turning away.

Richard had given Shaya no reason to inform the manager that the shade was perhaps as dangerous as the Phantom. Just as Shaya had found himself yesterday with no reason to tell Raoul and his cohorts that Erik's escape from Antoine's clutches was all too convenient. Why should he warn those who would not listen?

Guilt moved Shaya to the corridors near the stage, towards the rooms where the petits rats of the corps de ballet were scurrying between preparations for tonight's performance of *Faust*. He waited only a few moments before he found what he was looking for: Jammes. This time, it was her chasing after Julianne.

"You can't just accuse me of that and expect me to be fine!" Jammes called as the dresser headed towards Shaya. "I didn't mean to—"

Both women stopped when they saw the Persian. "Really?" Julianne asked, eyes on Shaya, her countenance full of fury. "Why don't we just ask him? Did you use what she told you – what *I* told her in confidence about *my friend* – to go to the Vicomte and his friends?"

"I did," Shaya replied. "I didn't know what they would do to confirm the information about Christine."

"It's still your fault. It's still all our faults," Julianne gritted out and rounded on Jammes.

"And so you're punishing me by—" Jammes stopped, biting her lip and blushing deeply.

"You told me you were done with me. Well now I'm done with you," Julianne said, sure and cold. Shaya had listened to many lovers' quarrels before but never one that made him feel so out of place as an interloper. "I'm done with all of you," Julianne added, pointedly looking at Shaya before she pushed past.

"Wait!" Jammes called as Julianne stalked off and turned a dark corner. Shaya followed out of habit, close enough to hear Jammes gasp. When he turned the corner to join her, he saw why: Julianne was gone. "Where did she go?"

"I am afraid to say," Shaya breathed, and a chill went down his spine. He could feel the darkness looking back at him, laughing as it made its plans. "You should leave. Go home."

"What?" Jammes asked in horror.

"Leave now. The Opera is not safe tonight."

The dark corridors backstage had never been so threatening. Raoul walked with one hand on Christine's arm and another in the pocket of his coat, ready to draw his pistol. He did not think that the fiend would attempt to take her now, but he could never hope to understand the madness that drove Erik. The denizens of the Opera whispered as they passed, which only made Christine look more sullen, but soon, he would free her. Soon.

"Don't you have things to see to?" Raoul turned at the sound of Christine's voice, realizing they had stopped in front of her dressing room. "Wherever you have him – don't you need to..." Christine swallowed her words, looking as if she might weep again.

"Philippe is attending to *him*," Raoul lied.

"And where will he be? When will I see him?"

"After. Don't upset yourself more thinking about it," Raoul replied, even as a single tear escaped down Christine's cheek. "This is all for the best. It's the start of a new life. A better life for all of us."

"It doesn't feel like a new start. It feels like the end of everything I love."

"I'll be here the whole time, right beside you as much as I can be. You won't be alone," Raoul offered, caressing her arms.

Christine shrugged him off. "Do you think I'm going to run off if you take your eyes off me? You know I won't. I'm not giving you any excuse to hurt him again. You can go."

"Let me at least stay until the curtain goes up. I promise not to get in your way," Raoul said with a smile. "I'm here to help."

Christine turned to her dressing room door. Both of them jumped as it opened, but it was only a dresser inside. An older woman with a ruddy complexion who looked relieved to see Christine.

"Louise? What are you doing here?" Christine asked, stepping into the room. "Where is Julianne?"

"I haven't seen her," Louise sighed. Raoul followed them into the dressing room, casting a glare at the great mirror. It did not move and nothing leapt out. Either Erik was waiting, or he was not there. "I thought I'd come to dress you and talk about this ridiculous rumor that tonight will be your last performance."

Raoul watched as Christine gave a tearful nod. Louise gasped before looking at him. "She wishes to be fully devoted to our marriage," Raoul explained, just as he had to the man at *L'Époque*.

"What about... Robert?" Louise asked, looking unconvinced.

"He can't give me the life I deserve. My heart isn't in the Opera anymore."

"How can that be? You sing like no one I've ever heard! You came here begging for any job you could find here, a little bedraggled thing come in out of the rain to my workshop. Now you're leaving?"

"There are things I love more than the Opera now," Christine whispered.

Raoul looked away at those words. She meant Erik – or thought she did. Why wouldn't she, when she was surrounded by all the evidence of his influence? Still, it filled Raoul with fresh resolve to end it all and claim what should have been his at the age of seventeen.

"Monsieur, are you going to remain here while a lady changes?"

Raoul looked up at Louise in surprise. "I am her fiancé."

"It's fine, Louise. We'll use the screen." The women did just that.

Raoul, to prove he was a gentleman, turned his back and went to examine Christine's vanity. It was a charming little collection of things she had. A vase of dried flowers. A brush.

A folded note.

Raoul glanced behind him, making sure the women were distracted before he opened the card and read the jagged letters scrawled in red ink.

Do not sing for him.

Raoul suppressed a grin as he pocketed the missive. So, Erik was here. And just as Raoul had hoped, he was livid that Christine was making a final performance dedicated to the man who had finally won her hand. It made Raoul want to laugh, to think of that monster stewing in impotent rage, excluded and denied as Raoul had been so many times.

Now it was Erik's turn for humiliation. When Christine sang, he would come for her. From somewhere in the shadows, he would come for her, and Raoul would be ready to end him for good.

Raoul stood back as Louise led Christine to the vanity, clucking over her as she finished her costume and started on styling her hair. Christine looked very much like a doll being painted and primped, but it brightened Raoul's heart to see even the illusion of a blush return to his beloved's cheeks.

"You look lovely, my dear," Louise said with a sad expression. "You'll be wonderful. I'll leave you to it." With a quiet nod from Christine and a sidelong glare at Raoul, the costumer left.

"Alone at last," Raoul chuckled. "Do you need to practice or warm up your voice? I confess I've never really considered the mechanics of all this."

"I don't sing until Act Three." Christine's eyes were now on the great mirror that Raoul had seen her disappear into before. Did she know its secret? Could she make it work? Why did she look like she was ready to cry again when they were so close?

"I can't do this," Christine whimpered, and Raoul could see she was trembling. "I don't want to do this! It feels wrong."

"It's only one last performance, a gift to him along with his life," Raoul countered, pulling Christine into his arms. She did not resist, but she made no movement to embrace him in turn.

"And then another and another," she muttered. "A hundred, then a thousand performances, day after day, as your wife. I cannot do that. I cannot pretend every day that I am anything but his..."

"Don't say that!" Raoul protested, reminding himself that, even now, his love was fighting the influence of a demon. "I know you are filled with pity for that wretched thing, but you must remember what he is and the evil he has done to you. When you are in the light of our new life, you will be free. We can love one another as we were always meant to."

"Raoul, please, why won't you ever listen?" Christine whined, and Raoul caught her chin with his finger. She was so lovely in her maiden's costume, her hair ornamented with pearls and white silk flowers, her sweet lips rouged red.

"Do you remember our first kiss? Under the apple tree at the edge of that old farm. You had blossoms in your hair then too. I said you were the most perfect thing I'd ever seen and you blushed, just like now."

"Raoul..."

"And you asked if I wanted to kiss you and you giggled, like the girl you were. I was dead serious when I said yes, and that I did not take a kiss lightly. I wouldn't kiss a girl I did not intend to marry. You frowned, and then I kissed you..."

"I remember." Christine's face was so sad it broke Raoul's heart.

"I still mean it." Raoul claimed her mouth. She was modest as she returned the kiss, letting him be the one to part her lips with his tongue and seek her. A good girl, despite all that had been done to her, assuring Raoul more than ever that she was ready to be his. God, he hoped Erik was watching, seeing what it meant for a true gentleman to show his love. Christine pulled away, hiding her face shyly.

"I'm sorry, I—"

"You cannot know how much I want you," Raoul went on, sighing as he pulled her close. "I wish I could have you tonight. Or right now even—" Christine pushed away, looking at Raoul in pure shock at such a suggestion. "You are to be my wife. It would not be wrong."

A knock at the door cut him off.

"Anyone there?" Philippe's voice called before he entered. Christine turned away immediately and took a seat at her vanity, resolutely reapplying makeup to her lips and avoiding the gaze of the men.

"Is everything prepared?" Raoul asked pointedly, trying to hide his frustration.

"It is." Philippe looked between Raoul and Christine. "Are you ready?"

"We are," Raoul answered with a smile.

"Is he there?" Christine asked, turning to meet Philippe's eyes. The hesitation in his brother's face made Raoul worry that Philippe was about to ruin the whole plan.

"He is," Philippe finally replied. "In his box. Hidden so he will not draw attention. Waiting to hear you one last time."

"Tell him I'm sorry," Christine whispered.

Philippe once again looked to Raoul before nodding in the affirmative. "I will."

"Come, Christine, it's time," Raoul commanded, hoping to avoid more tears. His fiancée rose and left the dressing room with the two men following after her.

"I hope you know what you're doing," Philippe muttered. "I don't want to have to be the one to save your foolish hide again."

"When have you ever saved me?"

"Exactly. I'm shit at it, so don't make me," Philippe said and turned away.

Christine was looking towards the stage, her back stiff and straight.

"I'll get out of your way now." Raoul received only the briefest nod in acknowledgement.

He did not go far. Rather, he took up a post in the recesses of the wings, nodding towards the other guards doing the same. They were all ready for the moment the ghost would try to take Christine, be it on the stage or off. It was time for the curtain to rise on what would undoubtedly be an unforgettable final performance for the infamous Phantom.

C hristine began *Faust* behind a screen, as nothing but a trick, the vision of a maid at her spinning wheel. It should have been easy to just sit there and be seen, but even that made her ill. She sensed the eyes of the audience upon her, an overwhelming wave of perception as they whispered.

There she is. The girl who ousted Carlotta. Who dazzled us all and now she's to marry and leave it all behind.

Christine closed her eyes and fingered the rough thread between her fingers as her prop spinning wheel whirred. The only eyes she wanted upon her were those of an angel, the angel she was singing to save and then to leave.

But she could not feel him.

The spotlight darkened, and Christine fled to the side of the stage, catching her breath. Maybe she was wrong. Maybe her nerves and guilt had the best of her. She kept to the wings, holding on during the interval. She could feel the way the chorus and other singers looked at her. She hid from the questions and closed her eyes, preparing herself.

Months ago, she had snuck up from the costume workshop, drawn by the music she loved so much. She had hidden in these same shadows and sensed something watching her through the whole performance. Now, there was nothing, and the music was empty.

Ever since she had spoken that deadly 'yes' to Raoul, it had all been empty. Not just the silent life stretching out before her, but all of it. She had been ready to leave the Opera far behind and run away with Erik a few days ago. Forsaking this for Raoul was so different. It was to keep Erik alive, because if he was gone, nothing mattered. But could she truly leave him so alone?

The brightness on stage made her wince when Christine made her first real entrance. She warbled her first few notes as Marguerite, said she was no lady, and refused Faust's hands. She glanced towards Erik's box. She saw Philippe there, with Richard beside him, and... Was that a shadow behind them? How could it be when she felt nothing? There was no magic, no prickle of ghostly eyes. Nothing.

The next interval came, and Christine searched the wings for wherever Raoul had secreted himself. He was watching her, assuring that she did not run – either to find Erik or out of the Opera entirely. She had considered it many times, especially when Raoul had propositioned her.

She was a ghost herself, drifting through the wings and avoiding other's eyes. Or a madwoman, groping through the shadows for a glimmer of hope. Then, around one corner she felt it, she swore – that prickle of danger and desire that only happened when Erik was near.

"There you are! You wandered off and scared me."

Christine turned, dejected, to see Raoul approaching, his smile so wide and warm it made her ill to look at it. "Do you swear that he's here?"

"What?" Raoul asked back as he blinked.

"I can't feel him." Christine realized how utterly insane it sounded. Maybe Raoul was right and she had gone mad. What sane woman wept at the thought of being forever separated from such a dangerous man? A woman who loved that man was the answer. "Do you swear he's here?"

"Of course," Raoul said earnestly. "He's here."

"I want to see him, please. I have to," Christine begged, and Raoul shook his head.

"That will only upset you. Why don't we get you some tea? That's what you singers like before you have to go on, isn't it?"

"That was how we poisoned Carlotta, you know. A drug in her tea to freeze her voice. I was the one that made sure her maid gave it to her," Christine confessed, hoping to get some sort of reaction out of the man who was looking at her like a wounded dog.

"The things that monster made you do make my blood boil. Come. I'll take care of you."

"I don't need to be taken care of!" Christine barked. "I need to see the man I'm throwing my life and soul away for before you take him from me."

"After," Raoul repeated, agitated, and Christine could not help but roll her eyes. Raoul dragged her back to her place in the wings and somehow tracked someone down to give her tea before retreating again to give her space.

Christine squirmed as the understudy for Adèle passed her by and avoided her eyes, gossiping with the baritone who was attempting to bring all he could to Valentin for the night. So strange that she barely knew the man who played her brother. Christine wished she could track down Robert or even Carlos Fontana for some measure of comfort, but all too soon, she was ushered on stage. The light of the chandelier stung her eyes.

"I would like to know who it was..." Christine began to sing, the music coming from the memory of her body and months of practice, but not her heart. Because there was no angel watching her, no phantom in the shadows following each note. She knew it in her soul.

She was passable, at least. Perhaps uneducated ears like Raoul's would think it was a fine performance, but Christine knew it was her worst. She faltered in support, wavered in pitch, and could barely muster the energy for the finale of the Jewel Song. She was a sleepwalker going into the love scene, her mind occupied with the terrible thought of the next romance she would have to perform. By the time she exited the stage, she was shaking in anger and dejection.

"Dear God, Daaé – I know it's your grand farewell but you could at least try," the man playing Valentin groused as the cast meandered backstage.

"Oh shut up, Julian." It was Robert, and Christine had never been happier to see the devil approaching.

"That's not even my name," the baritone grimaced.

Robert shrugged. "I don't care, fuck off. Are you alright, my dear?"

"No," Christine shook her head before embracing him. He held her in strong, comforting arms, and she almost laughed to imagine

how it looked for Margurite to be weeping into the devil's shoulder.
"Ah, so you aren't happy to have jilted me for what's-his-name on
such short notice?"

"No," Christine sniffled. "I'm not. It's all a mess, and now—"

"I'll thank you to take your hands off my fiancé." Of course,
now Raoul arrived, glaring at Robert as if he were a real rival. "She's
had a tiring few days making her decision."

"I'm sure she has. If it is *her* decision," Robert rumbled,
gripping Christine's side.

"What are you implying, Monsieur?" Raoul demanded.

Robert looked Christine in the eyes with no hint of mischief.
"I have heard from my sources in management that there are many
important people upset with the news. People I believe would have
been consulted."

Christine's blood began to quicken. Did he mean what she
thought he meant? But the only way Erik could have made his
opinion known of anything was if...

"Get away, degenerate," Raoul barked, and pulled Christine
from Robert's arms, marching them away.

"I'll tell Vincenzo you said that!" Robert called after them,
bewilderingly.

"You've been lying," Christine hissed as Raoul dragged her
behind a flat. "Erik is not here – at least not in that box."

"Why are you so convinced?" Raoul swallowed as he asked,
looking too nervous for an honest man.

"Because I cannot feel him watching." Christine raised her
hand to silence Raoul before he protested. "Don't tell me I'm
imagining things or that I'm hysterical! I don't know how, but I've
always *known* when he was watching. I can't feel him tonight, of
all nights, when I'm supposed to be saying goodbye. And now,
Robert—"

"You can't listen to that cad," Raoul scoffed. "He's just making trouble."

Chrstine's face hardened, along with her heart. "He has no reason to lie. You do. You have every reason to convince me to go through with this charade and agree to be your wife because... You lost him, didn't you?"

"You don't know what you're talking about," Raoul gritted out, his dark expression and tone all the confirmation Christine needed.

"I've been such a fool, but I'm done," Christine snarled and made to leave. Raoul caught her by the arm. It was then that she felt it, like drops of frost down her spine. "Get your hands off me now, Monsieur."

"No." Raoul's eyes were as cold as she'd ever seen them. "You will sing and he *will* come for you."

"And you'll kill him this time? Because he escaped you and your idiot companions." Christine tried to wrench herself away, but Raoul's grip only tightened as he pulled her close again, lips pursed, jaw tight.

"Because you will not humiliate me again," Raoul seethed. "All of Paris knows that you're promised to me now. I will have you in the eyes of God as my true wife."

"He'll come for me before that happens." Christine could not help but smile, a familiar shiver running under her skin.

"That is my dearest hope," Raoul replied, death in his tone. "And then you will come to your senses."

"You will never believe me, will you? When I tell you I love a man that isn't you?" Christine said softly. "Nothing I've ever said or done has ever mattered, because *you* decide what I feel and what I am. I'm a whore and a madwoman and not myself when I am with him, but I'll be a virgin remade and a sweet helpmate when I'm yours. Well, I refuse. I will be who I choose to be."

"Even if it kills him?" Raoul sneered, and Christine finally managed to yank herself free of his grasp.

"Even if it kills me," Christine declared, a strange feeling of freedom lifting her heart. "To live a life lying every day is no life at all. And I will not have it."

She stalked away, escaping into the crowd of chorus members and dancers preparing for the dark sabbath of the *Walpurgis-nacht* scene. It had always been her favorite part of the Opera that she didn't sing in, this orgy of darkness in an opera so concerned with the immortal soul. She closed her eyes and listened and tried to feel her angel, but the fleeting sense of his presence was gone. But it had been there, and she knew it would return.

Christine kept her eyes fixed on the stage, feeling the faint heat of the footlights on her face. She only looked away when Louise ushered her off to change into her final costume – a plain prison shift. She undid her hair, letting it fall wild and free down her back, and wiped off the makeup that had hidden her pallor.

Soon enough, Christine was on stage, and the orchestra was starting. She was a madwoman, thrown in jail for the unspeakable crime of killing the child she had borne; fathered by a man with the help of the devil, a man who had left her when she had become inconvenient. Faust came back to save Marguerite, with the devil in tow, offering her all the comforts and pleasures of the mortal world, and she refused.

The searing beam of the limelight hit her. Christine closed her eyes, reaching out with her heart, and sang for the angels.

She heard the way the audience gasped at the new fire in her song. She looked into the wings and saw Raoul watching, his face twisted with jealousy. He wanted her there on the earth like Faust, only to be his, and she called on the angels above to save her soul instead.

"*Angels pure, angels radiant, carry my soul to heaven!*" she sang with all her heart over the protests of Faust and Mephisto. Hooded demons circled as the audience watched in rapt awe. "*God of justice, I give myself up to you! God of mercy, I am yours! Forgive!*"

In reply, the heavens thundered.

Christine's eyes turned, along with all those in the audience, to the source of the noise – what had sounded so ominously like an explosion from above. They held their breath as the orchestra's notes faltered and jumped when the noise came again. It was coming from above the great dome of the theater, shaking the blazing chandelier so hard it began to swing.

"Get out!" Christine turned to see Armand Moncharmin standing in his box, waving and screaming at the stunned audience below. "Get out now!" he bellowed as another boom echoed from above. Pandemonium broke out in the stalls as the great contraption of crystal and brass shuddered and swayed. It was coming down.

"Listen to him! Go now!" Christine screamed as a fourth terrible blast sounded from above while the audience pushed and panicked to get away from the center of the auditorium. It was chaos all around her too, as the chorus and actors scrambled and yelled. Out of the corner of her eye, Christine saw Raoul striving through the crowd to reach her. She turned to the chandelier again, but she did not scream. She sang a prayer as a final blast sounded.

"*Pure and radiant angels, carry my soul to heaven!*" she sang as the icon of the Opera's power and grandeur plummeted from the heavens, blazing for one brilliant second before its light was extinguished. It hit the seats with a deafening roar of twisting metal and shattering crystal, and the entire theater was plunged into darkness.

Everyone screamed except Christine. She had no time to even consider it before a hand covered her mouth and another gripped her waist. Away from the blazing world into darkness, they fell. Her angel had come for her.

12. Drowning

Erik braced himself for the pain as they crashed through the trap door, and he was not disappointed. His knees cracked against the boards, and Christine's weight pushed the air from his lungs as she landed atop him, locked in his arms. It set off his wounds and made his head ring. If there had been any light, his vision would have blurred. He hauled Christine up with him as she groaned.

Was she hurt? Was she confused? Did she not know her prayers had been answered? Such beautiful prayers offered up in radiant song in defiance of that vile boy. Christine had pushed him away, and Erik had known and he had heard, and now, she was back in his arms.

Above them was screaming and thundering feet that made the stage above them tremble, and none of it mattered because Erik had her back and he would never let go. Even when she struggled to turn to him, he did not let go. He pulled her into their embrace again and muffled the cry he knew would come as he triggered the second trap door.

They landed on their feet this time, just as a cry came from above. Had they been seen? The stagehands, they had lights of their own to use down here, lights that weren't connected to the gas lines. Erik could see them distantly in the dark, like fireflies. He did not want to kill them if they came close. Fireflies were so beautiful in the summer, but it was spring and he had a task at hand, didn't he?

"Who is there?" a voice called, angry and dangerous. "Stop!"

Erik seized his love, dragging her away from the voice and towards their dark road. They had to run, so he made them run, dodging between the ropes and sets and great gears below the stage. It was too busy here, even with the distraction above. It was still loud. He could still hear the screams and chaos above. He could not stop and savor the fruits of his work, alas.

Another sound and they veered again, Christine stumbling behind him. They came to a door into a narrow stair and Christine stopped, forcing Erik to finally face her.

Fear clutching his heart, Erik let Christine go, and she rounded on him. Immediately she pushed off the hood that hid his face, exposing that he wore no mask. He stood before her, exposed as the chaos he had caused echoed above them and the woman who had either betrayed him or been stolen from him looked into his face once more. How different it was now from the sunset by the seaside...

"I did what I had to do," Erik said before she could berate him, bracing for her fury as he had braced for the fall.

"So did I." There was no anger in Christine's voice, only contrition. The thorn of doubt that had wedged itself between Erik's ribs since Perros was suddenly so much smaller. "I'm so sorry—"

He kissed her before she could say more. Kissed her living, eager lips with more hunger and desperation than ever before. Christine was there in his arms again, and that was all that mattered. The chaos above was silent, the wreckage was far away, as their breath became one in the warren of illusions below the stage. She pulled back, touching his cheek so tenderly.

"I thought you were—" she began just as a cry sounded nearby. Erik recoiled from her hand, the hate that had burned like a furnace in him all day reigniting.

"We have to move. They're coming." Erik grabbed her wrist once again as they continued down.

"Who is coming?" Christine asked breathlessly.

"The police – they're all over."

They made a sharp turn that took them into a room that he was sure Christine had never seen before, given that so few people in the Opera knew it existed. The central controls for all the gas lights in the Opera gave the impression of something like an organ, which was why it was called that. And like the other organ far below them across the lake, this one had a ghost to tend it. The figure wearing the black coat and hat along with a white mask turned to them as they entered and sighed in relief.

"What on earth—" Christine gasped as the other Phantom stepped away from the gas organ and removed her mask. "*Julianne?*"

"I'm sorry I wasn't able to dress you. I was needed elsewhere," Julianne muttered before Christine flew to embrace Erik's grudging accomplice.

"You helped?" Christine asked, her face falling as she saw the unconscious gasman in a pile on the floor.

"Someone needed to turn off the lights so he could get you away," Julianne explained. "It had to be the ghost. We'll be compensated for our work, he promised."

"You had other help?" Christine asked.

"And now the ghost has to run," Erik interjected. "Both versions. You remember your task now?"

"Wait until they come in and see the Phantom, then run like hell," Julianne replied with a determined nod. "Then cast off the costume before walking out with everyone else."

"Wait, what?" Christine protested as she looked worriedly between the two of them. "You could be killed!"

Julianne squeezed her hand and smiled. "I made my choices. I'll explain it all one day soon, I hope."

"Thank you, Mademoiselle Bonet." Erik pulled Christine away as she gaped at her friend. "And tell her—"

"I will. Don't make me regret this," Julianne admonished in return.

"Wait! Who else is involved?" Christine demanded as Erik pulled her out the door opposite the one they had entered. They slipped into a hidden passage, then down. There was no time to talk or explain, only to run, the lantern providing only the most meager of light as they descended and finally slipped into a dark passage. "*What is happening?*"

"What's better than one distraction? Two!" Erik laughed. "They've been all over all day, so many gendarmes infesting my opera like rats. But I learned from the rat catcher, they can't resist a bright blazing light! So I gave them one, and some darkness too. Quite poetic, I thought."

"Erik, how did you bring down the chandelier?" Christine asked breathlessly, and Erik looked over his shoulder and grinned. "Who helped you?"

"I set the charges, according to plan. I just needed someone in the dome to flip the switch. She was happy to help, just like Julianne was. The gendarmes and the firemen will look up in the dome and down at the gas organ for the terrible Phantom and they'll chase a shadow. Then he'll disappear, and two women will walk out of the Opera together."

"Adèle. You got *Adèle* involved in this too?" Christine gasped.

"She was deeply interested in what I would do to my brother," Erik assured her, turning back to their dark path. "I don't know if it was a lie, promising to kill my dear brother. I hurt him already. Not as much as he deserves, but there's time. Or I hope there will be. They asked me to hurt the Daroga and your new fiancé too, for standing by and making it happen, playing with that monster like he was a loaded gun and then acting so shocked when it went off and hurt someone. I'll certainly keep that promise."

Finally they came to a stair, narrow and close, and Erik pulled her down after him once more. Christine cried out as she tripped and faltered at the final step, stumbling into Erik's embrace again. She was so alive and real in his arms, and the weight of her when he lifted her up was so solid. He didn't care that the effort made his wounded arm scream or his lungs tight. It was faster this way. He could not have her hurting herself and he could not let them be caught. He would never be caught again.

"Just a little bit further, and we'll be home." Erik smiled at the thought of home, even if it was not safe anymore, with detectives and little noble brats on their way down to invade it. They would be so surprised when they arrived. "I know it's dark. Don't be afraid."

Christine made a sound and tightened her grip around his neck. Was it a sob? Was she scared? She had not been scared the first time he brought her below. She had been in this same white shift then, when he had sung to her all of their journey. When he had been an angel leading her to bliss, not the unholy thing carrying her now.

"*Siúil, siúil, siúil a ruin. Siúil go socar agus siúil go ciúin,*" Erik sang to her softly, feeling her relax even as she heaved another weeping breath.

It was chaos like Shaya had never seen. The audience streamed from the auditorium in a mad, screaming rush, the only light coming from firemen with their emergency lanterns trying to get in. The police shouted, the crowd pushed, and all the while, the wreckage of the great chandelier smoldered. Shaya could see it all from center stage where he stood. No one had stopped him when he rushed there, they were all too busy with Erik's perfect disaster of distraction.

Shaya had watched from the stalls as Erik had, somehow, brought down the chandelier, turned off all the lights, and kidnapped Christine right off the stage. Erik the Magician at his most deadly. Shaya had run backstage. He had to find Raoul before the boy went after Erik alone and got himself killed.

"The lights! Bring back the lights!" Shaya heard someone yell and turned to see Firmin Richard rushing through the crowd of dancers and chorus. Philippe de Chagny was beside him.

"Monsieur!" Shaya cried, rushing towards Philippe as the Comte abandoned the manager. "Where is your brother?"

"He was supposed to be waiting back here to kill that creature!" Philippe railed. "Was he taken too?"

"I don't believe so." Shaya looked around desperately. In the stalls, Moncharmin was leading the firemen to stem any blaze that might ignite from spilled gas or an errant spark around the chandelier's wreckage and look for injured. No one seemed to have been beneath the thing when it fell, thanks to the manager's warning scream. Richard was barking orders at gendarmes and firemen in the wings. But no Raoul. "He must have started after him alone. I'll go—"

"How? The girl disappeared into thin air *again*!" Philippe yelled. "I thought he could only do that with the bloody mirror!"

"That's where Raoul has gone!" Shaya gasped. He turned to go just in time for a fireman to barrel into him, pushing him aside to get to Richard.

"Monsieur! The gas is back on! He turned off the whole organ!" the man cried, and Shaya cast a look towards Philippe.

"How do you know?" Richard demanded, rounding on the young, red-faced man.

"We went down! A brigade of us, to check the gas, and we saw him! He ran, but we'll have him soon enough!"

"That can't be." Shaya watched as Richard and Philippe exchanged equally suspicious looks.

"Show me where he went. I'll go," Philippe volunteered to the fireman. "Persian, you go look for my brother, and please..." The elder noble gripped Shaya's arm and looked earnestly into his face. "Keep him safe. For me."

"I will." Shaya hoped it was a promise he could keep.

With no more hesitation, Shaya rushed into the halls where the lights were slowly being relit. No one marked him – everyone was either trying to flee or find someone. They didn't care about the Persian roaming backstage. He came quickly to Christine Daaé's remote dressing room and knew he was right by the noise beyond the half-open door.

"Open up! I know you can open, you piece of shit!" Raoul was yelling as he pounded his fists against Christine's mirror. "Let me in!"

"There are better ways down, Monsieur," Shaya said, and Raoul spun to glare at him, absolutely feral with rage. "And it will do you well to calm yourself if we are to travel them."

"He has her! I saw him take her right from the stage!" Raoul screamed in return. "He knew somehow! Did you warn him?"

"I did not." Shaya raised his hands to calm the beast before him. "The only one I warned was you. I told you this was a stupid plan, and now, we have to do something I have avoided for weeks."

"You know how to get into his house," Raoul hissed. "Your secret road that you never wanted to show me."

"It will surely be a trap; I want you to know that. Erik knows we are coming and he'll be ready."

"I don't care," Raoul growled. "I swore I would end this tonight, and I keep my word."

"You may regret such a promise. Are you still armed?"

Raoul pulled his pistol from his pocket to show Shaya that he indeed was. "I am ready."

"Remember, keep your hand at the level of your eye," Shaya admonished. "Especially in the dark."

Shaya turned back to the hall and did not look back as Raoul followed. It was still madness backstage, but as soon as they descended a level, it was as quiet as a tomb. Shaya easily found a small lantern to ignite, and with it they moved into the shadows. It was clever of Erik to plunge the Opera into shadow, Shaya mused. As clever as the disaster with the chandelier he had caused to draw away all the men meant to keep him from escaping.

They soon came to the area below the stage, where ropes and huge gears moved the machinery and sets. In the flickering light of their lamp, the wheels and rigging cast ominous shadows that seemed to dance...

"There's someone up there," Raoul whispered. Shaya froze, eyes scanning the distant dark. Sure enough, there it was: a shadow in a felt hat.

"Stay back. He's not on our side," Shaya hissed, hiding the light of his lantern as the shade moved with clear purpose between the machinery. "Get down."

They hid themselves behind one of the huge gears, holding their breath as the interloper moved past. What was he doing now? Shaya shuddered to think. After several long minutes of waiting, Shaya was certain they were alone and signaled Raoul to rise from their hiding place.

"You know who it is?" Raoul demanded when they began to move again.

"I have theories, but they're not important. Did you say anything to Christine about the plan?"

Shaya looked over his shoulder to see Raoul swallow awkwardly. "Somehow, she knew Erik wasn't watching and she became hysterical again."

Shaya paused at the top of the stairwell that would take them downward to the third cellar and the secret door, the ominous sense of repetition that had dogged him all day surging again.

"Have you ever stopped to think that..." Shaya sighed. "That she believes this is love. Honestly believes it. Maybe that's not so different from real love."

"No one could love that thing – you know that just as well as I," Raoul snapped. "So no, I have never even bothered to consider it because it's insanity. She's been manipulated and used and defiled. That's all."

"I admire your faith," Shaya muttered as they began to descend. He had experienced faith once too. In the Shah and in his God and that he was doing right, even when all evidence and logic pointed in the other direction. It had to have been right and righteous back then, just as now. Because otherwise...

"How close are we?" Raoul asked as they arrived at the third cellar, where set after set hung in narrow rows.

"Very. We're looking for a stone wall from *Le Roi de Lahore*."

"You think I know what different sets look like?'

"It looks Indian. I think it's towards the back." Shaya's lantern illuminated forests and markets and distant castles until, at last, they came to the right place.

Shaya pressed against the false stone as he had seen Erik do and, sure enough, the trap door opened to reveal an entrance to utter darkness.

"Are you sure?" Raoul asked quietly.

"I'm sure that if we go in there, there will be no coming out the same way. We will have to fight him or break in. Something awaits us."

"I'm ready." Raoul drew his pistol. "But I shan't mind you going first, as it is your discovery."

Shaya scowled but did not argue. He heaved one leg, then the other, into the hole and fixed the handle of the lantern around his thumb so he could grip the ledge as he lowered himself. There was no indication at all how far down the passage went, but it had to be at least two stories if it went to the fifth cellar and Erik. With one final breath for courage, Shaya let go.

The fall was long, and his knees and ankles smarted when he hit the cold ground, but he lived. That was something.

"I've made it down!" he hissed upwards, trying to make out Raoul's shadow as he followed through the passage. Shaya raised his lantern and jumped at the sight of a shadow also holding a light right in front of him. Stumbling back, the lantern dropped – and so too did the light belonging to the other. Shaya scrambled as the metal clanged against the hard floor, his heart suddenly pounding in terror. "No..."

"I'm following!" Raoul grunted above him as he prepared to drop. At the same time, Shaya raised the lantern to see his own face reflected in a mirror. One of many.

"Don't—" he began to cry out, but it was too late.

Raoul landed on the floor beside him, looking around the mirrored chamber in confusion. "Where—"

Shaya gestured for silence, listening for any sound through the walls. The lights were not on yet. The torments had not begun.

"This is worse than I could have ever thought," Shaya told his companion, as quietly as he could manage. "Do not make a sound. We cannot let him know we are in here."

"Where are we?" Raoul asked in the barest whisper.

"The torture chamber. The one he used to drive men mad in our rosy hours of Mazenderan."

Christine didn't want to let go of Erik when he lifted her from the boat, then put her down outside the house on the lake. She wanted to hang on to him and feel that he was real and solid and alive as long as possible. If she held him, she could reach him and calm the storm in his mind that had propelled them through the dark. The rage that had brought the great chandelier crashing down.

Christine shivered from the cold and to recall that sight. It had been horrifying, and at the same time, glorious, to see everything brought to ruin. There was no going back now, for any of them.

At last they entered the house, and Christine sighed in relief. Erik stalked through the parlor with some urgent purpose, checking the corners and the walls as if he might find some adversary waiting there, muttering softly to himself. He paused at the wall to the left of the organ and smiled strangely before turning to Christine at last. He was a mess, at least what she could see, his hair unkempt and matted, and a smear of blood on his ravaged cheek.

"I'm sorry I'm not more presentable. So much to do, no time to dress properly," he said with a shrug as she stared.

"Erik, did they hurt you?" she asked as she approached, wary of alarming him.

"I've had worse." Erik looked at his wrists, where fresh red marks were visible above his old scars. Carefully, Christine reached out to touch the wounds, trying to hold in her tears as he winced before allowing her to touch him. Her fingertips grazed his livid flesh, and he let out a shaking breath as she stepped close.

Slow and tender, Christine unfastened Erik's red robe to reveal that he was in shirtsleeves underneath, the same white one he had been wearing when they had taken him. It was clear because of the hole in the right arm and the hasty bandage he had affixed around his bullet wound.

"I'm so sorry," Christine murmured, reaching for the wound. "I can't imagine how awful it was to be chained—"

"It was not your crime, it was theirs," Erik replied with unnerving calm. "All you did was remind me what the world thinks of me and what a monstrous place it is. I should thank you! Yes, you wanted me to be there, you asked for it and you knew I could never refuse you, but you are not at fault. They are." There it was, that chill edge to his voice and tension in his body that made Christine so afraid.

"And you punished them. Now you have me back," Christine tried as she stroked his arm.

Erik laughed, bitter and cold. "Their punishment has only begun. The chandelier, that was only act one. Don Juan has yet to reach his final triumph."

Christine's stomach fell at the mention of his horrible masterwork and she turned to the organ. There it was: the huge score written in blood-red ink, open above the keys, with scrawled notes and designs.

Erik strode to the instrument and flipped to another page, revealing not music, but a diagram of the chandelier, its five counterweights... and the means to destroy them.

"You said it all went according to plan. You were able to bring the chandelier down because you built the devices years ago," she muttered sickly.

"I've modified them through the years, when I've had new ideas." Erik sounded so cheerful and proud it terrified her. "I told you, didn't I? I have worked on my *Don Juan* for a very long time, my great triumph. Just like Wagner and his *Ring*! Wagner ended his ring cycle with the death of the gods and the burning of the entire world. I have not yet penned my finale, but there is one scene I always thought to include. Much in that Wagnerian fashion..."

"We don't need that. It's over." Christine forced herself between Erik and the terrible score, trying to bring her angel back to her as she always had before. His eyes came back into focus, fixed on her. "Erik, please—"

"Did any of them hurt you?" Erik asked abruptly, as he caught her hand and examined her. "It matters. I was extremely specific with that boy about what I would do if he hurt you."

"No. Raoul..." Christine swallowed, afraid to lie and worried what the truth would inspire. "I think he drugged me in Perros. I thought I fainted but I don't know how I was asleep for so long."

"Of course he did," Erik said, deadly and dark. "I'm sure I know who supplied your aristocratic hero with the means to make a woman insensible and easy to use."

"I woke up in the carriage, Shaya was there. We were back in Paris and they told me they had you. Erik, I was so scared!"

"I knew he was lying, that little rat," Erik growled, tightening his hold on her hand. "He said you were relieved. He said you were happy."

"It wasn't true!" Christine cried, gripping her lover's hand. He wasn't looking at her eyes though, but at her bare fingers.

"I heard the happy news of your engagement this morning." Erik's voice was as dire as she had ever heard it.

"Please, you have to know, it wasn't true, whatever you read or heard," Christine whimpered, tears filling her eyes again. "I thought I was saving you. I agreed to it because I love you! He took my ring before I woke! Erik, I swear—"

"How far did you intend to go to save me?" Erik demanded, finally meeting her eyes, as fire sparked in his gold ones. "How far did he push his rights as your future husband?"

"He only kissed me," Christine pled, grabbing Erik by the arms. She wanted to shake the suspicions out of his foolish head and absolve herself of the shame. "But he wanted to take me tonight."

Erik seized her at the words, lips curling, his hands raking into her hair and he looked deep in her eyes, his own golden orbs incandescent with rage. "Would you have done it?" he demanded, hands shaking against her skull. "To save my miserable life, would you have gone to his bed? Like all the times you went to mine to save his?"

Tears streamed down Christine's cheeks as she shook her head. "No. I love you... but I couldn't do that. You saw – you saw me tell him I couldn't do it. I'm sorry, but I could never—"

Erik kissed her before she could say more. Kissed her hard, with more hunger and desperation than ever before, claiming her once again. It was a breath after drowning, Christine knew it, a gasp for life that had been so close to slipping away. She returned the embrace frantically, kneading her lips against Erik's and tasting their tears. He pulled away long enough to caress her cheek and show her that the fury was gone from his eyes.

"That's my girl," he whispered. "My beautiful, strong, perfect Christine. I should never have doubted you."

"I've always been yours." Christine kissed him again to prove it, starving and deep, wanting nothing more than to keep this contact forever. If she just kept kissing him, kept touching him, he couldn't be taken away again. He couldn't succumb to the madness she'd left him to. "I was so afraid. They said they were giving you to the police," Christine sobbed between kisses.

"It doesn't matter. I have you back now." Erik pulled her tight against him, kissing her cheek and jaw and neck. "They won't ever take you again."

Christine gasped as his teeth grazed her pulse, just as his hands swept up to her breasts. She thought of the way Raoul had kissed her in her dressing room – the way he had been so confident that he was entitled to take her tonight because of a promise he had stolen with lies and threats. It lit a fire in her as Erik pressed his thumbs over her nipples, which grew tight under her plain costume. "They won't. I swear."

Erik made a noise low in his throat, something like a groan or a growl as he seized her thighs and began to yank her skirt up toward her hips. In turn Christine gave a small, sweet gasp as she felt the hardening of his desire between them. She deepened her kiss and wrapped her arms around him, suddenly frantic to show her dark angel that it was him she chose. She heard the rip of fabric as he divested her of her thin pantalettes and shivered at the feel of cold air on her legs, then cried out in slavish need when he touched her.

"Still mine," Erik purred as his fingers explored her cunt, drawing forth a slick welcome and dizzying pleasure as he did. "My Christine."

"Always," Christine mewled in reply as he filled her with three long fingers, sending lighting through her bones and banishing all logic from her mind. She was sure she would have collapsed had he not been holding her by the waist, not only from pleasure and need, but the sheer relief that she could still reach him. But she needed more. They needed more. "Erik, I—I need—fuck—"

"I need you too," he answered. He withdrew his hand so that she whined in protest at the emptiness, then gasped anew as he lifted her by her thighs and right onto the keys of the organ. A discordant, thunderous noise filled the house as Christine's weight settled on the keys. Her cry of pleasure joined the chorus as her fallen angel of music kissed her again and dipped his hand between them to free his cock. "Promise it again, my love."

"I promise," Christine cooed, desperate to be filled and to show him her love and trust as she locked her legs around him. She nearly sobbed at the pleasure as he drove his cock into her and at last filled her to the brim. The organ gave another wail, then began to echo the rhythm of his thrusts.

Christine could feel the music behind her, the keys of the instrument hard against her bared ass, but more than anything, she felt the vibration of the sound into her core. It screamed and pounded as Erik claimed her, her hips meeting his in frantic counterpoint, sending new notes screaming from the organ as she writhed and trembled.

"My angel," Erik panted against her throat before sucking a mark onto her neck. She keened in ecstasy as he fucked hard into her, her cries in perfect harmony with the cacophony surrounding them. He released his grip on her thigh and took her hand, pulling away from their kiss as he did. "My angel who keeps her promises."

Christine opened her eyes at the feel of metal sliding down her finger and saw, miraculously, her ring returned to her, now on her left hand, where a wedding band was meant to be. The gold glinted against the brass of the organ's pipes and she wanted to ask how, to weep at the sight of a promise restored. She wanted to swear to never remove it again, but she was too overcome with the breathless passion of their joining.

"Always," was all she could gasp out, and who knew if Erik even heard her over the din of the organ as he drove into her. The whole world screamed around them. Her whole body shook with every thrust of his cock. She was careening to her peak, her hips wild and her breath ragged as her lover took what was his and his alone. Christine was a woman possessed, in every sense.

"Let me see it. Let me feel it," Erik commanded over the noise and, as ever, Christine's lust responded to his voice, pushing her higher and higher. "Come for me, my angel. Let me hear it."

Christine screamed as she obeyed, guttural and wild as the climax took her. She held onto Erik for dear life as she bucked and clenched around him, and the sound of his voice joining hers only deepened and extended her ecstasy. It was music as he followed her over the edge, spilling into her in hot bursts, even as the organ joined, and the walls called out around them.

Christine was breathless and boneless as the climax subsided, her ears still ringing from the organ's powerful noise.

"Christine." The sound of her name was strangely distant and urgent. She forced herself to look up at her lover, worried, only to see his triumphant smile. A smile that remained as the voice came again. "Christine!"

"Raoul?" Christine asked in horror, looking frantically around the room and to the door. Erik withdrew from her with a bow as she stumbled to the floor, her heart racing in terror and shame. "How did he—the lake—" Christine stammered as Erik righted his clothes.

"Oh, he's not outside," Erik replied with a shrug. "They've already shown themselves in. Right down the path I knew they would take."

"I will kill you! You monster! I will rip your heart from your chest!" came Raoul's voice again, and this time, Christine could discern its source: the wall between the fireplace and the storeroom door. The empty space she had always wondered about. Somehow, Raoul was inside the walls – trapped.

And he had heard everything that had just transpired.

"I don't think you're in a position to be making threats, Monsieur," Erik laughed in turn as Christine sank to the floor, her cruel lover's spend still wet on her thighs. "Are you there too, Daroga? Haven't you told him where you are? Let me turn on the lights, so you can see my work better!"

The brightness blinded Raoul and he stumbled back from the mirror he had been pounding so uselessly as he listened to *them*. He blinked over and over, confronted by his red-faced reflection in the glass. He was a mess of fury, his clothes in disarray thanks to his struggles with Shaya. The man had dared to try to keep him from shouting when that thing's assault on Raoul's fiancée had started. Now, the older man was nursing a split lip courtesy of Raoul's elbow to the face.

"I told you to keep your mouth shut," the Persian seethed from the floor. "Now we are done for."

"There you are, Daroga. Astute as ever," the monster's voice rang through the hexagonal room. Or was it a forest? Raoul's brain could not reconcile what he saw with what he knew to be true. By some devilry of the mirrors and a tree wrought of metal in a corner, the torture chamber had become a jungle filled with bewildered, furious copies of the two men.

"Erik! What is going on? Where are they?" Christine demanded. Her voice was not so tender now, raw from all the screaming and weeping she had done since arriving. From the cries she had given like an animal howling in heat.

"We are in his torture chamber, Mademoiselle," Shaya replied as Raoul stalked back and forth, slamming his fists into the walls. It was warm, now that the lights were on, like a real jungle indeed.

"What? No. No, that was in Persia," Christine protested, because of course she knew *something*, but the monster had not told her everything. She knew only enough to pity him and open her legs, not enough to see reason and run.

"I perfected it there," Erik crooned. "But I started it here. I told you! I tortured for the Communards. They were fond of this place. My friend Laurent had the idea for the tree, actually. Well, he was not really my friend, in the end. I did kill him, quite near where you are standing. I foolishly thought I was doing some good. Can you imagine?"

"Erik," Christine said, her voice soft now. Raoul did not want to imagine what she looked like after her exertions, but the picture came anyway. In his mind Raoul saw her with those big, sad eyes and her dark hair in tangles, dress ripped to expose her to the view of the lecherous fiend.

"When I came back here, I improved it as well. It was all part of my plans for my great triumph. I had so many plans in those first months. Plans to finish my work from that fiery night. I hadn't killed nearly enough of those useless, noble swine. I planned to put them in cages, make them go mad staring at their own faces and illusions of a world that's only there to kill and hurt them. I wish my dear brother were here to join them, but at least the young heir of the Chagny name will die burning, just like his father."

Raoul screamed at that, the noise echoing off the glass as he began pounding on it again, only for a sound even more awful than that of the creature defiling Christine to seep through the walls: Erik's laughter.

"I will kill you, you bastard!" Raoul bellowed as the laughter continued.

"Get a hold of yourself!" Shaya cried as he grabbed Raoul and shook him. "Acting like a madman will get us nowhere!"

"Oh no, Daroga – let him scream. It's such a wonderful sound! I've been wanting to hear it for so long," Erik cackled.

Raoul gritted his teeth, now determined not to give the monster the satisfaction of his suffering. In the silence, he heard a sob.

"Erik, stop, please. You don't have to do this. You've hurt him enough!" Christine wept.

"I don't think I have. In fact, I haven't even hurt him as much as I thought I did! I didn't kill the fool's father!" Erik went on hysterically.

Shaya let go of Raoul to turn to the wall where the voices were coming from. It would have been comical to see his confused face replicated so many times had it not been so bloody fucking hot.

"What are you talking about?" Christine asked as if speaking to a rational man and not a deranged monster.

"I always wondered why that fire took off as fast as it did that night. It turns out, I was just a distraction – a patsy! – to take the blame for the real criminal. Can you believe it? Do you know what I felt when I figured that out?"

"Liar! Don't listen to him!" Raoul yelled. Shaya delivered him a quick blow to the groin to gain some silence.

"Erik, calm down," Christine begged as Raoul collapsed. The floor – was it metal? It was searing hot, just like the walls. "Just look at me and breathe. We'll talk, and—"

"I was disappointed!" Erik howled, and Raoul struck the searing glass again. He was starting to sweat profusely from the rising heat and his endless rage. "I *wanted* to have been the one that delivered them all to Hades! I thought my Don Juan's great finale would finish the work, not begin it!"

"You don't need to finish anything! It's over!" Christine cried. "Erik, it's over! You have them where you want them and you've hurt them. You have me and you've proven your power!"

"And I will keep them there until I am done with them!" A crash sounded, and Christine gave a cry of alarm. "Would you like to see? Look in my window here and see. Tell me how they look in my lovely jungle!"

"I don't want to look!" Christine argued. "I want you to turn that thing off and stop this. I want to—"

"Talk? So we can fix it? So you can devise more lies and more placations to satisfy a world that hates me?" Erik sounded truly wild, like a man who could – and would – do anything. Raoul was sick and helpless and dizzy with the heat, furious to think how the creature had already abused her. "Or will you seduce me? Distract me from my path with a nice fuck?"

"Don't you dare touch her again!" Raoul found himself yelling. "You raping, murdering, degenerate villain!"

"Oh, you poor boy," Erik laughed, and his voice sounded like it was right in Raoul's ear somehow. "You don't even know how many times I've been ready to end your miserable life and our dear Christine has saved us all from the brink of devastation with her *charms*. Would you like to know about how I had her right under your snooping nose while you looked about her room? Oh, how she—"

The sharp sound of a slap cut off Erik's words. Then deafening silence on the other side of the wall. He was going to kill her or rape her again, Raoul was sure of it.

"How dare you. How *dare* you use me for your petty revenge like he used me as bait," Christine said at last, her voice unrecognizable. "I thought you were better than that - than all of this!"

"You were wrong. *I am the monster*, Christine. I always have been, always will be. The one I was made, the one I was born," Erik replied with terrifying calm. Raoul glanced to the Persian, who was just as transfixed. "*They* reminded me of that with their chains and their lies when they stole you from me! And now, I will not let them forget it!"

"Erik, for God's sake!" It was Shaya who cried out. "Have mercy! She's right! This is not who you are!"

"Are you a fool or insane?" Raoul demanded of the man beside him, ready to throttle him. He turned back to the wall and yelled instead. "No! For once, the beast is right! He is a monster! He knows nothing of mercy."

"I have given all of you mercy for decades!" Erik roared, and the very walls trembled. "I have held back from showing this cruel world just how terrible the monster they made is! I have hidden away and buried my rage and hate, but no longer! I am tired of mercy!"

Again, there was pregnant silence, the tension as oppressive as the heat of the torture chamber.

"If only my brother could see you now," Shaya chided. "Ramin showed you mercy, and I said he was a fool for it. At last, you prove me right."

"Erik, please," Christine pled, and Raoul could not banish the image of her falling to her knees before the creature. "We can just go. It can be over right now."

"Go?" the monster echoed, as disbelieving as Raoul. "You keep saying that. You keep planning to run away, but to where? I ran before. I've run my whole life until I came here. This is my *home*. The only home I have ever or will ever know. And it will be my tomb too."

"It doesn't have to be!" Christine argued desperately, and Raoul raised his hand to strike the glass again in rage. "There is a chance out there."

"Do you still believe that?" Erik asked, and it was the tenderness of it that shocked Raoul. "Christine, I can't—"

"We can! We—" Christine's entreaties were cut off by the sound of a bell, of all things, tolling mechanically.

"Someone is on the lake," the villain stated, and Raoul's pulse quickened. Was it the police? The managers? Who was as foolish as they to come down here?

"Oh, God. Erik, please help them!" It sounded like she was crying again. "No more! No more death. Whoever is out there – stop them! For me and for us!"

Raoul could not make out any word of reply but his heart leapt in hope at the sound of a door shutting. Was Erik gone? The silence stretched out as he breathed in air that scorched his lungs.

"Christine, you have to let us out!" Shaya cried, placing his hands against the glass then stumbling back at the heat from it. "It's these lights – they're making it too hot! They're electric! We'll die before he can even start his tortures!"

"I can't," Christine replied desolately.

"You can find a way! Please! Our lives are in your hands!" Shaya called, but Raoul was silent.

Was Christine hesitant because she knew what Raoul would do if he was freed? His pistol remained in his coat pocket, with its bullets still ready to fill Erik's skull. Did she honestly think this night would end with everyone alive?

Erik was going mad, he was sure of it. His head was full of screaming, a hundred ghosts and demons howling at him to kill or to flee, and he did not know who to listen to. The cool dark of the dock by the lake should have cleared his head, but he was now certain he had lost his mind, because the boat was gone. He had poled them across the lake in it on purpose, hadn't he? Because he didn't want anyone following the wrong way. His guests had to be shown right into the house – it was polite. Now, the boat was gone, and someone was on his lake.

Had he moved it? Was that the reason he now saw the slow progress of a light towards him? The lake was not dark. It never really was, thanks to the air holes that let in the light from above on the street or in the theater. In the glowing gloom, he saw the boat and the man polling it awkwardly with a lantern hung on the prow.

"Stop where you are and turn back," Erik heard himself say, his voice echoing like, well, a ghost, between the dark arches rising from the water.

"Who is there?" the interloper cried in return, flustered and furious. Erik knew that voice. As the boat drew closer to where it would trigger the trap, he began to make out Philippe de Chagny's features, though he was still far away. Of course he had come to save his brother's miserable life.

"Turn back now, Monsieur – I am warning you!" Erik called. To his surprise, the man stopped rowing and slowed. Again, Erik was certain he was losing his grip on reality because, despite his warnings, in the water he saw... himself. He saw the shadow – a black, inky stain – moving quickly through the water towards the unsuspecting Comte de Chagny.

"Where is my brother?!" Philippe bellowed as Erik tried to make sense of the vision. Was it a dream or a wish or madness?

"Go back," Erik began again. "And I promise—"

The boat overturned before Erik could finish, Philippe splashing violently into the dark water with a cry of shock. The Comte breached the surface, sputtering for air, before two pale arms pulled him under.

Erik dove into the lake, the cold of the water stabbing into his guts and stealing the air from his lungs. Swimming as fast as he could, he raced towards the struggle. Each time his head rose from the water was a new moment of terror and relief as the splashing continued again and again. And again. And...

Stillness, sudden and horrible. Erik increased his speed but he knew before he reached the body that it was too late. The shadow was gone, dissolved like some siren into the sea, and all that remained was the floating corpse of Philippe de Chagny.

Dead bodies are easier to move in the water – when they are limp and offer no resistance. Even as Erik hauled the man as fast as he could to the shore, he recognized the signs. His face was blue, his neck was bruised, and no matter how Erik pounded on his chest, he did not breathe or surrender the water filling his lungs.

Erik fell back from the corpse, unsure how long they had been on the shore or which shore it was. He had to go back. He had to tell Christine, but would she even believe him if he claimed a shadow had killed the man he had come out to save? Again he had fallen into the trap of mercy! Again the world of men had spit in his face for his efforts. It was all in vain now. It was all for nothing, because now there was no going back. Now, there was a crime on Erik's hands he could never undo.

Now, truly, everything was over.

13. Lux Æterna

"There has to be a way out. Where are you hiding it, Erik, you bastard?" Shaya muttered to Erik, wherever he was, and himself.

"Why would there be a door in a jungle?" The question from Shaya's noble companion was delivered with both derision and a not-insubstantial amount of delirium. "Why are you even bothering?"

"Because of all the places to die, here would be the most infuriating." Shaya continued to feel along the mirrors for some sort of latch or trigger to open the door. There had to be one – Erik used this place as an entrance to his home. It was just hidden.

"Do you think hell is this hot?" Raoul asked in a lilting, far-off tone.

"You could help, you know. Start on the opposite wall."

Raoul did not move from where he had sprawled on the floor. "Don't you think it will be that one? That's where they are." His eyes were clouded, and Shaya knew the man was thinking back to all they had heard. Shaya could still hear it too. The roar of the organ, the cries of passion... But more than that, he recalled the words of love.

"If we get out, what will you do?" Shaya asked earnestly. "And don't say kill him, I know that. What will you do if, by some miracle, Christine survives this too?"

"What do you mean?" Raoul asked back. "He made her a whore before and did it again to spite me. When she's free, she will repent her sin."

"She *loves* him, Raoul. You have to understand that now." Shaya replied, turning from the wall.

"She thinks she does, but it's just a sickness he's infected her with," Raoul spat back. "He has tainted her with depravity, twisted a poor girl's impressionable mind. She can't really love him, despite what she says. If she does, it is a crime she must absolve herself from." Raoul tugged on his undone collar, looking about the forest of reflections and iron branches with bleary eyes.

It's the ugliest thing I've ever seen, brother. To think it came from the mind of someone with such beauty in his soul. Ramin had said that to Shaya privately, after the torture chamber had been unveiled in Mazenderan.

"Wait, what was I saying?" Raoul stammered.

"That if her love is real, then it is a sin." Shaya was unsure if the boy heard him. He hoped he didn't. "Love is never a sin though."

"What do—" Raoul stopped as the sound of pounding came from the wall that separated them from the house on the lake.

"Are you still there?" It was Christine's distressed voice, and Shaya's heart leapt at the sound.

"Where else would we bloody be?" Raoul snarled back as he tried to stand. The poor thing was clearly not made for such heat, though it could be that his yelling and slamming himself against the walls had exhausted him more than it had Shaya.

"We're here! Where is Erik?" Shaya called back. It terrified him that someone was on the lake; he had nearly died there himself. Who would be foolish enough to follow them down?

"I don't know!" Was the fear in the girl's voice of the monster or for him? Perhaps it was both. "But I looked and—"

"Did you find a way out?" Raoul demanded.

"If I tell you, you must promise to use it to leave and never return," came the soft entreaty through the wall. "I don't want anyone else hurt."

"How can you ask that, after everything?" Raoul demanded, and Shaya very much wanted to strangle the fool on Erik's behalf. "He just said—"

"We promise!" Shaya called and met Raoul's incensed glare with his own. "No one else needs to suffer tonight! Just tell us."

"Do you swear? Both of you?" Christine asked, smart girl that she was. Raoul's mouth moved open and shut like a fish, and Shaya wondered how uncomfortable that was in the stifling air. Another noise made Shaya jump in fear. The door. "He's coming. Look on the floor! Under the tree by a root—"

"Christine—" Raoul began, but Shaya covered his mouth to shut him up and motioned for silence. They had to know what had transpired on the lake.

"You're soaked. Erik, what happened?" Christine asked on her side of the wall.

"It wasn't me," came Erik's listless reply, all the terrifying fire that had been in his voice now gone. What had he done now? "I swear, Christine, *it wasn't me.*"

"What happened?" Christine demanded again, sounding just as frightened as Shaya.

"Not here," Erik declared. Shaya cursed under his breath as he listened to the fading sound of steps and Christine's muffled voice.

"Come on, help me look for this exit she found for us," Shaya ordered, falling to his knees at the base of the iron tree. The roots and trunk were so hot it burned Shaya's fingers when he grazed them. He was grateful, even so.

He never would have thought to look there for an exit in the floor, but it made sense that Erik would have yet another trap door at his disposal. Shaya prayed that it at least took them somewhere to get them relief from this maddening heat and the illusion of the jungle that grew more real with every passing second. Shaya knew what this room did to even the strongest men, and he knew as well that he was not one of them. He hoped they had time.

E rik would not look her in the eye. It was something he did when he was ruled by fear, Christine knew. He stood in his bedroom, dripping, and looked at the rumpled sheets and the carved canopy. His eyes went anywhere but the woman who desperately needed to know what had transpired in the water and who still wanted to reach him.

He had looked so huge and fierce just moments ago, like a billowing sail filled with a storm of rage and hate. Now, he was deflated and bent. His shirt was so wet Christine could see through it to make out his scars and the new wound on his arm. "You're going to catch cold if you don't get into some dry clothes..."

Erik's shoulders moved as he gave a hollow laugh. "I don't think that matters anymore, my dear," he said so hopelessly it made her heart ache. "It's all over."

"Erik, please. I need you to tell me what is going on." He did not pull away when she gripped his arm and forced him to turn. "You were close to letting go and believing me when you went out. Who was out there?"

"He's dead now." Erik looked at Christine with wide, sad eyes in his corpse's face.

"You killed someone?"

"No. I *told you*," Erik protested, breath labored. "It wasn't me. It was the shade. It pulled him under and drowned him!"

"What shade?" Christine demanded, taking Erik by the arms as if she could bodily pull him out of this madness.

"The other ghost, the other me who has been haunting us! The one who hurt Jean-Paul and—" Erik stopped, shaking his head. "It doesn't matter. He's dead because of me. Now that boy will never forgive me."

"Who is dead, Erik? Tell me!" Christine's pulse quickened as her mind rushed to an inevitable guess.

"Philippe de Chagny."

Christine covered her mouth to stifle her sob, letting go as she did. It felt like releasing her grip on the one thing stopping her from being swept away in this flood of grief and pain and regret. "No..."

"Now you understand. We can't run, even if we wanted to. Your young hero will chase us down to the ends of the earth for his revenge." Erik said it so simply, as if he wasn't burying the last of their hopes. Or maybe, they had only ever been Christine's hopes. "Unless you let me kill him, that is. And the Daroga."

"No..." Christine shook her head as the world lurched around her.

"One man is already dead, my dear. What is a few more added to that number?" Erik went on, his voice dull and dreamy. "But you won't let me do that. Because it will kill you, to have so much blood on your hands and to know they died so that I could live and keep you. You and your dreams and hopes. Did you know I had given up dreaming before I met you and I was quite content? It was easy as a ghost. It will be easy to be a ghost again."

"What are you talking about?"

"It's simple, my love," Erik sighed. "Either they die or we all die. Yes, us included. I promise when we do, it will be quick. I don't think we will feel a thing."

"That is not the only way!" Christine cried in terror.

"Isn't it though?" Erik took her tenderly by the shoulders. His golden eyes were bloodshot and wild, even though his voice was sweet and calm. "If I kill them, we must both become phantoms.

We would hide here and wait and forget the world above. And you would die, slowly fading and losing your light; growing to hate me, missing the sun. Because you cannot be here always, my Persephone, even if you can never truly leave. Going down that road will destroy you, and in turn, it will destroy me. Day by day, we will die together if I let them go."

"And you think the only other choice is to *die* now?" Christine shrieked. "Erik, no! You told me that, whatever has happened to you, you always wanted to live. You wanted to keep breathing! You can't mean this!"

"But I do!" Erik nearly laughed in return, smiling as if a brilliant idea was blooming in his mind. "I have held onto my miserable existence for so long, my darling Christine, just long enough to find you. But I can't live if I lose you, and I will lose you. I know I shall. So why not end it now? We will be together forever on the other side. It will be perfect! We will haunt the ruins together!"

"Ruins?" Christine echoed in fresh horror.

"It's the great finale! Don Juan's final triumph over all those who shunned him for his sins. He has the last word as he brings the theater tumbling to ruin around them! Oh, it was meant to be so glorious... Laurent would have been so proud of how I meant to do it, how I used all his supplies."

"Erik, you are talking madness!" Christine shook him, trying just to bring him back to her and exorcise the demons that had filled him with such awful thoughts.

"No – I'm finally talking sense!" he cried as he threw off her hands and ran towards the parlor. "I'm finally showing the strength of my convictions and doing what I was always meant to do here: tear it down, all of it, and leave this gaudy palace in ruble when I turn the grasshopper. He hops so jolly high!"

"The grasshopper?" Christine echoed as she rushed after him.

"I thought it was funny, making such a little thing the instrument of their downfall. It's right there on the mantle if you'd like to look." Erik smiled as he nodded to a small casket above the fire, innocuous among all the other detritus and knickknacks he had hoarded there.

"I don't want to..." Christine exhaled, looking at the man she loved and seeing a stranger full of hate and madness.

"And yes, the scorpion is there too. I always meant to use it, but I never could. I never could forgive them enough. And now, I'm so glad I didn't! I wanted them all to pay, in my heart, and now they will. Or some of them. The Opera is surely empty by now. Or maybe it isn't. The Daroga will know! Daroga, are you alive in there?"

"What madness now, Erik?!" Shaya's voice came through the wall.

"Erik, please, stop! Listen to me and calm down!" Christine whimpered, stepping in front of Erik as he darted towards the mantle. Her body was ready to give out with the absolute fear and panic filling her, but she pushed it down and away, gripping Erik for dear life. "You cannot do this! I will not allow you! One person is dead already! It is enough!"

Erik stared at her as if he didn't recognize her, eyes unfocused and lost. "I should play his requiem first! It will serve as all of ours too," Erik cried, turning to the organ as Christine rushed after him. "I've always been suspicious of working on a requiem. Mozart's killed him, they say, because he wrote it for himself. I never wanted to start one because it might be bad luck, and now... Well, another man's work will have to suffice. I hope you do not mind."

"Erik, stop talking like that!" Christine protested as he picked up the score of *Don Juan Triumphant* off the floor where it had fallen in their throes of passion. Even now, with a new crisis at hand, it made her flush with fury and shame to think how he had used her and her love. At least she had found the plans in there that she had hoped would save two lives.

"At least I'll be able to finish the finale as it was meant to be heard," Erik laughed. "Should I play it as well, before we finish our time in this life and I turn the grasshopper?"

"No!" Christine wailed. "I will not let you do this! Erik!"

He did not hear nor see her. The notes of the organ filled the house, the thundering cry of the Dies Irae, and Christine fell to her knees with a sob. What was she supposed to do? Erik was out of her reach, lost so deeply to madness and pain that it was as if he were dead already.

He was a ghost again, an angel and a dream she could not keep or hold or love in the light. He always had been. And yet, Christine had always, stupidly, dreamed he could be more. When she had let go of all the other dreams that she had built her fragile life on, there had still been that. There had still been *him*, but she had to admit it now – Erik had never been there. It had been an illusion, a phantom that had kept up her hope.

Maybe he was right, and there was no reason to breathe any longer. Her father had given up on living and become a ghost to her, bit by bit, until he joined her mother. Christine had lived in a dream for years, a half-life, waiting for an angel. Then he had come. At last, she had been saved. Then the truth, again, had brought her so much pain...

The music went on, and Erik's voice rose in song. Christine closed her eyes on tears at the beauty of it and the memories the sound inspired. Memories of pain. And love.

It hurt so much now because she loved him and had for so long, and even with all the pain, she had been *alive*. She had felt joy and love and hope as well as the pain, because that is what it meant to live.

Erik sang on, lost in the music of death even as his breath
became something so beautiful. There could be no happiness
without the suffering, no summer without winter's chill, no choirs
of angels without a requiem. How could she reach the man who
had taught her that? How could she make him hear her over the
deafening music of death and despair?

"I've found something!" the Persian hissed, and Raoul started
from his stupor. It was beautiful, the sound of the organ and
the voice of heaven. It was louder here than in church and so
strange that there should be a requiem playing in the depths of the
jungle. "Did you hear me?"

"I heard you," Raoul grumbled as the angel on the other side of
the wall began to sing of eternal light. "Dear God, that's beautiful.
Is it a requiem?"

"It will be ours if you don't move right now!" Shaya began to
bodily drag Raoul towards the hole he had dug in the ground.

"There could be insects or snakes in there! It's not safe!" Raoul
scoffed and he was not prepared for how sobering the slap he
received in reply was. He blinked. This was not a jungle... "How did
you find that?"

"Get in now, before your brain melts further!" Shaya
commanded.

Raoul, good sailor, did as he was told and scrambled through
the little trap door at the base of Erik's iron tree.

The dark, cold air of the cellar they found themselves in was
even more bracing than the slap, and Raoul collapsed with relief
to be free of the torture chamber. He didn't hit the floor, however.
Instead his body slumped over something round he couldn't make
out, given he was utterly blind in the darkness.

"Now where are we?" the Persian asked as the music continued above. Raoul groped at the thing he had fallen onto, trying to understand. Wood. Rough, bowed wood like a ship's hull. Smaller planks though. It was round and girded by – was that steel?

"I think we've found his wine cellar! These are barrels! God, where is the stopper? I need a drink before I die."

"Why would he keep barrels down here?" Shaya muttered next to Raoul in the dark. As their eyes adjusted, Raoul could make out his companion's outline as they both groped over the nearest barrel for the outlet. Finally they found a cork. Raoul squinted in the dark as the Persian rummaged through his pockets. "I have a knife somewhere..."

"I have matches." Raoul began to search his waistcoat pocket.

"This doesn't feel like a wine barrel." Shaya was hopefully prying out the cork.

"How the hell would you know? Doesn't your prophet forbid that?" Raoul found the matches at last. He was so parched he was giddy at the thought of any liquid on his tongue. "Here we are, let's see—"

"No! Don't!" the Persian cried.

Raoul dropped the matches. "What on earth?"

"It's not wine!" Shaya's voice was full of new fear as he grabbed Raoul's hand in the dark and pulled it to where something that was certainly not liquid was pouring from the opened cask. "Smell that."

Raoul grabbed a handful of the sandy substance spilling onto the floor and sniffed. Thank God Shaya had stopped him from lighting the match. "This is gunpowder! Fucking hell, how many barrels are down here?"

"Enough to bring the whole Opera crumbling down on top of us with a single spark!"

"Why would he have such an arsenal? Unless he intends to use it..."

"He said he would end his opera burning down the world when he was raving!" Shaya hissed. "And he means to end things tonight."

"We have to warn her!" Raoul stumbled back towards the light and the trap door up into the chamber. "Help me up! Christine!" he cried as Shaya boosted him back into the sweltering, mirrored room. "Christine! You have to listen to us! You have to stop him! Are you there?!"

Raoul didn't care if the monster heard him, only that Christine did. No matter what she had done or what that thing had convinced her she felt, she would not allow murder and destruction on this scale.

"I'm here!" came her wrenching cry in return, close to the wall.

"Christine, listen to us!" It was Shaya who called out as Raoul hauled him up through the trap door. "He has a cache of gunpowder under the house! He has the means to kill us all!"

The music stopped, and Raoul held his breath. Already the heat of the torture chamber was making him dizzy once again. Or perhaps it was the image in his mind of Erik turning slowly to his captive where she stood by their prison.

"And he intends to use those means, very soon," came the voice of the demon. How could Raoul have thought it an angel before? The sound was pure evil and hate. "When I turn the grasshopper, the spark will ignite those barrels, and the whole Opera will hop with it."

"And the scorpion?" Christine asked in return, as if reciting a riddle Raoul had not heard the start of. "What does it do?"

"Makes the barrels unusable. But there will be no need," Erik laughed.

"Christine, find that thing! Turn the scorpion!" Raoul yelled, desperate for hope. "Don't let this coward kill us all!"

"A coward, am I, Monsieur?" Erik cackled. "Come and face me as we all die! You will beg me for your precious, useless life, and I will say no!"

"Let me out and I am happy to do just that, you vile creature!" Raoul screamed in return. "I will rip your heart out with my bare hands, do you hear me! I will cut off that monstrous face as a trophy and wave it through the streets and the world will thank me!"

"Ha, and you call me the monster," Erik laughed again.

"He is a monster because you have made him one!" Christine cried in turn. "But *you* don't have to be one or do this!"

"Christine, stop trying to reason with this thing!" Raoul screamed in fury. "He is beyond hope! Do you hear me, Erik? You are damned and doomed! You will rot in hell for your sins! The murdering coward and his—"

The arm around Raoul's neck cut off his words, squeezing the air from his throat. "That is enough from you!" the Persian ground out as he choked Raoul, causing his knees to buckle as his vision tunneled into black and white. "Erik! I'm ridding you of your audience!"

Raoul wanted to scream and fight. He tried to! But he could only paw at the arm around his neck and gurgle his protests as consciousness began to leave him. *What an awful way to die*, came his final thought, not knowing if he would ever wake.

"What have you done in there, Daroga?" Erik asked, blinking at the return of silence. "Please don't say you've killed him before I could."

"He is alive and unconscious," came Shaya's exhausted reply. "I did it to give you a chance to listen to this woman!"

"He won't," Christine said calmly. "Because he *is* a coward."

Erik turned to look at Christine, slowly advancing from his place by the organ. The music of the requiem had been like a respite – a balm on the wounds eating at his soul or a break in the fever. Or a final prayer before the end. He still was not sure. He could see Christine clearly again, beautiful and devastating as always.

Her long, unbound hair was a dark contrast to her rumpled prison frock, and yet, she looked like a warrior standing tall on a battlefield. Her jaw was set and her eyes resolved as she stared at Erik across the room. "Did you hear me, Erik? *You are a coward.*"

"A coward?" Erik echoed softly as he moved towards her, his wounded pride stoking his indignation. "I have endured and faced things no one could imagine."

"And you ran from them," Christine spat, and Erik clenched his fists.

"I ran to survive." Erik came within arm's length of his beloved, waiting for her to flinch or cower in the face of his monstrousness. Christine only raised her chin in further defiance.

"You did, and I admired that so much about you. How you chose to live in the face of such pain. How you could see the beauty in the world and live for it." Christine shook her head sadly. "But it was fear that moved you further and further into the dark, until you were nothing but a shadow."

"Not for you," Erik protested. "I came out of those shadows *for you*!"

"Not all the way. Not enough," Christine shot back. "You pulled me down into this endless night with you. And I let you! Because it was this strange honor and terrifying burden to be loved like that. To be yours. But not anymore."

"Christine..." Erik whispered, a torrent of maddening emotion filling him again as he tried to understand.

"If this is your path – if you are determined to end it all in some terrible act of hate for them and despair for yourself – I want no part of it!" Christine spoke with a voice like iron. "I am leaving. I would not be Raoul's prisoner in life and I will not be yours in death!"

To his utter shock, Christine turned, strode to the door, and opened it. It was simple as anything, but it was like a knife to Erik's heart to see her go.

"No!" Erik cried as he rushed after her, grabbing her hand and falling to his knees before her.

"I will make my own choices!" Christine bellowed in return, wrenching away her hand. "I do not know what life is left for me outside that door, but I would rather face it and fight for it – for even a few more *seconds* – than let you take it from me!"

"It's the only way!" Erik repeated, the words thick on his tongue as he grabbed for her skirts. "We have to end it to be free! And I will take everyone who trapped us in this cage of fate with us!"

"Spare me your poetry!" Christine yelled back. "I don't want to hear it – not if you're going to use it to justify killing yourself! And *me*, for God's sake! I want to live! And I deserve to *try*, no matter what sort of mess I'll make of it or pain I'll feel. The men in that room who you hate and all the strangers you want to destroy – they deserve to live! They deserve a chance! And so do you!"

"How can you say that?" Erik pleaded. He could barely see her beautiful, furious face through his tears and he could not understand how she could still see a way out. "How can you look at all of this and see anything but ruin and sin?"

"Oh my poor, unhappy Erik, how can you not know?" Christine asked in return, her voice and face softening at last. "How can you ask that, when it was you who taught me to see beauty behind ugliness?"

The cacophony that had filled Erik's skull since Perros was suddenly silent. The world was still and quiet as Christine looked at him with utter pity and resignation.

"What?" Erik asked as Christine knelt with him, taking his hand.

"You have helped me, always, to be brave," Christine began as she touched his face, new tears glinting in her forest eyes. "You taught me to see beyond fear, to keep breathing and doing and *living* when the pain was too much. You taught me to see beauty, and I found it in you. I fell in love with that."

"I didn't teach you bravery," Erik breathed back, in awe of her once more. "It was always there."

"Nevertheless, because of you, I was brave enough to see. I loved you. I still do and always will," Christine went on, and Erik held her hand tighter.

"You make it sound like this is a final goodbye." It was one thing to rave and plot and dream of their end and fear any world without her, but to have it happen was another thing entirely, and it hurt like nothing before.

"Because if you do this – if you refuse to see – it is. You ask me to stay and die with you if I love you, and Erik..." Christine swallowed back a sob and her hands were warm and solid in his. They shook as she held him, and he hung onto her, because if he did not, he would fall forever.

"Christine, please," Erik breathed even though he did not know what it was he was begging for.

"I have worn my love for you like a chain, a weight of iron dragging me down to the bottom of the sea, to a place where there is no light or breath," she began, each word another cut to his soul. "And I have let it, because I thought I deserved the void – that I deserved this terrible, hopeless love – because of the darkness in you and the darkness you fostered in me. Drowning down here was my penance, my punishment for loving your darkness and letting it feed the darkness in me. But I was wrong."

Christine steadied herself, breathing deep as if before a song.

"I love your darkness because it is yours. Because I see what is beyond it and I forgive it. I forgive the mistakes of the man you were and, beyond all reason, I love the man you are. And I hold on to hope for the man you could be. That is who I need: the man who you can become if you just *forgive them*."

"Who?" Erik asked in wonder.

"All of them – Raoul and Shaya and the cruel, cold world. Let go of your revenge and fear and hate," Christine begged, her forehead against his. "You helped me be brave enough to hope. You showed me how to be brave enough to love. For me, if you love me... Be brave enough to forgive."

Erik heaved a sob, clinging to her to keep from falling, his heart tearing to shreds again and again as the demons and ghosts and better angels fought within him. If he loved her? How could she doubt that, and yet, how could she ask something so impossible?

He was a creature of the dark, abandoned and broken. A phantom. A monstrous thing wrought by humanity's cruel hand. How could he let go of the fear that had sustained him? How could he not answer the world's hate in kind? How could he step into that light she spoke of when, over and over, it had done nothing but burn? Yet, how could he refuse her any wish?

"I cannot live in a world without you," Erik wept.

"Then don't. I will not die here in the darkness with you, Erik. I want you to live with me in the light."

Her words were like dawn in his heart, the soft creep of sun after night's long chill. He felt it, the touch of that first sliver of light on the dark places in his soul that had ruled him for so long. But no longer. For Christine, he would let the light burn his hate away.

"Yes," Erik gasped, nodding against her, and she embraced him fiercely in turn. "Yes," he repeated and she kissed him.

Had Erik ever been kissed before? He did not know, for this was so different, so new. Christine's lips pressed against his deathly skin, and he came alive in a way he never had before. His heart surged as he embraced her, tasting their tears and the breath of life from her lips. She kissed him, and the shackles and cages fell away. The light eternal of her love saved him, right there on the floor, hidden away beyond the lake.

"Help me," he begged as he pulled away, breathing deep. For the first time in days (or maybe in forever) he was determined to breathe as long as he could. "Christine, I don't know how. I don't know what to do."

"The scorpion. Show me where it is." Christine pulled him up with her as she rose. "Promise me it will make everything safe."

"I promise," Erik rasped, still gripping her tight as he stumbled to the mantle and opened the second casket to reveal the bronze scorpion waiting. "I've had it there so long. I meant to turn it one day..."

"Now – we'll turn it now," Christine commanded, and Erik steeled himself to obey. She did not hesitate as she lifted his hand and set it upon the figurine, and so he did not wait either. He had waited long enough for this. It was time.

Together they turned the scorpion. The second the gear clicked and the mechanism began to work, Erik collapsed towards the mantle in relief as one more vise around his heart broke away.

"It's done," he panted as Christine threw her arms around him and kept him from falling. The sound of rushing water below the floor filled the house and the barrels that could have ended them all were drowned and disarmed.

"It is. It's all done," Christine repeated, relief and joy and love in her voice. "Keep breathing. Just keep breathing, my love, and let it end."

Erik's chest heaved as he obeyed her, her head moving up and down with the rhythm as she pressed her cheek against his heart and held onto him tight. It was a new birth, breathing with her and for her, trying to be the man she believed he could become.

The water slowed beneath them, and Christine pulled back to stroke his face before kissing him once again, wondrously gentle and kind as she always had been. But there was something different to her now, a strength and a sureness Erik had only ever glimpsed before. If he had stepped into the light at her urging, she was the sun. And oh, how she blazed now.

"Now, show me how to open the door. We need to let them out."

"As you wish," Erik stammered, leading her to the wall. He could feel the heat radiating from the hidden room of mirrors. "Are we sure that the boy – Raoul – that he's not conscious?" It would be much harder to take their next steps, whatever the hell they were, with the young man trying to kill them.

"Shaya, are you there?" Christine called, eyes still on Erik. "Is he still unconscious? And can you promise to be reasonable when we open this door?"

"I swear it," came the Daroga's instant reply.

Erik braced himself, doubtful as always.

"Open the door, Erik," Christine commanded. "Don't be afraid. I'm here. I'm not going anywhere."

Erik groped for the hidden switch on the side of a painting to turn off the electric lights, then triggered the door with the mechanism he'd hidden behind a drum mounted next to the painting. The wall swung open, and hot air blasted from the darkened space as the Daroga tumbled out. Behind him, on the

floor, as promised, lay the man who still wanted nothing more than
to see Erik dead.

"You did it," Shaya wheezed, bent double as he struggled for
breath. He was looking at Christine with as much awe as Erik. "You
made him hear."

"I did not make him do anything," Christine countered, her
hand still tight on Erik, her voice calm. "I asked."

"And you said yes." Shaya turned to Erik, his face ashen beneath
the sheen of sweat. He'd even removed his customary Astrakhan
hat along with his jacket. "Didn't you? I have to confess, I'm not
feeling entirely well—"

Shaya collapsed to the floor in a heap. Christine gave a cry
and rushed to his side to feel his pulse. Erik faltered, unmoored
with her hand in his as he remained standing. He was whole. He
was his own, even if he was but a mere reflection of Christine's
compassionate light. All that mattered now was to do all he could
to keep it burning.

"Let me help," he muttered as he joined her in attending to the
man who had hunted him for so long. He would not let him die
tonight.

S haya woke at the taste of water, dusty and stale and the most
wondrous thing he'd ever had on his tongue. He grabbed the
cup that someone was holding to his lips and blinked, blearily
trying to regain his senses. Above him, he saw gold and silver stars.

"Careful now, Daroga, or you'll make yourself sick," came Erik's
calm voice. Shaya did not have the strength to be startled when he
looked up into that hideous and familiar face above him, the man's
long, lank hair doing nothing to remedy his funereal appearance.
"Here, let me refill that," Erik went on kindly and poured more
water from a jug set beside them.

"Was I at your mercy for long?" Shaya asked, trying to keep his dignity even though it was incredibly hard just to sit up.

"Only a few minutes," Erik replied.

"Don't over-exert yourself though, or you'll be right back on the ground." The words came from Christine Daaé as she swam into Shaya's vision.

"Thank you," Shaya said before he forgot again. Christine gave him a beatific smile, as if there was nothing to be grateful for.

"Is the young man intact?" Erik asked, nodding towards (Shaya assumed) the torture chamber.

"He won't wake for a while, I don't think," Christine answered. "But he's alive and breathing."

"Well, that is a pity."

Erik sprang up at the intruder's voice. Shaya forced himself up to see that Christine, in her threat to leave, had left the door of the house wide open. And another ghost had walked right in.

At the entrance to the parlor stood a shade – a poor copy of Erik – in a black felt hat and cloak. His mask was black too; a simple domino. Shaya looked between the two phantoms and was unsurprised to see Erik's lips twitch into a smile.

"Am I still seeing things?" Shaya asked sickly. The shade entered the room, his steps squelching as if he had water in his shoes.

"No, Daroga, you are not. I believe you are familiar with the Baron de Martiniac," Erik answered easily as Christine gripped her lover's arm.

Shaya blinked again, rising as much as he could, because of course – *of course* – it was Erik's lost brother who had taken on his dark mantle to haunt his steps.

"I knew you'd recognize me eventually." Antoine removed his disguise and cast it to the floor, revealing clothes that were as sodden as Erik's. "Blood connection and all that."

"I should have guessed." Shaya looked at Christine and Erik to see no shock in their faces at the information. "That it was you lurking about. Spying on your own brother."

"So everyone here knows?" Antoine asked. "That's disappointing. I was hoping for a more dramatic revelation. I guess you've made things terribly operatic for all of us this evening, haven't you, Erik? Thank you, by the way, for letting me in so I could hear that wondrous finale, whoever left this open."

"It was my mistake," Christine hissed, formidable and furious. "What are you doing here?"

"I wanted to confirm everything was going to plan and ended up listening to you save all our necks, for one thing," Antoine answered with a shrug as he strode into the parlor, looking around curiously. "What a marvelous little flat you've built. Now, I am grateful to you, dear girl. It would have been quite an annoyance to die tonight after all the trouble I've gone through to ensure my comfort in life."

"What are you talking about? Plans and trouble," Shaya demanded. "Last I heard, you ruined plans by letting this one escape."

"He let me escape on purpose," Erik answered thoughtfully, putting together some puzzle that was still obscure to Shaya. "He wanted it to look like it was his mistake. He was very careful."

"I told you. I knew you wouldn't kill me – you have too soft a heart," Antoine replied. Shaya wanted to laugh at that, but Erik smiled as if he had been given a compliment. "You're even weaker than I thought. You were supposed to kill the Chagny brothers, not keep trying to save them."

"You killed Philippe," Christine murmured. Shaya looked frantically between Erik and the other man as he circled the room, peering into the torture chamber where Raoul lay prone and insensible to the operatic drama unfolding.

"Philippe is dead?" Shaya asked in horror. "He was the one on the lake..."

"Yes, and I had to make sure he never left it." Antoine knelt next to the man whose brother he had just taken away. "As I said, I had hoped *both* these idiots would be dead by now, but you continue to disappoint me."

"Dear God, why?" Christine cried as Antoine looked over the man he had deprived of a beloved brother. "They are your friends. Your family."

"Money," Erik answered in utter disgust. Antoine gave a crooked smile and a nod. "My brother has none left, he's wasted it all. So he planned to marry the sister for her share. But when he saw an opportunity to take more than her dowry – to kill both Chagny heirs and have everything pass to her, and therefore to him – he leapt on it."

"They were right: you are smart," Antoine confirmed. "Family trait."

"You sent men to their deaths so you could steal an inheritance?" Christine's voice was thick with pain and contempt. "You disgusting, evil man!"

"Rich words from a woman fucking a living corpse," Antoine sneered. Erik started towards his brother only for Christine to hold him back. "Now, I believe it's time to rid the world of dear, sweet, stupid Raoul. Don't worry, I'll let you do it, brother. Consider it a gift to make up for all the time we've missed."

"No." It was not only hearing Erik say it that shocked Shaya, but the pure conviction in his voice.

"Is this little attack of conscience so severe that you'll actually give up ending the miserable life of a man who would have had you paraded down the streets being flogged if he could?" Antoine laughed.

"I have made a promise." Erik turned to Christine with love and devotion in his unearthly eyes that took Shaya's breath away. "No more death. Not at my hands."

"Then you won't stop me doing it, I guess." Antoine rose from beside Raoul with a calm expression, pulling the pistol from the unconscious man's coat pocket as he did. "I'm so glad I found this. Mine was all wet. I hope he has enough bullets."

"Put that down, Antoine," Erik ordered even as his brother aimed the gun at his head. "Christine is right. No one else needs to die."

"Oh, at least two more do, for me to get what I need." Antoine replied easily. Shaya tried to rise and failed, his exhausted body choosing the worst possible time to give up on him.

Erik sighed powerfully. "Of course. I imagine you'll need my head or something to present as evidence to get that first son's share that I've denied you by my mere existence."

"Sadly, yes. I want you to know I did entertain a few delusions of letting you live to run off with your whore." Christine's face hardened at the insult, and Shaya's head and stomach continued to turn. "Alas, I have a debt to Richard now for his help. I hope you'll understand. This foreign shit will need to be disposed of as well, I guess. I can't have you chittering about." He gestured with the gun towards Shaya.

"You would kill your own brother?" Christine asked.

"He doesn't care. He used me before, to remove his family." Again, Erik's voice was calm and resigned. "He set the fire, or stoked it, the night our father died. I always wondered why he was calling out 'my son' before I found him. Now, I realize he was calling out for you. Because you left him to die too."

"Can you blame me?" Antoine laughed. Shaya expected Erik to make some snide remark, but none passed his lips. Perhaps the gun pointed at him was having some effect.

"And what about me?" Christine asked, and Shaya could see how tight she was holding Erik's hand, even as hers shook.

"You, dear Christine, I will take my time with," Antoine replied, and that made Erik snarl. "I want to know what sort of magical cunt you have to drive so many men to madness. After I've sampled, I'll decide if you'll live or if I'll put you in a mad house. Sabine will join you eventually. I can visit you both at the same time. Now—"

The shot was deafening in such a small space. It echoed on the pipes of the organ and deep into Shaya's bones, radiating from the pistol gripped in his hands. Christine screamed and grabbed the man she so clearly loved, shielding him and hiding her eyes from the sight. Antoine seemed only mildly surprised to look down at the red stain blooming on his chest.

"Damn," the monster mumbled as he collapsed to his knees. Shaya fired again, just to be sure, adding another hole to his chest before Antoine fell dead to the floor, a trickle of blood seeping from his mouth.

Shaya fell as well, his gun clattering to the floor as he did. He met Erik's eyes and saw a new sort of admiration there. "What have you just done, Daroga?" Erik breathed as he continued to cradle Christine against him.

"I lost my brother because of you," Shaya panted, clinging to the back of a chair as the world spun again. "Now, at last, we are even."

"And you have saved my life again," Erik murmured.

"Earn it," Shaya managed to say before his body gave out entirely.

He found himself in a fog; not truly asleep, but unable to move or speak. He could only listen. He heard weeping and soft, soothing words.

"It's over now..."

"Not yet."

He tried to open his eyes as he was lifted up and placed somewhere soft and comfortable, and more cool water was poured down his throat. He could only see shadows. A ghost holding an angel, two lost souls who had found one another, united at last.

"You have to go, my Christine. You can't stay here." The words were so sad and resigned.

"You could come with me," the angel protested.

Shaya's vision began to return, and he saw them more clearly. Erik holding Christine close, his hand against her cheek as he kissed her forehead.

"It will be better this way," Erik consoled her. "I have to be that man - the one you know I can be and to do that." She kissed him before he could continue, and Shaya marveled at the sight.

"I love you," Christine wept, and Shaya knew it was true.

"There is one thing I must ask of you if I am to do this. If *we* are to do this..." Erik murmured and took up Christine's hand. Shaya saw the glint of a gold ring on her finger as Erik placed a tender kiss on her palm. He whispered something in his lady's ear that made her heave a sob before kissing him again.

Shaya wanted to sit up and see her answer whatever the request was that had so undone her, but the effort of watching alone was too much. Indeed, it felt wrong to intrude on such an intimate moment. He closed his eyes, just a blink, but darkness began to take him.

He did not hear the answer. He did not know the question.

14. Eurydice

Raoul dreamed of screams and sweltering jungles and gunshots and floating. In his dreams, Christine came and went, snatched away over and over by the monster's shadow. He tried and tried to wake and warn her – tried to blow out the matches that would light the spark and kill them all – but he was helpless. He couldn't move, and a sweet-smelling cloth was on his face again and again and it made him so tired...

They were all going to die. He was going to kill Erik. Someone was already dead. Erik had played their Requiem and it had been so beautiful.

Who had died? Why did Raoul feel already like something had been ripped out of his chest? Where was his voice? Why could he not make a sound with Erik's song in his ear and Christine's wanton cries echoing in his dreams? He tried. He tried and tried, and finally, it was he who screamed.

"Raoul! Stop!" a female voice cried as gentle hands took him by the shoulder.

"Christine?" Raoul asked, blinking to reality to make out the dark-haired woman holding him.

"It's your damn sister." Sabine was wan, her eyes red-rimmed and sunken, and her expression was furious. "Of course you ask after her."

"Where is she? Is she alive?!" Raoul demanded, shaking his sister. The effort of moving made his stomach turn, and had there been anything in it, it would have been swiftly emptying itself. He fell back on the bed – his bed? – and rubbed his aching head. "Tell me she is alive."

"She is, unfortunately," Sabine replied. "She's waiting downstairs. I wouldn't allow her near you after she showed up with you on our doorstep with that awful Persian. I should have sent her away with the police as well."

"He's alive too? And with the police?" Raoul balked. "Has he been arrested?"

"Not yet, just answering questions, about—"

"What of Erik? Where is the fiend? Dear God, what happened? I have to speak to her! Christine!" Raoul called out and tried again to rise, only for another wave of sickness and dizziness to claim him.

"Raoul, I'll bring her up, but first, you have to know..." Sabine's voice was unsteady with emotion.

"Where is Philippe?" Raoul asked frantically. It was unlike his big brother to not be hovering like an old woman when he was ill. Sabine, to his surprise, answered with a sob and threw her face into her hands.

That feeling from the dream – of a void, of something vital missing from the world, like a part of his flesh had been carved out of his chest – returned in full force as Raoul sat up fully in his bed and looked at his sister, dressed in black, weeping by his bedside.

"Where is Philippe, Sabine?" His voice sounded so small and lost, and he found that he was trembling. Sabine only shook her head, another wail lost in her hands. "No... no, it can't be! Where is he?!"

"Raoul." He looked up to see Christine in his doorway, her face a mask of sorrow and sympathy. She looked so different from when he had last seen her on the stage, properly dressed in a simple gray frock and looking as ill as Raoul. She had seen too much, at last, and been changed. Just as they all had.

"Where? How?" Raoul demanded as Sabine continued to cry. "What did Erik do to my brother?"

"I'm so sorry," Christine began, eyes gleaming. "The firemen looking for us found his body on the edge of the lake—"

"No!" Raoul screamed, rising from the bed and nearly collapsing as he did. Christine was there to catch him in an embrace, holding him tight and stroking his hair like he was a child. He felt like a child, like the foolish teenager who had asked why his father was not coming home from the hunting party. The teenager that Philippe had held and told it would be alright. "No. He can't be dead!"

"I'm so sorry, Raoul. I'm so sorry," Christine cooed in his ear as his tears began to flow. "We think he was trying to save you and—"

"He was there because of you!" Sabine hissed to Christine. "They were both there because of *you*."

"I'm sorry," Christine repeated, sincere and soft. "I'm so sorry for both of you."

"It was him!" Raoul cried, springing back and stumbling. His head was on fire again, like in that godforsaken torture chamber where he had burned while Philippe had... "Erik! He killed Philippe just like he killed our father!"

"Raoul, calm down. You're sick and exhausted." Christine sounded like she was talking to a crying child. Raoul wanted to strike her for it, so he flailed his arms and someone caught him. "You aren't talking sense."

"Erik drowned my brother!" Raoul screamed as two women forced him back into his bed, for he was too weak to resist. "I'll kill him for this! I'll have his head!"

"Raoul!" Sabine shouted through tears as Raoul flailed in her grasp. "Stop raving! Where is the doctor?"

"He's here." Christine's voice was far off. When had she left? How was she here? How were they all alive when Philippe was dead?

"Where is he? Where is the murderer?!" Raoul railed, vision blurred and swimming as stronger hands took him by the shoulder. "I will extinguish that demon's eyes forever!"

"Raoul, it's over. He let us go. You and I," Christine said. But that was impossible, because Erik had killed and burned and lied and stolen to make Christine his and his alone. How could that thing have let them go?

"I need to find him! I'm going to kill him for this!" Raoul screamed. His brother was lost, and it was all that monster's fault. He screamed, words lost as he struggled and flailed against the hands holding him down.

"I'm sorry for this, Monsieur, but it will help you rest," a male voice said. There was something over his mouth, and Raoul recognized the smell of the drug he had used on Christine. He tried to struggle but he was weak and limp and lost and he could not scream anymore. He could not see.

Despite stolen minutes on couches and in parlors, Christine still felt as if she had not slept for days. She'd be glad to be back in a familiar bed soon. The cold of early March was refreshing, keeping her awake for a few steps more. She breathed in the fresh air and savored the simple joy of walking free and alone, even for a few moments.

She hadn't had such a pleasure since the journey to her father's grave in Perros and she had not felt this free for... it felt like months. A season at least. Christine had spent all of winter tied to the Opera, sometimes by choice and sometimes by bond. Now, the branches of the trees were pregnant with buds ready to burst into bloom, and everything was different.

Christine braced herself when she came to the door on the *Rue Notre Dame Des Victoires*. Once again, it looked so different in this new light. She knocked hesitantly, having lost her key who-knows-how-long ago. She hoped Adèle was not mad at her for making her get up, but it was not Adèle who answered the door. It was Julianne, dressed in the same clothes as the night before.

"Oh, thank God," her friend gasped before embracing Christine. "I was so worried. Are you—"

"I'm fine," Christine exhaled as she hugged Julianne back. "Are you alright? I'm glad you saved me the trip to find you."

"I'm well. It all went to plan. I gave the gendarmes a merry chase and met my compatriot."

"I wanted to stay and watch the chaos, but Julianne was adamant we get back home." Christine looked up in relief to see Adèle standing inside by the fire. The bruises on her beautiful face were still there but fading. What was more, the defiant gleam had returned to her eyes. "Come here, my dear girl."

Christine flew from Julianne's arms to Adèle, earning a soft grunt of discomfort with the force of her embrace. "I'm sorry!"

"I forgive you," Adèle whispered into her hair. "I'm just glad you're safe. I didn't expect to see you here so soon."

"I need to stay here if you'll let me. Just for a night or two." Christine pulled away, avoiding Julianne's gaze.

"Of course," Adèle said.

"But why?" Julianne demanded, and Christine fought to hold in her tears. "I thought that he was taking you away or... well, he didn't say. He wasn't in a very talkative mood."

"He needs – wants – me to be up here," Christine said with great difficulty. Just the thought of telling the story – all the sins and mistakes and absolutions and promises – made Christine want to expire. "Don't ask me yet. I can explain, but not yet."

"Take all the time you need," Adèle replied, and Christine caught her giving Julianne a look. "Though you must tell me one thing. I did my part in that disaster, and I was glad to wreak my havoc, but I didn't do it for free. Antoine – is he dead, like your ghost promised he would be?"

Christine met the eyes of her friend, taking in the hint of fear in her gaze, as well as the righteous anger as she waited. "Yes," Christine answered, the sound of gunshots and a body falling to the floor echoing in her mind. "But not by Erik's hand."

"As long as he's gone," Julianne spat. "Good riddance."

"I..." Christine stopped herself. She had fought so hard to save lives, and still, two men were dead, men who would never have the chance to right any wrongs in the world or see the face of a brother. But to Adèle, Antoine had been beyond the pale, a man cruel enough to risk her life and soul and career to take vengeance against. "I won't tell you how to feel."

"Thank you," Adèle said. "Let's just all be glad it's over."

"Almost," Christine sighed. "There are a few matters left to handle before—" Again the words caught in Christine's throat, emotion overcoming her along with exhaustion. "I just need to rest."

"Your bed awaits. Come on." Adèle gestured to Christine's room.

"I don't want to put Julianne out if she's staying there," Christine protested.

"Oh, she'll be fine." Adèle gave her a surprisingly roguish smile. "Come along."

Christine found herself ushered to her old room and deposited on the bed. It was heaven compared to the chaise in the Chagny parlor, but it didn't feel like home. Home was far away, below the streets, and she could not go back.

"Where is Raoul in all this?" Adèle asked as Christine relaxed onto the pillow. Julianne was lurking at the door, Christine noted, before closing her eyes.

"I've been with him all morning. I needed to be there when he woke, but the doctor says he'll sleep for a while. I was not welcome at his house. Understandably. I'll—" Christine yawned, days' worth of exhaustion overtaking her. "I'll go back in the morning while the arrangements are made."

"What arrangements?" Julianne asked from far away as Adèle placed a blanket over Christine. Dear God, she wanted to sleep for a week.

"The wedding," Christine muttered and slipped into sleep.

Shaya woke before dawn. It was understandable – Darius had ushered him into bed before the light had left the sky. Now, he could smell food cooking in their little kitchen, and it was a small miracle. Shaya rose stiffly and shuffled down the hall, still aching and drained from the exertions and tragedies of the previous days. The sight of Darius working diligently over the stove to prepare tea and āsh was beautiful in a way Shaya was not prepared for.

"What have I done to merit this?" Shaya asked gently as Darius stirred.

"Not dying, for one," Darius replied without looking up. "I have told you many times: I would be quite put out if you expired without my permission."

"Why? I've brought nothing but discord and displacement to your life as long as I've been in it." Shaya smiled despite himself as Darius looked at him with the affectionate annoyance Shaya had become familiar with long ago. Yet it was not until now that he had recognized the love behind it. "Oh."

"Sometimes I think you are a terrible detective," Darius sighed. "At least when it comes to observing the people closest to you."

"I think you might be right," Shaya said thickly. "I was wrong. About Erik. And Christine."

"Were you now?" Darius continued to spoon ochre sauce over the meatballs.

"He chose to let us all live, because of her and her love," Shaya mused, thinking back to how Christine Daaé's words had made him weep in that terrible room of tortures. "He changed. He chose to be the man who deserved her love. Ramin's too."

"Well, that is encouraging, but I sense there is more to this and your time with the police yesterday that you declined to discuss," Darius countered. "I haven't retrieved the papers yet for the day, but I imagine they will carry dark news from the Opera."

"Philippe de Chagny is dead by the hand of a man who cannot be known or named outside this room: Antoine de Martiniac," Shaya answered grimly. He took a seat at the table, suddenly exhausted once again.

"Why is that? I didn't even know he had returned to Paris."

"As far as anyone knows, that must remain what we tell others. Otherwise suspicions shall arise, and I do not want to explain to anyone but you... why I killed him." He waited for Darius's face to darken with shock or disapproval. He only kept stirring the āsh as it thickened. "And I don't regret it."

"I didn't assume you would. It was justice, was it not?"

Shaya nodded. "I believe so. I must."

"What happens now?"

A knock at the door interrupted Shaya's search for the answer. Darius looked between Shaya and the pot in front of him with an unmistakable message that he was busy and Shaya had to answer his own damn door for once. Bemused and weary, Shaya did just that.

The man leaning against his doorframe was thin and tall, and behind his beard and glasses, his skin looked pale. But it was the golden eyes that still gave Erik away, despite his disguise.

"Is that āsh I smell? Darius must be relieved to have you home," the man Shaya had been ready to kill yesterday and ended up killing for said in an exhausted tone. He looked as if he was barely able to stand, and Shaya wondered if under the mask Erik looked even sicklier than he had when he had left him at the gate out of the Opera's underground, with Christine weeping by Shaya's side.

"We'll fix you a bowl if you come in and stop alarming my neighbors," Shaya admonished. Erik stepped inside the flat and collapsed into a chair, groaning in either relief or pain, Shaya could not be sure.

"I've always wondered what it looked like in here," Erik muttered, and Shaya raised an eyebrow. "Oh, I've known where you lived for years, Daroga. It's quaint. Lovely location, but I have to say these furnishings are rather pedestrian."

"Pardon me for not having an entire organ installed," Shaya grumbled as Darius peeked into the parlor. He gave both men a shocked look, clearly noting how unwell Erik looked. "Get this fool some tea."

"Thank you," Erik replied. Darius left for the kitchen and Shaya surveyed his rather melodramatic guest. "I hope he is not too concerned. I myself never thought I would be dying for love."

Raoul wanted it all to have been a dream. He kept his eyes closed as he listened to the steps of the servants and the quiet murmur of the household beyond his door and told himself that the phantasmagoria of the last few months was the product of a fevered brain. He had consumed far too much brandy and sweets after they had returned home from Christmas Eve services (at Philippe's insistence, of course). Sabine had chided them for it, but she had joined in too, stealing a few bites of apple tart from the feast that Cook would be sad to see eaten early.

That meant it was Christmas morning. It was a special day, a day just for the three of them. Philippe had promised Sabine that today he would not mention his affair with Sorelli or insist that Raoul make another appearance at the Opera. Raoul knew better now, after the nightmare, than to follow that road. He would also be so glad to not have Antoine lurking about to leer at his sister.

Raoul imagined it, walking down from his room just like when he was a child to find Philippe already at the breakfast table. His cheeks would be ruddy, not pale. His eyes would be bright, not clouded and blank. There would only be laughter coming from his mouth, not an endless trickle of water from the lake that had taken his life...

Raoul sat up with a cry, trying to banish the image from his head. The valet asleep in a chair next to his bed jumped up.

"Where is my brother?" Raoul cried, and the young man looked so stricken it made Raoul's stomach wrench with grief. "Where is Philippe?!"

The man ran from the room as Raoul stumbled from the bed, his legs unsteady under him. Outside his window, the sky was a pale gray, giving no clue as to the position of the sun. Was it morning? How long had he slept in that drugged stupor? He would have that doctor's head for making him insensible when there was so much to do.

"Raoul!" He looked up as Sabine rushed into the room and caught him. "Get back into bed."

JESSICA MASON

"No! I need to see Philippe," Raoul roared, even as he collapsed into his sister's arms. She was crying again already. How dare someone make her cry.

"Raoul, please don't make this harder," Sabine begged. "Don't you remember?"

"I remember a nightmare," Raoul protested as his own tears began to fall. "I remember you telling me – you and Christine – you told me..."

"He's gone, Raoul," Sabine sobbed as the two of them fell to the floor, holding one another the way they had as children. "I saw his body. They are preparing it for the funeral tomorrow. He's gone."

Raoul had never wept like this. His mother had died before he could know her, and his father had always been a distant, somber figure. But Philippe...

Philippe had been the sun in their family's sky. He had been warmth and joy and laughter, and now it was all just *gone*? No more nights at the Opera or jokes about Raoul's frowns or muttering over the morning paper or worrying for the family name. It was all over, and Raoul had not even had the chance to say goodbye...

Raoul cried and cried with his sister, wishing he had not been forced to sleep for so long, because now he was awake and the peace of sleep was such a distant thing. How could he sleep soundly in a world where his big brother was not there to protect him and guide him? A world where the man responsible for Philippe's death still breathed.

He rose when there were no tears left in him, resolve solidifying in his gut. Grief could wait. Raoul had justice to pursue.

"Where did my man go? I need to dress at once," Raoul asked, trying to sound composed. If he acted like he was in control of himself, eventually he might feel that way. Sabine gave no answer, so Raoul rang, and the same a servant who had been attending him before appeared. "Get me my clothes."

"You need to rest." Sabine stood and straightened her black dress. "You had an ordeal."

"I've rested enough. What bloody time is it, anyway?"

"It is ten o'clock on Saturday morning. You've been asleep for nearly a day," Sabine answered. Raoul could hardly make sense of such a span. They had gone to the Opera on Thursday, and it had felt like weeks that they had been in that hot, horrible, mirrored room. Now it was over.

Christine had told him it was over, he remembered that from the delirium of his first waking. She had said...

"He let us go?" Raoul asked aloud as his valet began to dress him. It was impossible.

"You mean the fiend responsible for all of our misery freed you both?" Sabine asked back. "That is what she and that foreigner say of the matter, but they have given me no details beyond the fact that this *Phantom* held you all captive for a span, then somehow had a change of heart."

"I don't understand it either," Raoul muttered as he buttoned his shirt. The last awful thing he remembered was Erik threatening them *all* with death. They had found the gunpowder and learned of the scorpion and the grasshopper. Then Shaya had choked him unconscious, the bastard.

Raoul rubbed at his throat as he finished his final button, recalling the expert way the Persian had subdued him. Somehow, in the time he was asleep, Christine had been able to broker their freedom.

"Where is my fiancée?" Raoul asked.

"You cannot be serious," Sabine scoffed. "You still mean to marry that woman after all of this?"

"If I do not marry her, it was all for nothing," Raoul hissed in return. "Now where is she?"

"I sent her away to sleep at whatever hovel she calls home," Sabine snapped. "But she returned today, and I've had her waiting in the kitchen. A place appropriate for someone of her breeding."

"With the *servants*?" Raoul balked.

"You're lucky I didn't send her to wait in the kennel."

"You would do well to show some respect for your future sister."

"I would rather cut out my own tongue," Sabine replied with more hate in her face than Raoul had ever seen. "Go grovel to her yourself – I refuse to share a room with that whore."

Raoul scowled at his sister and left the room. He was the head of the family now, and she had a duty to obey him as much as she would her husband. At least now Raoul had the power to stop her marriage to Antoine. That was some consolation.

"Has the Baron de Martiniac visited since I've been indisposed?" Raoul asked the valet at his heels.

"No, Monsieur le Vi-Monsieur le Comte. No one has heard from him or seen him for days."

Raoul's frown deepened. He would not put it past Antoine to run away in shame after being the one who let Erik go. Perhaps he had heard the grave news of Philippe and was hiding away with his guilt. Or he knew that, now that Philippe was gone, there was no place for him in this household.

"Please let the rest of the staff know that he is not to be admitted without my permission," Raoul said, still finding his voice to be unsteady.

"Yes, Monsieur le Comte." The valet nodded before disappearing down a hall as Raoul prepared to enter the kitchen.

The memory he had tried to return to before waking was still vivid in his mind: of the three remaining Chagnys together by the dying fire, stuffing their faces with dessert and laughing. He wished he could remember what Philippe had joked that had made Raoul nearly choke on a tart, but it was gone. It was all gone and it would only fade more.

He paused with his hand on the handle, pushing back the grief that hit him like a wave. He had to fight the undertow. He had to be strong. There was no one else left who could be. He straightened his spine and composed his face and pushed on.

Christine was seated by the kitchen fire reading when he opened the door, a book of prayer, if Raoul was not mistaken. She was in a plain, conservative brown dress with a high collar, and her hair was fixed nicely, though her cheeks were still pale.

Raoul began to think that she looked so different from how she had been in the house on the lake, but it occurred that he had only imagined her appearance. He had imagined her head thrown back in wanton pleasure just as he had imagined her pretty face stained with tears. But he could not imagine what she could have done to free them.

The last time he had *seen* her had been before the final act of *Faust*, when she had said she would rather die than live a lie married to Raoul. Her words of love had only been for the monster.

"Good morning," Raoul said darkly, and Christine looked up. Her expression was one of sympathy and kindness, but also apprehension.

"You're finally awake." She rose, her head demurely inclined, and came to him. "I cannot say enough how sorry I am for your family's loss."

"We will speak of that later," he grumbled. "Right now, I need to know how we are both alive."

"I imagine you do," Christine sighed. "Shall we walk outside while I tell you? It is not too cold, and I've always wanted to see your gardens."

"As you wish." Raoul followed Christine into the mild morning air. "I think you will like these gardens even better when they are in bloom," he remarked as they strode quietly through the rows of pruned shrubs and roses.

"I think it's beautiful now, for what it is, as well as what it will be when the sun returns," Christine replied. "That is the great task of living in a land where winter always comes, isn't it? To love it as much as the spring."

"I'm not sure what you mean." Raoul's head was beginning to ache.

"It doesn't matter. Before I tell you what transpired, I need you to promise to trust me and to not..." She swallowed as she stopped in her stride, emotion filling her face. "To not judge me too harshly."

"What was the price of our freedom, Christine?"

"He wants me to live." A single tear slipped from Christine's eye. "There was no bargain, Raoul, no price to be paid. I spoke to him from my heart and begged him to change. To be a better man for the sake of our love."

"And?" Raoul asked coldly, hating each word. "Perhaps you are innocent, my dear Christine, but many a man has promised to change to win a woman's forgiveness or favor."

"I told him I would be with him, live my life with him. I turned the scorpion and gave him my soul one last time, and he—" Christine choked back a sob, rushing to seat herself on a stone bench among the budding lilacs as she shook.

"What did he do?" Raoul asked, finally moved by her distress. "Did he abuse you once again?" Christine shook her head vehemently even as Raoul took her into his arms.

"He told me I deserved a life in the sun, with a good man by my side," Christine cried against his shoulder. "He said I had to live it above, and that no phantom could share it with me."

"What?" Raoul pulled back, examining her face for a lie.

"Don't you understand? He let us go so we could live up here, alive and in peace, in the light of day," Christine whimpered. "Where his shadow could not follow."

"He wants us to be together?" Raoul asked in awe. "Do you? After all you said about this life being a lie? Would you still take me?"

"I don't know." Christine shook her head, holding her hand to her chest. It was only then that Raoul saw she was once again wearing Erik's gold ring. "I have wanted and feared so many things, but I never—"

"If this is what he wanted, it will be for the best." Raoul's mind raced. Now that they knew where Erik was, it would be no hard thing to send in the gendarmes and have him arrested! "We have a chance at a new life. Perhaps we can find some joy in all of this. Some hope in all this despair."

"Perhaps," Christine breathed. "I couldn't bear it, though, to be in Paris. Everything here reminds me of him and the Opera. How could I go about as your wife with the Palais Garnier right there in the center of town, mocking me with my failures and follies, and everyone gossiping behind my back?"

"Then we'll leave!" Raoul exclaimed, grasping her hands, as she presented him with yet another solution. "We will go on a world tour. Newlyweds do that all the time, don't they? We'll start in Sweden, take you home for as long as you need, and then we can go wherever we want to!" Raoul was delighted by the idea and all its possibilities.

They would leave, and meanwhile, in Paris, Richard would see to it that Erik was in jail. Raoul could return home briefly – on business, he would say. Then he would choke the life out of Erik like he had done to Philippe.

"I'm not sure," Christine stammered.

"We can make new memories until it's time for our family to grow."

Once again Christine's face fell and she shook her head sadly. "I don't think—"

"What is it?" Raoul asked and Christine bit her lip as if ashamed. "Are you worried about how he defiled you? It won't take. I've heard doctors say. He forced you, didn't he? With his lies and voice and powers. A woman can't get with child when it's against her will!"

Christine looked at him, wide-eyed, as if she had never heard this information, the poor, innocent thing. "Raoul, I—"

"Monsieur le Comte," the butler's voice echoed through the gardens, and Raoul had never wanted so much to strike a servant.

"What? What could possibly be important enough for you to intrude on a grieving man and his fiancée?" Raoul barked.

"There is a visitor for both you and Mademoiselle Daaé who insists on being seen," the butler replied. "It's that Persian fellow."

"Shaya? Why is he here?" Christine asked, concern filling her face. She did not wait for Raoul and rushed inside, finding her way to the parlor where the Persian was waiting, looking grim and tired.

"What is the meaning of this?" Raoul demanded. There were still missing pieces to the story, he realized – pieces that Motlagh would need to provide.

"I am glad to see you up and about, Monsieur," Shaya began, somber. "I must extend my deepest sympathies over the loss of your brother. I know that pain and I am so sorry."

"Thank you." Raoul said, terse. "Now. I have questions. I know why Erik let us live, but why didn't he kill you?"

"To please Mademoiselle Daaé," Shaya answered with a faint smile to Christine. "Just as I know she would undertake many things, to bring him joy."

"What are you talking about, Shaya?" Christine asked shakily. "Why are you here?"

"He came to visit me this morning in my flat—"

"He came to your goddamn house?" Raoul clenched his fists. "Please tell me you have come here to tell me you shot the thing on the spot and he is dead?"

"No, Monsieur," Shaya sighed. "But he is dying."

"No!" Christine cried, grabbing Raoul's hand for support. "He can't! He promised he would live and—"

"He promised he would try, my dear, but..." Shaya shook his head. "You should have heard him, the both of you – the way he spoke and the joy in his voice to think of your new life."

"What do you mean he's dying?" Raoul pushed, pulling Christine to him as she began to weep.

"He wished to stay alive long enough to know of your wedding," Shaya went on. "But he says he is dying of love, and that his heart... it cannot bear the light you have given it. He asks only one thing of you, Mademoiselle: that you bury him with that ring and let the world know, somehow, of his passing."

Raoul held Christine tight as she cried, just as she had held him. It was better this way, wasn't it? This way her heart would be truly free, and Raoul's revenge was assured. He had already taken it, apparently.

"She will do it, of course," Raoul answered for Christine, holding Shaya's gaze. "We are to be married as soon as it is done. Then we will leave Paris and begin anew."

Christine had attended too many funerals in the twenty-three years of her life. Her mother's. Her grandparents'. So many old patients and friends of Doctor Mainville. And of course, her father's. She had stood by the grave at that somber affair and wept.

Now, she lingered on the fringes of a much grander event, her face veiled as mourners entered to pay respects and pray for the soul of Philippe de Chagny.

It had felt wrong not to come, even though Christine had been told quite clearly by Sabine that she was not welcome. She didn't much care what Sabine thought of her at this point, given how much she still had to disappoint the woman. Hiding herself in the back was the better option.

Christine wondered sadly if this was how Erik had felt all his life: hiding in the shadows and keeping to the edges, avoiding the eyes of those that hated him. She did not think that everyone from the Opera hated her, the few that had come, but she did not want to face Sorelli's furious gaze even so.

It was Moncharmin who came to represent the managers. Richard was, if the gossip was to be believed, hiding in shame after his contract had been revoked with the Opera. The minister of Fine Arts blamed him for the chandelier, and he had been punished accordingly.

Christine listened as the notes of the requiem wafted out the door and closed her eyes on her grief. It didn't feel real, any of it: the pain of the past and the promise of the future. She would not believe it until every last duty was done and she was alone with her husband at last.

Such a strange thing to think – having a husband. Was she too young and too foolish? Was this all a mistake? Would she regret it forever? She hoped not.

She raised her veil and turned away from the church. It was a fine, lonely building in the *Faubourg Saint Germain*, where the Chagny family had been interred for many years and hopefully would be for many more. Christine had never taken the time to really observe the neighborhood that Raoul and so many other well-heeled Parisiennes called home, including the one she needed most to speak with. In truth, it was not so different from the rest of Paris, with buildings of creamy white and gray, windows decorated in Romanesque details, and steep, blue-gray roofs and wrought iron rails. It was all variations on one distinct tune that only this city knew. Christine was going to miss it.

Carlotta's house was not as fine as the Chagny manor, of course, but it was well-appointed, and the maid was stoic as she led Christine to her mistress. The once-great diva was ensconced in the parlor, sipping tea and looking out the window at the Sunday traffic.

"I'm glad to see you are doing better than I last heard," Christine said without ceremony. "Did it work?"

"The cure for the poison you gave me, you mean?" the woman asked back. Her voice was thin and unsteady, but it was a voice, nonetheless. "What do you think?"

"I think it will be a long time before you sing again, but that one day, you might."

"One day," Carlotta replied. "And you? When will you sing again, little witch? Last I heard, a ghost kidnapped you and tried to burn down the Opera."

"My brief career is over, you'll be happy to know."

"And you are leaving it for marriage. You never struck me as this much of an idiot." For once, there was no malice in the woman's tone, only a sort of world-weary jadedness.

"Perhaps." Christine's stomach filled with butterflies as she considered. "But my reason for singing is gone. At least for singing at the Opera. Why not try something new that I have chosen?"

"You'll miss it," Carlotta shot back. "I warn you. The applause and the glory and the gold. All of that is better than sitting around day in and day out, waiting for some man to come home and mount you so you can spit out his heirs and wither away in obscurity. That's the real hell."

Christine sighed. "Or I could spend my days and nights seeing the wide world with a companion and an equal? I know for sure I won't be spitting out heirs."

"Well, at least that's lucky." Carlotta gave a small cough. "Will you miss the music? You always seemed to enjoy it to your fill."

"I am leaving a career in the opera, not music. Music is an angel that travels with me always. I could not leave it if I tried."

"Dear God, you're a strange one." Carlotta took another sip of tea. "Did you come here to gloat or see your good works?"

"I came here to apologize." Christine shrugged. "I have hated you since I met you. I wanted what you had just like you wanted what I took. I saw you as a rival and treated you with the same cruelty you showed to me. I was wrong for that, and I am sorry."

Carlotta regarded Christine, her eyes sharp and discerning, before giving the slightest – and haughtiest – of nods. "Be absolved then, you useless creature. Now, go off to ruin yourself better than I ever could."

"Thank you."

"And I am... sorry too, for what I did."

"I forgive you," Christine said easily. Carlotta raised an eyebrow. "Not because you deserve it, but because I do not want my soul weighed down with that hate anymore. I am tired of it."

"Fair enough. Goodbye, Christine Daaé. Good luck."

Christine was grateful for the blessing, such as it was. She needed all the luck she could find for the journey ahead. Once again, she walked, slow and steady, through the streets. Cherry blossoms were just ready to bloom as the sun peeked through thin clouds to kiss them.

Erik had lived in this city for so long and never seen the flowers bloom under blue skies in the spring. Now, he never would.

Christine's stomach sank as she approached Raoul's home once again, replacing her veil so that she could slip like a shadow among the mourners just beginning to arrive. Raoul was in the study, looking over papers and sighing.

"There you are," Raoul smiled. "I was just going over the train schedules. There is one to Brussels tonight. Unless you want me to stay and help?"

Christine dug her nails into her hand and shook her head. "No, please. Shaya will be help enough."

"Are you sure? You don't have to do this alone." It was kind, but there was still something in his voice and a spark in his eye that made Christine shake her head. He wanted to see his rival dead, and Christine could not give him that satisfaction.

"I must."

"Well, then, I will go to Brussels and meet you there. There is a hotel by the train station. I'll find a priest and witnesses."

"I'm sure you will take care of it," Christine muttered, and Raoul gave one of the few real smiles she had seen since they had returned from the Opera. It made her heart hurt as well. "I'm going to go try again with your sister before I go home and..." Christine hesitated, not sure of which details to give. "Shaya will meet me at the Opera."

"I will see you tomorrow then?" Raoul asked before smiling. "My future wife."

"Tomorrow, yes," Christine echoed. The dangerous man Raoul had become melted away, and the boy she had loved by the seashore so long ago returned. She did not pull back when he bestowed a chaste kiss on her lips before taking her hand to lead her from the study and towards the waiting crowd. "Raoul?"

He turned back to her and she let go of him. "Yes?"

"I know this will be hard to do alone, but you will survive and be stronger for it," Christine said. "Goodbye."

Raoul merely smiled and turned away, leaving her alone by the door as he went to attend to his guests. Christine found herself shaking as she contemplated what lay ahead.

Sabine was in the large drawing room, looking up at a portrait above the fire of a woman who looked strikingly like her. Her late mother, perhaps. Sabine had buried both parents as well, Christine realized, and now her brother too.

"I haven't had a chance to tell you how sorry I am, Sabine." Christine summoned her strength. "Philippe was a good man—"

"Don't you speak to me of my brother," Sabine hissed as she rounded on Christine, her eyes stony and furious. It reminded Christine of the madness she had seen so often of late in Raoul, and it broke her heart.

"I am sorry. I still have to say it."

"What you have to do is get out of my house," Sabine snapped. "Why are you even here?"

"To confirm my plans with Raoul for our elopement. Tomorrow." Christine waited for the woman to slap her or scream or even laugh. She only stared in disappointment. "We mean to travel to Brussels and—"

"You have taken one brother from me, my fiancée is still missing, and now, you wish to take the only good man I have left in my life?" Sabine said. "No. I won't allow it."

"Raoul is set on it. I must," Christine stammered. "I made a promise."

"Promises are to catch gulls with," Sabine sneered, and Christine flinched. "Break it."

"Why would I do that?"

"Because you will destroy him." Sabine's face was not only angry; it was twisted with grief new and old. "You don't love my brother, not the way he deserves. You are doing this because you think you must fulfill some vow to a murderer. But you will *ruin*

Raoul even more than you already have. If you just leave now, our family name has some hope, but if you marry him, it will be gone. There will be no legacy to pass on to your children."

"I can't have children," Christine blurted out, and Sabine was stunned into silence. "I would know, by now, if I could, and I can't."

"So you will ruin our family's name and end our bloodline, and all for what?"

"What do you suggest?"

"You have some secret errand at the Opera tonight, don't you? I heard you blubbering about it. You have to bury the man who killed half our family."

Christine winced at the words but nodded.

"It's going to overwhelm you," Sabine went on. "It will fill you with such grief that you will be moved to end the engagement. It was under false pretenses, anyway, given that you are barren. You will write all this in a letter that I will deliver to my brother while he waits for you, and you will – I don't know. Go off to a convent."

"A convent? Really?"

"I don't care where you actually go, only that you leave and never return to this city or our lives," Sabine growled. "Do this, and you are forgiven, and I won't have to spend the rest of my life making yours a living hell in return for what you've done."

"I will... consider it." Some tether had been cut, and Christine was suddenly caught in a new current as she floated free. "I will send word later tonight."

"I trust you will make the right choice. It will be a novelty for you," Sabine sneered.

Christine sighed. There was one more thing she could tell Sabine de Chagny, regarding the fate of her own fiancée; the man whose body now rested under the Opera. But maybe that was too cruel. Sabine would realize soon enough that Antoine was never coming home, and she too would be free.

Christine slipped from the house, not looking behind her as she began the long trip towards the Opera, for the last time. Her feet were tired, as was her body. She had slept poorly last night in her empty bed, tormented by nightmares of all that awaited her today. But she had to keep going. She had always been good at that.

Months ago, as autumn had just taken Paris into her deathly embrace, Christine had walked a similar path. She had managed to get lost a few times, back then, but she had found her way to the place she was meant to be. To the Opera. Now, she went again, to fulfill a different promise to a different ghost she loved just as deeply.

It was almost spring. She stopped along the Seine, among the trees growing by the river, just to appreciate the flowers daring to bloom first as the sun returned. She gathered a few: snowdrops, crocuses, and narcissus. She would need them.

It always amazed her: the sight of the Palais Garnier as she turned down the *Avenue de L'Opéra*. Even though she knew her so well, the great empress of art astonished Christine with her size and grandeur. She held so many dreams, this palace of excess and splendor, and just as many nightmares and ghost stories. Christine would miss her: the golden angels and grimacing masks, the nymphs holding their lanterns, and the great copper dome beneath Apollo's lyre.

Christine would remember it always though, holding it in her heart wherever the road led her. She did not know, even now, where that would be. She had come here sure of one thing, one destination, and a ghost had helped her find it. Just like the first time.

Shaya was waiting for her right where he had promised to be, near the ramps towards the subscriber's pavilion. There was another man beside him, also Persian.

"It's all prepared," Shaya said. "This is Darius, Mademoiselle Daaé. The only person in the world kind enough to tolerate me for decades."

"It is nice to finally meet you, Darius. I have heard about you," Christine smiled. "Thank you both for coming and for your help."

"Do not thank us yet – there is still work to be done," Darius replied. Christine nodded and steeled herself. For the last time, she walked along the Opera's edge, to the place that had been her secret door towards home. The place where she had taken refuge months ago, and had, by some divine intervention, been found by an angel.

And a chief groom. Christine smiled to see Jean-Paul busy at work in César's stall, whistling to himself as he shoveled hay. He looked slightly worse for wear, from whatever Antoine had done to him, but he was healing.

"César likes Delibes the best, I think," Christine called, and laughed when Jean-Paul jumped and then jumped again to see the infamous Persian behind her.

"Mademoiselle! I had heard you were taken! Now you're consorting with this character?" Jean-Paul cried. "And looking like you're going to a funeral, the lot of you! What's going on?"

Christine held her breath, unable to answer for fear. Her hand shook as she felt for the ring on her finger and pulled it off. She would need to give it to Erik so soon. So very soon...

"You're right, old friend. They do look rather dour."

Christine's heart jumped higher than Jean-Paul at the sound of the voice from the shadows. He stepped forward into the fading twilight, mask affixed and not a hair out of place in his immaculate regalia. She ran to him, not caring that Jean-Paul looked as if he would faint away on the spot. Nothing else mattered, except that her angel had found her again.

"I'll change there," Christine whispered as Erik embraced her.

"Change where?" Jean-Paul asked as Christine pulled away to look between Erik and Shaya. She didn't even know where they were bound.

"The Madeleine, of course," Erik replied, golden eyes filled with love and wonder. "You were promised a marriage at the Madeleine, my love, and I did not wish to disappoint you."

15. Promise

S haya, at last, had found himself inside the great edifice of the
Madeleine; a Roman temple built to worship a different God
with a grand statue of a woman above its altar. It was a magnificent
place, even as the evening fell and what few parishioners were left
filtered out. Darius smiled at the gilded ceilings and inscribed
mottos above the pews, and so did Shaya. Despite their faith's
prohibition on graven images, he was not immune to the beauty
here.

"I'll be right back." Shaya noted as he walked from their seat
that the other guests had arrived. Armand Moncharmin looked
more relaxed and revived than he had seen him in weeks. Strange
indeed, for a man who now had to steer the National Academy
of Music alone, but maybe it was better that way. Maybe it was
because Robert Rameau was beside him.

Shaya, for his part, did not know if he would ever not be tired
again. Despite hours of rest, it did not feel like the whirlwind had
stopped at all. There had been the hours with the police and the
hours of planning and arguing with Erik, a chore in itself. Along
with that had been tasks grim and pedestrian.

It was right that he and Erik had been the ones to move
Antoine de Martiniac's body to the communard's prison cells across
the lake, leaving him the gold ring on his finger that matched the
one Christine had been sworn to return. Already the body had
begun to decay, and soon the rats would render the face
unrecognizable under the white mask it now wore. The Opera

Ghost was dead, and if (or when) Raoul de Chagny came to gloat over his enemy's body, he would never know it was a different man who had also sought the end of the Chagny line.

Shaya found his way behind the altar to the small changing room (he was sure the Catholics had some complicated word for it, but he didn't know it) where Christine had been whisked away from their party upon arrival. Adèle Valerius and Julianne Bonet were there, waiting as their friend changed. It filled Shaya with fresh guilt to see the fading bruises on Adèle's face when she looked at him, and he immediately bowed his head in contrition.

"She's nearly ready," Adèle said.

"Good. But I came to speak to you, to both of you," Shaya replied humbly. "To express my regret for the part I played in your pain, Madame Valerius. I am sorry. I cannot ask for forgiveness, but I am sorry."

"You're the one who killed Antoine?" Adèle asked back. Shaya gathered the strength to meet her eyes. He could still feel the gun in his hand, the reverberations of the bullet finding its target, and the surety of that awful moment.

"I did."

"Good. Now apologize to her." Adèle nodded towards Julianne, who gave a scowl.

"I don't need—"

"I need to," Shaya said. "I used Jammes and you because I thought it was righteous, and for that, I am sorry too."

"Thank you," Julianne muttered. "I'm sure Cécile will be happy to hear that – if you ever find her. I don't believe she'll ever return to the Opera."

"Really?" Adèle asked, perking up in interest.

"I'm sure Meg Giry will be happy to take her place in the row," Julianne answered. Adèle took the other woman's hand and squeezed it.

"As long as that's the only place she's taking," Adèle remarked and somehow made it sound bawdy, much to Shaya's confusion and delight.

"Will you and Mademoiselle Jammes reconcile?" Shaya watched as Adèle gave the other woman a rather reproving look before Julianne sighed. From where she was dressing, he heard Christine give a huff as well. Shaya recalled the last time he had listened to Daaé from the other side of a divide and smiled. "If you ask me, you deserve someone who will love you in the light."

"I agree," Adèle said.

"As do I." Christine emerged from behind a screen, resplendent in a dress of white that glowed in the candlelight. She smiled at Shaya and Julianne.

"Oh! You look perfect," Adèle breathed.

"You're welcome," Julianne smiled. "I do hope your wedding will end more happily than Lucia's." Shaya smiled at the joke, recalling the famous scene in Donizetti's opera when Lucia di Lammermoor emerged to madly sing herself to ruin after killing her new husband. Allah, Opera was such a grim affair.

"I think it shall," Christine murmured as her friend adjusted her bodice and produced a veil. "Our opera is not of the current style, where every love story ends in tragedy and every heroine dead. Ours will be far more akin to Mozart's. At least that is my hope."

"Mine too," Adèle said fondly. "Though I will admit that this is not the ending I would have expected."

"Do you have any advice? For married life," Christine asked as Adèle took her hand.

"The times of love are the easy ones," Adèle began with a sigh. "The hard ones are the times when you run up against the parts that are harder to love and the times of sorrow. You must meet them *together*. And grow."

Christine looked downward, overcome as she clasped her friend's hand. It moved Shaya to see it, just as it had moved him to see Christine in his hated enemy's embrace and realize that his hate was a weight he no longer wished to bear.

"Are you ready?" They looked up to see the young priest at the door. He appeared only slightly less amazed at the whole situation than when Shaya had approached him about the wedding.

"Not really, but I don't think I ever could be," Christine replied.

"I know how you feel," Father René chuckled. "I am happy to be performing your marriage. To the right man, I hope."

"That I know for sure," Christine smiled. "Shaya, before we begin, there are two more things I must ask of you. If you don't mind waiting. Father, may I have some paper and a pen?"

E rik had expected to be nervous tonight, but the absolute storm of anxiety he felt at the moment was like nothing he had ever experienced. There was a vise around his heart and an entire hive of bees in his spine. It was not just the suffocating fear that always came with being above ground and being seen by the living – he had to get used to that now – it was even more than that. He was standing in a house of God awaiting *his wedding*. It was an event Erik had never even dared to imagine in his wildest dreams.

He had dreamed, a few times, of seeing his Christine in the sun, of loving her in her world. For her, he would make that real, because she desired it. It was the hardest thing he had ever done, promising to join her in the light, and finding the impossible path. Yet it was almost done.

It had felt like madness when they made the plan. When they realized they had a body at their disposal who had pretended to the Phantom's legacy. Through Antoine, the Opera Ghost could die, so that Erik could live. He had been afraid the moment they had decided on it; when he knew that his love would have to play one last role to free them all. So he had asked her – begged her – to grant him one promise in consolation: to marry him. And she had said yes.

Now, Erik was waiting in front of an altar, his back to the largest crowd he had been part of in nearly seven years. There were five people present, now that Adèle and Julianne had come to sit down, which Erik watched from the corner of his eye. Shaya made six, as he walked down the aisle. Was his face serious for some terrible reason? Had Christine changed her mind? She would be right to do so. Erik didn't deserve this. He didn't deserve her.

Shaya spoke quietly to Robert Rameau, who gave an amused smile and nodded before leaving his seat. Erik braced himself as the Daroga and the manager beside him both walked towards Erik, looking rightfully hesitant.

"She wanted Robert to walk her down the aisle," Shaya said before Erik could ask. "He's played her father enough times, she thought it was close enough to count."

"I think it should." Erik looked at the men who were staring at him uneasily. "And?"

"And she wanted to make sure someone would stand beside you," Shaya answered. "If you needed it."

"I believe it is up to you to choose," Moncharmin added.

It had been an impulse to invite the manager. Erik had sought Moncharmin out the day before, in order to make his amends with the man who had saved Erik from taking more lives. The man had been relieved when Erik had told him the Ghost, or at least one ghost, intended to leave the Opera. He had asked if he meant to follow Christine. Erik had answered honestly, by saying yes, that he would go with her as a husband, and would Moncharmin like to be a witness? To Erik's shock, the man had agreed.

"I appreciate your presence, Armand," Erik began, still unsure of himself. "But I should like to have the Daroga here. If he is willing."

"Of course," Moncharmin smiled. "I think my memoirs would have already strained credulity. I hope it is not bad luck to say in advance that you have my congratulations and good wishes."

"Not at all. I much appreciate the sentiment," Erik muttered. "I need it."

"She also told me to tell you to stop worrying – not that you would," Shaya added. Erik gave him a gentle glare as Moncharmin returned to his seat.

"I confess, Daroga, I would never have imagined we would find ourselves here." Erik looked around the opulent church that somehow was theirs for this quiet evening before the dawn of spring.

"At your wedding to a woman so far above you in virtue and kindness you might as well be a stone marrying the sun? Or in a church?" Shaya replied, and it took a moment for the spark of humor to ignite in his eyes.

"Both. Nonetheless, I am grateful to whatever powers brought us here."

"He would be happy for you. I know that," Shaya said softly. "Or wherever he is watching from, he *is* happy. I can feel it."

"That is the greatest gift you could give me, Daroga," Erik answered as moisture edged his eyes. "And you have given me many a gift in the past few days."

"None so great as the one you will soon receive." Shaya nodded towards the priest, who had emerged to take his place and eye Erik nervously. "Ready, Father?"

"We are," the priest replied.

"And we have not been struck down yet on this holy ground, so I think we can proceed," Erik joked and enjoyed both Shaya's glare and seeing the young father go a bit paler. Then he turned to see Christine on Robert Rameau's arm, and there was nothing in the world but her.

Erik had never witnessed anything more beautiful than her. The way her dark hair set off the white of her gown, the small bouquet of early spring blooms in her hand, the brightness of her smile behind her lace veil. Erik was so inadequate; so small and unworthy in this glittering holy place with such an angel looking upon him. But he would not run from her, not today. Not ever again.

Christine met him before the priest, and with shaking hands, Erik lifted her veil to reveal her beaming face and shining eyes. Christine handed her bouquet to Robert, and her hands shook too as she then lifted to Erik's mask. It was only right that he should enter into this unveiled as well, was it not? Even if it terrified him. Erik nodded, and Christine removed the mask from his face then handed it to Shaya. No one screamed, no one gasped, and Christine smiled.

Father René began to speak in Latin, and Erik barely listened. The blessings and ritual did not matter as much as the simple miracle that Christine Daaé was here with him, ready to trade her name for his.

"In the presence of God and the witnesses here gathered, I ask that you state your intentions," Father René said in French when the blessing was done. "Have you both come to enter into marriage without coercion, freely and wholeheartedly?"

"We have," Erik and Christine answered as one, not looking away from each other.

"Since it is your intention to join in the covenant of Holy Matrimony, join your hands and declare your vows." Erik was quick to obey, and the feel of his love's palm against his, of her holding him, real and alive, gave him strength.

"Do you, Erik Gilbride, take Christine Daaé to be your wife? To cherish always and be faithful to, in good times and in bad, in sickness and in health, to love and to honor, until death do you part?"

"And beyond it. I do." Erik glanced to the poor priest, who seemed unprepared for such a deviation. The young man looked kindly back to Christine, who continued to grin even as tears trickled over her pink cheeks.

"Do you, Christine Daaé, take Erik Gilbride to be your husband? To cherish always and be faithful to, in good times and in bad, in sickness and in health, to love and to honor, until, well—"

"To the stars and beyond, I do," Christine answered.

"You may now exchange your rings," Father René declared. "And I am, uh, told you have vows you wish to speak of your own. Please proceed."

Erik braced himself, pulling the gold ring that had already held so many promises for them from his pocket, and placed it on Christine's left hand.

"Christine, I cannot swear to you that, as my wife, you will never hunger, or suffer, or weep. I cannot swear that the path ahead will be kind. But I do swear that I will walk it with you, wherever it may lead. I will protect you and cherish you. I will respect and adore you. I give myself to you as your husband, knowing that I cannot ask you to be mine..." Erik swallowed, and Christine squeezed his hand, smiling through tears. "For you are your own. I ask only that you choose to walk in this world next to me, through all its joys and trials, and I will walk next to you in turn, endeavoring each day to be worthy of the honor of calling myself your husband."

Erik heaved a sigh, tears flowing freely down his bare face. Christine prepared herself in turn as Adèle rose and handed her another plain gold band. Erik had not even considered the matter of his own ring, but it fit perfectly. He would never remove it, he knew for sure.

"My Erik, I will walk with you. We shall never want for shelter, for I swear to be your home, as you are mine. We will never be without hope or strength, for we will find it in each other. I swear to be patient, to be brave, and to meet you with love as we grow and learn and change. I swear I will love you, my angel, forever and a day."

Erik wished more dearly than anything he could kiss her now or fall at her feet in gratitude and amazement.

"I...uh..." the priest stammered. Erik glanced at the man, who looked just as affected by feeling as the couple he was meant to join. "You have spoken your vows and exchanged rings as a token of your devotion. Now in the eyes of God and these witnesses, I pronounce you husband and wife."

They met in a kiss that eclipsed everything, lips joining as their souls too were bonded as one. Erik held her, his wife and salvation, his reason and his light. No words or vows could express how much he loved her, or his gratitude that she somehow loved him in return. Her forgiveness still baffled him. Perhaps that was the magic of her love and the miracle of her compassion. The beauty of her grace.

Erik drew away, his forehead against Christine's, meeting forest eyes that were full of tears. Tears of joy now, after all the sorrow he had caused.

"I will earn this, I swear it, my love. Forgive me, for all I was before," he sighed. Christine gave him a humoring look, for she had forgiven him days ago, in the dark beyond the lake. Still, he sang to her, his voice rising through the church in the first phrase she had ever heard from her angel of music. The count's line from *The Marriage of Figaro*.

"*Contessa, forgive me. Forgive me*," he sang. "*Forgive me*."

"*I am kinder than you,*" Christine sang in return with no hesitation, her voice more beautiful and full of feeling than he had ever heard it. "*I will say yes... I will say yes.*"

And then together, as one, they sang. "*Ah, all are happy, and ever shall be so.*" Their voices rose in harmony in a melody of love and compassion, echoing with hope. It was as sure a vow and a consummation as any ceremony in Latin, and it echoed up past the saints and sacred symbols to the heavens that heard.

The crowd that had gathered to witness them wept as well, at the beauty of the song and love. At least that was what it seemed when Erik bothered to glance away from the woman who was now his wife. His angel. His Christine. His forever.

His promise.

Shaya approached the door of the Chagny house for what he deeply hoped was the last time. Evening had fallen and the air was once again cool, letting go of that warm glimpse of spring that had been there in the afternoon. Warmth remained in his heart, thanks to what he had seen in the church. It was strange, he knew, to have spent so long hating a man and planning for his demise, to now be committed to giving him a future with his wife. Shaya would adjust. He was still the Daroga of Mazenderan, and he was even better at keeping secrets than discovering them.

The butler gave a powerful sigh when he saw Shaya at the door. "The wake has ended and Monsieur le Comte has left on a personal trip and will not return for a long while," the man drawled, his face unmoving.

"I understand that. I ask only for a brief moment with Mademoiselle Sabine," Shaya replied. "Tell her I have a letter for her she has been waiting for."

"Very well." The butler showed Shaya into the parlor, where he waited. It was empty, now that half the men who had plotted there for the Phantom's demise were dead. Shaya had not attended Philippe de Chagny's funeral. He had been too busy burying another man, but he intended to visit the tomb when he had time and offer his prayers.

"Good evening, Monsieur." Shaya turned to see the Vicomtesse standing proudly in her mourning black, waiting at the threshold.

"Mademoiselle de Chagny," he nodded. "Thank you for seeing me. I have a letter for your brother—"

"From Christine? Thank God." The woman gave a deep sigh of relief as she took the offered envelope. "Does this mean I shall not be seeing that cursed woman again?"

"That is her hope. Give Raoul this. Tell him I said it was done. Page five." He handed Sabine a folded copy of *L'Époque*, the evening edition that had just been printed.

The obituary she would find there was brief, and even so, the subject of it had argued over the wording, for it was not Erik who was dead, but the Phantom of the Opera. Shaya's position had been that phantoms could not die, and that, for Erik to be reborn in the life he was about to pursue, he had to die first.

"Is there anything else?" Sabine asked stiffly, folding the papers under her arm.

"Yes, there is," Shaya began unsteadily. "Your fiancé, Antoine—"

"He's not ever coming back, is he?" Sabine guessed before Shaya could confess.

"Do not wait for him. And do not mourn," Shaya answered. "He is not worth your tears."

"He never was." Sabine looked more relieved than anything, and that was a consolation to Shaya. He gave a final bow to the woman.

"Tell your brother for me that I wish him peace," Shaya said before he received a curt nod of dismissal.

He walked home along the Seine feeling light. Lighter than he had in years, or even decades. It was strange, to be so without a purpose. There was no quest now. No revenge to seek or monarch to serve. It was... lovely. He could do whatever he chose now, even though he had no idea what that would be. It felt good to have the choice at all.

He walked across the *Pont de la Concorde* and cut through the Tuileries to the *Rue de Rivoli*. Perhaps he would spend tomorrow at the Louvre or walk in the gardens as they prepared to bloom. He always liked this time of year, when the world seemed to hold its breath, bursting with the promise of life. Had Darius ever been? He should really know that sort of thing.

There was already tea brewing in a pot when he entered the flat. Darius rose immediately to pour Shaya a cup, smiling kindly as always.

"How was it?" Darius asked.

"Easier than I thought."

"Good. I was worried. It took you so long," Darius chided as they took their seats by the fire.

"I walked. I wanted to think and, well, enjoy the city," Shaya replied, and Darius raised an eyebrow. "What can I say? Perhaps Paris has grown on me at last."

"Does that mean we shan't be departing for home, or even someplace near to it, now that you are done with everything?" Darius asked before taking a slow sip.

Shaya smiled. "There was something Christine said in her vows: *we shall never want for shelter, for I swear to be your home, as you are mine.*"

"I did like that part," Darius murmured. When Shaya dared to look up, the other man was smiling warmly.

"We don't need to go home, Darius. Or at least I don't. I have all the home that I need right here," Shaya confessed.

"Well, that is a good beginning."

C hristine took the key from the drowsy attendant at the front desk with a smile. The hotel was convenient to the *Gare du Nord* station and the train that would take them from the city in the morning. The brass and marble in the lobby reminded her of the Opera, strangely enough. More than once, the Opera had been compared to a train station in her construction. It was as appropriate a place to spend her wedding night as any.

"My husband and I wish not to be disturbed," Christine declared. The man showed little interest. It didn't matter; she just wanted to say it and have the words be true.

She had changed out of her wedding costume and back into her traveling clothes, so how was anyone to know she had been so changed today if she didn't declare it? She turned to said husband, who looked slightly overwhelmed by his surroundings.

Erik was trying, she could tell, to blend in as much as he could, with his mask adorned with a beard and spectacles, his hat low and his collar high. Still, Christine took his hand to offer comfort, and he squeezed hers tightly back. She led them to the room, but Erik pulled her back into his arms after she had unlocked the door, much to her surprise.

"I believe there is a tradition I need to uphold?" Erik whispered in her ear before scooping Christine up into his arms as she yelped in delight. He carried her over the threshold into their simple room and her heart fluttered.

The room wasn't much. It had a handsome bed and a little fire with chairs before it, and two tall windows in the Parisian style that looked out over the lights of the city. It was so normal. It was perfect.

Before her husband could let go, Christine lifted his mask from his face and kissed him. She loved the tenderness with which his lips responded, the tight hold of his lithe arms, and how she was sure that, if she tried, she could feel his heart pounding against hers. Just as she had expected, Erik set her down and slipped from the embrace, fussing with his hat, cloak, and gloves.

"Are you nervous for your wedding night, husband?" Christine asked, removing her heavy cloak, the one that had once been his.

"Very. The last time we made love was—"

"One of your worse moments, yes," Christine replied as Erik moved towards the window that gave them a view of the city. "You used me to hurt Raoul. You knew you could because I have always been weak when it comes to my desire for you. You knew that the first night you took me below, before I even knew your name."

"Christine..." Erik's voice was fraught with pain as he turned to her, and guilt was written across his mangled face.

"You regret it, don't you?" Christine demanded, calm and cool.

"I do. You know I do."

"And would you ever do it again?"

"Never," Erik swore, tentatively approaching and reaching for her hand. He had begged her forgiveness many times. She was sure he would continue asking it for a long time to come. She would give it.

"Then you are forgiven," Christine smiled, twining her fingers with his. "Now help me to make a new start. I will show you how."

Erik stared at her, golden eyes full of wonder and anticipation. "I await your command, dear wife."

"Let me see you, husband. All of you. No need for any modesty now."

He kept his eyes locked with hers as he obeyed, and she knew it gave him strength. It gave him peace to be commanded by her, to be the object of her love and desire and care. She smiled as he unbuttoned his shirt and waistcoat and removed all the layers in one smooth action. The scarred skin of his chest and arms took on the color of old ivory in the dim light from the oil lamp by the bed and the low fire, and it was beautiful. His thin, long frame and tight muscles, the marks and scars of a life lived so painfully. It was all *Erik*, and she loved it.

"Perfect." Christine swore she saw him blush as he busied himself with his shoes. His hands hovered at the fastening to his trousers. "Help me first," Christine intervened. Erik's shoulders relaxed and a sly smile appeared on his lips.

"It would be my honor," Erik breathed as he knelt before her, and Christine fought to keep her breath steady. He raised the hem of her dress and kissed it, like he was a pilgrim paying homage at a holy shrine, and it made Christine swoon. "Would you like to sit, dear wife?"

Christine tried to be graceful as she took one of the chairs by the fire and Erik remained prostrate before her. It was impossible now to conceal how her breath had grown rapid and her cheeks red, especially as her husband removed her shoes for her. Christine shivered as Erik's gentle hands slid beneath her skirts and ghosted up her leg to her garter, undoing it with ease before pulling down her stocking. To her utter amazement, he kissed her foot when it was exposed, tender and worshipful.

Erik repeated the action with the other stocking, bestowing another supplicant kiss on her other foot. Christine wanted to command his hands to find their way between her thighs again to let him discover how wet and ready she already was. At the same time, she wanted this all to last forever.

Erik rose and helped her up again, transferring his focus to the many buttons of her jacket and blouse with far more confidence than he had exhibited when attending to his own clothes. He kissed her collarbone softly when it was finally exposed to the air, then her arms and chest. Her skirts left her next, falling to the floor in a pool. Finally they freed her of her corset, leaving only her chemise and pantalettes. Erik lifted the former from her body, exposing her heavy breasts and tight nipples to the air before granting them the attention of his mouth.

Christine wrapped her arms around her husband as he licked and suckled at one breast and then the other, using his teeth and tongue expertly to make her sigh and coo in pleasure. He caught her around the waist at the exact second her knees grew weak and caught her, carrying her to their wedding bed as she caught his mouth in a kiss.

Erik kissed her as he laid her down, his hands sweeping over her skin, deft and soft, but all too soon, his mouth was gone from hers to shower her body once again with kisses. She adored the attention he paid to every curve and crevice, from the bend of her arm to the soft curve of her belly right above her ruff.

He slipped off her pantalettes, following the slow removal of the fabric with his lips and tongue all the way down her legs then back up as he parted her thighs to take his place between them. Her hips rose in anticipation, but he paused, face hidden against her skin.

"May I taste you, sweet wife?" Erik asked, his voice a symphony. "Will you let me serve you?"

"Yes," Christine panted, dizzied by the knowledge that, even now, when she was bare and needy under him, she was still in control, still mistress of her fate and choices. "Yes, my love. My husband."

Christine's blood and lust surged as her husband's mouth descended ravenously on her sex. She could hear and feel it, how wet she was for him as he licked and sucked and made her writhe. She gripped the brass frame of the bed with one hand and twined her fingers into his dark hair with the other, her legs splayed out as he devoured her with the same pure adoration that he had shown all night. She had never felt more honored – more served and cherished – as she felt now, as her husband worshiped her with his mouth to bring her pleasure and show his love.

Her body convulsed as she began to come, the pinnacle building slowly as Erik added his fingers to his efforts, filling her so sweetly and touching those places inside that made Christine helpless. She bucked and arched as she climaxed, Erik humming in pleasure and pride as she did so, provoking more spikes of bliss. Just as slowly as it had begun, he eased her down from the peak, now with gentle kisses to her belly and thighs as she caught her breath.

"So beautiful," Erik breathed against her skin. Still light-headed with lust, she pushed herself up from the bed, focusing on the debauched face of the man looking up at her. He was a sight: his long hair falling in his face, nearly concealing his missing nose and terrible scars.

"As are you, my Erik," Christine said, and he blinked in disbelief. It was all the prompting she needed. "Let me show you."

Her husband did not resist as she reversed their positions, laying him out on the bed, prone below her. She kissed his lips, tasting herself there, then his neck and chest, licking his nipples and ministering to his scars.

"Oh, Christine..." he sighed, as ever in awe of her touch.

"Your Christine," she breathed against his taut abdomen, breasts now against the bulge in his trousers. "Your wife."

He only groaned as she moved against him, her nipples catching on the fabric as she continued for a few moments longer.

She smiled at how compliant and eager he was when she finally undid the fastenings and freed him of this last scrap of clothing. His perfect cock sprang free, blushing and hard just for her, with moisture already beading at the tip. She gave it one long lick, savoring the tang of him as he had savored her. It was tempting, to keep her mouth upon him, but she had a marriage to consummate tonight.

"Look," Christine commanded, sliding up her lover's long body and touching his cheek. His eyes were unfocused at first as they opened, perhaps more so as Christine kissed him. Those perfect golden eyes cleared as she drew back, gazing down at him below her in the lamplight and seeing all of him. He glanced nervously at the light and it made Christine even more sure of her next move.

"I—" Erik began, and she placed a finger against his lips to stop his protest.

"Watch," she said. Erik relaxed and complied. He watched in wonder as Christine straddled him and guided his hard member into her tender sex. She was sensitive from coming already, but that only made her feel every vein and ridge of him as she lowered herself on his length. "Eyes open, my husband, so you can see," Christine gasped, fighting not to let the pleasure overwhelm her.

"I see an angel, a goddess," Erik began, then moaned as Christine began to move her hips. "I see my wife."

"And I see you," Christine keened in return as Erik began to meet her with shallow thrusts. She loved all the ways they could join, all the different joys their bodies could find together, but having him like this was special and always had been. It was not just the pleasure it brought her to be so utterly filled, or how good it was to ride him at whatever pace she chose. Making love like this meant he could not hide and she could see the face and the scars of the man she loved.

"Christine," he breathed, grabbing her hand as their speed increased. He bucked up into her and she undulated above him in turn.

"I see you. Erik, I see all of you," Christine nearly sang, her sweat beginning to glisten on her skin as she arched herself to take him deeper, faster. "I see your scars and your darkness and your beauty and your love and your sins and I love it. Do you know that, my husband? Can you see that right now?"

"Yes!" Erik cried, his free hand coming between them so he could rub that magical nub with his thumb, causing Christine a new explosion of pleasure that nearly made her scream.

"See it, Erik. See how I love you," Christine whimpered, refusing to look away from his teary, adoring eyes. "Entirely."

She let go as Erik came, joining him in the orgasm that pulsed through them. So many times before, her pleasure had engulfed her in beautiful silence, a tidal wave of delight and peace that took her from the mortal world and into the realm of angels. But not now. Finally, she was present. Pleasure coursed through her blood, and she stayed on the earth, experiencing every second of it as her lover poured out his climax inside her. It went on and on, the spasms of her cunt, the bucks of his hips, and the delirious joy of being one with him.

At last it was as it should be. Christine was joined in body and heart and soul to the man fate had linked her to so long ago. She was not lost, not subsumed or fading. She was herself and her own. She chose him, right now, and would continue to, as long as her soul endured.

Raoul had slept on the train, thanks to a bottle of brandy and his general exhaustion. So now, he found himself wide awake in the wee hours of the morning at the hotel in Brussels, glowering at the city as he waited for dawn. Even so, he was not expecting a knock at his door. His heart surged at the sound – could it be Christine already? Had burying that thing finally freed her heart and had she rushed to him on the next train?

It took Raoul a moment when he threw open the door to understand that the familiar woman looking at him across the threshold was not his fiancée, but his sister. She was still in black and looked as dour as when he had last seen her.

"Sabine, I told you: you cannot tell me who to marry or interfere!" Raoul growled as he retreated towards the fire.

"I don't need to interfere. Your Christine isn't coming," Sabine replied, and Raoul spun to her in shock. "I came to bring you home."

"What are you talking about?"

"Here." Sabine handed him a letter addressed in Christine's delicate hand. "Read it."

"Where did you get this?" Raoul sputtered. "Did she—"

"Your Persian friend brought it."

Raoul stared at the words on the paper, his brain struggling to put the words into focus.

My Dear Raoul,

I regret how this letter must reach you, but I think it is for the best to say my goodbyes in this way. When you return to Paris, I will be gone, and I ask that you do not try to find me.

I cannot be your wife. I feared it was true before, but the burial and my final moments at the Opera confirmed it in my heart. I love a man you hate, and I will love him until my days are done. What is more, you deserve a wife who can bring you heirs as much as she can give you her whole heart, and I can do neither. It is better for you and your family for us to part.

I am so sorry, Raoul, for all the grief I have brought you and all you have sacrificed in my name. I pray you find the strength to forgive me, yourself, and all of us, for what has transpired. I pray you thrive and grow and find joy and build the life you deserve. Do not forget the brave young boy who saved my scarf from the sea. Make him proud.

~ Christine

Raoul read and reread the letter, trying to make sense of it. He had arrived in Brussels buoyed by one single hope, one single spark of light in all the vile darkness: that Christine would be his, finally. And now, she was gone.

"Did Motlagh say where she was going?" Raoul asked numbly, looking at the letter for some clue. "We spoke of going north. To her homeland."

"She was quite clear she did not want to be followed. Are you going to listen to her for once?" Sabine's voice was sharp as a slap.

"How do I know this is not some deception?" Raoul demanded. "She has lied before."

"Then why in the name of God would you still want her?" Sabine cried, and unmanly tears stung his eyes.

"I... I don't know. It is one thing to be denied my revenge, but to also be denied my prize for all I have endured is another." Raoul ignored his sister's grunt of disgust. "Now I have nothing."

"You have your life, you fool! You have a future free of that cursed trollop." Sabine grabbed his shoulder and forced Raoul to look at her. "You have a chance to save our name and our family. You should be thanking her for that."

"But Erik—"

"Your Phantom is dead!" Sabine drew a folded newspaper from the folds of her traveling cloak and presented it to Raoul. "Look!" *Erik is dead.*

The words were there, as plain as day, in the pages of *L'Époque.* The obituary that the monster had asked for so that some strangers could know a man named Erik lived and died. Even that was more than the thing deserved.

"So it truly is over." Raoul was as unmoored as when he had learned Philippe was gone, for all his ideas about what his future would be now had to change. How could that be? How could the story have ended without his involvement or action again? He had woken after the torture chamber to learn Christine had saved them all. He had learned from the Persian that the beast was dying. Now, while he was looking away, he had lost Christine as well.

"It is. Now come home. There's a train back to Paris in a few hours," Sabine entreated. "Come home, and we can start again."

"Apparently I must," Raoul sighed. He looked out the window towards the dark sky and found himself wishing more than anything that he was on the deck of a ship, counting the stars as they sailed north. Vincenzo would be there laughing, and at home, Philippe would be alive.

"This is for the best, Raoul," Sabine declared once again, tugging at his sleeve. "You have to know that."

"The best would have been if I had never come home at all and just stayed away at sea." Raoul's soul darkened at the words. "Or if that creature had never been born."

Sabine forced him to look at her once again. "We can't change what happened, little brother. We can only control what happens next."

"You're right." Raoul let himself be led to where a carriage was waiting. When the carriage door slammed closed, it was as final as when they had placed the stone on his brother's tomb. Something had ended. Raoul's hopes for the future had died. Yet he remained.

Or a version of him remained. Christine had seen it, Raoul knew, the ways she and Erik and their intrigues had changed him. He was the Comte de Chagny now. A man hardened by suffering and loss, broken-hearted and growing colder every day. He understood why Christine had wanted him to remember the boy who had thrown himself into the sea for her scarf.

If he had that boy here right now, Raoul would throttle him and tell him to not bother at all with heroics or chivalry, least of all young love. He did not care to make that child proud, as he had been asked to do. Raoul had a legacy to uphold of the Comtes de Chagny before him whom he had barely avenged.

That boy was a ghost, and Raoul would not let any more phantoms haunt him.

E rik jolted awake as searing light hit his eyes. He blinked and hid behind his hand as he tried to see through the brightness while Christine stirred beside him. What the hell was happening? Where was that blasted illumination coming from? He lowered his hand, eyes stinging as his vision adjusted, and saw that there was no intruder or device of torture in their little room. It was only the first rays of the morning sun blazing over the roofs of Paris.

"What is it?" Christine asked from beside him, and Erik's attention snapped to her.

Her hair was a mess, and there was a mark on her cheek where she had slept on the crease of a pillowcase. Her eyes were bleary as she yawned, and when she covered her mouth, it made the sheet fall away to expose one bare breast to the golden glow from outside. The sunlight brought out the reds in her hair as it brightened her cheeks, and she smiled at him. It was the single most beautiful sight Erik had ever seen.

"It's morning," he breathed.

"It is," Christine smiled back.

His joy at seeing his wife in the dawn light evaporated as Erik realized she could see him too. He could feel the sun burning against his bare skin. He was exposed! He had to leave! He had to *run*!

"Erik, breathe!"

When had Christine pulled him into her arms? He didn't know, but there she was, shielding him and holding him close. Inhaling and exhaling slowly so he could match his breath to hers. She held him and kissed his hair and stroked him. Slowly the panic ebbed, even as the room grew brighter.

"I'm sorry," Erik murmured against her breast, and she clucked in reproval.

"I asked you to be with me in the light. We both knew it wouldn't be simple, or easy." Erik drew back, forcing himself not to wince as the sun caught his skin once again. "All that matters to me is that you are here and that you stay here. That you keep trying."

"I had forgotten." Erik dared to look towards the window and the blue sky beyond it. "The sun – how bright and warm it is."

"It is time you remember then." Christine rose from the bed, pulling Erik after her towards the window. "How does it feel now?"

"Standing naked in the daylight next to the most radiant creature on earth? Humbling, for one." Christine scowled and wrapped her arms around him, waiting for more. "It feels like a new life, like being reborn."

"Good. That's a start," his wife said with a smile. "Our train leaves at ten. I'm glad you woke us early."

"And why is that?" Erik asked back. It would be a miracle if they made it to Rome without incident, and he fully believed they would. Because his angel filled the world with miracles.

"Because I wanted to say goodbye to this city before we leave her behind, and I want my husband to make love to me in the morning light."

Erik could not help but laugh. Just those words: another miracle, as wondrous as kissing her and tasting her laughter mingling with his. He drew away smiling, and the warmth of the sun did not burn his unmasked face. It felt like hope, not a punishment. Like spring.

"I love you, my remarkable wife." Erik kissed his Christine once again. Perhaps people looking across the street could see them. Perhaps they gasped at seeing a maiden in death's embrace, but Erik did not care, and neither did his wife. They knew the truth, and he smiled to think it as their lips parted and she laid her head against his heart. "My salvation and my hope."

"I love you, my poetic husband," Christine sighed in return. "My angel."

Erik pulled her close and breathed deep as they looked out over Paris towards the dawn.

The Beginning

Erik and Christine's continues in...
ANGEL'S FLIGHT

Acknowledgements

To Tamsin, who I love the most and is the best daughter ever and who helped write this sentence: I love you more than anything.

To my wife Heidi, my angel and my rock, who sees me for all I am: I love you to the stars and beyond.

To Marlon, Lemon, and Dewey: thanks for the moral support. Thank you to my parents and extended family for their constant support of my career.

Thank you to Ana for listening to me whine about these characters and letting me make you cry. Thank you to Lisa, Saba, and especially Jordan for your help in editing. Thank you to Andrea, Miriel, Ariana, Kaitlyn, Laal, Angie, Germaine, Lynx, Nenia, and all the incredible members of my Patreon for your support and love of this series. I hope I continue to earn it.

Thank you to everyone who has read *The Phantom Saga*. Yes, every single person. You have taught me so much and given me the gift of your time, energy, and attention. I could not be more grateful that you've helped me realize the dream of being a part of Phantom's legacy.

And finally, to Gaston Leroux, for the story that changed my life: *grand merci, mon ami.*

Don't miss out!

Visit the website below and you can sign up to receive emails whenever Jessica Mason publishes a new book. There's no charge and no obligation.

https://books2read.com/r/B-A-RZHV-TDBXC

Connecting independent readers to independent writers.

Did you love *Angel's Fall*? Then you should read *Erik's Tale*[1] by Jessica Mason!

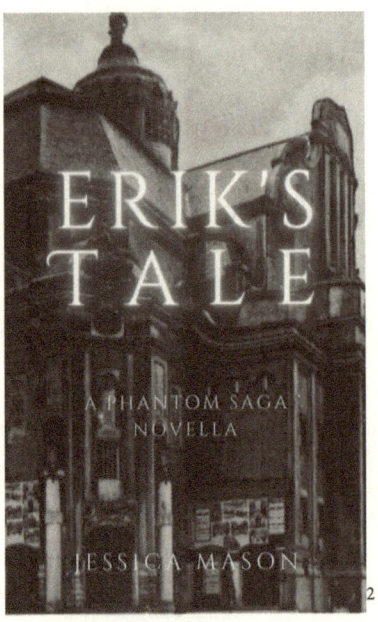

[2]

Before he became a Phantom, he was simply Erik. Before he found the Opera, he wandered the world. In this companion novella to the love story of The Phantom Saga, Erik, the legendary Opera Ghost, tells the story of his life in his own words.

Born deformed to a mother who despised him, the bastard son of a cruel noble, then sold into a freak show to perform as "The Living Death," *Erik's Tale* is one of tragedy and loss. But it is also the story of hope found in the darkest of moments through music and an unquenchable desire to survive.

A wanderer in search of belonging, Erik journeys from the musical grandeur of Vienna and the debauchery of Carnivale in

1. https://books2read.com/u/4DDYvg

2. https://books2read.com/u/4DDYvg

Venice to the mystic hills of Ireland and the dangerous underground of India. Erik searches for hope that his life can be more than ugliness and death, joining the commune of Paris and serving the paranoid Shah of Persia on a perilous journey marked by catastrophe, triumph...and love.

Erik's Tale invites readers into the Phantom's life before the opera as it has never been portrayed, with diverse characters, surprising twists, rich historical detail, and heartbreaking romance.

Also by Jessica Mason

The Phantom Saga
Angel's Mask
Angel's Kiss
Erik's Tale
Angel's Fall

About the Author

Jessica Mason lives near Portland, Oregon with her wife, daughter, and corgi. She has studied opera, practiced law, and has worked as a fandom journalist and podcaster, among many varied careers. But first and foremost she has always been a storyteller. When she manages to stop writing, she enjoys gardening, travel, music, and witchcraft.

Find her on social media: @ByJessicaMason

About the Publisher

Murmuration Books is an independent publisher bringing readers, steamy, spellbinding, spooky, sensational stories. We are committed to diverse themes, new authors, and creative takes on old ideas.

For more, visit Murmurationbooks.com

www.ingramcontent.com/pod-product-compliance
Lightning Source LLC
Chambersburg PA
CBHW020543120726
47903CB00001B/99